# HELLFORGED

*"Hellforged* is the total package." —*Fantasy Literature*

"This series is becoming highly addictive!"
—*RT Book Reviews*

"A highly satisfying whole: action, adventure, suspense, Welsh mythology, humor, and pitch-perfect characters that live and breathe on the page." —*Bitten by Books*

"I cannot wait to see what is in store for my new favorite demon hunter!" —*Intense Whisper* . . .

"Jam-packed with action." —*Night Owl Reviews*

"Vicky is the kind of kick-butt heroine fantasy lovers can get behind . . . A novel lovers of fantasy, urban fantasy, and paranormal fiction in general won't want to miss."
—*Romance Reviews Today*

# DEADTOWN

"Fresh and funny, with a great new take on zombies."
—Karen Chance, *New York Times* bestselling author of *Tempt the Stars*

"A must-read . . . This heroine totally kicks butt!"
—Phaedra Weldon, author of *Revenant*

"Fast, fun, and feisty." —Devon Monk, author of *Hell Bent*

"An incredibly realized world and a cast of vivid characters. I can't wait for the next book!"
—Chris Marie Green, author of *Deep in the Woods*

"Nancy Holzner is a master of characterization and I'll be buying her next book the moment it hits the shelf."
—Ilona Andrews, *New York Times* bestselling author of *Magic Rises*

*Ace Books by Nancy Holzner*

**DEADTOWN**
**HELLFORGED**
**BLOODSTONE**
**DARKLANDS**
**HELLHOUND**

# HELLHOUND

**NANCY HOLZNER**

ACE BOOKS, NEW YORK

**THE BERKLEY PUBLISHING GROUP**
**Published by the Penguin Group**
**Penguin Group (USA) LLC**
**375 Hudson Street, New York, New York 10014**

USA I Canada I UK I Ireland I Australia I New Zealand I India I South Africa I China

penguin.com

A Penguin Random House Company

HELLHOUND

An Ace Book / published by arrangement with the author

Ace Books are published by The Berkley Publishing Group.
ACE and the "A" design are trademarks of Penguin Group (USA) LLC.

For information, address: The Berkley Publishing Group,
a division of Penguin Group (USA) LLC,
375 Hudson Street, New York, New York 10014.

ISBN: 978-0-425-26280-1

PUBLISHING HISTORY
Ace mass-market edition / November 2013

PRINTED IN THE UNITED STATES OF AMERICA

10  9  8  7  6  5  4  3  2  1

Cover art by Don Sipley.

*To Steve, with hope for better times ahead*

# ACKNOWLEDGMENTS

Much of this book was written during a time of crisis, due to my husband's multiple health issues and hospitalizations. I'd like to thank the hospital staff who helped us through some really tough times. At Cayuga Medical Center: all of the ICU staff, as well as Chris, Coby, Katirae, Theresa, Arlene, Nathan, David, Tim, Mike Ronald, and Josh Hamilton. At UPMC Shadyside Hospital in Pittsburgh: Pam, Lorreece, Chelsea, Troy, Keith, Ebony, Laurie, Debbie, Sheila, Alexa, Angela, Bridget, Patricia, Dara, Maureen, Marlene, Karen, Sally, Nicole, Audrey, Linda, Amanda, Lisa, Ryan, Laura, the amazing staff of the cardiothoracic ICU, and all of the physicians who worked so hard to restore his health. I know I've forgotten some names—and I'm sorry about that—but I'm grateful to each and every person who took care of my husband during a difficult time.

Thanks also to the wonderful people of the Well Spouse Association for understanding, hugs, prayers, and much-needed support. Anyone caring for an ill spouse will find a warm welcome at www.wellspouse.org.

I appreciate the patience, understanding, and assistance of everyone at Ace.

Friends who've stuck by me have my deepest love and thanks: Michelle Brandwein, Kathy Giacoletto, Margaret Strother, Jeanne Mackin, Nicola Morris, Sydney Chase, Keith Pyeatt, Carlos Thomas, Kaysi Peister, Deborah Blake, Jessica Woodhouse, Janis Kelly, Mark Butterworth, Peter Munroe, Jane Rogers, and Sharon Choe.

Love and thanks also to my family, including my wonderful in-laws.

# 1

A PHONE THAT RINGS JUST BEFORE DAWN NEVER BRINGS good news. That's true even if you live where I do—Deadtown, Boston's paranormal-only district. Deadtown wakes up when the sun goes down, and by five in the morning most of the zombies, vampires, and other paranormals who live here are home behind their blackout shades, pulling on their jammies and ready to turn in for the day. Not dialing up their friends just to say, "Boo."

I stared at the ringing phone like I was expecting the thing to morph into a tarantula if I reached for it. The caller ID read BLOCKED CALL. No help there. Maybe it was a potential client wanting me to exterminate a demon—I could use the work. But norms don't make phone calls at this time of day. They wait until what they consider business hours. And by then I'm usually fast asleep.

One more ring, and the call would go to voice mail. I let it. I was in the process of pulling on my own jammies, and I didn't see any reason to let some ridiculously late (or early, if the caller was a norm) phone call rob me of my sleep. Of course, wondering who was calling and what they wanted would probably do that, anyway.

I watched the phone to see if the message light would start flashing. It didn't. Instead, the phone began ringing again. And the caller ID still didn't have a clue.

Whoever was calling was going to keep trying until I either answered or unplugged the phone. I grabbed the handset (no tarantula) and pressed Talk.

"Hello?"

"Vicky, is that you? This is Daniel." A pause, like he wasn't sure I remembered him. "Daniel Costello."

"Daniel?" Of course I remembered him. Still, I couldn't keep the surprise out of my voice. Daniel Costello was a human I'd dated a few months back. Great guy, but things hadn't worked out. Last I heard, he'd moved in with Lynne Hong, a TV news reporter. And of course I was with Kane, my werewolf boyfriend.

That is, if our relationship managed to survive the next full moon.

But I couldn't think about that now. I refocused my attention on the voice on the phone.

"This hasn't hit the news yet," Daniel was saying, "but it will soon. There's been a zombie attack. Three people are dead."

"And by 'people' you mean . . . ?" A zombie attack *any-where* was bad news. But, unfair as it may be, the fallout would be less if the attack happened in Deadtown. Paranormals killing their own didn't attract much interest from Boston's powers-that-be.

"Sorry. Humans. A zombie killed three humans."

*Shit.* That meant hell to pay for all of us. Ever since a magically enhanced virus had been set loose on downtown Boston three years ago, the plague victims—called "zombies" because they'd lain dead and decaying for three days before reanimating—had lived with humans in a truce that was uneasy at best. Looked like that truce had been breached.

"Was it bloodlust?" I asked.

Zombies, despite their superhuman strength and their tendency to bounce right back from injuries that would kill a norm, aren't much of a threat to humans. *Unless* they catch a whiff of fresh blood. The scent stirs up an insatiable hunger that makes human flesh suddenly seem mighty tasty. Talk about your awkward social situations.

"We're checking out that possibility, but I don't think it was bloodlust. I'd like you to come out and look at the scene."

"Me? Why?" Daniel was more than a guy I used to date. He was also a city homicide detective. Not long ago, as a serial killer terrorized the South End, Daniel had told me in no uncertain terms to stay away from his investigation. The way he'd called me an amateur then still stung. Especially when I was the one who'd stopped the killer.

So why the sudden about-face?

"You'll understand when you get here," he said. "I don't want to say anything else before you've had a chance to view the scene. But if you end up thinking along the same lines I am, I want to hire you as a consultant."

"You suspect demon activity?" Of course he did. *That* explained the about-face. There was no other reason he'd call me in as a consultant.

But Daniel didn't answer my question. He gave me the address, on Lincoln Street in the Leather District, and urged me to hurry.

"I'm on my way," I said, pulling on a jacket.

GETTING OUT OF DEADTOWN WAS GOING TO BE A PROBLEM.

Even if Daniel was right that the story hadn't made the news yet, everyone knew *something* had happened. Sunrise was fast approaching, yet the New Combat Zone, the gritty strip between the checkpoints into Deadtown and human-controlled Boston, was packed with zombies. At this time of day, the monster bars were all closed and the street was usually deserted. Now, throngs of zombies milled around, making the Zone look like Street Party of the Living Dead.

Except the mood was anything but festive.

I tapped a zombie on the arm. He was tall and could see over the heads in the crowd. The face that turned to me—spongy, gray-green skin with deeply sunken cheeks, bloodred eyeballs protruding from their sockets, thin lips pulled back from yellow teeth—looked like a vision out of a norm's worst nightmare. But I'm not a norm, and here he was just your average man, or monster, on the street.

"What's going on?" I asked.

"Protest." Recently, several zombie groups had organized marches against the restrictions placed on Deadtown residents. The first demonstration or two had been covered by the press, but then media attention had wandered elsewhere. Zombies marching through Deadtown? Big deal. As long as they stayed on their own side of the border, no one cared.

This gathering wasn't like the marches, though. For one thing, there were no signs. No speeches shouted through bullhorns. And the feeling in the air was one I could only describe as menace. Real anger was simmering here. Things could get ugly, fast.

I moved into the crowd. The zombie's hand clamped my shoulder.

"Don't bother," he said. "They've sealed the border."

Of course. If a zombie had attacked some humans, that's the first thing that Boston's paranormal-hating police commissioner, Fred Hampson, would do, even before he made any kind of official statement. But word spreads fast in Deadtown. Zombies heard about the restriction, but not why it had been put in place. And even if they knew a zombie had killed three humans, many would still be here protesting, anyway. After all, if one norm murdered another over on Marlborough Street, Hampson wouldn't seal off the entire Back Bay.

An amplified voice cut through the crowd's rumblings, but it wasn't to make a speech or lead a chant. "This is an unlawful gathering. Disperse at once and return to your homes."

The Goon Squad had arrived.

Deadtown's police force comprised joint zombie-human teams armed with exploding bullets—one of the few things that could kill a zombie, or at least make undeath not worth living. Now, Goons moved into the Zone, dressed in riot gear and carrying big-ass automatic weapons. With their faces shielded by visored helmets, you couldn't tell which cops were zombies and which were human. They all looked like storm troopers from an invading alien force.

The bullhorn repeated its commands. The crowd stirred,

restless, poised uncertainly between retreat and riot. The silence felt heavy with threat, like a gathering thunderhead.

"Let us through!" a man's voice shouted.

Somewhere, glass shattered.

A roar erupted from the crowd. Bodies surged toward the Boston checkpoint. The yelling resolved itself into a chant: "Let us through! Let us through!"

I struggled to keep my feet under me as shouting zombies shoved from all sides. I tried to move toward the curb, but it was useless pushing against a wall of tightly packed zombie bodies.

An acrid smell—was that smoke?—reached my nostrils. There was another crash of glass, and a group of zombies broke away, charging toward the buildings that lined the street. I ran after them. Ahead, a jagged, gaping hole marred the plate-glass window of The Wild Side, a monster bar. The breakaway zombies were storming it. They punched out the remaining glass and climbed inside. A minute later, they were back at the window. One clutched a cash register. Others passed beer kegs out to their friends.

The Wild Side wasn't enough for the looters. Zombies yanked at the locked door of Creature Comforts, the next bar over. Shit, that was *my* hangout. "Stop!" I screamed, my voice swallowed up in the din. Not that a group of rioting zombies would pay the slightest bit of attention to a lone, five foot six shapeshifter, even if they could hear me.

"Ram it!" someone shouted. Through The Wild Side's smashed window came—hell, was that the *bar*? Four zombies grabbed it and backed up, ready to use it as a battering ram.

"One!"

I rushed forward. If I could get between the zombies and the door . . . Who was I kidding? I'd end up squashed like a swatted fly against the door of my favorite bar. I watched helplessly.

"Two!" The zombies around me backed up, cheering, to give the looters more room. I stumbled back with them. I hoped Axel, the bar's owner, had insurance.

"Thr—!"

The looters never finished their countdown. The door

slammed open, banging hard against the wall. Axel's seven foot tall silhouette filled the wide-open doorway. Even from where I stood, the looters' gasp was audible as they froze. Axel stepped outside, shut the door behind him, and folded his arms. No gun, no riot gear, just a badass troll protecting his turf.

The looters fell back. Some disappeared into The Wild Side. Others rejoined the crowd. Axel stood there like the Colossus of goddamn Rhodes, his beady eyes promising trouble to anyone—zombie, vampire, human, whatever—who took one step too close.

Around me, the crowd headed for the checkpoint again. Someone shoved me from behind, and I almost fell. I lost sight of Axel as I concentrated on not being trampled to death in a zombie stampede. The bullhorn, still shouting commands, was barely audible.

Then, a burst of gunfire sounded.

Everything stopped. Voices cut off in mid-chant. Raised fists halted in mid-shake. For several seconds, silence reigned.

The bullhorn voice took advantage of the moment. "Go home. Proceed in an orderly fashion." A pause. "Sunrise will occur in less than eight minutes."

Around me, several zombie heads snapped up toward the pale gray sky. Here, the buildings were tall enough that it was still as dark as midnight on the ground, and most of the rioters weren't dressed for daytime. Zombies don't burst into flame or anything in sunlight. Instead, they're afflicted with zombie sunburn: orange skin, pocked with deep pits. Zombies aren't exactly pretty to begin with, but zombie sunburn hurts. And zombies don't heal.

The crowd had surged toward Boston as a single force, but now it dribbled away as the zombies returned to Deadtown. It seemed to shrink around the edges and thin at the center. A few zombies stood their ground, but no one continued the push toward human-controlled Boston.

"Excuse me," muttered a zombie. I recognized him as one of the looters, but now his hands were empty as he shoved them into his pockets. He stepped around me and, head down, hurried toward Deadtown.

I turned, watching him weave through the crowd, but I soon

lost sight as others joined him. The gates of the checkpoint into Deadtown stood wide open; the guards were letting everyone through without running their IDs. Within minutes, I was the only person standing in the street.

Smoke blew past. I checked to make sure Creature Comforts had survived unscathed. Axel saw me and raised one giant hand in silent greeting. Then he went inside and closed the door. As far as I could tell, there was no damage. But few of the other buildings in the Zone had fared as well. The door of a convenience store hung askew, boxes and broken bottles spilling out into the street. Conner's Tavern had a couple of broken windows, and smoke billowed from one of them. I hoped the sirens screaming our way came from fire trucks.

What were those zombies thinking? They weren't sticking it to the norms; they were demolishing paranormal-owned businesses. But rioters aren't practicing their logic skills. They're out for the thrill of destruction: the crack and give of splintering wood, the shriek of a hinge letting go, the blast and roar of hungry flames.

The demon mark on my right forearm buzzed. I knew—too much—about the high of letting go, of giving into rage and smashing whatever stood in your path. Even now, the demon mark urged me to pick up a rock, find an intact piece of glass, and hurl it through. Just for fun. Just to hear that sweet, sweet music of the crash and clatter.

*Do it,* a voice whispered inside my mind. The mark's buzzing ran up my arm like an electrical current. *No one's watching.* Of its own accord, my arm started to reach for a brick that lay near my feet.

"Stop it," I said out loud. I pulled my arm close to my chest and held it there, flexing my fingers, pushing out the feeling. That voice might be inside my head, but it wasn't mine. It was the voice of the Destroyer, the Hellion that had marked me, and I wasn't going to listen to its insinuations and commands.

I would not let the Destroyer rule me.

I looked around. The Zone was a mess, and I made myself see it for what it was. Not beautiful chaos, but needless waste. Waste that hurt those trying to scrape out a living here. I wasn't going to add to their misery.

Anyway, I had a job to do. As my demon mark subsided, I walked away from Deadtown, toward the checkpoint into human-controlled Boston.

I hadn't gone more than a dozen steps before four Goons in riot gear blocked my path.

"The border is closed." The Goon's riot helmet muffled his voice. "Go home."

Nobody pointed a gun at me—thank heaven for small mercies—but two Goons rested their hands on their batons. The fingers of the one who'd spoken to me twitched.

So did my demon mark. I took a couple of deep breaths to stay calm. Starting a fight with four armed Goons would not resolve the situation, unless the resolution I wanted was getting the crap kicked out of me.

"I'm a consultant for Boston PD," I said, wishing I had a badge or something to prove it. "I've been called to a crime scene. Contact Detective Daniel Costello. Homicide. He'll tell you."

The Goons didn't budge. Twitchy Fingers took a firmer grip on his baton.

I stepped back and raised my hands, palms out, to show I meant no harm. I opened my mouth to try to reason with them, but Twitchy Fingers advanced menacingly, his baton half drawn.

"Okay, calm down. I'm going home," I said. Daniel was a nice guy, but when doing him a favor meant getting my skull split open by an overzealous Goon, there was no question. I walked backward, unwilling to take my eyes off Twitchy Fingers, who matched me step for step.

A fifth Goon trotted over. "Is there a problem, gentlemen?"

Gentlemen. Hah.

Twitchy Fingers stopped and turned toward the new Goon, who was taking off his helmet. No, make that *her* helmet, I realized, as she adjusted her long blonde ponytail. I knew this cop: Pam McFarren, one of only two female zombies on the Goon Squad.

McFarren balanced her riot helmet on her hip and gave me a sharp nod. She turned back to the Goons. "Situation?" The way she barked the word sounded more like a command than a question.

Twitchy Fingers's baton went back into its holster. His arm dropped to his side. He hesitated, and then removed his helmet, too. The face inside was human. Figured. Most norms who join the Goon Squad don't do it because they want to "serve and protect" us monsters; they want to prove their toughness on Boston's meanest streets. "The subject refused to return to DA-1," he said, his voice sulky, as though McFarren had spoiled his fun. DA-1 was short for Designated Area 1, the bureaucratic name for Deadtown.

"And did it cross your mind to ask her why? Or was your plan to beat her into the ground and then make inquiries?"

The Goon looked at his feet, his lips pressed tightly together.

"I'll handle this," said McFarren. "You boys return to headquarters."

Twitchy Fingers shot her a hate-filled glare, but he nodded. He stared at me as though assessing which spot on my skull he would have whacked first, then turned away. He and the other three Goons shuffled toward the Boston checkpoint.

"Asshole," McFarren muttered when he was out of earshot. "We were sent in to prevent or contain a riot. We did the job, minimal violence. And he's disappointed he didn't get to break any heads."

"Thanks for calling him off."

She blinked and refocused on me, as though she'd forgotten I was there. "So why won't you go home?" She glanced toward Conner's, where firefighters hauled a long hose to the smoke-spewing window. "Bars are all closed."

"I'm not out for a drink." I explained that Daniel had called and requested my help. "I tried to tell that to the Goo—er, the officers, but they weren't interested."

"Yeah, why make a simple phone call when you can give your favorite weapon a workout instead? Sheesh." She snorted, then unclipped a cell phone from her belt. A couple of calls later, she motioned to me. "You're cleared," she said. We walked toward the Boston checkpoint. "There are a couple of uniforms waiting for you on the other side of the checkpoint. Costello sent them to vouch for you, but word never got through to my boys."

"You've been promoted?" The way she'd sent those other Goons packing was a classic demonstration of pulling rank.

"To sergeant." She raised her chin with pride, but then her forehead creased in a scowl. "'Course, some of the guys say it's affirmative action bullshit. Promoting a PDH who's also a woman nails two birds with one stone." PDH, or *previously deceased human*, was the politically correct term for zombie. "But I deserve it. I worked hard for my promotion. I have to be three times as tough, or they think I'm soft."

Looking at McFarren in her riot gear—her broad shoulders, her narrowed eyes, the determined set of her jaw—*soft* was the last word that came to mind.

She sighed. "All this unrest in Deadtown lately. It's really split the squad in two. Half the guys sympathize with the zombies. The other half would like to bomb Deadtown into oblivion. The split isn't even along human-PDH lines." She shook her head. "But here's the thing about being a cop: You can't take sides. All you can do is uphold the law."

"Even if the law is unfair?" A zombie had killed some norms, and now every single Deadtown resident was guilty by association.

McFarren shrugged again. "I never said the law was perfect. Sometimes it's necessary to tilt the balance a little to keep the peace or ensure the greater good. I can live with that."

"But what if it tilts too far?"

"That's the day I leave the force." The steel in her expression suggested that would be the day *after* hell froze over. "In the meantime, I have to keep knuckleheads like that guy"—she jerked a thumb over her shoulder, toward where Twitchy Fingers and I had faced off—"from beating the crap out of innocent people, just because he can. I think I see your escort."

We'd reached the checkpoint. On the other side, two uniformed cops waited. McFarren went over to speak to them, then she motioned me to come through. The guard swiped my ID and handed it back. The gate went up, and I stepped into human-controlled Boston.

# 2

THE LEATHERWORKERS WHO GAVE THE LEATHER DISTRICT
its name are long gone. Their old factories have been converted
into trendy lofts, bars, boutiques, and restaurants. The galaxy
of flashing police lights and yellow crime scene tape seemed
out of place here. The faces peering from windows reinforced
the sense of novelty.

As soon as I ducked under the crime scene tape, Daniel was
there. It had been a few months since I last saw him, but there
was no mistaking his curly, tousled blond hair or that high-
wattage smile. He gave me a quick, one-arm hug. When he let
go his smile lingered, but his blue eyes were full of worry.

"So what happened?" I asked.

"I'll walk you through and tell you what we've learned."
When I nodded and turned toward the scene, he put a restrain-
ing hand on my arm. "It's not pretty."

"I wasn't expecting it to be."

Still, his hand stayed in place and we stood where we were.
"Thomas Malone was the PDH involved," he said. "Did you
know him?"

I shook my head.

"Huh." Daniel seemed puzzled, even disappointed.

"Daniel, there are over two thousand zombies in Deadtown. I'm not going to know every single one."

"Sure, of course. But—Well, you'll see why I thought maybe you did. Anyway, Malone was part of the night crew at a warehouse in Dorchester. He and four coworkers have a Class B permit to go there for the overnight shift six nights a week."

A Class B permit was open-ended permission for a group of zombies to leave Deadtown for work purposes. Zombies are in demand as manual laborers for the third shift. They're strong—just one can do the work of five humans—and night is their natural "awake" time. The big plus: Labor laws don't insist on pesky expenses like health insurance or minimum wage for zombies.

Daniel showed me a list of names, the other zombies on Malone's crew. I didn't recognize any of them, either.

"So," he said, "Malone's work routine was this: Each night, an hour after sunset, a van would arrive to pick up the crew. The van came from Hub Transit—they've got a standing order to send a driver twice a night: first to pick up the crew and then to bring them home again before sunrise. Besides the driver, the crew's human sponsor made the trip each night."

"The sponsor is employed by the warehouse company?" Even with a Class B work permit, zombies couldn't leave Deadtown unless they were accompanied by a human.

"Was. He was shift supervisor."

*Was.* Okay. So the supervisor was one of the victims.

"And that's the van over there?" I pointed to a white vehicle that sat half on the sidewalk, its front crumpled against a lamppost.

"Yes. Last night, Malone and the others left Deadtown as usual. Records show they went through the Summer Street checkpoint at seven forty-six P.M. Hub Transit dispatched the van for the return trip at three fifty-seven A.M. Just past the intersection of Lincoln and Beach, Malone attacked the driver."

"And you don't think it was bloodlust." Maybe he was mistaken. It doesn't take much blood to set a zombie off. The driver might have chewed down a hangnail too far or gotten overzealous popping a zit.

"I'm sure it wasn't. There were four other PDHs in the van. We've taken a statement from each of them. No one smelled any blood before the attack. Malone was closest to the driver, sitting in the seat directly behind him, so I suppose there's a chance he smelled blood the others didn't catch. But Malone didn't act like a PDH in a blood frenzy."

"By which you mean, I assume, that he didn't try to eat the driver?"

"Right. Without any warning, he reached forward, gave the guy's head a twist, and snapped his neck."

And that would be how the van ended up accordioned against a streetlight.

Daniel continued. "The supervisor, who was in the front passenger seat, tried to take control of the van. Malone got his hands around the guy's neck and choked the life out of him. Another PDH tried to pull Malone off, but he couldn't budge him."

"Malone's a big guy?"

"That's what we understand."

Wait—the police didn't know for sure? "He's still on the loose? I thought you guys had him in custody." Okay, if a murderous zombie was running around the city, maybe I couldn't blame Commissioner Hampson for sealing off Deadtown. In his place, I probably would have made the same call. First time for everything.

Daniel gave me a funny look and said, "Not exactly. Let me finish telling the story."

"All right." But I was wondering why he'd called me in. "So far, I haven't heard anything to indicate demon activity. Demons don't possess zombies, if that's what you're thinking about Malone."

"Just give me your opinion after you've heard all the facts and taken a look at the scene."

I nodded.

"After the van crashed, the PDHs all clambered out. Malone's coworkers followed procedure and put on their masks." All zombies who worked outside of Deadtown were required to carry surgical masks, saturated with eucalyptus, to overpower the smell of blood if they found themselves in the vicinity of an injured human. The masks are sealed inside an easy-open plastic pouch, and zombies who carry them have to pass a speed test for putting them on.

"But not Malone, I take it?"

"Right. While the others were putting on their masks, Malone got his third victim, a human who'd run across the street to see if he could help. Tore the guy's head off."

It was a good thing the other four zombies got their masks on. Five bloodlust-crazed zombies rampaging through Boston was not what you'd call good public relations.

"One of Malone's coworkers tackled him. Two more piled on while the fourth, who was injured with a broken ankle from the crash, called 911. But even together, those three PDHs couldn't hold Malone down. He shook them all off and was back on his feet when all of a sudden he fell to his knees, clutching his temples." Daniel ducked his head, watching my face intently as he spoke his next words. "Vicky, two of the three zombies who were nearby heard crows cawing."

*Crows.* For a moment, everything stopped. My heart quit beating. My lungs forgot to take in air. And the harsh cries of a hundred crows echoed inside my own mind. "You think this was a Morfran attack?"

What Daniel was suggesting, if true, would be the worst kind of bad news. The Morfran, an evil, destructive spirit of insatiable hunger, is the power that animates demons and gives them their strength. You could say that, for demons, the Morfran is a corrupt version of the human soul. Morfran means "great crow." My race of shapeshifters, the Cerddorion, has battled the Morfran, keeping demons weak, from the very beginnings of time.

But the demons had other plans. For centuries, they'd bided their time, watching for signs and omens that their prophesied chance to rule the three realms—the worlds of the living, the dead, and the demonic—was coming to pass. Pryce Maddox, a demi-demon who calls himself my cousin, believed the time was now. And Pryce would stop at nothing to be the conquering emperor.

When the Morfran possesses a person, it drives its host to kill. The spirit also has a free-floating form, which takes the shape of massive crows. Free-floating Morfran can be imprisoned in slate, and that's where much of the Morfran had remained, locked away by my ancestors and guarded by generations of shapeshifters. But last winter, Pryce had discovered how to release the Morfran. He freed huge amounts of the spirit and sent it to Boston to feed. Crows are carrion eaters, and the Morfran's favorite snack turned out to be zombie flesh.

The Morfran was one of the few things that could kill a zombie. And many zombies, some of them my friends, had died before I managed to subdue the Morfran, dividing it and binding it inside the slate headstones of one of Boston's oldest cemeteries.

New Morfran activity suggested Pryce was making a move.

Daniel watched as I processed these thoughts. Finally he spoke. "Something attacked him, but I don't know what. That's why I asked you to come and have a look."

"Malone's dead, I take it."

He nodded. "Are you okay to view the body—or what's left of it?"

I'd seen zombie Morfran victims before. Daniel's comment when I arrived—"it's not pretty"—was a finalist for understatement of the century.

"Sure," I said, steeling myself.

Daniel offered me a eucalyptus-treated surgical mask, the kind the zombies wore. I waved it away. Morfran attacks leave behind a stomach-clenching stench, but that would help me tell whether the Morfran really had killed Malone.

I could already smell it from where we stood. Around the edges of the expected smells—exhaust, garbage, the blood of Malone's victims—lurked a foul odor redolent of sourness and decay.

Daniel opened the pack and removed the mask. He put it on his own face, covering his mouth and nose. His eyes watered from the eucalyptus fumes, and he blinked to clear them. Together we went to inspect the scene.

Ambulance workers were removing the driver from the van. A gurney waited nearby, ready to receive the body. Another gurney, draped with a white sheet and now being wheeled toward the ambulance, probably carried the shift supervisor. Not far from the van, in the street, another sheet covered a lump the size and shape of an adult man. Six feet away, a smaller sheet hid an object the size of a soccer ball.

"That's the third victim's head?" I asked, pointing.

Daniel nodded.

There was no sign of Malone's body. Not at first glance, anyway. You couldn't put a white sheet over what I was looking for.

Beyond the headless human body, a large puddle of black goo covered the street. It looked like a truckload of tar had spilled there. I walked toward it, noticing two things as I went: Flecks of the black stuff speckled the van and nearby buildings, and the dead, sour smell I'd noted back at the police line grew stronger. It made the air a viscous, putrid fog.

Although it was full daylight now, I opened my senses to the demon plane—and staggered back a step. If the smell was bad in my reality, here it was unbearable. I covered my nose with both hands and scanned the area. In this perspective, the morning light dimmed to an ashy gray twilight, smudging the scene with filth. Demons can't materialize in daylight, so I didn't expect to see any hanging around. I didn't; the streets and sky were empty.

If the Morfran had been involved in what happened here, the spirit was gone now.

From the looks of what was left of Tom Malone, the Morfran *was* involved, I thought as I pulled back from the demon plane. Back in human reality, the smell was less overwhelming, and I let my hands fall to my sides. I inspected the black slime that covered the street. Crime scene technicians, swathed in protective gear, combed through it, picking things up with tweezers and dropping them into evidence bags. Daniel showed me what they'd collected so far: bone fragments. Scraps of cloth. A clump of hair. A tooth.

"You're right," I told him. "It sure as hell looks like Malone was killed by the Morfran."

A Morfran attack has three stages. First, the attacking spirit gouges out chunks of flesh and enters the victim, causing pressure to build inside the head. As this screaming headache grows, more Morfran enters the body and feeds. The pressure in the head increases, filling the entire body with agonizing pain. Finally, the pressure becomes too much, and—*kaboom!*—the victim explodes. Leaving exactly the kind of mess now gunking up Lincoln Street.

We walked back to the scene perimeter, away from the slime

and the smell. Daniel removed his mask and stuck it in his pocket.

Something was bothering me. "You remember the stages of a Morfran attack, right?"

He nodded. "Entry, feeding, explosion."

"You said two of the witnesses heard crows. Did anyone say anything about *seeing* crows attack Malone? You know, materialized Morfran."

"I asked. No one saw anything like that."

"Then what about wounds spontaneously opening up on Malone's body, like he was being slashed by an invisible knife? The Morfran doesn't always materialize when it attacks."

"All they said was what I told you. Malone dropped to his knees, clutched his head, and then . . ." Daniel gestured toward the zombie's remains. "I see what you mean, though. Unless the witnesses left something out, it doesn't follow the pattern." He ran a hand through his hair, then shrugged.

"I need to interview the zombie witnesses," I said.

Daniel gave me a half smile. "Does that mean you want the job?"

"What job?" a man's voice asked from behind me. "Costello, what's this paranormal doing outside DA-1? The code level's at red, you know."

"Shit," muttered Daniel. Then he raised his voice. "So, Foster, you finally decided to answer your phone?"

I turned to see the bald head and perpetual scowl of Daniel's partner. Daniel believed they'd been put together because he, Daniel, was thought to be too sympathetic to paranormals. Foster, who had no such scruples, had reported Daniel several times for violating department policies regarding those of us whose DNA reads something other than "human." Those department policies had been created by Commissioner Hampson, who'd like nothing better than to send in the wrecking balls and knock Deadtown off the map.

Foster kept his beady eyes on me. "My phone battery died. Now, are you going to keep violating the Code Red, or are you going to call some uniforms to escort this . . . creature back to DA-1?"

*Creature.* My demon mark blew up like a firecracker, and

I had to grab my own right arm to stop myself from hauling off and punching that scowl off his ugly face. Give him something to spice up his goddamn report.

Daniel laid his hand on my shoulder. "Vicky's on the exceptions list. You'd know that if you'd bother to check."

Foster continued his stare-down like he was daring me to start something.

"She's on a list of approved consultants," Daniel went on. "An expert on demons. She's worked with us in that capacity before."

That was true. If you define "working with" as being dragged out of bed by the Goon Squad and marched to their headquarters for questioning. At least this time Daniel had picked up the phone and called me.

"Vicky." Daniel turned to me, and I broke eye contact with Foster. "We need your help on this." He named a per diem rate. "Save receipts for any expenses that come up. You'll get reimbursed. And you shouldn't have any more trouble getting through the checkpoints. Once this goes through, you'll be on the permanent 'clear' list."

"And that means?"

"Your approved status remains the same, no matter what the code level."

"Until revoked," Foster added, savoring the words.

"Yes, until revoked," Daniel snapped. "Just like your detective's shield is good until it's revoked."

Foster's snorty laugh showed how little he feared that happening.

Daniel lightly touched my arm, turning me away from Foster. We started walking toward Deadtown. "I'll see you back to the checkpoint, then start on the paperwork right away. I'd like you to come out and interview the witnesses tonight, as soon as it's dark."

Behind us, Foster snorted out another laugh. I turned to glare at him. The detective's eyes gleamed, as though he was seeing a vision of Daniel wrapped like a mummy in miles and miles of red tape.

# 3

AFTER SUNRISE, DEADTOWN BECOMES A GHOST TOWN.
(Well, not literally—ghosts are one of the few paranormal
beings you *won't* find here. Arawn, lord of the dead, does a
pretty good job of keeping the shades of the departed within
the boundaries of his realm.) But today, even though the sun
had been up for more than an hour, the streets were crowded.
And the mood wasn't what you'd call festive.

Zombies gathered in small groups, some listening to street-
corner orators, others looking like they were ready for trouble
the moment somebody else started it. Most were bundled up
against the skin-damaging sunlight, wearing wide-brimmed
hats, sunglasses, scarves or bandanas, coats, gloves. They
looked more ready for a polar expedition than a political
protest.

But protest was in the air. Deadtown residents were beyond
fed up. And they were getting ready to do something about it.

Snatches of speeches faded in and out as I passed:

"... *Previously Deceased Humans. Hear that?* Humans.
*Unlike some others around here, we're human, and we deserve
the same rights we had before the plague* ..."

*". . . no longer willing to play the scapegoat for every crisis in Boston . . ."*

*". . . take back what's ours! Before the plague, I owned my own business and two homes. Now? By law I can't own anything. I work as a manual laborer. How 'bout you? How many here have similar stories?"*

A zombie turned to watch me walk by, then nudged another standing next to him. Their heads moved as they tracked me; even with their eyes hidden behind sunglasses, the hostility was palpable. I stopped. Putting my fists on my hips, I faced them, returning their stares. It wasn't a challenge, simply a message that I would not be hurried on my way by a couple of zombies who didn't like the looks of someone like me in their neighborhood.

I can't help it if I look like a human. Most of the time.

After ten or twelve long seconds, the second zombie turned back to the speaker. The other watched me for another heartbeat or two. Then he also turned around.

I let out the breath I hadn't realized I was holding. Then I continued down the block.

At the intersection, I paused. If I turned left here, a few minutes' walk would take me to Kane's town house. Kane, the monster I loved . . . or thought I did. Like many werewolves who held professional jobs, he worked norm hours. Usually he'd be at his office by now. But that office was near Government Center in the human part of town, and Deadtown was locked down tighter than a maximum security prison. Kane wasn't on any Code Red exceptions list. As a high-profile lawyer working to secure civil rights for paranormals, he had too many enemies in the Police Commissioner's Office. So right now, he was either working from home or making his own street-corner speech, one urging calm and using the courts—not violence—to redress grievances.

I wanted to see him. Five minutes and I could be there. I'd go up to the front door and pull out my key . . . I sighed. No, I wouldn't. Even though Kane had given me a key to his place months ago, I wouldn't use it. I'd ring the bell. And the reason why was the same reason I stood on this corner, unable to make my feet move in the direction I wanted to go.

After years of on-again, off-again dating, Kane had told me

he loved me. That he wanted to take our relationship to the next level. And I, world champion of commitment-phobes, had managed to admit I felt the same way. So why wasn't I running to be with him now?

Why, indeed.

A couple of weeks ago, I'd followed Pryce into the Darklands, the realm of the dead, to try to stop him from recreating his lost shadow demon and reclaiming his power. I'd failed. Not only did Pryce have a shadow demon again, that shadow demon was the biggest, nastiest Hellion I'd ever had the misfortune to encounter. Although I'd killed Difethwr, the Destroyer, Pryce had managed to resurrect the Hellion, binding himself to it in the process. The Destroyer and I went way back—more than ten years ago, the Hellion placed its mark on me, the mark that made me want to smash things when I didn't keep it under control. When Pryce brought the Destroyer back to life—bigger and nastier than ever—my little anger-management problem boiled over.

These days, dating me was on a par with dating an active volcano. Any little thing could trigger an explosion, like when I'd surveyed the destruction in the New Combat Zone and wanted to join in. But the Destroyer's claim on me wasn't the worst of it.

When I'd disappeared into the Darklands, Kane followed me there, determined to bring me home. But the realm of the dead doesn't issue tourist visas. To get in, he'd made a bargain with Mallt-y-Nos, aka the Night Hag, a psychopomp who drives wandering spirits of the recently departed into the Darklands. Mallt-y-Nos is a hunter. She loves nothing more than to chase terrified, disoriented souls through the night, her pack of hellhounds snapping at their heels. As his price of admission to the Darklands, Kane agreed to serve the Night Hag as one of those hellhounds for a year and a day.

When he made the deal, Kane had no way of knowing what he was getting into.

He knew better now.

The Night Hag's hellhounds are creatures made of pain. Fiery, agonizing pain miles beyond anything imaginable. The burning drives the frantic hounds onward—running, running from the pain—but no relief ever comes. The hag intensifies the torture to force the hounds to obey her commands. It's the kind of pain that pushes everything out—thoughts, judgments, even sanity—consuming all. I knew, because I'd experienced it. To enter the Darklands, I'd made my own bargain with the Night Hag. She'd forced me to shift into a hellhound and then run me across the border.

Now, Kane had experienced it, too. Just once, but once was enough to break nearly anyone. And for the next twelve full moons, his werewolf form would be twisted, over and over again, into a monstrous hound that knows nothing but pain.

The Night Hag hates me because even though I fulfilled the terms of our deal, things didn't turn out in her favor. She's vowed that her hellhounds will tear me to pieces. And she's waiting until the next full moon, when her pack will have an extra member: Kane.

He'll be forced to obey the Night Hag's command; the pain won't leave room for anything else. I know it, and he knows it.

There's no way around it: *I love you* doesn't stand a chance against *Sorry, but in a few days I'll be forced to hunt you down and kill you*. Was it any wonder we were avoiding each other?

With a heavy heart, I crossed the street and headed home.

IN MY BUILDING'S LOBBY, I NODDED GOOD MORNING TO Clyde, the doorman, who was stationed at his desk. He was eating, as zombies do, but Clyde's sense of decorum was such that he never wanted to be caught snacking on the job. He stashed a crinkly cellophane bag in the desk and brushed some crumbs off his uniform.

"Good morning, Ms. Vaughn," he said. I'd asked about a hundred times for him to call me Vicky, but to Clyde being on a first-name basis with tenants was as much a faux pas as picking one's nose in public. "Mr. Kane stopped by while you were out."

My heartbeat surged. "Is he upstairs?"

Clyde pursed his lips. He'd been a minister in his former, pre-plague life, and becoming a zombie hadn't changed his moral sense one iota. Although he'd never uttered a judgmental word, he'd let me know in no uncertain terms what he thought when I gave Kane a key to my apartment. In fact, he was letting me know right now. If you've never gotten a disapproving look from a holier-than-thou zombie, you haven't really lived. Still, once you get past the disapproval, Clyde's a good guy.

"No," he finally said. "He seemed very concerned with that business out there." Clyde waved a hand toward the door, whether to indicate the zombie unrest in Deadtown or the state of the world in general I couldn't tell. "He requested that I inform you he'll telephone this evening."

As the rhythm of my heart settled back to normal, I wondered whether it was pleasure or anxiety that sped it up in the first place. Both, probably. At any rate, Kane knew I usually slept during the day, so he was assuming I'd come home from wherever and fall into bed. Which was exactly what I intended to do.

If only he were there to fall into bed with me.

I wished. In the days since we'd returned from the Darklands, Kane and I had barely been able to look one another in the eye, let alone touch each other. It was like each of us was afraid the other would break.

Maybe we would.

A sigh escaped me before I squared my shoulders and thanked Clyde. His expression softened, as much as it's possible for a zombie's face to go soft. "Is everything all right, Ms. Vaughn?"

*No.* These days, nothing was within shouting distance of all right. But I pasted on a smile and nodded. "Fine."

Clyde tilted his head skeptically, as if trying to see inside mine. "If I can be of any assistance. I'm a trained counselor, you know . . ." He blinked, as if suddenly remembering his place, and nodded sharply.

"Thanks, Clyde." My words seemed to embarrass him. He shuffled papers on his desk and wouldn't meet my gaze. "Well, have a good day," I said. He didn't reply.

Walking across the lobby to the elevators, I wondered how long it had been since either of us had had a truly good day. Was there such a thing in Deadtown?

# 4

I COULD HEAR JULIET'S MOVIE SCREEN–SIZE TV BLARING
through the front door as I inserted my key. One of the disad-
vantages of having a 650-year-old vampire for a roommate was
her simultaneous fascination and boredom with contemporary
life. Juliet was intrigued by modern technology, which was
why she bought the biggest, flattest, highest-definition television she could find. But during her many centuries of undeath,
she'd seen it all—aside from intermittent "fascinations" (her
word) with home shopping channels or the latest reality show,
she couldn't sustain interest in what was on. In other words,
she loved her TV but couldn't care less about the content. She'd
turn it on, crank up the volume in all six speakers, marvel at
the quality of the picture and the sound, and then wander off
to find something else to do. Seeing as the sun had come up
hours ago, she was undoubtedly tucked into her coffin, dead
to the world, leaving me to risk going totally deaf in the time
it took to cross the living room, pick up the remote, and turn
the damn thing off.

*Good thing our neighbors are vampires, too,* I thought,
opening the door and wincing against the assault of sound.
Once a vampire resumes the shroud for the day, nothing dis-

turbs him until sundown. At least I didn't have to deal with angry neighbors pounding on—or more likely through—the walls.

To my surprise, Juliet was still up. She sat in the dark room, blackout shades drawn, her face tinged by the flickering bluish light from the screen. She didn't notice me come in; she was absorbed in some nature program, absentmindedly eating popcorn from a bowl in her lap.

I switched on the overhead light, and she turned toward me, blinking.

"Can you turn that down?" I shouted.

She leaned forward and picked up the remote. Several clicks later, I could actually hear myself think.

"What did you say? I couldn't hear you over the television."

Before I could think of a suitably sarcastic reply, a large white bird hopped onto Juliet's shoulder. "It was a little loud, I guess," the falcon said. "But those surround-sound speakers are brilliant." He cocked his head and fixed his sharp gaze on the bowl in Juliet's lap. "May I have some more popcorn?"

"Hi, Dad," I said, as Juliet offered a kernel to the hooked beak.

Yes, my father is a white falcon. A *talking* white falcon with rainbow-colored eyes.

He hadn't always been a bird, of course. Although I come from a race of shapeshifters, Dad's condition was unheard of, even among our kind. For one thing, only Cerddorion females have the ability to shift (it arrives with all the other joys of puberty). For another, when I change shape, the animal brain takes over. If I shifted into a falcon, I wouldn't be sitting in anyone's living room, watching TV, eating popcorn, and making conversation. I'd be out hunting mice or whatever it is falcons do. Real falcons, I mean.

But my father had done something that no one among the Cerddorion—hell, no one of *any* species—had ever managed to do. He'd hijacked the body of a falcon to come back from the dead.

After my father, Evan Vaughn, was killed by the Destroyer, whom I'd foolishly summoned in my eighteen-year-old know-it-all mode, Dad spent ten years in the Darklands, first serving in Arawn's court and then, when his shade had been

marked for reincarnation, hiding out in a cave. More than anything, Dad wanted to keep his spirit from being cleansed of its
memories and recycled into the body of a newborn infant.
When I followed Pryce into the Darklands, Dad helped me
track him down. But the closer we got to Tywyll, Arawn's
capital, the stronger the pull of reincarnation became. The
magic that gave Dad a body in the Darklands drained away
from him, and his spirit was in danger of dispersing into nothing. In fact, I thought I'd lost him forever.

But no Vaughn has ever quit without a fight. Dad knew that
the Night Hag required three items as my price of passage out
of the Darklands. One of these was the white falcon of
Hellsmoor, a magical bird that could enter places from which
others were barred. The hag demanded I bring her the falcon,
along with a magic arrow and Lord Arawn's hunting horn, to
make her nightly hunts more amusing. To Dad, the falcon
looked like an escape plan. He bound his spirit to the bird's
body and hitched a ride back to the world of the living.

A brilliant idea, with one big downside. That downside was
currently sitting on my living room sofa pecking popcorn from
my roommate's hand.

Juliet scattered some popcorn across the coffee table, and
Dad hopped over to peck at it. Juliet stretched and stood. "My
coffin calls," she said. "What time is it, anyway?"

"Nearly eight."

"No wonder I'm tired. I should have reinterred myself hours
ago. But the program your father and I were watching was just
so . . . fascinating." Uh-oh. It sounded like Juliet was starting
a new television obsession. Well, at least it would be cheaper
than the time she bought every single product labeled "As Seen
on TV."

She waved good night and went down the hallway. A
moment later her bedroom door clicked closed.

I sat down on the sofa where Juliet had been and picked up
the popcorn bowl. Only a few crumbs left at the bottom. I set
the bowl on the table.

"What were you guys watching?" I asked my father.

"A show about birds of prey. Their habitats, behavior—that
sort of thing."

"Feeding habits?" I doubted wild falcons had much popcorn in their diet.

"Let's gloss over that part," he said, popcorn spilling from his beak. "I figure, though, that if I'm going to be in this body, I have to be able to pass myself off as an actual falcon when needed. If I act like myself, I'll end up as a sideshow attraction."

"Or the Night Hag's pet." Dad had escaped from the Night Hag, but she was a huntress at heart and would never quit trying to get him back. Although she didn't know the falcon was my father—almost no one did—she'd offered me a trade. If I returned the white falcon to her, she would release Kane from his servitude as a hellhound.

Kane, free of pain and subjugation.

Her offer was tempting, I had to admit. I'd take her up on it in a heartbeat, except for two things. One: The falcon in question was my father. And you just don't hand your dad over to an evil, vindictive spirit, even if it means freeing your boyfriend from same. Two: Obscure, ancient prophecies hinted that a white falcon had a role to play in the coming war among the realms. Unfortunately, said prophecies were obscure enough that we didn't know exactly what that role would be—or even if Dad was the falcon referred to. But when hundreds of thousands of lives are at stake, you don't sit around playing guessing games.

Still . . . there was Kane. The warmth that made his gray eyes glow when he smiled. His courage, the courage to go to hell and back—for me. His sense of fair play. His belief in justice. The Night Hag wanted to destroy all that, to strip away everything that made Kane who he was, leaving nothing but a shattered, empty shell.

It almost made me think it would be worth it, worth *anything*, to wrest Kane from her power.

For three weeks, my thoughts had circled in that endless loop: Dad . . . the prophecies . . . Kane. Over and over again. I thought I'd have time to plan a strategy. But now the full moon was approaching, and I still didn't see any way out of this mess.

It didn't help that Dad had made me swear to keep his return a secret. I hadn't told a soul, not even Kane. Not even Mab, my aunt and demon-fighting mentor—and I told her *everything*.

Mab knew I'd brought the white falcon out of the Darklands, but she didn't know Dad had come with it.

Dad, done inspecting the coffee table for popcorn kernels, perched on the back of the sofa and preened his feathers.

"Have you told Mom yet?" I asked. When Dad wasn't hanging out at my place watching TV, he spent most of his time staking out the suburban neighborhood of my sister, Gwen. Mom had left her retirement condo in Florida to move in with the Santini family for a while, helping Gwen's daughter, Maria, adjust to the shapeshifting abilities she was starting to manifest. Mom and Gwen had both remarked several times on the large white falcon nesting in the area. But my promise to Dad kept me silent. As far as I could tell, Juliet was the only one besides me who knew—and I suspected that had something to do with her willingness to make popcorn.

"Of course I'll tell your mother. I'm waiting for the right moment."

"Dad, there *is* no right moment. When a bird opens his beak and starts talking, it's bound to be a shock. When that bird says, 'Hi, honey, I'm home. Did you miss me?' it's guaranteed to up the voltage."

"I don't see what's so strange about a talking bird. Parrots talk."

"But they don't have conversations. Anyway, you're not a parrot."

"Damn right." Dad puffed out his chest. "You won't hear me begging for a cracker." He eyed the empty popcorn bowl. "I wouldn't mind a cheeseburger, though."

"If I'd known you were here, I'd have brought you one." The white falcon had a magical ability to go anywhere he wanted— locked doors and walls be damned—but hadn't yet mastered the art of calling ahead.

Besides hanging out, getting fed, and watching TV, there was another reason my father spent time in my apartment. I asked about it now. "Dad, have you looked at the book recently?"

I didn't have to name the title. He knew which book I meant: *The Book of Utter Darkness*, an ancient volume written in the language of Hell, which outlined the history of the conflict between demons and the Cerddorion—from the demons' point of view. It contained prophecies of how that conflict would end, prophecies that were now coming to pass left and right. It was this book that mentioned the white falcon.

The book and I had a history. For years, it had fascinated me on Mab's library shelf, the only book I was forbidden to read. When I was eighteen and considered myself a highly trained demon slayer, I took the book down and, leafing through, conjured a demon. I guess my intention was to show there was no demon I couldn't take down. The demon that answered the call was Difethwr, the Hellion that marked me and killed my father. I'd vowed never to touch the book again, and for years I didn't, but the times it prophesied were now upon us. At Mab's insistence, I went from avoiding the book to studying it. We needed to find out what was coming and how we might counter it. But the book was full of tricks. You couldn't read it the way you'd read a normal book; you had to stare at the unfathomable words until a meaning took shape in your mind. Sometimes the meaning didn't come. Sometimes it came in riddles—riddles that tried to trip up and fool the reader into believing whatever meaning the book was pushing.

Lately, whenever I looked into the book, one of two things happened: Either I stared at its pages until I went cross-eyed, getting nothing, or else the book hit me hard with a vision of destruction so terrible and all-encompassing it left me shaking for hours. Not exactly surprising, then, that I was back to avoiding *The Book of Utter Darkness*. Since Dad was willing to spend time with it, I was happy to hand it over to him. He'd perch on the back of a kitchen chair, the book open before him on the table. For hours at a time, he'd stare at the book with that predator's gaze, turning pages with his beak.

"I looked at it for a little while," he said now, "before my show came on."

"Anything new?"

"Hard to tell. The book doesn't speak to me, to Evan Vaughn, I mean. Everything I get from it goes straight to the falcon part of my brain." Mab said the book referred to the white falcon, but in all my terrible visions of a burning land-scape terrorized by demons, the falcon had never appeared. "I get flashes of imagery," Dad continued, "but they're filtered through the falcon's perception, so it's hard to know what they mean."

"What kind of imagery?"

"Darkness, mostly. But it's not the kind of darkness that makes the falcon want to return to his nest. I guess that means it's not night. It's a darkness that grows thicker and thinner, that burns my lungs."

"Smoke." There was plenty of smoke in my visions. They showed the entire East Coast in flames.

"Yeah, smoke. It must be that. But it's damn frustrating, Vic. The falcon doesn't have any words for anything. He's driven by instinct. He knows hunger, hunting, sleeping, danger." His head turned almost all the way around, toward the TV. "That's another reason I was watching the nature show. I was hoping it would give me some insight into how this body's brain works. So I can interpret its images and feelings better."

I nodded. "So this darkness, or smoke—does it come with a feeling of danger?"

The falcon cocked his head as Dad considered. "Yes. The burning feeling in the bird's lungs makes him want to fly higher. But he doesn't want to flee. He's not afraid. Instead he's . . . excited. And hungry. But . . ." For a moment, I could almost see Dad's face—his real face—superimposed on the falcon's, frowning as he struggled to express his meaning. "But not like the kind of hunger that wants a cheeseburger or, you know, a rat. The feeling isn't in the bird's stomach; it's . . . I don't know where it is. But the only way I can describe it is hunger."

"Weird." I understood how hard it was, trying to use the human mind to interpret an animal's perceptions. When I came out of a shift, I had exactly the same problem. "In your visions, is the falcon's hunger ever satisfied? Does it feed?"

"That's a good question. The short answer is no, it doesn't. But there's a jolt of attention, followed by excitement. The feeling a falcon gets when its vision locks onto a mouse or a rabbit or whatever moving in a field below."

"When it spots its prey."

"Exactly. Then everything blacks out. The book drops the curtain, so to speak, and I can't see what caught the bird's attention. I'll tell you one thing, though. When I come back to myself, I'm ravenous." His hooked beak opened and closed. "In fact, I think I'll go out and get that cheeseburger now. Maybe a couple."

"Munchies?" Dad may have been stuck in a falcon's body, but he didn't share his host's taste for raw, still-squirming meat. Dad's favorite hunting ground was Munchies, a fast-food restaurant in Deadtown, where one of the zombie short-order cooks had taken a liking to him. Dad hadn't spoken or anything, but whenever the white falcon appeared, the cook would toss a cheeseburger upward and watch admiringly as the bird caught the food in his talons and climbed into the sky.

The falcon glanced at the clock. "Shoot, I missed Munchies. They close an hour before dawn."

"They might be open today. Half of Deadtown's zombies are milling around out there." And when zombies mill, they get hungry.

"I noticed that when I flew into town. What's going on?"

I filled him in. "Daniel, he's a homicide detective, thinks the Morfran is somehow involved. From what I saw at the scene, I suspect he's right. But from witness accounts, it doesn't sound like a straightforward Morfran attack. So I'm going to interview the witnesses tonight. Maybe that will help us understand what happened."

His falcon eyes bright, Dad nodded. "You should take another look at the book, Vic. New Morfran activity might be an omen."

"You're right." A wave of weariness washed over me, and all I wanted to do was crawl into bed. "I will. But later." I needed to sleep. If I even glanced at the book right now, while I was tired and weak, it would attack. Once my mind was clear, I'd try again.

Dad left, hoping to scrounge a cheeseburger or two, and I got ready for bed. I thought about contacting Mab at her home in Wales to tell her about the zombie attack and its possible Morfran connection. She'd want to know. But I decided to wait. It would make more sense to talk to the witnesses first. That way, I'd have a better idea of what we were dealing with.

Right now, the only thing I knew for sure was this: Whatever it was, it couldn't be good.

# 5

I WOKE UP AROUND FOUR IN THE AFTERNOON, AFTER A long sleep blessedly free of dreams. No zombies rioting in the Zone. No visions of Boston burning. No flashbacks to the sheet-covered bodies or stinking black slime of Daniel's crime scene. Those images decided to wait until I opened my eyes, when they all came rushing back, reminding me of the problems crowding around and clamoring for my attention.

Rolling over and clamping a pillow on top of my head wouldn't do anything to make them go away. I know. I tried.

That left one option: facing them. By the time I'd hit the shower, pulled on a pair of jeans and a T-shirt, and downed two mugs of black coffee, I felt almost ready to do just that.

I still had some time before I went to meet Daniel at the Tremont Street checkpoint, so I thought about which weapons to take on tonight's expedition. I wasn't going demon-hunting, so I didn't need my usual assorting of daggers, a sword or two, and bullets, all in demon-busting bronze. Still, it would be dark soon, the time when demons are free to enter in the human plane, and you never know when one might materialize in your face, waving its claws and spewing its sulfur-and-brimstone halitosis. I'd bring along a bronze-bladed dagger or two, just in case. A pistol and a couple of magazines of bronze bullets couldn't hurt either.

But one weapon was a must-have for tonight: Hellforged, an obsidian dagger that, true to its name, had been fashioned by demons in the depths of Hell. Centuries ago, the Cerddorion had stolen it from a Hellion, and it was the only tool we had to control the Morfran.

Hellforged rested in my hand, its polished black blade gleaming. The first time I ever touched this dagger, it leapt away from me like a skittish colt. Hellforged had a mind of its own, and my early attempts to use it were clumsy. But we'd learned how to work together. Now, a quiet vibration thrummed through the dagger as I held it, but it didn't twitch or jump. I slid it into its ankle holster, hoping there would be no need to use it tonight.

Hellforged could call and hold the Morfran, but only slate could imprison the spirit. For that, I had a specially made slate plaque, commissioned by Mab from a local witch in Wales. The plaque looked like something your grandmother would hang in her gingham-curtained kitchen. Surrounded by a painted border of curlicues were the words HOME SWEET HOME. The curlicues were magically charged symbols that strengthened the slate and increased its capacity to hold the Morfran. HOME SWEET HOME had no magical significance; it was my aunt's idea of a joke.

Okay, so Mab doesn't have the world's sharpest sense of humor. She's still a formidable demon fighter.

I tucked the slate into my jacket's inner pocket. After checking again to make sure my weapons were secure, I went to meet Daniel.

THE SCENE IN DEADTOWN HADN'T CHANGED MUCH SINCE this morning. All the zombies who'd usually be working the night shift were restricted to DA-1, thanks to the Code Red, and every single one of them seemed to be out on the streets. The mood was tense, the air buzzing with that electric feeling that happens right before lightning strikes.

I kept my gaze on the pavement in front of me, though I could feel heads turn to track my path. I ignored occasional pushes, choosing to interpret them as harmless jostling on a crowded sidewalk, despite flares from my demon mark that urged me to turn and punch whoever had shoved me.

Then someone stopped in front of me, deliberately blocking my path. *Uh-oh,* I thought, raising my eyes, *here it comes.* My demon mark goaded me to reach for a weapon. I balled my hand into a fist, but kept my arm at my side.

"Hi, Vicky. Jeez, how loud do I have to shout your name? I called you, like, three times, and then I still had to stop right in front of you to get your attention."

"Tina." My fist unclenched. Standing in front of me was the teenage zombie who'd briefly been my apprentice before a new shiny object had come along to distract her from demon slaying. Lately, though, she'd been trying to get back in my good graces, even studying demonology on her own time. I was glad I hadn't gone for a weapon. Tina could be annoying, but she was basically a good kid.

Tonight she wore purple skinny jeans and a tight T-shirt bearing the slogan CODE RED? KILL IT DEAD! spelled out in rhinestones. It looked like Tina had found yet another new shiny object. Literally.

"Nice shirt. Is it a political statement or a fashion statement?"

"Both, of course. Duh. Plus an artistic statement, too. I made it, and I'm selling zillions of them out of my Etsy store. Mostly to norms, if you can believe that." Her gray-green face creased in a scowl. "Although I can't tell whether they want to stand in solidarity with us in Deadtown or just, you know, look cool." Her expression brightened. "Hey, you want one? I'll let you have it for fiftee—uh, ten percent off."

"I don't think I'm cool enough to wear that."

Tina tilted her head as she appraised my outfit. "Yeah, you're probably right. Anyway, here." She thrust a piece of paper at my face.

"What's this?" I took the flyer and held it where I could read the thing without going cross-eyed.

"A unity rally. Your boyfriend is organizing it. He's all about, like, nonviolence and coming together and not splitting into factions and stuff. It'll be awesome."

I studied the flyer. Tina was right—the rally was meant to

inspire Deadtown residents to work together for equality. I'd figured Kane would be doing something like this, but it felt weird to hear about it from Tina. He would've told me about it if we'd managed to have a conversation since Code Red was imposed; I knew that. But with all our problems, conversation was exactly what I'd been avoiding. *Hell, say it, Vicky*—what I'd been fearing. My heartbeat sped up, and all I wanted was to see Kane's face, to feel him in my arms. The zombie witness interviews could wait. My need to find Kane, to push away all the terrible things that had come between us, was bigger and more urgent than any homicide case.

"Do you know where—?" I started to ask.

Tina snatched the flyer from my hand. "Hey, you didn't say anything about this part. Didn't you see it?" Her sparkly pink fingernail pointed at a name in the list of speakers. Tina Terror—the stage name she'd chosen back when she aspired to become a zombie pop star. "Kane invited my school to send a speaker. You know, to give the paranormal youth perspective. My whole school voted, and they picked me! It would've been unanimous except some of the sophomores thought it'd be funny to write in Jenna because she's, like, so shy and there's no way she'd get up on a stage. Anyway, I won. There I am, on the list right there. It's okay to use Tina Terror, don't you think? I mean, even though I gave up singing it's still got name recognition. Like, people would look at the flyer and be like, 'Tina Zawadzki—who's that?' But if they see Tina Terror, they might go, 'Oh, yeah. That singer chick. I remember her.' Know what I mean?"

Somewhere in Tina's flood of words, my plan to drop everything and find Kane got washed away. It would be silly to go rushing through Deadtown, trying to find him so he could sweep me up into his arms and tell me everything was all right. This wasn't some stupid movie, and everything wasn't all right. Everything was a million miles from all right.

I watched the zombies filling the streets of Deadtown. Tina, still chattering about the rally. A woman in a nice suit, her shiny brown hair carefully cut to frame her monstrous face, who'd clearly once been some kind of professional. A group of men in Red Sox jerseys, gathered around a radio listening to the game. A young couple holding hands. Kane could hold rallies to bring them together—he was good at that sort of thing—but who was going to save them from a demonic spirit that saw them as nothing but food?

That would be my department.

I told Tina I had to go, but I promised to be at the rally. Then, still aching for Kane, I walked away from Deadtown.

THERE WAS TROUBLE AT THE CHECKPOINT INTO HUMAN-controlled Boston. The norm guard wouldn't let me bring my weapons through.

Daniel, who'd been watching for me, came over as we were arguing.

"What's the problem?" he asked, showing his detective shield. "She has clearance. I checked the database this afternoon—she's on the list."

"*She* is." The guard's jaw was set so hard it was amazing he could get any words out. "But her weapons aren't."

Daniel's glance went to me, and I folded my arms. "Tools of the trade. I need them."

"Three concealed daggers, plus one concealed handgun with extra ammunition," the guard continued, as though I hadn't spoken. "And if you look at the list, nothing by her name clears her for bringing a weapon into Boston." He motioned to Daniel, who stepped up beside him in the booth. The guard turned his back to me, blocking my view of the screen. "See? Nothing about weapons. I can't allow her to bring those through."

Daniel argued. He threatened. He made phone calls. He cajoled. But the police didn't have any direct authority over border security, and the guard remained unmoved. "Either she hands over those weapons, or she stays in DA-1."

"Okay, look," I said. "I won't take the bronze daggers or the gun. But this dagger"—I showed him Hellforged—"isn't a weapon. It's a ritual tool, an athame. Go ahead and look at it. The blade is dull. You couldn't slice a tomato with it, let alone hurt a norm."

The guard ran his thumb along the blade. When no blood appeared, he shrugged. Maybe he got my point, or maybe he was tired of arguing and wanted to get back to watching videos on his smart phone. But he said, "Okay."

I hated handing over my other weapons. Daniel made sure I got a receipt for them. I suspected that wouldn't mean much, but there wasn't time for me to run home and lock them in their cabinet. We'd wasted too much time already.

Daniel led the way to a double-parked black panel truck. When I reached for the front passenger door, he shook his head. "We ride in the back." He opened the rear door and gestured for me to climb in.

I stopped and peered inside. The interior looked comfortable enough, with several rows of plush seats and a video screen at the front. But there were no windows. Not along the sides, not in the wall that divided us from the driver's compartment, not in the back doors that Daniel now held, waiting for me to enter.

"Good thing I'm not claustrophobic," I said. Well, not *very* claustrophobic. "Um, do the lights stay on after you close the doors?"

Someone in a front seat twisted around to face us. Foster. I hadn't noticed the dome light gleaming off his bald head. "Don't tell me a creature of the night is afraid of the god-damned dark."

Daniel ignored his partner's remark. "Yes, the interior is fully lit," he said to me. "But we're required to travel this way—even Foster and me. The detention center is in a secret location. Only a few people, at the very highest levels of security clearance, know where it is."

"And we'll never make it there if you don't get in," Foster griped. "Not that I'd care if we left you behind. I still think it's a lousy idea, hiring one of your kind."

At that, I climbed into the van. "And what kind would that be, Foster? Shapeshifter? Woman? Or the kind who could save your ass in a demon attack?" Foster's mouth dropped open, but no words emerged. "Now that I look at it that way, maybe you're right. Maybe I should stay home and leave you dangling out there as demon bait." If the only thing I accomplished tonight was annoying this bigoted detective, it'd be a good night's work.

Daniel grinned like he was thinking the exact same thing as he climbed in behind me. As soon as the door shut, Foster picked up a phone and spoke to the driver, who peeled away fast. I lurched sideways into a seat, and Daniel grabbed the seat beside it. Foster smirked at us, then turned to face the front.

*Jerk,* I thought, buckling myself in. Wherever we were going, and whatever happened there, it was going to be one hell of a long night.

# 6

I WAS RIGHT ABOUT IT BEING A LONG NIGHT. BY THE TIME
we reached our destination, I'd already suffered through what
felt like several lifetimes of Detective Foster's charming company. First, we pulled over in a deserted underground garage
somewhere so the driver could frisk me. I thought I was going
to get a hard time about Hellforged again, but he wasn't looking
for weapons. He was checking for a cell phone or other GPS
device that could transmit information about our location. Daniel got the same treatment because he'd left the "secure area"—
I assumed that meant the back of the van—at the checkpoint.
Foster stayed inside, radiating his pleasure at our humiliation.

Once we got underway again, Foster's presence stifled any
attempts at conversation. Every possible topic seemed off the
table. We couldn't talk about our personal lives, because Foster's ears would be wide open for any mention of Kane, and
Daniel's girlfriend—a TV reporter—was barely a step above
paranormals in Foster's worldview. Family, work life, the unrest
in Deadtown, even the case we were investigating, it all felt
like material that Foster could smear and twist into something
nasty in his report to Commissioner Hampson. So we sat in
silence.

"Do we get any in-flight entertainment?" I asked, pointing at the screen at the front of our compartment. I was joking; I assumed the screen was a computer monitor for police business.

"Good idea," Foster said and reached for a control.

Daniel groaned as a video game loaded. "He does this every time."

Zombie Kill. Clever name for a game that was all about killing zombies. By machine gun, by bomb, by machete, by fire—every sort of damage you could inflict on a body was directed at staggering, oozing, decaying ghouls-from-beyond-the-grave. Men, women, even zombie kids were obliterated as Foster worked the controls. He whooped as he decapitated an undead toddler clutching a ragged teddy bear.

"Ignore him," Daniel advised. "I've learned to pick my battles."

I didn't want to cause Daniel any problems at work. So instead of tearing the controller out of Foster's hands and breaking it over his bald head, I leaned back and closed my eyes. I pictured Foster in Deadtown, surrounded by zombies. Real ones, who'd laugh at his puny machete. And first up was Tina with her rhinestone gun. I smiled. CODE RED? KILL IT DEAD! would make quite the fashion statement sparkling across Foster's forehead.


THE PARANORMAL DETENTION FACILITY WAS UNDERground. Or at least that was my impression as I walked through the place. Like the van there were no windows anywhere. Harsh fluorescent lights glared down from the ceiling on tiled floors and cinder-block walls. Daniel walked beside me as we followed Foster through a labyrinth of corridors. We made so many turns I could've sworn we were back where we started when we came to a massive metal door.

"This is the maximum security wing," Daniel said.

"You really think witnesses, who didn't commit any crime, deserve maximum security?"

Daniel glanced at Foster, who watched him closely. "No, I don't," he said. "But I don't make the rules." His words reminded me of what Pam McFarren had said earlier. The rules weren't perfect, but unless they crossed a line you couldn't pick and choose.

A buzzer sounded, and a light by the door lit up. Gears turned and clanked. The heavy door slid open.

We stepped into a corridor lined with metal doors on both sides. Each door had a small, barred opening, about five and a half feet off the ground, shuttered by a gray metal plate. Behind us, the door shut with a resounding clang.

The silence felt as heavy as the door that sealed us in.

"Let's get this over with," said Foster. He went to the guard station, where two norms sat behind thick glass. "We're here to do some interviews," he said into an intercom. He paused, then turned to Daniel. "Which one you want to start with?" he asked.

"Andrew Skibinsky."

"We'll start with number 721," Foster said into the intercom.

One of the guards stood up. A moment later he was escorting us down the hallway. He stopped in front of a door with 721 stenciled on its surface and slid open the metal plate over the window. "Skibinsky," he said. "You got company."

He opened the door. Daniel went inside. Over his shoulder I could see a narrow cell, six by ten at most. A toilet and sink occupied one corner. A cot was bolted to the side wall. There was no other furniture.

Skibinsky didn't react to our entry. He sat on the cot, one leg resting across the other, examining his ankle. A splint held it straight, and a long row of black stitches wound its way crookedly up his leg.

The door shut behind us. Foster stayed in the hallway, but he watched us through the bars.

At the sound of the door closing, Skibinsky tugged his pants leg over the ankle splint and looked up. It's hard to guess a zombie's age, but I'd say he was in his midthirties. He had thinning, sandy hair and a sparse mustache. A scar marked the bridge of his nose, but it had healed, so he must have had it before he became a zombie. He wore a plaid flannel shirt, jeans, and work boots. His red eyes went back and forth between Daniel and me.

"I see the doctor has been by." Daniel gestured toward the zombie's ankle. "How does it feel?"

Skibinsky's forehead wrinkled. "When can I go home?"

Daniel ran a hand through his curls, looking uncomfortable. "We won't keep you here any longer than is absolutely necessary."

"'Absolutely necessary.'" Skibinsky snorted. "I know what that means. I ain't never getting out of here. This is the place zombies disappear to, right?"

"You haven't disappeared, Mr. Skibinsky. You're a witness, here for your own safety."

"Yeah, right. Guess that means you told my wife where I am."

Daniel said nothing.

"Just like I thought. Poor Deb. She must be half out of her mind with worry. And I didn't even do nothing." When Daniel didn't reply, Skibinsky snorted again. Then he looked at me. "Who are you?"

"My name's Vicky Vaughn. I live in Deadtown, too."

"You look human. What are you, a werewolf?"

"I'm a shapeshifter. I change form, like a werewolf, but I can change into any creature, not just a wolf. And my shifts aren't tied to the full moon like theirs are." I wasn't in the mood to give a lecture on the differences between the Cerddorion and werewolves, but maybe this zombie would look at me with less hostility if he understood I was a paranormal, too.

"Vicky is an expert on demons," Daniel said. "She's here to help us determine whether there was demonic involvement in what happened last night."

Skibinsky laughed, a deep baritone chuckle. "You mean horns and pointy tails and pitchforks—that kinda shit? I didn't see nothing like that."

"Just tell me what happened," I encouraged. "When did Mr. Malone start acting strange?"

Skibinsky's amusement vanished. "How 'bout when he snapped the driver's neck? That strange enough for ya?"

"So before that, he was his usual self, is that what you're saying?"

A shrug was his only reply.

I decided to back up a bit. "How would you describe Mr. Malone? What kind of guy was he?"

"Well for starters, I wouldn't describe him as 'Mr. Malone.'"

Who the hell calls a zombie 'Mister' anything? When the bloodbags start using 'Mister,' you know you're in trouble." He glared at Daniel, even though I was the one who'd spoken. "He was Tom. Tommy to his ma. She lives out in Revere, but she comes into town to take him out for the day, first Sunday of every month. Guess she won't be doing that no more."

Silence stretched through the cell.

"If you don't like Mr. Skibinsky," I said gently, "what should I call you?"

My question seemed to surprise him, like he'd never expected anyone to ask. "Andy. Day I was born, Ma said, 'Put Andrew on the birth certificate, but we'll call him Andy.'"

"Andy, then. Tell me about Tom."

"He was okay. Quiet. A good worker. I liked being on the same shift with him. He did his share."

"And that's how he was last night?"

"Just another night at the warehouse." He examined his hands. Though the skin was zombie-green, they looked strong, with short, square nails. Hands that worked for a living. "You gotta understand. I was there to do my job. Not study my coworkers to see if maybe one of 'em was gonna suddenly turn into a homicidal maniac."

Fair enough. "Tell me about the ride home."

"Home." Another snort. "I wish to Christ it was a ride home. I'd be asleep in my own bed next to Deb, like I should be." Resentment flared up, then flickered away. "It's like I already said. Just an ordinary night, until Tom up and killed the driver." He scratched his chin, thinking. "Wait. There was one thing I noticed. Tom seemed a little . . . I don't know. Twitchy. In the van after work. He kept bouncing his leg. I was sitting next to him, and it bugged me, so I told him to quit it. He did, but then a few minutes later he started again. I was about to remind him to knock it off when he killed the driver. And then everything went to hell."

"You don't know what set him off?"

"It wasn't bloodlust, if that's what you're thinking. There wasn't any blood until after the van crashed. And like I said, I was right beside him. If there was blood for Tom to smell, I'd have smelled it, too."

"Okay, so Tom broke the driver's neck. What happened next?"

"I yelled, 'What the hell do you think you're doing?' Or something along those lines. I tried to pull him off. At the same time, Weisner—the norm who's our supervisor—grabbed for the wheel. Tom let go of the driver and locked his hands around Weisner's neck. There was no pulling him off then. The boss's face turned purple. His eyeballs bulged out like one of them cartoon characters. I punched Tom, hard, trying to make him let go, but he didn't even feel it. We crashed. The next thing I remember is sitting on the sidewalk, tugging at my mask because I'd put it on crooked."

"That's when you broke your ankle?"

"Yeah. I felt it about ten seconds after I got my mask on straight. Hurt like hell then." He pulled one leg on top of the other again and ran a finger along the line of stitches. "The bone was sticking clean through my skin. Compound fracture, the doc called it. He bolted everything back together, but I don't know how well it'll hold my weight."

"Did you see the attack on the third victim?" I asked.

He let his leg fall back to the floor. "I wish I hadn't. The poor son of a bitch came over to see if we needed help. He was asking if I was okay, reaching out a hand to help me up. I was trying to explain about my ankle when Tom loomed up behind him, looking like . . . Hell, I don't even want to say it, but it's true. Tom looked like a monster, like one of those dumb-ass movie zombies had walked off a screen and into the real world. He grabbed the norm and tore his head off his shoulders. Poor bastard didn't even have a chance to scream."

Foster moved on the other side of the door. Probably imagining himself in the world of Zombie Kill, charging onto the scene with a machete.

"There was blood everywhere." Andy paused, tilting his head. "Now, there's something strange—Tom didn't even seem to notice it. He wasn't wearing his mask, and you'd think the smell would have driven him nuts. The way it was all over him, all over the ground, he should've been chewing his own arm off, know what I mean? But he didn't."

"What did he do?"

"The other guys, they tackled him. Piled right on top of him. But he shook 'em off—all three—like a dog shaking off fleas." Andy seemed to go inside himself as events unspooled in his mind. "I remember this part like it was happening in slow motion. The guys who'd tackled Tom were sprawled on their asses. Tom got up. He stood there, covered in blood, staring at the headless body at his feet. Still no sign of bloodlust. Then, all of a sudden, his head jerked up and he looked at the sky. The way he looked up, like he saw something that scared him, made me look, too. But I didn't see nothing. Then Tom kinda groaned. He had his hands on his head, like this." Andy made two fists and pressed them hard against his temples. "He dropped like someone had whacked his knees from behind with a baseball bat. He curled up into the whatchacallit—the fetal position—and started shaking. And then he just . . . blew up." He blinked rapidly, like he was trying to clear the vision away.

"Andy," I said, "this is important. Before Tom clutched his head, did you notice any injuries appearing on his body?"

"What, like my ankle? Nah. The accident didn't touch him. Neither did the fellas taking him down."

"Not from those things. I'm talking about wounds that suddenly appear, chunks of flesh gouged out from no apparent cause."

"I didn't see nothing like that." His red eyes widened. "Oh, you mean like at the concert last winter? The one for . . . what was it called?"

"Paranormal Appreciation Day."

That earned another snort. Not that I disagreed.

"Yeah, that. I was working, so I didn't go, but I heard about it. All those zombies that got killed . . ." His red eyes widened. "That was some kind of demon attack, wasn't it?"

"Sort of." I didn't need to go into the details of how the Morfran was the spirit that animated demons. The popular understanding was that demonic crows had attacked the concert. It was close enough.

"In our previous interview, you told me you heard crows cawing," Daniel prompted. "When precisely did you hear them?"

"Right after Tom blew up. It was like *Blam!* And then this burst of cawing right away, like the noise had scared a flock somewhere. But you're saying maybe it wasn't crows. Not real ones."

"Maybe," I said. "But maybe not." From what Andy was telling us, Tom Malone's death bore some of the hallmarks of a Morfran attack, but there were also significant differences. "The cawing you heard may have been exactly what you thought—some crows roosting nearby were startled by the sudden noise."

Andy's expression showed his doubts. "I never would've admitted it an hour ago, but I guess I was lucky, huh? Them crows could've gone for me next."

I didn't have any more questions, and I needed to process what we'd learned. I held out my hand, and Andy shook it. "Thank you for your help, Andy. I'll get word to your wife."

"Like hell," Foster muttered from the other side of the door. Damn. I'd forgotten he was there, listening in.

Daniel shook Andy's hand, too, and I knew he'd help me find Deb Skibinsky. Maybe he was thinking about how his girlfriend, Lynne, would feel if he didn't come home some night. Maybe he was thinking of the families of the other zombies—God knew how many—stashed in this underground complex. Anyway, it was the least we could do, and Daniel knew it.

# 7

WE LEFT ANDY SITTING ON HIS COT, CONTEMPLATING HOW close he'd come to being Morfran chow. If it was the Morfran.

"Is there such a thing as coffee in this place?" I asked Daniel. He nodded and led the way to a cafeteria. Despite my hopes that we could ditch Foster, he followed.

I poured steaming coffee into the biggest paper cup I could find and added a sleeve so it wouldn't burn my hand. Daniel insisted on paying. "It's on the department," he said.

"In that case . . ." Foster tried.

"Use your own expense account," Daniel said.

We sat down at a small table with two chairs. Within a minute, Foster had dragged over a chair from another table. Okay, I thought. There was no shaking the guy. I would've liked to bounce my thoughts off Daniel alone, but it wasn't like I was saying anything off the record. Still, I didn't have to welcome Foster to the conversation. I angled my chair so my back was toward him.

"It's like I told Andy," I said to Daniel. I swallowed some coffee. Hot. Strong. Bitter. Exactly what I needed. "What happened to Malone *almost* sounds like a Morfran attack."

"But that 'almost' bothers you."

I nodded. "Nothing in Andy's description indicates the first stage of a Morfran attack. And that stage is crucial; it's how the Morfran gets inside its victim to feed."

Daniel waited while I gathered my thoughts.

"Andy was right there. He was watching Malone. There's no way Malone could have experienced that stage without Andy noticing." I sipped my coffee. "I've been on the receiving end of stage one, Daniel. It hurts like hell." That attack had been cut short by Mab, who'd saved my life by drawing the Morfran away from me. "All I could think about was protecting myself from whatever was tearing at my flesh."

Foster heaved a sigh, as though he wished the Morfran had won that battle. I scooted my chair closer to Daniel.

"I know what you mean," Daniel said. "I saw it happen at the concert. The PDH I observed was frantic, twisting and ducking and trying to bat the crows away."

"Exactly." I suppressed a shudder at the memory of all that pain. "From the description we just heard, it sounds like Malone was attacked from the inside."

"Can that happen?"

"The Morfran can possess humans." Daniel's lips compressed into a grim line, and I knew we were thinking the same thing. A human police officer we'd both known, not exactly a friend but a good cop, had been possessed by the Morfran. And if the Morfran comprises the soul of a demon, you can imagine what it drives a person to do. The cop had become a serial killer, tormented by the Morfran until he ended his own life.

"You think it can possess PDHs, too?" Daniel asked.

"That's the trouble—I don't see why it would. Zombies are nothing but food to the Morfran. And since the Morfran is always ravenous, it doesn't make sense that the spirit would dwell inside a zombie without consuming it. Unless . . ."

Daniel leaned forward. "What?"

"Unless some kind of sorcery is involved."

Behind me, Foster spewed coffee. Some landed on the back of my neck. "First demons, now sorcerers? Why are we wasting money on this freak?"

I ignored him as I gathered my thoughts. Sorcerers command demons. Or try to. It's a dangerous business, and sooner

or later most sorcerers get their heads handed to them—
literally—by the demons they attempt to force into servitude.
One sloppy gesture, one incantatory syllable uttered off-pitch,
and the demon seizes the opportunity to attack its so-called
master. As the drops of coffee cooled on my neck, I kinda
wished Foster would try his hand at sorcery. He wouldn't last
one summoning.

"A highly skilled sorcerer *might* be able to bind the Morfran
to a zombie," I said to Daniel. "Instead of feeding directly on
the zombie, the Morfran would feed on the acts of destruction
it drove its host to commit."

"Turning the zombie into a killing machine."

Foster whooped with laughter. Instead, he should've been
cowering under the table. Zombies are incredibly strong and
nearly indestructible. A zombie driven by the Morfran would
make an unstoppable weapon.

"If the binding is imperfect," I said, "eventually the Morfran
would turn on its host. That may be what happened last night."
I drained the last mouthful of coffee from my cup and stood
up. "Let's talk to the next witness. Maybe he saw something
Andy didn't. I don't want to follow this line of reasoning too
far if Malone's death turns out to be an ordinary Morfran
attack."

Foster stood, too. "'Line of reasoning,'" he mocked. "Could
you enlighten me as to which part of what you've said has
anything to do with reason?"

"What's your problem, Foster? Don't you believe in
demons?" It'd almost be worth the expense of paying a sorcerer
to send a few Harpies to visit the guy and change his mind.

Foster thrust his ugly face within an inch of mine. "I believe
hiring you is a waste of taxpayers' money."

My demon mark flared. I'd show this jerk ugly. I wanted to
get Foster in a headlock and ram his face into the cinder-block
wall. Over and over, until his skull was cracked, his nose was
a mushy pulp, and his teeth crunched under my boots. How
satisfying that would—

"Leave it alone, Foster." Daniel's voice brought me back to
myself as he stood and stepped between us. "Vicky's a col-
league, whether you like it or not." He offered me his arm, like

a Victorian gentleman going for a stroll, and we strolled right past Foster. I hoped a fly would invade his wide-open mouth as we passed.

"Ready for the next witness?" Daniel asked as we left the cafeteria.

"After that exchange, I'd be delighted to converse with another zombie."

"Me, too. This guy didn't see as much, though." We waited for the heavy metal door to open and return us to the maximum security wing. When we were through, Daniel continued. "He was sitting in the back of the van, behind—"

"Hey, Detective." The window in Andy Skibinsky's door was still open. The square, barred opening in the door framed his face. "Got a minute? There's something I forgot to tell you."

"That window shouldn't be open," Foster said, coming up from behind us. He moved to close it.

"Wait," Daniel said. Surprisingly, Foster paused. "What is it, Andy?"

"Could you come back inside? It's not somethin' I feel like shouting across the hall."

"I'll get a guard." Daniel set off toward the guards' station.

Andy looked at me and smiled. A zombie's smile is never a pretty sight, but something in his face unnerved me. "Are you all right?"

"Great." His smile broadened until it threatened to split his skin. A tic jittered at one corner of his mouth. He glanced from me to Foster, then back.

Daniel was returning with the guard, who sorted through his ring of keys. Andy pressed his face against the bars, straining to see them. The tic had moved to his eye. The black tip of his tongue protruded from his lips, and he was panting. His fingers twitched where he gripped the bars.

"Wait," I said, putting out an arm to hold the others back. "Something's not right."

Andy snarled. He shook it off, and the smile reappeared. "Come on," he wheedled. "Just open the door."

"Andy, what's happening?" I said.

He ignored me, his eyes fixed on the guard. "Open the door."

"I'm shuttering that damn window," Foster said. He reached for the metal plate.

"Open the door!" The two steel bars snapped off like plastic in the zombie's fists. His arm shot out into the hallway, his hand grasping. It found Foster's tie and clutched it.

Foster screamed—or tried to. The best he could manage was a gurgling sound as strong zombie fingers tightened their grip.

Inside his cell, Andy roared. The sound was way too intense to come from the throat of one zombie. The scream was wrapped in a sound like the cawing of a hundred angry crows.

*Caw caw caw!*

"Morfran!" I shouted.

Foster's heels did a rapid-fire tap dance against the tiles.

The guard reached for his gun.

Foster's eyes bulged. His tongue protruded from his purple face.

The guard fired, hitting Andy's elbow. With a howl, he dropped Foster and withdrew his arm.

For a moment, all was quiet. I opened my senses to the demon plane. Dozens of crows screamed, but I couldn't see them. They were *inside* Andy. And that meant there was no way to help him.

The best I could do was trap the Morfran when it emerged from his body. I drew Hellforged and readied the slate.

*Bam!* The door shook as Andy threw his body against it.

"Open the doooor!"

*Caw caw caw!*

A bulge appeared in the door where Andy had dented it.

*Caw caw caw caw caw cawcawcaw!*

More dents, faster. A crack of light opened at the top of the frame.

I felt sick, waiting, my ears ringing with the racket of screams and caws. There was nothing I could do for Andy, no way to help.

The crack of light widened as the door buckled. The guard braced, his gun pointed at the door.

A moan, low and drawn out, then silence.

"Andy?" Daniel said.

"My head. Oh God, my head. I'm sorry. Tell my wife . . ." The words dissolved into another moan. The sound built in pitch to a scream.

Hellforged felt slippery in my sweaty palm. I knew the agony Andy was feeling. But I couldn't get the Morfran out of him. All I could do was wait.

The screams came fast, a single, continuous sound. Like a siren, rising and falling and rising again without a pause. I wanted to cover my ears, block out the blare of his pain. So much pain. But I couldn't. I had to be ready.

Then it happened. With a *boom!* and a wet, tearing noise, the Morfran burst from Andy's body. Black goo shot past the cell door and splattered the ceiling and walls. Furious cawing filled the air as crows the size of eagles shot out of the cell.

I raised Hellforged in my left hand and circled it clockwise over my head. *Come on, you bastards,* I thought, drawing the deadly spirit toward me. The racket quieted a couple of decibels, and I felt a drag on the dagger. I glanced upward. The crows were circling, circling, following the motion of my arm. I concentrated, pulling them in.

The drag on Hellforged increased as the dagger pulled more of the Morfran into its orbit. The crows moved closer to its blade. A tingle of cold whispered against my fingertips. The icy feeling crept into my hand. Next, my wrist ached with a cold so intense it burned. When the feeling shot up my arm, I transferred the dagger to my right hand.

*"Parhau! Ireos! Mantrigo!"* Pointing Hellforged at the slate, I shouted the incantation to bind the Morfran. A sword of icy pain slashed across my chest and down my right arm. A streak of blue lightning erupted from the dagger's tip and slammed into the target. The slate jumped a foot in the air. It clattered to the floor, shuddering. It shuddered again and then lay still. A curl of bluish smoke, almost lazy, wafted toward the ceiling.

Silence settled over the hallway.

I sheathed Hellforged and rubbed the lingering cold from my arms.

Daniel rose from where he'd been crouching against the wall. Spots of black stuff—the remains of Andy Skibinsky—dotted his tie and the side of his jaw. He took out a handkerchief and rubbed his face.

The guard had fainted, but he was alive. We went to Foster. He lay on his back, gasping for breath. His suit was clean, no black goo, but there was a wet spot on his trousers where he'd pissed himself.

"He's all right," Daniel said. He was too nice a guy for me to imagine there was disappointment in his voice.

"Andy's broken ankle," I said. Daniel looked at me, uncomprehending. "It was a compound fracture. That's how the Morfran possessed him. Last night after it exploded out of Malone, it entered his wound."

"But you got it, right?" He gestured toward the slate.

I opened my senses to the demon plane. The dingy corridor grew dingier, smells of sulfur and brimstone assaulted my nostrils. The air was full of sounds—screams, cackles, howls, shrieks. Demons were out and about, tormenting their victims. But the sounds were all distant; there was no cawing, not even an echo. No trace of Morfran here.

"I did," I said, pulling back from the demon plane. "This is a certified Morfran-free zone." A thought struck me. "But we don't know whether any of the other witnesses were possessed by the Morfran when it left Malone's body. Were there other injuries?"

"They got banged around some, but nothing like Skibinsky's fracture. On the other hand, they're . . . you know, zombies."

I did know, of course. Because zombies don't heal, every zombie in Deadtown carries around cuts and scrapes, or worse. If the Morfran could possess a zombie by entering through an open wound, there wasn't a single zombie in Boston who was safe.

# 8

BACK AT THE CHECKPOINT, I WAS ASTONISHED WHEN I PRE-
sented my receipt and actually got my weapons back. Two
daggers, a pistol, and two magazines of bronze bullets. I
couldn't believe it.

"You've got connections now." Daniel smiled, but grimness
touched his expression. "I'll make sure the clearance list spec-
ifies you're allowed to bring Hellforged through. Tonight
proved we need it."

"Good." I didn't need an argument each time I went through
the checkpoint. Especially with my demon mark springing to
life at the slightest provocation. "How much paperwork will
that take?"

"It shouldn't be too bad. At sunrise they're going to lower
the restriction level from Code Red to Code Yellow. But I want
to make sure you and Hellforged have clearance at all levels."

Code Red meant that all paranormals were confined to
Deadtown, no exceptions. Or so I'd thought until Daniel actually got me through. Code Yellow lifted restrictions on all
non–previously deceased, so any paranormal who wasn't a
zombie could come and go. In between was Code Orange,
which gave clearance to certain Deadtown residents on a pre-

approved list. Kane was on the Code Orange list. Normally I wasn't, but my new Code Red clearance would trickle down through the other colors. Cool.

"Hampson's calling it yellow?" I was surprised. "Even after another Morfran possession tonight?"

"It's not entirely up to Hampson. As commissioner, he makes the initial call, but the guy hates paranormals so much he'd keep it at red all the time. There's pressure on him not to overdo it. The mayor's office, for example." Mayor Milliken's daughter had been caught in the zombie plague and now lived on my block. "And businesses that employ werewolves don't like their staff to miss too much work. Some of those companies have a lot of pull."

Nice to see we monsters occasionally had somebody on our side.

"Of course," Daniel continued, "Foster's probably singing a song to Hampson right now about what happened tonight. So you're right—Hampson might try to keep the code level where it is, or go down half a step to orange. But so far no word of that has come through. I think it'll drop to yellow."

With another promise to get official approval for me to carry Hellforged into Boston, Daniel said good night. Between the checkpoints, the New Combat Zone was strangely quiet. Nobody lingered on the street. Buildings were dark. Boards covered the windows smashed in this morning's riot. The only place open was Creature Comforts. I paused, wondering if I should stop in. I wanted to see how Axel was doing. Plus Juliet was probably there, along with half the vampires of Deadtown, hunting among the humans who visit the bar to mingle with the monsters. Even if word of the riot scared casual thrill-seekers away, there'd be a good supply of vampire junkies offering themselves up for dinner.

I wasn't in the mood to watch vampires flirt with their prey. I needed to figure out what was going on with the Morfran. And to do that, I had to go home and spend some time with *The Book of Utter Darkness*. A shudder went through me, and I almost ran to Axel's front door to yank it open, greet some friends, have a drink, engage in mindless conversation. Anything to avoid that damn book.

But the Morfran's reemergence meant fate was pushing

onward. And only the book could show me the signs to watch for and suggest where they were pointing.

Shoulders hunched, I trudged toward the checkpoint into Deadtown.

On the other side, zombies thronged the streets. Tomorrow's Code Yellow would mean nothing to them. There were no zombies on the Code Yellow list. It wasn't until things calmed down to the level of Code Green—normal restrictions—that zombies could leave Deadtown. And that was only with a permit and a norm sponsor.

So it was no wonder, I thought as I pushed through the turnstile and stepped into Deadtown, that the zombies gathered here were giving me dirty looks.

If you've ever gotten a dirty look from a zombie, chances are it took . . . oh, about a week before the possibility of a good night's sleep returned. And here were six or seven of them all trying to outdo each other with nightmare-inducing scowls.

I can scowl, too. I did, and I kept walking.

One zombie, a beefy guy in camouflage pants and a black T-shirt, stepped off the curb. I stopped and looked him straight in the eye. He was even more scary-looking than most zombies. The right side of his face looked like it had been attacked with a cheese grater, and there was a golf ball–size hole in his neck. I didn't blink as we locked stares.

"I saw you leave before, after they called the Code Red." His voice came out in a growl. "What are you, some kind of spy?"

My right forearm began tingling. "You think spies waltz in and out where everyone can see them? I had business to attend to."

"Business?" His fingers clamped into a fist. "What kind of business?"

"None of yours, that's for damn sure." Who the hell did this guy think he was? The tingling intensified, rapidly heating as it spread up my arm. Sunburn. Flames. Molten lava. Before the feeling reached "nuclear meltdown," I slowed my breathing and started counting. *One . . . two . . . three . . .* I pushed down the burning, fast-rising anger. Anger that wasn't mine. Wasn't me. The anger of the Destroyer.

The zombie got in my face. "I said, 'What kind of business?' "

*Four . . . five . . .* My demon mark blazed with pain. I could almost smell charred flesh. *Six . . .* I bit the inside of my cheek.

Two of his friends were behind him now. He reached out and gave me a shove—almost gentle, but hard enough to let me feel his strength.

Shit, what number was I on? My arm burned. Six. I remembered counting to six. *Seven . . .* If I gave into this rage, it would possess me. I'd become a puppet of the Destroyer. *Eight . . .* But damn it, so what? This zombie was a bully. I hate bullies. I quit counting and clenched my fists. I'd like nothing better than to pound his head into the pavement, over and over until the left side matched the shredded right. Until I heard the crack of his skull fracturing. I'd stomp his brains into mush and then—

"What's going on?" a woman's voice asked in a tough, don't-mess-with-me tone, as someone stepped between me and Mr. Ugly.

I blinked away the image of the zombie's broken body turning to pulp under my boots. The pain still surged; the rage still wanted out. I closed my eyes and swallowed hard—once, twice, three times—trying to regain control. *Breathe, Vicky.* Better. A little.

When I opened my eyes, I got an extreme close-up of the face of Pam McFarren, the Goon Squad sergeant. Her expression was a strange mixture of annoyance and concern. "You all right?" she asked.

I nodded. I was still focused on swallowing and didn't trust my voice.

McFarren turned to Mr. Ugly and his friends. "Go home. I don't know what you think you're doing, but you're only making things worse." Four other Goons, all zombies, flanked her in a line, their backs to me. Nobody moved.

"Go on!" she shouted. "Get out of here. Now!"

Feet shuffled; zombies fell back. Mr. Ugly made an over-elaborate bow, like something a ham actor would do in a Shakespeare play, and backed away.

The male Goons advanced, making sure the zombies dispersed.

McFarren spun around to face me. This time, her face was pure anger. "Again?" she sputtered. "What the hell did you think you were doing? Picking a fight with a guy like that, when all his buddies are itching to back him up. Are you nuts?"

I rubbed my demon mark. "Something like that. Look, thank you for stepping in again. I've been lucky you were around."

"Lucky? What the hell do you think luck has to do with it? I've got orders to protect you. As if I need anything extra on my to-do list right now. For some reason, you get special treatment, while I'm trying to keep the peace with a fraction of my usual staff."

I stared at her. "I didn't know."

She continued her tirade like she hadn't heard me. "All PDH patrols are working overtime. The brass is keeping our human partners off the streets for now. Too dangerous. And that's for trained officers who pack exploding bullets. I know you're not a norm, but you look too much like one to be playing chicken with a gang of pissed-off zombies."

"I'm sorry."

"You know what? I was wrong—you *were* lucky. I got word you'd passed through the checkpoint, and I could scrounge up enough cops to make those guys back off. But we can't be everywhere. This is the worst I've seen it in Deadtown. Everyone's at each other's throats. Tonight, two werewolves were critically injured when their pack tried to take on a group like the one you were just staring down."

*Werewolves. Kane.* But no, it wouldn't be Kane. He was a lone wolf who didn't belong to a pack. Relief opened some breathing room in my chest.

Maybe Kane's unity rally would do some good. Unity was exactly what Deadtown needed right now.

"Okay," I assured McFarren, "I promise I won't pick any fights with roving zombie mobs."

She gave me a long, hard look. "Don't joke," she said. "Something's brewing. I haven't felt this level of tension in Deadtown since I woke up after the plague."

MCFARREN WAS RIGHT. THE TENSION SHE DESCRIBED WAS everywhere. It was physical, like thick, oily smog hanging over the streets. Normally, an after-dark walk through Deadtown wasn't all that different from walking along other city streets. As long as you belonged in the neighborhood, people left you alone. Like anyone else, zombies had their own concerns: job, family, making ends meet, getting a little downtime, stuffing as much food as they could fit into their faces.

Wait.

That was part of the strange atmosphere. The zombies weren't eating.

A chill shivered up my spine. Deadtown without zombies munching away on junk food is like a spring day without birds singing. Eerie.

Yet it was true. The hot dog carts, ice cream trucks, and falafel stands that line Deadtown's streets were out in force, same as always. But there were no lines in front of them. The vendors stood listlessly, heads hanging, as zombies walked by, ignoring their offerings. The hot dog seller who usually ate his wares with one hand while serving customers with the other leaned against his cart, both arms dangling as he stared into space.

I stopped and asked if he was okay.

He shrugged. "Business is a little slow tonight, I guess." Hope stole across his face. "You want a hot dog?"

I didn't, really. But I bought one.

The hot dog seller got busy, slathering on mustard and onions. "You know," he commented, "most nights I eat a dog or two for every one I sell. But tonight . . ."

A group of zombies passed on the sidewalk. The smell of onions and steamed hot dogs wafted from the open cart, but not a single head turned. It wasn't just eerie; it was downright weird.

I overpaid for the hot dog and told the guy to keep the change, which got me a zombie grimace-smile. As I walked away, I bit into the hot dog. A little salty, but not bad. Maybe I should've made the guy's night and bought two.


ONCE AGAIN, I DIDN'T TURN DOWN KANE'S STREET. ONCE again, I thought about how much I wanted to see him, imagined the feel of his arms around me. And once again, I turned away.

Excuses? I had a fistful of 'em. It was late. He'd be sleeping.

He had a million things to do before his rally. With the restriction dropping to Code Yellow, he'd be up extra early to make up for work he'd missed today. The last thing he needed was a middle-of-the-night drop-in from yours truly.

I was in my building, waiting for the elevator, when I finally admitted the real reason I was avoiding Kane. We needed to talk. And I had absolutely no idea what to say.

# 9

MY APARTMENT WAS EMPTY—AND QUIET. NO TV BLARED.
As I'd thought, Juliet was out hunting. Dad was probably roosting somewhere out in Needham, near Gwen's house. I kinda
wished they were here, staring at the screen and scarfing popcorn, because then I could hang out with them and not do what
I knew I had to do.

Strange things were happening. The Morfran was possessing zombies and driving them to acts of violence before consuming them. My father had brought the prophesied white
falcon out of the Darklands and into the human world. Even
the fact that Deadtown's zombies had lost their appetites en
masse seemed like some kind of omen.

I couldn't put it off any longer. I had to consult the book.

*Please,* I thought, not knowing who or what I was beseeching, *not another vision.*

*The Book of Utter Darkness* waited on the kitchen table,
where it had been since Dad's last attempt to read it. You'd
think it would look innocent, ordinary. An everyday sight. Just
a book lying flat on a tabletop.

Not this book. It pulsed with menace—literally—like some
kind of force field emanated from it, rippling the air. When I

hovered my hand a couple of inches from its cover, icy sparks snapped against my fingertips. The snapping resolved into a rhythm, like a beating heart: *duh DUM duh DUM duh DUM duh DUM*.

The pulse traveled up my arm—buzzing through my demon mark, then going past my elbow, through my shoulder, down into my chest. It swirled around my heart, as though it were trying to hijack its rhythm.

*Duh DUM duh DUM.*

I shivered and pulled my hand away. The pulse faded. Feeling ill, I let both hands drop into my lap. I closed my eyes and rested my left hand on my right. The right was cold, stinging with the book's energy, but the left covered it like a blanket. Warmth dispelled some of the iciness.

I got up and went to the sink, where I grabbed a pair of rubber gloves. Juliet had bought them, not that she'd ever washed a dish in her life—or her undeath, for that matter. She'd seen on TV that the gloves would keep your hands soft and, later, was disgusted to learn they only performed this magical feat in the context of doing housework. She'd tossed them aside and forgotten about them.

But I'd discovered that the gloves were good for something else. They insulated me from *The Book of Utter Darkness*.

I pulled them on. They were hot pink—*not* what you'd call my color—and clumsy. But they let me touch the book without feeling like the damn thing was trying to grab me and pull me into its pages.

Of course, the gloves were also the most likely reason I'd gotten nothing from the book lately. They insulated me from the book's power—great—yet they probably also broke the psychic connection that let the book transfer information to its reader. I almost didn't care. The last several visions the book had given me had been horrible and so overwhelming they knocked me out of my chair. Boston in flames. Corpses littering the streets. Demons rampaging—attacking women, children. Smoke. Blood. Screaming. Death, death, and more death. I'd wake up on the floor, curled tight in the fetal position, covering my ears against the shrieks and demonic laughter. For one blessed moment I'd feel relief, like when you wake up from your worst-ever nightmare and realize it was only a dream. But relief fled as I remembered that what the book was showing me was real; it just hadn't happened yet.

That vision—Hell throwing open its gates, sending an army of demons to destroy the human world—was the final goal of Pryce's schemes. It wasn't a dream. It wasn't just a vision. It was his plan.

So I had to try. If I could find out how Pryce would turn those horrible visions into reality, I'd have a chance of stopping him.

I stared at my rubbery, neon pink hands. I'd probably have to do this without the gloves. I knew that, and the knowledge made the sick feeling in my stomach expand to fill my whole body. I did not want to touch that book. I'd rather jump into a pit of cobras.

But maybe the gloves didn't really do anything. The book sometimes remained silent for days or weeks at a time. Maybe it was in one of its sulky moods. I'd try once more with the gloves. If I didn't get anything, I'd bite the bullet and go barehanded next time. Tomorrow. I couldn't bring myself to touch it now.

I reached out and lay my gloved hand on the cover, testing. No pulse. No icy sparks. The sight was absurd—bright pink plastic on the pale leather cover. That cover had been crafted from the skin of some poor human who'd died centuries ago. He'd been flayed alive—the book had made sure to show me that in vivid detail.

Now, though, no visions rose up as I opened to a random page. It didn't matter where I began. It was impossible to read *The Book of Utter Darkness* like a normal book. For one thing, it was written in the language of Hell—a language forbidden to anyone outside the infernal regions. Google Translate doesn't do Hellish to English. But even if it could, it wouldn't have helped, anyway. *The Book of Utter Darkness* was enchanted. It released its secrets when it wished, as it wished. The book taunted anyone who opened it. It teased, it hinted, it tried to trick would-be readers. It didn't lie, but it fed out bits of information designed to confuse, to nudge toward false conclusions. The book knew I was its enemy, and it wanted a demonic victory every bit as much as Pryce did.

If I couldn't decode its secrets, they'd win.

I shoved such thoughts aside. Breathing slowly, I tried to let my mind go blank. I stared at the incomprehensible jumble of strange letters. The ink was a faded rusty brown, and I had a flash of insight—it had been made with the blood of humans. Many humans. They'd been destroyed to create a book foretelling the destruction of their world.

It was an ugly thought, one that weighed in my gut, hard and cold, as if I'd swallowed a lump of lead. But I put it from my mind. People had suffered and died to make this book, but their tragedies happened long ago. I couldn't do anything for them now. I was trying to protect others, people who lived and breathed and loved and hoped and walked the Earth now. Those who hadn't yet come to harm.

My mind settled back to blankness as I made myself stare. The letters blurred, then doubled. I blinked to uncross my eyes. Damn, I wished this thing had an index. Then I could just flip to the back and look up *Zombies, possession of by Morfran* or *Maddox, Pryce, how to thwart his evil plan*. Save a lot of time.

Turning the page sometimes helped. The new set of letters would be equally impossible to read, but sometimes a fresh page would send a flood of understanding into my mind. Or there might be a picture; the book was illustrated, but the illustrations seemed to change and move around at will.

Worth a try. I reached out with a hot-pink-gloved finger.

The page wouldn't budge.

I licked my finger—the rubber tasted gross, like licking a tire—and tried again. Nothing. I laid my hand flat on the page and slid it, but the page still refused to turn. I tried going back a page. Nope. Neither the right-hand page nor the left would move at all. It was like somebody had glued them down.

Damn it.

I knew what I had to do—not tomorrow, but now. My hands were sweating inside the stupid gloves, anyway. I yanked them off and threw them on the floor, where they lay like two beached pink whales.

"Talk to me, damn you!" I grabbed the page with my bare hand. I yanked it so hard I jerked the book off the table.

The page flipped easily. For a fraction of a second, I stared at another block of reddish-brown letters, my fingers resting on the page I'd turned. Then the book's energy slammed into me like a lightning bolt. A charge shot up my arm. Fireworks exploded in my demon mark. The room went black, then crimson, and then I was no longer in my kitchen. I wasn't anywhere at all.

*Rage.* The feeling seethed inside me like lava. It surged, filling me—hot, angry pressure building in my head. I wanted to explode. I wanted to smash something, anything, and my arms flailed around in the nothingness, searching for a target. Smoke, hot and yellow and sulfurous, billowed around me. Smoke that emanated from the hellfire blazing inside me.

I coughed, waving both hands through the smoke, swiping it away. As the billows parted, I smelled the coppery scent of blood. Lots of blood.

I stood on Boston Common, but the site looked more like a battlefield than a city park. I sniffed, tracking the source of the blood. On the ground before me lay a man, a human, his intestines spilling out of a gaping wound in his gut. His sightless eyes stared at nothing; his mouth hung open in surprise or horror or maybe just the slackness of death. Blood soaked his clothes and spread in a puddle around him. It reflected the light of nearby flames.

A scream made me look up. A woman in running clothes fled from a demon. She was fast, but the demon was closing in on her. It leapt in huge bounds, shaking the ground with each step.

I gripped the sword I hadn't realized I was holding and sprinted toward her.

The woman saw me. A flash of hope replaced the panic on her face. She veered toward me, pumping her arms and running harder. The demon followed.

*Now.* I raised my sword and charged. The woman gasped as the blade sank into the soft flesh of her belly. It sliced through her organs as easily as it had done to the man I'd killed moments before. I yanked out my sword, and her hands went to the wound, cradling the gleaming pink and gray viscera that slid out. Her eyes registered astonishment, then betrayal as her own blood coated her hands. She moaned and fell to her knees. She toppled over sideways. One soft sigh, one final gush of blood, and her heart stopped forever.

The demon had caught up to us. It snarled at me, baring its long yellow fangs. "That one was mine."

"You were too slow. Our leader rewards the quick." I sneered at its hideous face. "Go chase some old lady with a walker. That would be more your speed."

The demon howled and lunged at me. My sword burst into flame. Demon flesh sizzled as the creature's clawed hand touched fire. It shrieked and jumped back.

"Go!" I shouted. "Before I kill you as unfit to serve."

It spat at me, but I waved my sword and the gob of demon phlegm sputtered in the flame. The demon's wings unfurled and lifted it into the air. After a last growl in my direction, it flew off toward the harbor. A moment later, smoke swallowed its form.

I stepped over the woman's body and looked around for something else to kill. Something human, preferably, though I didn't care.

A buzzing in my arm drew my attention to my demon mark. The red scar was moving. It grew and changed its shape. The mark became the face of the Destroyer.

"Well done, shapeshifter," it said. The face grinned, and the burning inside me shone through its eyes. "Finally thou hast embraced thy destiny."

# 10

WHEN I CAME BACK TO MYSELF, I LAY ON THE KITCHEN floor. Again. Inches from my face an empty rubber glove reached for me like the hand of a dead man. A bright pink dead man.

*Shit.* It was the only thought I could muster. *Shit, shit, shit.*

I sat up, as achy and stiff as if I'd really just fought a battle. I rubbed the elbow I must have whacked when I fell on the floor. As I did, I glimpsed my demon mark. It took the shape of the grinning Destroyer's face, as it had in my vision. *No!* I blinked, and the face was gone. The mark looked like it always did—a small red burn scar that puckered the flesh of my forearm. But it felt strange, as though something were stirring there. Some presence, some creature waking after a long sleep. The presence moved under my skin, exploring. With it awakened a feeling I barely knew how to describe. Like a superheated itch, but deep inside where no scratching could relieve it.

I sat on the floor, inhaling deeply and rubbing my forearm, willing the feeling to subside. I focused on the soothing strokes, on making the sensation disappear. It didn't, but gradually it decreased. The itch dulled and sank deeper. I rubbed and rubbed, making it smaller, until the itch was no bigger than a pinprick. When the feeling stilled enough that I could ignore it, I climbed back into my chair.

*The Book of Utter Darkness* lay open on the table. An illustration now stretched across both pages. It was a detailed, hand-painted scene from that appalling vision. There I stood, spattered with blood, the woman I'd murdered lying at my feet. Fires burned on all sides, framing the scene. Above, a flying demon disappeared into the smoke. I held my sword aloft, its flames reaching into the sky and running along the tops of both pages. On my forearm, as vivid and detailed as a tattoo, leered the Destroyer.

A single word formed in my mind, appearing letter by letter as if scrolling across a marquee: *D . . . E . . . S . . . T . . . I . . . N . . . Y.*

No. *Not* my destiny.

I slammed the book shut. I grabbed the gloves and piled them on top, as though those rubber hands would hold the book's filthy visions inside it. I would *not* let the Destroyer take control. In whatever war was coming, I would *not* fight on the side of Hell.

A word whispered through my mind like the echo of a breeze: *destiny.*


I NEEDED TO TALK TO MAB. MY AUNT HAD ALSO STUDIED *The Book of Utter Darkness*, and her time with it stretched across several centuries. Mab rarely told me about anything she'd gotten from the book. But surely, *surely* if she'd ever had a vision like this one, a vision that showed me slaughtering innocent people and fighting alongside my sworn enemies, she'd warn me. Wouldn't she?

The book revealed different things to different readers. It was time for both of us to lay out everything we knew. Maybe if we put together all of the puzzle pieces we'd each seen individually, we'd get a clearer picture. Because I sure as hell refused to swallow the vision it was trying to feed me.

There was one problem, though: To talk to Mab, I had to be asleep. My aunt was old school—no cell phone, no landline, and nothing like a computer in her house. The only way to get in touch with her was to use an ancient Cerddorion method of psychic communication. When Gwen and I were kids, we called it the dream phone, using it to keep our conversations going each night after Mom had turned out the lights. Because the dream phone makes use of the parts of the mind that become active when the body is asleep, we could get our rest and keep gossiping together halfway through the night.

Now, sleep seemed about as possible as reassembling those zombies who'd been exploded by the Morfran. For one thing, it was barely two A.M., and I usually didn't climb into bed until after dawn. Tonight, of course, that wasn't the real problem. Even with every light in the apartment on, I didn't dare close my eyes. The moment I did, I saw the shocked betrayal on that woman's face as I drove my sword into her belly.

A vision. It was only a vision, sent by a book that hated me and wanted to confuse me. A book, made by demons, that wanted the demons to win. It had given me false visions before—visions not of something that came to pass but of something the book wanted to happen. One of its tricks. If I bought into the idea that the book's visions were inevitable, it became harder to see other possibilities, harder to find ways to thwart its prophecies.

I knew that. I'd learned to resist accepting such visions and whisperings from the book. But tonight was different. Tonight, I hadn't simply watched the vision unfold; I'd participated in it. I'd fought on the wrong side—and I'd liked it.

The admission slashed through my gut like a knife, like the way my blade had stabbed those innocent people. I'd liked it. I'd felt free and powerful, with no restraints on my behavior. Free to kill. Free to destroy.

My demon mark itched, and I rubbed it impatiently. I didn't want that seed of pure rage inside me. I knew now how it felt for the seed to grow and blossom, to fill me with its bitter fruit. I knew how it felt to be nothing more than an extension of the Destroyer.

I inspected the mark. Was it bigger? It looked redder, but that was probably because I couldn't stop rubbing the damn thing. I went to the bathroom and dug out a tube of aloe vera gel I'd bought last summer, after a romantic weekend on Cape Cod had left me as red as the lobsters Kane and I had eaten at a fancy waterfront restaurant. I squirted out a dollop and massaged it into the spot. Coolness spread across my skin, and the itch receded. It didn't go away, but it pulled back inside. It was the best I could do for now.

I'd put the gel back in the medicine cabinet and started to close the door when something caught my eye. A bottle of sleeping pills. Normally, sleeping pills didn't do a thing for me, but these were magically enhanced, the kind I give my clients to make them sleep soundly while I run through their dreams exterminating nightmare demons. I used them myself from time to time when my schedule got so messed up that I couldn't remember whether I was supposed to sleep during the day or at night. These worked. One pill, and I'd be snoozing away within ten minutes. But wrapped in a warm cocoon of drug-induced, magically enforced sleep, would I be able to use the dream phone? I'd never tried.

Still, there was no chance of talking to Mab while I was sitting bolt upright in a chair, too scared to blink. I poured myself a glass of water, swallowed the pill, and washed it down.

Five minutes later, I lay in my bed, the lights off and the covers pulled up to my chin. I pushed all thoughts from my mind except my aunt and her colors. Each member of my race has a pair of colors, specific to the individual, that you use to call someone on the dream phone. Mab's were blue—a strong, vibrant cobalt—and bright silver. Sleep lapped at the edges of my consciousness like a calm lake on a summer day. A blue lake, reflecting silvery glints of light. *Blue and silver. Blue and silver.* I slipped into sleep as though diving into that warm lake, surrounded by blue and silver swirls.


I WAS A MERMAID. THE THOUGHT DELIGHTED ME. LONG strands of silvery hair floated around my face in the blue, blue water. I looked at my tail, covered with glimmering scales in an intricate pattern of silver and iridescent blue. Beautiful. I giggled, sending a column of bubbles toward the surface.

*Giggling?* questioned an incredulous voice somewhere inside my mind. *You're not a giggler.*

I giggled again for the fun of it and to see the pretty silver bubbles rise. Then I jackknifed my body and streaked away. My powerful tail propelled me through the water. My silver hair streamed behind me like a comet's trail. I swam and swam through the blue water, loving my speed and strength.

From the corner of my eye, I caught sight of a form swimming beside me. Turning my head, I saw an old woman. How strange. I stopped and floated above the lake's bottom, inspecting my companion. Mab. It was Mab. But she wasn't a mermaid like me. Her long black skirt belled around her ankles; two feet stuck out awkwardly past the hem. The sight of my aunt—her short gray hair all wild and floaty around her face, her efforts to retain her dignity by holding her skirt in place—set off another giggling fit. Mab didn't giggle with me. She didn't look happy at all. She scowled at me through the giggle-bubbles and pointed toward the water's surface. Then she swam upward.

I watched her go, her black boots kicking as she ascended. I started to swim away. But something, the flash of my blue-and-silver tail, made me pause. The colors that surrounded me, that *made* me, they belonged to Mab. I was here for Mab; I couldn't let her go. With a flick of my tail, I followed her.

As soon as my head broke the water's surface, I became myself again. No mane of silvery hair, no iridescent tail. My legs thrashed for a moment until I remembered how to use them. I treaded water and looked around.

"Over here, child," Mab's voice called. She sat on the shore, no more than thirty yards away. I swam toward her in a slow breaststroke. Too slow. But when I dove beneath the water, my mermaid form didn't return. Pity. Swimming as a mermaid had been like flying. Now, I was reduced to clumsy thrashing.

Still, I made it. I got my feet under me and waded to my aunt. She sat on the sand, her knees drawn up and her arms wrapped around her shins. Water dripped from her hair and ran down her face in rivulets. Her scowl remained in place. She looked funny, but her expression killed any urge to giggle.

"Are you on some kind of drug?" she asked, her voice cross.

"It's just a sleeping pill, the kind I give clients." I conjured a towel and handed it to Mab so she could dry her hair. "Bedtime isn't for hours, and I needed to talk to you."

"I'm certain you realize the effects of trying to communicate while under the influence, so I'll spare you the lecture. Here's your towel." She handed me a pizza.

"Oh." Suddenly the giggles welled up again, and this time

I couldn't suppress them. "Good thing you didn't rub your hair with this." The idea of Mab, her hair coated with tomato sauce and draped with strings of cheese, was just too much. I dissolved in a fit of laughter, dropping the pizza. It sprouted four legs and a head and grew a hard green shell, then lumbered into the water. My laughter subsided to hiccups, and I felt a little mournful watching the towel/pizza/turtle go. I was hungry, and that pizza had looked good. A whiff of oregano and garlic hung in the air.

"Enough nonsense," Mab snapped. Kind of like a turtle, actually. I covered my mouth with both hands to hold the laughter inside. She was still dripping, and the phrase *mad as a wet hen* came to mind. I'd never thought about what it meant before; now I had a very vivid picture to last me for life. I fought the smile that tugged at my mouth. "I'm assuming that you had a reason for contacting me," she continued. "Unless you've taken up recreational drug use—in which case I'll be on my way."

"No, Mab, don't go. I'm sorry. There was a reason, an important one." I couldn't for the life of me remember what it was. My mind was crowded with mermaid tails and furious wet hens and snapping turtles and towels that turned into pizzas. I stalled while I tried to find the thread that brought me here. "Why are you all wet?" Her scowl deepened. "No, wait. What I mean is . . ." I concentrated, feeling like I was hunting for words in a bowl of alphabet soup. "How come you're here, *inside* my dream?" Usually, dream-phone conversations took place on neutral ground, a kind of borderland between the participants' psyches. In a typical dream-phone call, I could see my aunt in her own surroundings (day or night—Mab was the only person I knew who could place and receive calls while awake). In the same way, she could see me in mine. Tonight's situation was entirely new to me.

"It's the strength of the magic supplementing the pill you took. It must have been very well spelled. That's good when you enter a client's dreamscape, but not so good for this form of communication. The signal of your call came as usual—your colors rose up in a mist—but when I answered I found myself deep underwater, swimming beside a mermaid with your face." A tiny twitch that might have been a smile tugged at her mouth.

"Most unexpected, I assure you. It took me several seconds to regather my wits."

I wished I could regather mine. I stared at my bare feet, trying to remember why I'd called Mab. I counted my toes. *When I get to ten,* I promised myself, *my mind will clear. Deep breath. Okay, this little piggy went to market . . . that's one.*

I wiggled my toes and moved on to the next one. *This little piggy stayed home . . . two.*

My toes seemed to be wiggling of their own accord. I watched, fascinated. *This little piggy had—*My toes turned into pigs. Miniature ones. They remained attached to my feet, but they made a racket with their squealing.

Cool.

"Mab, do you see that?" I pointed at my wriggling, squealing toes. A thought made me snicker. "I've heard of pigtails, but not pigtoes."

"Child." The sharpness of Mab's voice silenced the pigs and turned them back into toes. "Look at me."

I did. She wasn't wet anymore, but she still looked mad. I lowered my eyes, ashamed of my spaciness.

Mab held my face in her hands. "Look at me," she repeated. "Look in my eyes."

All right. I could do that. Mab's eyes are blue, not amber like mine. In her irises, I could see both the blue and the silver that make up her colors. Pretty. My aunt had been a beautiful woman once upon a time.

A spark flared in Mab's eyes. I felt a snap, like a tight-stretched rubber band breaking. My gaze locked onto hers. She reeled me into a world of blue and silver. For a moment, I had an image of a mermaid caught on a fishing line, but then all images, all thought exploded in one great blue-and-silver flash.

I blinked, and the colors cleared. I felt my aunt's cool hands on my cheeks. I blinked again, and her face came into focus.

"How do you feel, child?" She watched me closely.

I considered. No aches, no pains. No bubbling wellspring of giggles. My head felt clearer, too.

"Better. Good, actually. What did you do?"

"I drew out some of the magic that was clouding your thoughts."

"You did? Are you okay?"

"A bit dizzy, but I'll be fine. However, with its magic removed, the pill you took will be less effective. So let's get down to business before you wake up."

Business. Right. With that word—*business*—I remembered. Part of my message had to do with my new job as a police consultant. "The Morfran is back."

Mab put a hand to her forehead and closed her eyes, as though waiting for some dizziness to pass. "It's attacking the previously deceased again?"

"Yes, but with a difference." I explained how the Morfran had possessed two zombies, driving them to kill, before consuming them.

"You're certain the Morfran is doing this?"

"I saw it. When the second zombie exploded, the room was full of Morfran. I used Hellforged to stow it in that slate plaque you gave me."

"Good." She rubbed her temples, frowning. "Good that you caught it, I mean. It's very bad that this is happening, however."

"That *what* is happening, Mab? What's going on?"

"Have you received any information about this from the book?"

I shot her a look to show her I didn't appreciate the way she avoided answering my question. But when I saw how she was holding her head, I softened. I'd been drunk with magic—enough to transform my normally empty dreamscape into Hallucination Street in Psychedelic City—and Mab had siphoned off the excess and taken it into herself. She was probably feeling way more off-kilter than "a bit dizzy." Yet she barely showed it.

I glanced at my toes, which remained toes. I almost wished they'd turn back into little piggies so I could giggle at them and not think about that damn book. "Nothing about zombies and the Morfran. But I had a new vision."

"Tell me."

"It started off like the others. Boston burning. Dead bodies everywhere. Huge demons running rampant. Same old story. Yadda yadda yadda."

I kept watching my toes, studying their shape, to block out the picture of Boston become Hell. Mab's cool hand touched my forearm and gave it a light squeeze. Mab wasn't the touchy-feely type. She knew this was hard for me. I swallowed the lump that seemed to be stuck in my throat.

"I fought, Mab. In the vision, I fought on the wrong side. And I . . ." I couldn't bring myself to say the truth, that I'd enjoyed it. I shrugged. "In the vision, it felt right."

"Child." Mab's voice was so soft, so gentle, like I was some fragile object that would shatter if you breathed on it too hard. That scared me almost as much as the vision did. "You must never forget the book's malevolence. It's trying to shake your resolve, make you dispirited and unsure."

Something wet ran down my cheek. I wiped it away. "It's doing a good job." More wetness, more wiping. "Mab, I'd rather jump in front of a train than have that vision come true."

"Of course you would. Don't you see, child? The book fears you. It would like nothing better than for you to believe you have only two options: jump in front of a train, as you put it, or join the demons in the coming apocalypse."

"Apocalypse?" I don't know why the word surprised me; it was the only way to describe the devastation I'd seen in those visions. Still, it sent a shiver along my limbs.

"The end times foretold in *The Book of Utter Darkness*. The final struggle between demons and our kind. The book wants you to believe this struggle will end in the devastation of humanity, but remember, child: Many paths stretch forward from where you stand now. It's up to you to choose the one you'll take."

Mab was trying to rouse me, give me confidence—I knew that. But I didn't like her metaphor. Yes, I was standing at a crossroads with multiple paths leading in different directions. But from here, I couldn't see where any of them led. What if I started down one, with the best of intentions, only to find the Destroyer at its end, waiting with open arms?

Beside me, Mab rose to her feet. I tilted my head to look up at her. She swayed and stepped sideways to steady herself, a residual effect of the magic, I guessed. But her expression was determined. "I'd hoped for a little more time to gather my strength," she said, "but that is not to be. The signs are too strong."

"What signs?" I squinted as my aunt's form thinned. A deep

rumble shook the ground, and Mab staggered. Earthquake? No, it was coming from the outside. My sleeping body was snoring—and that meant I was about to wake up.

"There's no time, child. I'll tell you when I get there."

*Get where?*

"I'll have Jenkins ring with the arrangements."

"What arrangements? Mab, what are you talking about?" Snores and snorts shuddered the air and ground. The lake sloshed into whitecaps. A fissure opened beside me. Mab fractured into a mosaic portrait of herself; the blue-and-silver pieces faded around the edges, going all wispy and cottony and floating apart.

"The arrangements for me to travel to Boston." Somehow, her words, quiet as a distant murmur, found me through the thunderous booming that broke apart my dreamscape. "So I can lend my support. It's time for you to accept your role."

"What role?" The fragments of my aunt drifted away like dandelion seeds. "Mab, don't go yet. I need to know what you're talking about. *What* role?"

"Why, child, haven't you realized? You're the Lady of the Cerddorion."

# 11

MY EYES FLEW OPEN. I BOLTED UPRIGHT IN BED, CLUTCHING sweaty handfuls of sheet. My heart pounded in my ears like wild horses galloping through my brain. "Mab!" I wanted her to come back and explain what was going on. But even as I shouted her name, I knew she couldn't hear me. She'd left my dreamscape, and so had I. Two thousand miles away in Wales, she was starting her day—greeting Rose, who'd already been in the kitchen for an hour, telling Jenkins they had urgent arrangements to make. Did she really say she was coming to Boston? Or had my drugged-out dreamscape thrown her last words at me, like it had made me a mermaid and turned my toes into wriggling piggies?

I rubbed my eyes and checked my bedside clock. Two forty-eight A.M. Groaning, I flopped onto my pillow and pulled the covers over my head. *Sleep!* I ordered myself. *Sleep now!*

Yeah, right. Like that was going to work.

The command got lost in the storm of questions that swirled through my mind. Why was Mab coming to Boston—assuming I'd heard her right? Who was the Lady of the Cerddorion, and what did she have to do with me? It had to be a hallucination.

Yet Mab had pulled most of the magic out of me, and I'd felt lucid enough after that.

I wished I could say the same thing now.

Maybe Mab's exit from my dreamscape had released the magic she'd siphoned off, and that's what made me hear crazy things as she left. The thought slowed my speeding heartbeat a little. That was probably it. It was too early to call the Welsh pub that would send a message to Mab's remote estate, but I'd do that later. Just to make sure she hadn't really said she was coming to Boston.

Because if she hadn't said that, she also hadn't said that other thing, about the Lady of Cerddorion, whatever that was.

Feeling reassured, I sat up again. The room tilted a little, and I closed my eyes before it started spinning, too. Didn't help. My bed felt like the Tilt-a-Whirl ride that had left me with a dizzy head and a queasy stomach at a seaside fair when I was eight. Damn sleeping pill. I opened my eyes and pressed down on the bed with both hands, as though that would hold it still.

No way I'd be going back to sleep now. For me, three o'clock in the morning was like midafternoon for the norms. I'd had a nap, and my body didn't want more sleep. The residual effect of the sleeping pill and its magic said otherwise. It left me with a foggy head, heavy limbs, and a mind that refused to sleep. Not a great combination.

I heaved myself out of bed and staggered across the hall to the bathroom. A steamy shower provided some relief. But as I toweled off, my head still felt like someone had stuffed it with soggy cotton balls. Maybe a walk in the cool night air would clear it.

I dressed in jeans and a black T-shirt, then threw on a light jacket. In front of my weapons cabinet, I paused, looking over my collection of knives and swords. Pam McFarren was right—there was so much anger in the streets, and I couldn't afford to look like a target. Twice now, somebody had looked at me and seen a punching bag.

So how best to shut down a fight before it started? To a zombie, a knife is about as scary as a toothpick. A semiautomatic pistol would be the best thing to hold back an aggressive zombie in a bad mood. I carried bronze bullets, not the exploding "zombie droppers" that could kill a zombie if you fired a whole lot of them fast enough. Even so, most zombies would think twice about getting aerated with a dozen new holes.

I shrugged off my jacket. I chose the biggest, meanest-looking pistol I owned, a Magnum Desert Eagle .44, and buckled on its shoulder holster. If I left the jacket unzipped, it was almost as good as carrying a neon sign that read DON'T MESS WITH ME. Given the mood out there, would that be a deterrent or a challenge? Whatever. All I knew was I'd rather face a zombie mob than climb the walls of my apartment.

AS SOON AS I STEPPED ONTO THE SIDEWALK, I HEARD MY name. I looked along the nearly empty street—the crowds seemed to gather near the checkpoints—and then I saw him. Kane picked up his pace as he walked toward me. He wore an open trench coat over his expensive suit. His silver hair gleamed in the moonlight.

Moonlight. The waxing moon was a reminder of how little time was left before Kane's bargain with the Night Hag forced him to become one of her hounds.

I tried to smile as he caught up to me, but I knew my face reflected the despair, fear, and guilt I saw in his. Still, his touch was warm as he folded me into his arms. I pressed my face into his chest. His scent was all Kane—fresh air and pine woods— not the charred brimstone of a hellhound.

Kane stepped back. Reluctantly, I let go.

"I'm glad I ran into you," he said. "I've been trying to get in touch."

*Tell me you want to sweep me off my feet,* I wished. *Pick me up and carry me through the streets back to your place. We'll close the bedroom door and not come out for a week. We'll push away the Night Hag and Pryce and the Morfran and everything else that's driven this wedge between us. We'll be so close nothing will ever get between us again.*

I didn't say any of that. Instead, I asked what was up. We started walking in the direction of his town house. His hand brushed mine but didn't grasp it.

"Two things. First, I got this for you." He held up something that looked like a pendant. From the end of a leather loop dangled a charm. It was made of metallic threads woven into a complicated pattern, with various crystals knotted in. "It's a protection charm," he said, lifting the loop over my head. "To keep you safe from malevolent spirits. I commissioned it from Roxana Jade." He arranged the pendant so it rested over my heart. "Promise me you'll wear it."

"All right." If it brought him a little peace of mind, I would. Although privately I had my doubts. I knew Roxana. She was one of Boston's most skilled witches. But I knew where I would place my bet in a contest between any human and a spirit as ancient and spiteful as the Night Hag.

"Second, I wanted you to know that I've hired some witches to cast a protection spell over your apartment for each night of the full moon. Four witches, one for each element. Each is the top-ranked witch for her element nationally. I've got a list of their names." He dug around in the inner pocket of his suit jacket. "Here it is." He held it out to me.

"Kane, how much did that cost?" A fortune, no doubt. Maybe two.

"The cost doesn't matter. I need to make sure you're safe. I need to do it now, because . . ."

He didn't finish the sentence, but I knew what he was thinking: Because once he transformed into just another hellhound in the Night Hag's pack, he'd be forced to obey her orders. Including the order to kill me.

I looked at the list. Roxana Jade was on it, but she was the only local. For the others, Kane must be paying travel expenses, hotel, food—all that on top of whatever ridiculous fee they were charging. I stopped and shook the list at him. "This isn't necessary, Kane. It's a waste of money."

"Vicky—"

"I can't even promise I'll stay home on those nights. I might have to work."

"You can't possibly have scheduled any jobs for the full moon—for *this* full moon. If you did, reschedule. I'm sure your clients would understand."

"Not demon extermination. I'm working as a consultant for the police. The zombie murders—" Kane scowled. He was all about the proper terminology and hated it when I said *zombie*. I tried again. "The PDH who killed those humans was possessed by the Morfran. Those damn crows drove him to kill before they fed on him. So the cops asked me to help them figure out what's going on."

"Which one?"

"What?"

"Which cop asked you to help?"

"Daniel Costello."

Kane's scowl deepened, and something flared in his gray eyes. Jealousy? But that was ridiculous. Kane knew Daniel and I had gone on a few dates. But he also knew that was ancient history. I'd made my choice. I'd chosen Kane.

I tried to dredge up a little pleasure at the thought that Kane was jealous, like maybe it was a sign that we still had hope of a normal relationship. But it didn't work. Any jealousy was one more vapor in the noxious cloud that held us apart.

"You don't have anything to worry about," I said.

Kane laughed bitterly. "I've got so many things to worry about I couldn't even count them all between now and next Tuesday."

"Well, me running off with Daniel isn't one of them."

His look softened. He pulled me to him as we continued down the street. "I'm sorry. I know that. I don't doubt your feelings for me. I mean, I don't doubt them tonight." His fingers tightened on my arm. "It's me. After I become that . . . that *thing*, after the Mistress of Hounds forces me to attack you— How could your feelings *not* change?"

"That hellhound isn't you."

"It is, though. Or . . ." He chewed his lip, searching for the right words. "It's like I'm trapped inside it. I feel what it feels, see what it sees. Most of the experience is pain—" His voice broke, and he shuddered. He swallowed hard, his body tense. "Pain and instinct. But it's like some part of me, the part I think of *as* me—my mind, my emotions—gets shrunken down and locked inside. I'm there, but I can't control what the hellhound does."

I stopped. He waited beside me, his arm still around my shoulders as he stared into the distance. "I understand," I said. When he wouldn't look at me, I reached up and gently turned his face toward mine. "I do." Apprehension dimmed his eyes, but he nodded. He knew I'd felt the same pain when the Night Hag had transformed me into a hellhound to drive me into the

Darklands. It had been agonizing, maddening. But the Night Hag didn't want merely to hurt Kane. She wanted to break him.

"If she forces me, Vicky"—he didn't say to do what, but we both knew what he meant—"I'll experience every second of it. I'll remember it the next day. Forever. I . . . I couldn't live with that."

*You don't have to.* I could release him from the Night Hag's power by giving her the white falcon. Yet how could I turn over my father's spirit, so recently liberated from the realm of the dead, to the same kind of torment? And what if giving up the falcon meant my horrible visions of war and death would come to pass? I wanted to tell Kane about the Night Hag's offer, but that would be dangling false hope. I didn't fully know what was at stake. Unable to see a solution, I was paralyzed.

So I didn't say anything. I put my arms around him and held him until he stopped shaking.

"Thank you," I whispered, "for trying to protect me. I love you."

He groaned and pulled me closer. "I love you, too," his lips murmured against my hair.

If only that were enough. If only we could stay like this, so solid, so close, until everything that threatened us melted away and simply ceased to be.

But that wasn't going to happen. Kane sighed, and that quiet sound expressed worlds of frustration and anxiety. We stepped apart, but he held my hand as we continued walking.

"Where were you headed?" he asked. "I'll walk you there. There are too many people out looking for trouble tonight."

At one time, I'd have bristled at the idea I needed an escort. But right now, I understood the depth of his need to keep me safe.

"Just out for a walk. I know, I know." I put my fingers to his lips to stifle his objection. "I had a bad session with the book and needed to clear my head. I've got protection." I pulled open my jacket to show my gun.

"I noticed. I'd prefer you didn't put yourself in a situation where you need to use it."

"Me, too. But this is my neighborhood, and I'm not going to hide indoors like a scared little kid. I'll be fine." Before he could argue with me, I changed the subject. "Did you hear they're lowering the code level to yellow in the morning?"

He nodded. "I need to put in a full day at the office tomorrow. I'm behind on work. I've been planning this rally."

"Tina told me. If anyone can bring unity to Deadtown, it's you."

"I don't know about that. But I have to try. If we can channel all the energy from the current unrest into something constructive—" He stumbled, and I realized how tired he must be.

"You've been up all night, and you're planning to be at work in, what, four hours?"

He checked his watch. "Three. I need to get an early start."

"Then I'll walk you home. You can't save the world if you're falling asleep on your feet, you know."

He didn't argue. We walked the couple of blocks to his town house in silence, his hand warm in mine. With each step, the cloud I hated so much rose up between us again.

At the door, he kissed my cheek. It felt stiff, formal, like a man kissing an elderly aunt he didn't really like. I put my hands on his face and turned his head, sliding my lips across his skin until our mouths touched. He made a soft sound, half sigh, half moan, and pulled me to him as he parted his lips. We kissed with a deep hunger—hunger to regain the closeness we'd somehow lost, to blow away the cloud and really touch each other again.

And yet, when he drew back and looked at me, hopelessness dulled his eyes. Or maybe it was just exhaustion. Either way, he gave me a squeeze and stepped away, letting me go. He didn't gather me into his arms and carry me upstairs. Although I knew that couldn't happen, not now, my body ached with disappointment. Kane smiled sadly and said, "You say I want to save the world, and maybe I do. But I swear, Vicky, I'd send the whole world to hell if it would keep you safe."

Then he went inside. As he was closing the door he paused, gazing out at me, but I could barely see his face through the cloud of our mutual despair.

# 12

MY WALK WITH KANE HAD DONE NOTHING TO CLEAR MY head. I kept wandering through the streets of Deadtown, aimlessly I thought, until I realized my feet were taking me toward Creature Comforts.

The streets grew more crowded the closer I got to the checkpoint, but I kept my head down and this time nobody bothered me. Maybe it was my Magnum. Or maybe it was the Goons on every corner. Whatever, I was glad to avoid trouble. Pam McFarren would be proud.

I whizzed through the checkpoint, feeling a little guilty it was so easy when all those zombies behind me couldn't even pass into the Zone, not since yesterday's riot. On the other hand, I thought, kicking away shards of a broken bottle, the mood was still ugly, and the Zone hadn't yet recovered from yesterday's damage. Axel had held his own, but he was only one troll. Next time, he might not be so lucky. I hated to agree with Commissioner Hampson, but maybe it was a good idea to keep zombies on their own side of the barrier until things simmered down.

As I'd noticed earlier, Creature Comforts was the only bar

in the Zone that was open for business. Things would be hopping inside. The crowd might be rowdy. Knowing that Axel frowned on bringing weapons into the bar, I zipped my jacket all the way up to my chin. If I needed the gun, it would be there. But I didn't expect to need it. Axel doesn't allow any nonsense.

As I stepped inside, inhaling the familiar, comforting scent of old beer, stale smoke, and a slight whiff of human blood, I stopped in surprise. Aside from a couple of vampires holding court to three adoring junkies in the back booth, I was the only customer. Axel lounged on a stool at the end of the bar, his large hands around a glass of beer, watching the overhead TV. He acknowledged my entrance with a short nod, and then stood, picked up his beer, and walked behind the bar.

"Where is everybody?" I asked, taking a stool.

"Not here." He rummaged around in a refrigerator, then held up a bottle, his eyebrows raised.

The beer he offered was my usual—a lite beer that tasted just a shade beerier than carbonated water. I'm not all that big on drinking. Tonight, the way that sleeping pill had messed with my head, I didn't want to compound the problem with even a miniscule amount of alcohol. "No thanks," I said. "How about a club soda with lime? Make that a couple of limes." *Wow, Vicky, you really know how to live it up.*

Axel gave me a look that suggested he was worried I'd go all crazy on him—not—and rattled some ice cubes into a glass. He gave me my drink, three lime wedges adorning the rim.

"You all right?" I asked. "After last night, I mean."

"Fine."

I looked around. The bar seemed fine, too. Same dim lights, sticky floor, crooked chairs, and vinyl-seated booths I knew and loved. Here, you could almost believe that all was right with the world.

Axel reached to lower the volume on the TV.

"Don't bother," I said. "If you're watching it, I mean."

I was in the mood to sit and stare into my drink, and Axel isn't what you'd call a big talker, anyway. Well, not unless Mab is here to chat with him in whatever language Scandinavian trolls speak. Then you can't shut the guy up. I wondered again if I'd heard Mab right, if she really was coming to Boston. The more I thought about it, the more I was sure I'd imagined it. That and her Lady of the Cerddorion comment. None of it made any sense.

Axel leaned against the counter behind the bar and returned his attention to the TV. He was watching one of those competitive cooking shows, where teams of chefs race to outdo each other to perform culinary miracles. Axel watched intently, not even blinking.

"Thinking of opening a restaurant?" I asked.

His eyes didn't leave the screen as he shook his head. "Reminding myself why I'd be crazy to try."

I could see what he meant. On the screen, flames shot upward from a pan as two chefs screamed at each other. One of them grabbed a plate of pasta and hurled it across the kitchen. The scene made Axel's job of tossing out anemic vampire junkies and breaking up werewolf fights look positively placid.

I turned back to my drink, drawing a line with my finger through the condensation on the glass. The show was easy to tune out—I wasn't really interested in people throwing fits about overcooked linguini. Instead, I squeezed a lime wedge and stirred the cloudy juice into my club soda. What was going on with the Morfran? How was it managing to possess a zombie like Tom Malone or Andy Skibinsky and control its host's actions before consuming him?

Pryce was behind this—he had to be. He was the one who'd sent a huge quantity of the Morfran to Boston last winter. When the spirit had attacked the zombies at the Paranormal Appreciation Day concert, I'd acted as quickly as I could, using Hellforged to trap it in the old slate gravestones of the Granary Burying Ground. I'd mopped up most of it, but some had gotten away. Maybe that little bit of escaped Morfran had found those zombies and driven them to kill. But why would the Morfran change its behavior?

An uneasy feeling clenched my stomach.

I'd told Daniel that sorcery was a possible cause. Pryce's father, Myrddin Wyllt, had been a wizard, well versed in the sorcerer's black arts. When Myrddin died, Pryce absorbed his father's life force and knowledge. In the Darklands, I'd seen Myrddin's spirit emerge from Pryce's body to cast a spell.

Could Pryce be using Myrddin's sorcery to bind the Morfran to zombies?

There was one way to find out. I had a spy in the demon plane.

A spy I hated to summon, because it always gave me twice as much trouble as information. My very own personal guilt demon, an Eidolon with the unlikely name of Butterfly.

The uneasy feeling in my gut grew. I let it. Worry, anxiety, any kind of malaise—all these things are like catnip to an Eidolon. When a wave of nausea rose from the pit of my stomach to my throat, I knew *now* was the time. I jumped off my stool and rushed across the room, past the vampires and their acolytes, to the back hallway. I passed the door marked BOOS and shoved open one marked GHOULS. The bathroom was empty—good. Stomach churning, I leaned on a sink and commanded, "Butterfly! I summon thee here from Uffern!" Uffern is what demons call their own plane.

The sick feeling tightened into a ball. I braced. A black butterfly with razor-sharp wings tore from my body, shooting out from the region of my solar plexus. *Damn*, that hurt. It bounced off the wall and whacked the side of my head. Then it flew up near the ceiling and hovered there.

"Whaddaya want?" it asked in an irritable voice.

I reached with shaking hands to turn on the faucet. By the time I'd splashed some cold water on my face, I felt better. As I reached for a paper towel, the black butterfly landed on my shoulder.

"And what'd you conjure me in the ladies' room for? I ain't a lady. I ain't *comfortable* in here."

"Too bad." I wiped my face with a handful of paper towels, then leaned forward to look in the mirror. Dark purple circles ringed my eyes. Clinging to my shoulder was a large black insect, with a six-inch wingspan and the hideous face of a demon—beady eyes, a tusked snout, a mouthful of pointy teeth. "I need some information, Butterfly."

The demon cringed at the nickname. To an Eidolon the most important thing—besides gorging on its victim's feelings of guilt and anxiety—is its own dignity. If you don't take a guilt demon seriously, if you mock it and call it names, it loses some of its power over you.

Or at least, that's the theory.

I'd first conjured this particular Eidolon several weeks ago. Then, as now, I'd needed information about happenings in the demon plane. Unfortunately, in calling it to me I'd drawn a bit too deeply on my feelings of regret and remorse, and ended up with a teensy little demon infestation. Butterfly was keeping a toehold in my gut, always ready to snack on my baser feelings. In a way, I couldn't blame the demon. The way my life had been going lately, my gut-level emotions were an Eidolon's dream of an all-you-can-eat buffet.

"Oh, *you* need information, huh? That would be the same 'you' who calls me names, tries to starve me to death, and threatens to kill me with one of your dozens of nasty-looking bronze weapons. Why should I lift a wing to help you?"

"I don't know. 'Cause you like my pretty face?"

Butterfly's braying laugh sprayed demon spit in my ear.

*Gross.* I swatted the demon from my shoulder and grabbed more paper towels. As I wet them and scrubbed out my ear, Butterfly flew up to the fluorescent light fixture, bumping against it a few times. My turn to laugh. "Must be hell for a demon to manifest in the form of a creature that's attracted to light."

"I manage." Butterfly tore itself away from the light and landed on the edge of a sink. Its black, serrated wings quivered. "I like this form. Good mobility." Usually Eidolons manifest as a giant maggot, with a demon head and a second toothy mouth hidden in its belly. The Eidolon sits on its victim, the demon head taunting while the belly-mouth munches away on the shame, remorse, and despair that arise. The worse the victim feels, the better the Eidolon eats. "That dumb nickname you gave me lets me take this shape. So I don't even mind when you call me B . . . Buh . . . you know."

"Sure. The name you can't bring yourself to say." I was getting fed up with this conversation. "Cooperate, or I'll come up with a different name for you, like Horse Poop."

"Try it. I'll manifest in a big, steaming pile in the middle of your bed. On your pillow, maybe." The demon chuckled at the thought. Conjuring this demon was a mistake. I thought of the gun under my jacket, and my demon mark twinged. One bronze bullet, and I'd finally be rid of this pest. My hand on the pistol grip, I wondered how miffed Axel would be about one little bullet hole in the ladies' room wall. And possibly another in the ceiling. Maybe two. Butterfly was fast.

A tap sounded on the door, which cracked open an inch. I let go of my gun and pulled my jacket shut. "You all right?" Concern threaded Axel's gruff voice.

"I'm fine."

"I thought I heard voices."

"That was me. I'm, um . . . practicing a speech. For the unity rally." It was the only reason I could think of that I'd be standing in front of a bathroom mirror, talking to myself. Butterfly put two legs over its mouth, trying to hold in the laughter. It staggered on its other four legs and fell over sideways. "Really, Axel, I'm okay." I raised my voice to cover the sound of demonic laughter. "I'll be out in a minute."

After a moment's hesitation, the door closed.

Butterfly lay on its back, howling with laughter, its legs kicking the air. "That's the lamest excuse I ever heard. Hey, do you think that later on you could feel, you know, *dumb* about it? Idiotic, even? Those feelings are delicious."

Anger welled, and I thought again of my gun. "Forget I conjured you. And stay out of my emotions. I'll kill you, I swear."

Ever seen a butterfly look skeptical? That was the look the Eidolon gave me. My anger skyrocketed, and my demon mark flared into a bonfire. I wanted to make Butterfly hurt, bad. Okay, the gun would get me banned from Creature Comforts, but I didn't have to shoot the Eidolon. I could swat it with my shoe and smear demon guts across the sink. Squashing the demon wouldn't be fatal, but it might teach the damn thing some manners. I reached down and pulled off my shoe.

Butterfly felt the change in my mood. It launched from the sink and flew around my head, then alighted on the farthest stall door. "You know, you really need to look into an anger-management class or something," it said. "You're not safe to be around."

"Then quit infesting me. Whether I call you or not, *just leave me alone*!" I shouted. I punched the door open and stomped out into the hallway. I hurled myself back onto my barstool. It wasn't until I slapped my shoe on the bar that I realized I hadn't put it back on.

Axel stared, one eyebrow raised. I opened my mouth to explain, but I couldn't think of a single reason why my supposed speech about unity would end with me taking off my shoe and screaming, "Leave me alone." So instead I drained my club soda and asked for another.

He picked up my glass and, giving me a funny look, sniffed it. I took the opportunity to study my fingernails. The one on my right index finger was looking a little ragged; had I been chewing it lately?

Axel put the empty glass in the sink and took a clean one from the shelf. He filled it with ice and club soda and sniffed it again, then cut a couple of lime wedges.

On the television above the bar, the closing credits for the chef competition show were rolling. The picture cut to a shot of the police commissioner, Fred Hampson, all dressed up in a dark blue suit and staring into the camera. He had a narrow face, with deep bags pulling down his eyes and a thin mouth made thinner by his grim expression.

"This is a public safety announcement," he said. "Until further notice, a curfew is in effect for Designated Area One. Starting immediately, all previously deceased residents must be off the streets and in their homes from two hours before sunrise until two hours after sunset. Extra patrols will be dispatched to the area to ensure compliance.

"In addition, the code for Designated Area One is now yellow. I repeat: Code Yellow. All previously deceased humans are restricted to DA-1. Other paranormals may pass through the checkpoints with proper identification. At this time, twenty-seven of the previously deceased remain at large."

A list of names, organized alphabetically, scrolled up the screen. *Wendy Abingdon. Mario Bello. Oliver Burnes.* As the list went by I didn't see any names I knew.

Hampson's face reappeared. "If you encounter any of these fugitives, you must inform the authorities immediately. Call 911 or the Paranormal Reporting Hotline." A phone number flashed across the bottom of the screen. "Anyone with knowledge of the whereabouts of a fugitive who fails to make a report may be subject to arrest. Thank you for your cooperation." Again, the list of names scrolled up the screen.

"What a prick."

That wasn't Axel's voice. I looked up to see who'd spoken. Not a vampire; they'd left and taken their groupies with them. But Butterfly—now in its giant maggot form—had slithered onto the barstool beside mine. The Eidolon sat there in all its maggoty glory, fat and white and glistening grotesquely. Its demon face leered at me.

"I hate guys like that." Butterfly gestured with its chin toward the TV where Hampson had spoken. "Always convinced he's right. He's a prick, but there's not a remorseful bone in his body. No guilt, no regrets. You know what would happen if everybody was like him? There wouldn't be any Eidolons, that's what. We'd starve out of existence."

"Why are you still here?"

Axel, who'd just set my drink down, gave me a sharp look.

"Not you," I said. "That thing." I gestured toward the next stool.

Butterfly chuckled. It was exactly the kind of sloppy gurgling sound you'd imagine if you ever happened to think of a chuckling maggot. "He can't see me."

Oh, great. If they choose, personal demons can manifest only to the person they've infested. The victim can see and hear them, but they're invisible to everyone else. That's the option Butterfly was taking, making me look like a crazy woman talking to herself.

"I mean that guy," I said, changing my gesture to sweep vaguely toward the TV. "Hampson. Why couldn't Boston have a police commissioner who's more sympathetic to paranormals?"

Axel grunted, but he didn't look convinced. I smiled weakly and picked up my club soda.

"Mmm," Butterfly said. "Embarrassment—tasty." The demon had slithered closer to me. Now its second mouth sucked at my arm. I yanked away and grabbed some cocktail napkins to sponge off the slime where it had touched me.

Axel turned from the television to watch me flailing around. I picked up my glass and wiped away the water ring beneath it.

I thought about explaining to Axel that I was dealing with a giant invisible maggot sitting on the stool next to mine. The guy's a troll; he's probably seen weirder things. But I couldn't think of any way to phrase it without making myself sound pure batshit crazy.

"Maybe that's because you *are* pure batshit crazy," Butterfly said. "Calling a terrifying demon B . . . Buh . . . some silly pet name is proof of that."

Of course. Eidolons can read their victims' thoughts. That's how they get access to a person's deepest, darkest secrets to exploit them. I didn't have to talk to Butterfly; I could just think at it.

*Okay, Butterfly, listen up. The fact that you haven't gone away suggests one of two things: (a) you're willing to share some information or (b) you've got a death wish. If it's b, I'm happy to oblige. I'll pull out my gun and pulverize you with bronze bullets until there's nothing left but a puddle of demon goo for Axel to mop up. He won't ban me after I've explained—he'll congratulate me.*

"Such a charmer. No wonder you're a failure at relationships." A pointy black tongue snaked its way from the second mouth toward my arm, eager to taste the feelings that jibe brought up. I leaned back and twisted away, out of reach. Butterfly heaved a put-upon sigh. "By 'information,' I'm assuming you mean the latest goings-on of Pryce and the Destroyer, since that's what you asked me to watch. I might know a thing or two, but I'm too hungry to remember it, so—"

*No. You're not snacking on me. The only thing you're making me feel right now is pissed off, and you don't like me when I'm angry. Remember what happened on top of that mountain between the Darklands and Uffern?* I was referring to a time when I'd opened myself fully to the Destroyer's rage. I'd been so brimming over with anger and fury and lust for destruction that my own personal demon had jumped out and run away from me in terror.

"All right, all right. But I *am* hungry. At least push over that bowl of peanuts so I can reach them."

Anything to keep that disgusting belly-mouth away from me. I grabbed the bowl of peanuts that sat on my left and dragged it over so it sat in front of the stool on my right. The Eidolon fell into it face-first, looking like the most disgusting pig at the trough.

"I heard that."

*Sorry.* I'd have to work at shielding any thoughts I didn't want the demon to overhear. Like the thought that I wasn't sorry one bit.

I glanced at Axel, but he didn't seem to notice the peanuts magically disappearing. In fact, he was conspicuously *not* looking in my direction.

Butterfly straightened, smacking its lips. "Better." The demon belched loudly. "But physical food gives me heartburn." A nauseating stench of peanuts, bile, and sulfur wafted through the air. Axel didn't notice, not even a twitch of his nose, but I was tempted to put a cocktail napkin over my face. I settled for propping my elbows on the bar and resting my chin in my hands, steepling my fingers over my nose.

*You'd better have something useful for me.*

"How 'bout this: Pryce and the Destroyer have been fighting each other for dominance."

*You told me that weeks ago.* When Pryce had resurrected Difethwr in his quest to regain his shadow demon, the Hellion had been furious to find itself bound to someone it considered a lesser being. I'd been hoping they'd stay locked in that struggle— fighting each other kept them both out of the human world.

" 'Have been,' I said. Things change. They've come to some sort of agreement. I mean, I'm not privy to their terms— personal demon like me, either one of 'em would just as soon step on me as look at me—but they've stopped fighting."

*The Destroyer has agreed to be Pryce's shadow demon?* That surprised me. The leader of the Hellions bowed to no one. I couldn't imagine it was content with being Pryce's sidekick.

"Difethwr isn't a shadow demon. It's more like a partnership. They're bound to each other, thanks to whatever happened inside that cauldron thing." Pryce had resurrected the Destroyer by trapping hundreds of demons in a magical cauldron. As those demons merged into a Hellion, Pryce bound that Hellion to him by jumping into the cauldron himself. "They've accepted they're stuck with each other—for now, anyway. Neither is subordinate to the other. But they hate each other. You ask me, I think each one's waiting for the chance to gain the upper hand."

Well, there was a little bit of comfort. Although they'd been allies in the past, being bound together changed everything. One or the other would make a power grab, and they'd start fighting again. It's hard to wage war against humanity when you're locked in a battle for supremacy over your other half.

"Yeah, except for one thing," Butterfly said, and I realized my private thoughts were leaking into its hearing. I concentrated on shielding them better. "I mean, far be it from me to be the kind of demon who dashes people's hopes"—Butterfly paused to snicker, since dashing hopes is one of the things Eidolons do best—"but Pryce and Difethwr are united in their ultimate goal."

*Which is?*

"To rule the three realms, of course. To make the Darklands and the Ordinary part of Uffern."

Part of Hell, in other words.

*I bet you'd love that. The human world would become your playground.*

"Well, that's a bet you'd lose, sweetheart. Pryce isn't what you'd call fond of personal demons. He calls us 'puny' and 'weak.' He wants to build a mighty demon army, and he scoffs at using personal demons as foot soldiers. Fine with me—I don't want to be a foot soldier. I mean, can you imagine this body in uniform?"

I tried. I failed. I was glad.

"Yeah, exactly. So before Pryce attacks the Ordinary, first he plans to conquer the Darklands. He wants to use that cauldron of transformation, the one that brought back Difethwr, to create an army of Hellions. He'll round up all personal demons, march us into the Darklands, and force us into the cauldron to be transformed. I don't want to be transformed." The maggot looked at me, and I couldn't help thinking that any transformation would be an improvement. "I don't figure you've got much chance of stopping him, but who knows? You might get lucky."

*Thanks for the vote of confidence.*

"Hey, I can read all your doubts and fears. I'm just echoing what worries you, deep down." Butterfly paused to scarf some more peanuts. "Anyway, for some reason, Pryce sees you as an obstacle to his plan. He's all obsessed with some old prophecy or something. He believes he has to get rid of some lady before he proceeds."

Some lady? That sounded nuts. Unless . . . *Wait, do you mean the Lady of the Cerddorion?*

Butterfly belched again. "I dunno. All he says is 'the lady.' Anyway, that's why he's working with that wizard."

"Myrddin?" Oops. Hadn't meant to say it out loud, but if Axel noticed, he didn't let on. *That's Pryce's father. When the old man died, his life force became part of Pryce.*

"Yeah, Myrddin. In Uffern, the wizard can detach from Pryce, float around on his own as a spirit. But when Pryce crosses the border into the Ordinary, the old man has to re-integrate. You know, cram his spirit back into Pryce's body."

*So Pryce has been entering the human realm. Do you know what he's doing here?* This was what I wanted to know—whether Pryce was somehow binding the Morfran to the possessed zombies.

"You think I tag along, like a little lost puppy looking for a home? I told you, I do *not* want to get on that demi-demon's radar. All I know is it's got something to do with zombies."

Bingo. Drawing on Myrddin's vast knowledge, Pryce was making the Morfran possess zombies, turning them into killing machines. It occurred to me that the Morfran-possessed zombies we'd seen so far were guinea pigs. Myrddin and Pryce hadn't found the right spell to make the Morfran fully inhabit the zombies. Instead, the Morfran turned on its host, feeding on the zombie's body and destroying it.

*So where is he, do you know? When he comes into the human plane, I mean.*

"Spying on you, sometimes. Thanks to that demon mark on your arm, the Destroyer always knows where you are. And the Hellion's not shy about sharing that information with Pryce. I'd watch my back if I were you. Could be you're the lady Pryce wants to get rid of."

No. Not me. I was not the Lady of the Cerddorion.

"Yeah, I tend to agree," Butterfly sneered. "As someone who knows you, mind, heart, and soul, I've gotta say *lady* ain't the word that comes to mind."

Damn. My private thoughts were slipping out from behind the shield again.

"But Pryce doesn't always tail you," Butterfly went on. "There's another place he goes. He goes there a lot."

*Where?*

"Beats me. Like I said, I keep my distance. I got no ambition to be the first demon he tosses in that cauldron."

The only thing worse than being saddled with a personal demon was being saddled with a cowardly personal demon.

"Now you're back to insulting me. After I come at your beck and call and do you a favor." Butterfly eyed the half-empty bowl of peanuts on the bar, then gave me a sidelong glance. "Bet that makes you feel guilty, huh?"

*Not in the slightest.* I made a mental note: Practice shielding my thoughts.

"Hah, good luck with that." Butterfly sniffed in my direction, searching for any palatable emotions. Then it sighed and buried its face in the peanut bowl. Soft, wet, smacking sounds filled the room. *Gross.* As the Eidolon fed, its body faded. It looked up at me, semitransparent, peanut crumbs coating its chin. "I'll let you know what I find out. In the meantime, try to calm down a little, okay? All that anger isn't good for you. Not to mention me." Smacking its lips, Butterfly faded to a dirty smudge on the air. Then the demon was gone.

So Pryce, Myrddin, and Difethwr were working together. That was the bad news. But they hadn't yet perfected their method for turning zombies into mindless, bloodthirsty, unstoppable killing machines, since the Morfran destroyed any zombie it drove to kill. That was . . . well, not exactly *good* news, but I'd take it. If Butterfly could give me an address, I might be able to surprise Pryce and stop him before he made any more progress.

A throat cleared. Axel stood in front of me. "You're out of peanuts," he said, nodding at the bowl. "Want more?"

I thought of Butterfly, facedown in the bowl, slobbering all over the peanuts. Traces of demon spit still glistened inside.

"No thanks," I said. "I think I've gone off peanuts for a while." Probably for the rest of my life.

# 13

THE SUN WAS COMING UP AS I WALKED THROUGH NEAR-deserted streets toward home. Hampson's curfew must be working. I saw plenty of Goons, dressed in riot gear and patrolling in pairs, but not another soul. The Goons watched me go by, but they didn't bother me. The curfew applied only to zombies, so they had no reason to stop me.

The lobby of my building was also deserted. For the first time I could remember, Clyde wasn't at the doorman's desk for his day shift. And for all the times I'd squirmed under his former minister's gaze, I realized now he still saw himself as a shepherd of sorts, watching over his flock. Clyde looked out for his tenants; he took care of us as best he could. Without him at his post, crossing the marble floor of the lobby felt like trekking across miles of empty, frozen tundra.

Upstairs, I didn't hear the TV blasting as I unlocked the door. As I stepped inside, the lights were on, but the television was off. "Juliet?" I called, taking off my jacket. "You home?"

"In the kitchen," she called.

"All right, Vic?" came Dad's voice from the same room.

I hung up my jacket and put away the Magnum and its holster, then went into the kitchen to join them.

Dad perched on a chair, *The Book of Utter Darkness* open on the table in front of him. Across the room, the microwave dinged. Juliet took out a plate of cheeseburger sliders and carried it carefully over to Dad. She shut the book and pushed it aside, then set the plate down in its place.

Dad snatched up a slider and gulped it down.

"Rough session with the book?" I asked.

"Not rough so much." He swallowed another cheeseburger. "But trying to read that damn thing leaves me ravenous. Afterward, the falcon part of me cannot get enough to eat."

"Did you see anything new?" After the last vision the book had given me, I was almost afraid to ask.

"A little. The smoke was thinner, and I could see more of what was happening on the ground. Lots of fighting." Had he seen me killing humans? A jolt of anxiety hit as his rainbow eyes regarded me, but there was no way to read Dad's feelings in the bird's face. "Now, remember, this is my interpretation of what the falcon perceived. But I'm pretty sure I saw demons slaughtering humans. And fighting alongside the demons—"

"Don't say it, Dad." The rush of panic made me talk fast. "I've seen it, too. But it doesn't have to happen that way. Remember, Mab says the book tries to trick us. And in your case, everything gets filtered through the falcon's perceptions."

"So you don't think the zombies will turn against humans and join the demons?"

"Wait. You saw *zombies* attacking humans?"

"They make awfully impressive soldiers. They're strong and practically indestructible. Nothing stops them. They keep coming and coming, focused only on killing, like in a horror movie." He swallowed the last slider. His head swiveled to find Juliet. "Got any more of those?"

"They're already in the microwave." She grinned at me. "Who knew I was such a good hostess? Maybe I should give a party."

Dad's head swiveled back to me. "So what did you think I saw?"

"Doesn't matter. But I think I should tell Mab about this right away."

"Oh, there was a voice mail from her." The microwave

dinged, and Juliet paused to remove another plate of sliders. "Well, not from her but from someone calling on her behalf."

"Jenkins?"

"Could be. I saved it so you could listen."

"Thanks." I picked up the kitchen phone and put in the code to retrieve messages. In a moment, I heard the voice of Jenkins, Mab's major domo, giving me information about her flight number and when she was due to arrive in Boston. I grabbed a pen and some paper, then played the message again and wrote everything down.

"Mab's coming to Boston," I told Dad as I hung up the phone.

"Excellent!" he said. "I'd love to see the old girl. When?"

"Tomorrow evening. Her flight gets into Logan at six thirty." A thought occurred to me. "If you want a family reunion, you really should tell Mom about . . . you know." I opened my arms as though they were wings and flapped them a couple of times.

"You're right. And I'm gearing up to do just that. Won't be long now." He looked at the kitchen clock. "Is that really the time? I've got to fly to Needham. I do enjoy watching Gwen get the kids off to school in the mornings. Thanks, Juliet, for the chow. See ya, Vic." The falcon launched himself into the air and disappeared through the kitchen wall. Even though I knew the white falcon had the ability to pass through barriers that held others back, it was always disconcerting to see that.

The microwave dinged.

"I don't suppose you want these." Juliet held out a steaming plate of sliders.

"Nope."

She picked up a mini cheeseburger and nibbled at the edge. "Ugh," she said, wrinkling her nose. "Your father prefers these to rats?" She tilted her wrist, and the sliders slid into the trash. She set down the empty plate and rubbed her hands together. "Anything else you want microwaved? Anything at all. I'm getting quite accomplished at the technique."

"I'm good, thanks. Microwaved food before bed gives me indigestion."

She peered into the trash can. "I can't say I'm surprised. Maybe I'll have to rethink that party."

"If you want to host a party, hire out Creature Comforts. Axel could use the business. I expected to see you there tonight, in fact, but the place was practically empty. Where were you?"

"I was there early on. But the norms are keeping their distance from Deadtown these days. I had to go farther afield to hunt."

"But . . . the Code Red."

"Please. Any vampire thwarted by the humans' silly little checkpoints can't be older than a century or so. We play along when it suits us. The rest of the time . . ." Her eyes glazed, then she smiled. "The rest of the time we are 'like the fox, / Who, ne'er so tame, so cherish'd and lock'd up, / Will have a wild trick of his ancestors.' "

"Shakespeare?" Juliet was obsessed with Shakespeare. After more than four centuries, she still carried a grudge about the way he'd distorted her life story in *Romeo and Juliet*. For starters, she complained, the title should have been *Juliet*. But she'd memorized every one of his plays, and dropped Shakespearean quotes into casual conversation like other people drop brand names.

"Who else? Bonus points if you tell me which play."

"Not a clue."

"*Henry the Fourth*, part one, of course. I know you've seen it. I dragged you to a performance at Boston University last year. But I think you'd fallen asleep by this act."

"What sleep? You elbowed me in the ribs so many times it took a week for the bruises to fade."

"I had to. Do you have any idea how loudly you snore?" She yawned and did a cat-stretch. "Speaking of sleeping, I think I'll go and resume the shroud."

" 'A thousand times good night!' " I said, pleased with myself for remembering a line from Juliet's own play.

"Um, sure. Whatever," she said, and left the kitchen.

I went into the living room and called Kane. I expected to leave a message, but he picked up. There was warmth in his voice as he said my name, but also a guarded tone. "Is anything wrong?"

"No, nothing." Nothing besides the usual, which was everything. But no need to rehash all that now. "I was going to leave a voice mail. I'm sorry if I woke you up."

"You didn't. I'm getting ready for work."

"Did you get any sleep at all?"

"Some. I'll catch a nap on my office couch this afternoon if I need it. So what was the voice mail about?"

"Mab's coming to Boston. I'm meeting her plane at six thirty."

"Tonight?"

I had to stop and think before I replied. Kane was getting ready for his day, but I hadn't been to bed yet. "Tonight" for him was "tomorrow" for me. "Yes. In about twelve hours."

"I'll drive you there."

"Kane, you don't have to do that. You said you're tired. And you've got your rally tonight."

"That's all under control. I want to, Vicky. I like your aunt. And I want to see you. We only have three days left . . ." His voice trailed off, and my mind finished his sentence. *Before the full moon.*

"All right." I wanted to see him, too. I wanted to spend a couple of hours together free of tension and anxiety, without the lengthening shadow of impending terror stretching over us. We arranged to meet at his office at five. We'd grab a quick bite (dinner for him, breakfast for me), and then take his BMW out to the airport in time to meet Mab.

"It's a date," he said. As we hung up, I kept thinking how nice, how normal that sounded. And how very far beyond my grasp.

TERMINAL E, LOGAN AIRPORT'S INTERNATIONAL ARRIVALS terminal, was crowded. People packed the area elbow to elbow, watching intently each time the doors opened to reveal newly deplaned passengers, most arrivals looking tired and disoriented as they wheeled out trolleys piled with luggage. Bored kids chased each other, running up and down the lobby or twining through the crowd.

Mab's plane was late. We'd been waiting over an hour, sipping coffee from paper cups and watching the board for updates. Kane made half a dozen phone calls, checking the progress of his assistants in setting up for tonight's unity rally. He even managed to nap for ten minutes, his head resting on my shoulder, as we sat in hard plastic chairs. Carefully, so as not to wake him, I curved my arm around his shoulders as I watched the evening light fade through the big plate glass windows.

Kane snorted awake and sat up straight. "Is she here yet?"

"The board says her plane landed a couple of minutes ago. It'll take some time to deplane everyone and get through customs."

He stood and stretched. "Let's watch for her, anyway."

"You don't want to keep resting?"

He shook his head. "It'd be better to move around a little."

His hair was ruffled where his head had lain on my shoulder. I stood and smoothed it.

"Thanks," he said, flashing me a grin. His fingers went to his blue silk tie, making sure it was straight. "Don't want your aunt to think you're dating some slob."

We walked over to join the waiting crowd. Kane stood beside me, close but not quite touching. I twisted to see beyond the people standing in front of me. As I did, my shoulder brushed his side. He put his arm around me and pulled me to him, smiling with a deep-down warmth I hadn't seen since our return from the Darklands. I smiled back. For a moment, it felt like we were the only two people in the airport—hell, in the whole world—as that warmth flowed between us. It felt so good. This was us, Kane and me, and all the worries and things that stood between us melted away as he bent his head to brush his lips against mine.

"Get a room!" shrieked a high-pitched voice. A boy darted away, giggling.

Kane straightened, but his smile remained. He turned back toward the door.

"Let me know as soon as you see her," I said. Kane was a head taller than me; he had a better vantage point.

He nodded, the smile still playing around his lips. Maybe, I thought, just maybe we could find our way through this whole hellhound thing.

"There she is," Kane said, nodding toward the door.

I caught a glimpse of gray hair through the crowd. "Mab!" I shouted, jumping up and down and waving. Strong hands closed around my waist and Kane lifted me up. Mab squinted at the crowd, then her eyes registered that she'd spotted me. A small, tight smile curved her lips (my aunt is not a grinner), and she raised her hand. Kane put me down, and we made our way to a spot along the wall where she waited.

Tiny smile in place, she opened her arms to me, and I ran to give her a hug. She stood stiffly, as always, like she was allowing my hug instead of receiving it. But that was Mab. The bones of her back felt small and fragile, like a bird's, but there was a strength in her that belied her age. She gave me her customary quick pats on the back—*onetwothree*—and held me at arm's length. Her eyes sharp, she inspected me. "You look tired, child. Have you been getting enough sleep?"

I smiled. It was a traditional greeting from my aunt. Other people say, "Hi, how are you?" Mab asks about nightly hours of REM. No surprise there. She's fought demons long enough to know how it messes up a person's sleep schedule. "I'm fine. How was your flight?"

"Long. But less traumatic than my previous journey here." The last time Mab traveled to Boston, she'd made her way physically through the collective unconscious, the region that borders everyone's dreamscapes. It's dangerous territory to cross, home to the stuff of nightmares. Better to brave airplane food and lousy in-flight entertainment options.

"Welcome back," Kane said, stepping forward and extending his hand. "It's wonderful to see you again." As Mab shook his hand, he pulled her into a one-armed hug. I smiled to see my aunt's eyes widen over his shoulder.

"Oh, my," she breathed, pressing a hand to her chest, when he released her. He flashed his million-watt grin and stepped behind her luggage cart, which was loaded with a large suitcase and an old-fashioned trunk, the kind ladies in floor-sweeping skirts used to pack their tea dresses and ball gowns for ocean crossings. With Mab, though, such a trunk could carry only one thing.

"You brought weapons?"

"That's what took so long in Customs. Fortunately, I was carrying papers saying they're bound for an exhibit at the Higgins Armory Museum in . . . er . . ."

"Worcester. It's a city about an hour west of here." I'd given a couple of sword fighting demonstrations there. In fact, I'd put the curator in touch with Mab when he expressed interest in one of her swords that I'd mentioned in conversation. She must have had Jenkins give him a call. "Are they? Going to be shown there, I mean?"

"Perhaps one day. But I have use for them first."

"I don't know if we can get them into Deadtown," I said. "The border is pretty tight right now."

"You can keep them in my office," Kane said. "It has a secure vault for sensitive papers and things." Good idea. That would give us a cache of weapons—mine—in Deadtown and another beyond its boundaries.

I linked my arm in Mab's and we headed for the exit. Kane followed with the trolley.

The zombie came out of nowhere.

One second we were winding through the crowd, and then people were screaming and scattering as a huge zombie in a Bruins jersey charged straight at us. His bloodred eyes were fixed on Mab; his twitching fingers reached for her throat.

I yanked Mab to the floor and rolled toward the zombie, tripping him and sending him sprawling. Kane leapt onto the guy's back while he was down. I glanced toward my aunt to make sure she was all right. She was on her knees, working the lock on her weapons trunk.

With a roar, the zombie threw Kane off and climbed to his feet. A series of shots popped from the left, and the zombie staggered back as holes appeared in his torso and the side of his head. Who the hell was shooting? Blackish stuff oozed from the wounds. But the bullets weren't zombie droppers, because this zombie shook his head and looked around. His eyes locked on Mab. He staggered toward her.

More shots, followed by a woman's scream.

Twenty yards away, a security guard stood, his legs planted, both arms braced as he aimed his gun.

"Hold your fire!" I yelled. Idiot, shooting in a crowded airport. The bullets only ventilated the zombie, but they'd do a lot more damage to any of the hundreds of norms caught in the panic.

Kane tackled the zombie from behind, and the creature fell again, rolling back and forth as he tried to shake Kane off. Kane punched him, and the zombie stopped moving.

Then, the fallen zombie clutched the sides of his head. Morfran.

"Kane!" I shouted. "If he starts shaking, take cover." Damn, I wished I had Hellforged.

Maybe Mab had a weapon in her trunk that could help us. I turned to see if she'd gotten it open.

A second zombie, this one a woman, stood over Mab, choking the life out of her. My aunt's face was purple. Her eyes bulged like they were about to pop out of their sockets. She clawed at the viselike hands locked around her neck.

"Let go!" I launched myself at the female zombie, who stood rigid and unmoving. I hit her in the throat, but she didn't flinch.

I went for her eyes, pressing into them with my fingers. No reaction.

Mab gurgled. Her tongue protruded from her bluish lips.

I pulled at the zombie's hands, trying to pry them away. It was like trying to bend bands of iron.

Frantic, I looked around for the security guard and his gun. The hall was empty.

"Mab," I sobbed, digging at the zombie's locked fingers. "I can't—"

From overhead came a piercing cry, the call of a falcon.

Before I could look up to locate it, a white shape plummeted downward. It slammed into the zombie, knocking her backward. She let go of Mab, who collapsed sideways on the floor. The falcon's talons were locked into the zombie's face. She shrieked and hit at the bird.

Mab dragged in a long, shuddering breath.

The female zombie's shrieks intensified, and the sound changed into a harsh, constant cawing. A dozen dark shapes blasted from her wide-open mouth. Crows. The white falcon was after them like a shot. He chased them, grabbing crows with his beak or his talons and hurling them squawking to the ground. Each lay in a heap of inky feathers, as still and silent as a broken toy.

He was killing them. Dad was killing the Morfran.

Mab rubbed the purple finger marks on her throat. "Are you all right?" I asked. She nodded and pressed a key into my hand. She tried to say something, but her voice was barely a croak. Licking her dry lips, she gestured toward the trunk.

The lock was stiff. As I wiggled the key, trying to make it turn, I realized the cawing had stopped. I scanned the hall. Overhead, I didn't see the falcon, but neither was there a single crow. To my right, the female zombie lay curled on the floor, clutching her wounded face and moaning. Kane still pinned down the other zombie, who no longer tried to rise. Hands clamped to either side of his head, the male zombie was shuddering in a way I didn't like.

"Get away!" I yelled to Kane. *"Now!"* In my peripheral vision, I noticed the cautious approach of two airport cops, their guns drawn and shaking. "You, too," I shouted, waving them away. "Get back!"

The cops turned and ran. Kane stared at me like he couldn't believe I was telling him to let the zombie go. But when the screaming started, rising in pitch like a demon choir practicing scales, he leapt up and sped toward me. I twisted the key. The lock gave, and the trunk opened. I spun the cart around to shield Mab, and Kane joined us, crouching.

One, maybe two seconds later, the Morfran blew the zombie apart.

Something splatted against the trunk, knocking its cover shut. Black slime spotted the floor around us. Huge crows shot upward in a frenzy of cawing. They circled near the ceiling. The white falcon sped into their midst. As the predator tore into them, caws became shrieks.

I opened the trunk and pawed through the contents. Long swords, a couple of cutlasses, a rapier, a two-handed claymore. Half a dozen daggers. Most were bronze-bladed. Nothing with an obsidian blade like Hellforged, but that would be too much to hope for. Hellforged was one of a kind. "Which weapon, Mab?" I asked, grabbing a random dagger and holding it up.

Mab didn't even look at me. Her gaze followed the white falcon as he seized and tore the Morfran. "Not a weapon, child." Her damaged throat could scarcely emit a whisper. I had to lean in close to hear her. "A leather glove. Put it on, and quickly. That's the falcon from the prophecies."

I found the glove. The dead body of a crow, its breast torn open, thumped to the ground beside me. Its black eye lost its sheen and dulled into death.

The hell with Dad's secret. I'd kept it long enough. This new development—that the white falcon could actually *kill* the Morfran—was important. "That falcon is also—"

The falcon landed, perching on the trunk. He stretched out his wings, folded them, and shook his feathers. Then he looked my aunt in the eye.

"Hello, Mab," the falcon said. "Long time, no see. Welcome to Boston."

# 14

"EVAN?" MAB RASPED.

My aunt is most definitely *not* the fainting type. But her injuries, combined with the look of utter surprise and bewilderment that crossed her face, made me reach to catch her, just in case. She huffed and pushed me away.

Kane stared, mouth open.

Dad turned his falcon's head and cocked it, as though listening. His rainbow eyes looked into the distance. He spread his wings.

"We'll talk later. Gotta go. Say hi to Juliet for me, Vic."

The huge bird launched himself into the air. His wings flapped, carrying him toward the ceiling. The ceiling wavered, like ripples in water. The falcon passed through and disappeared.

Two faces turned to me.

"I guess I owe you both an explanation." But I had no idea where to start. Instead I gestured at the female zombie who lay on the floor clutching her face and rocking from side to side. "First, though, we need to get her secured. And call Daniel. He needs to know about this."

The look my aunt gave me made me want to crawl into the

trunk and close the lid over me. I glanced at Kane for support, but the hurt in his eyes made me wish I hadn't. My fingers tightened around the soft, thick leather of the glove I still held.

"Put that away," Mab whispered. "And lock the trunk." Her gaze slid sideways. The airport cops approached us, their guns drawn. That must have been what made Dad fly off. I hoped they had somewhere we could hold the female zombie while we waited for Daniel to arrive.

But it wasn't the cops that worried Mab. Before they got two steps closer, a howling, baying sound filled the terminal. The men froze, glancing around in terror. The noise seemed to surround us, approaching from everywhere at once, until galloping hooves cut through the din. Beside me, Kane caught his breath, then groaned.

The Night Hag was coming.

Inside my shirt, the protection charm grew hot against my skin.

"Victory! The glove!" Mab got some voice into her words, but the effort must have hurt her throat.

I threw the glove into the trunk and slammed the lid. After two desperate jiggles, the key turned, locking it shut.

Two hellhounds bounded into the terminal.

The charm burned my chest. I grasped the chain and pulled it outside my shirt, where it glowed like a miniature sun.

More hounds ran in. The pack skidded to a stop not ten feet away. They crouched and snarled, snapping their teeth. But they didn't come any closer.

I reached for Kane's hand. "Are you all right?"

"The moon's not full yet." His tone was grim, and there was strain in his voice. Together we stood.

The galloping hooves slowed to a walk, then halted. For a moment, there was silence except for hellhound whimpers and growls. Then, the Night Hag burst through the outside wall. Her horse screamed; flames shot from its nostrils. And there was the hag herself, her hood thrown back to reveal her death's head skull, an eerie light glowing in its eye sockets.

She'd obviously chosen her moment to make a dramatic entrance. The footsteps of one airport cop echoed as he raced out of the terminal. The other was already gone.

Mab struggled to stand. Kane let go of my hand as he

reached down and got one arm around her. Gently, he lifted her to her feet. She leaned on him for a moment, then straightened and stood on her own. His hand found mine again. Together the three of us faced the Night Hag.

From her mount, the hag scanned the terminal. As she turned her head, flesh covered her face and her hair grew long and silky. Her dress filled out, as her shape morphed from skeleton to young woman. But there was no beauty in her youth. Her gaze locked on me, her features twisted in fury.

"Where is he?" she snarled.

"Where's what?" Hard to sound tough when your voice comes out in a squeak. The charm glowed on my chest, its heat penetrating my shirt.

"My falcon. The one you stole from me." She pointed an accusing finger, and one of the hounds barked. The others leapt to their feet and joined in, straining forward. I glanced at Kane. His eyes were squeezed tightly shut, as though that would block out light and sound both.

"Silence!" roared the hag.

The hounds yelped and dropped to a shivering crouch. Kane flinched, but he opened his eyes. He regarded the hag with a steady gray gaze that must have cost him every ounce of strength and will he could muster.

But the hag fixed her own gaze on me. Her face had changed, sagging into middle-age. Bags pouched under her eyes; her jawline drooped into jowls. The fury remained, however.

I cleared my throat to steady my voice. "The falcon escaped. Don't blame me if you couldn't hold on to him."

"Liar!" The word exploded through the room, and the hounds cried out in pain. Beside me, Kane gasped, then pressed his lips in a tight line. I squeezed his hand, trying to offer reassurance neither of us felt.

The hag now wore the face of a cruel old woman, the kind who stalks through fairy tales and children's nightmares. "I've been tracking that bird. He comes to you. I demand you remove whatever spell you've enchanted him with and return him to me."

"There is no spell. The falcon is free. I handed him over to you as per our bargain. What happened after that isn't my problem."

"She's right, Mallt-y-Nos." Mab's voice rang out clear and

strong. I looked at her in surprise. Five minutes ago, she'd been crumpled on the floor, barely able to whisper. Now she stood tall and straight, like a warrior queen rallying her troops. "My niece is no witch." Her brows came together in a frown. "She can't even boil water with a seething spell. Surely you don't believe she's capable of weaving the kind of spell required to bind the white falcon of Hellsmoor."

*Um, thanks, Mab.* It was true, I sucked at spellcraft. But as desiccated skin flaked off the hag's face, revealing the creepy skull beneath it once more, focusing on my weaknesses didn't seem like the best way to make her leave.

"You." Mallt-y-Nos turned her hideous face to Mab. "I should set my hounds on you this moment. It would please Lord Arawn no end if you were driven back into his realm."

"But you won't, and we both know why." Mab's calm voice thrummed with a deep resonance that echoed off the terminal's walls. "It is not yet my time."

"Your time!" shrieked the hag. "It was your time centuries ago!"

"Perhaps. But that time came and went, and here I stand."

"You cannot cheat Arawn forever," intoned the bare skull. "You are not immune to harm."

"Again, perhaps. But that harm will not come from you."

Moments passed, and the Night Hag's face returned to youth. She looked like a sulking teenager. Then she threw back her head and let out a scream of rage. Windows shattered. Flames burst from the mouths and ears of her yowling hounds, and Kane staggered backward. My arm met Mab's as we moved to support him. But Kane stayed on his feet.

"Felt that, didn't you, hound?" the hag sneered, her beautiful young eyes glinting cruelly.

"The moon isn't full yet," he said again, pushing out each syllable through gritted teeth. Sweat beaded on his forehead. "I'm not your hound."

"So you say. But your body tells you otherwise." Her silvery laugh rang with menace. "It knows your Mistress. Shall I make you kneel before me, here and now?"

She pointed, and Kane's whole body went rigid. He clenched his jaw and grunted, trembling with effort.

"On your knees, hound!"

With a gasp, he bent at the waist, as though taking a terrible blow. His knees began to buckle.

"Stop it!" I shouted. I stepped in front of him, hoping to shield him with my protection charm. "Leave him alone!"

The hag made a sweeping motion with her hand, as though batting away a mosquito. There was a loud crack, and the charm blew to pieces.

Behind me, Kane groaned. The sound held bottomless depths of pain.

The Night Hag's aging face grinned a terrible grin.

Anger flared, and my demon mark glowed crimson.

"Mallt-y-Nos, you abuse your power." The words came from Mab, but the growing haze of anger around me distorted her voice. It sounded deeper, her Welsh accent stronger, and it echoed through the hall. "Desist, or face the consequences."

I almost laughed. No matter how impressive Mab's voice, what made her think the Night Hag would listen to her? There was only one way to deal with this damned spirit.

A tongue of flame leapt up from my demon mark.

I had no intention of waiting around for the Night Hag to agree to play nice. I was going to kill her for what she was doing to Kane. It was so simple. Destroy this horrible creature, and she'd never bother us again. That was the answer. That was *always* the answer. If something gets in your way—kill it.

Hurt it. Crush it. Destroy it.

My demon mark blazed with hellfire. I used its flame like a blowtorch to blast the hinges off Mab's trunk.

"Victory, don't!" Mab shouted. Her voice sounded like her own again.

I ignored her and ripped off the lid, then tossed it aside. I seized the hilt of a steel-bladed sword. Steel—perfect. The hag was a spirit, not a demon, and the touch of steel would make her feel unbearable agony.

And feel it she would. Over and over, before I destroyed her.

I laughed.

I hefted the sword, looking forward to feeling her flesh give way as I drove the blade into her body.

But the hag, still atop her huge steed, was too high. All right. First the horse, and then the rider. I aimed for the beast's massive chest.

"*No*, child!"

I charged.

Something black flew at my face, blinding me. I stumbled, losing my bearings. A sharp pain stung my cheek. Another sliced into my sword arm. The sword was snatched from my hand.

I stopped, confused. My vision cleared. My aunt stood between me and the Night Hag, brandishing the sword.

At *me*?

Rage reddened my vision. All right. If she wanted to fight, we'd see who won. My aunt or not, I'd had enough of the bossy old lady and her Mab-always-knows-best attitude. She needed to get the hell out of my way.

My demon mark spurted a geyser of flame. A flick of my arm, and I'd burn her to ashes. But no. What I really wanted was to beat her at swordplay. I reached into the trunk for a weapon. Another sharp pain bit my arm.

"Jeez, what is *wrong* with you?" The question buzzed close to my ear. "Have some respect for your elders, why don't you?"

So that was the black shape that had flown into my eyes.

"Get out of my way, Butterfly," I snarled. "Or you're next."

"Okay, sure. Go ahead. Kill your conscience. Then this"— the black butterfly flew through the jet of flame and landed on my demon mark—"will take over completely." The insect started tap-dancing on the mark, all six legs jumping furiously. It tickled—but it also soothed and cooled. The red haze of anger cleared a little. The flame sputtered and shrank.

And there I stood, reaching for a weapon to do battle with my aunt, one of the people I loved most in the world.

Head hanging, I let my arm fall to my side. Butterfly's question was a good one: What *was* wrong with me?

The answer, of course, was in the faint red mark where Butterfly was stamping out the last sparks. The Eidolon looked up at me and winked. "Listen to me, kid. I may be a pain in the ass, but I'll keep us both out of trouble." Its sharp black wings lifted it into the air, and then it dive-bombed me and disappeared somewhere in my gut.

*Oof.* That never felt pleasant.

But it was miles better than what I'd be feeling if I'd attacked Mab.

I raised my eyes to hers. There was forgiveness there, but also a wariness that made me want to curl up in a ball and weep. My aunt didn't trust me.

The Night Hag cackled.

Behind me, Kane groaned. He lay on his side, panting, his ashen skin slick with sweat. I leaned over him. His eyes flickered open. "I didn't kneel," he whispered. "I couldn't stand, but I didn't kneel."

I reached out a hand—my non–demon marked hand—and smoothed back his beautiful silver hair.

"You are mine, hound, whether you will it or no," the Night Hag said. She was old again, pinched and wrinkled, her voice shrill. "And your precious Victory doesn't care. She has the means to release you, and yet she refuses." She cackled evilly. "She would rather see you suffer. And oh, you will. I will make you suffer beyond anything you've endured. Your will is strong; it will be my pleasure to break it."

Kane swiveled his gaze to me, a question in his eyes.

"Has she not told you? Weeks ago, I offered her a bargain. Your freedom in exchange for the falcon. *My* falcon. Clearly, she has made her choice, hound. And she has not chosen you."

"Leave us, Mallt-y-Nos." Mab's voice had again faded to a whisper. She'd fitted the lid back on the trunk and she sat on it now, her shoulders slumped. The steel sword lay on the floor beside her. "You have no business here."

"Oh, but I have. There is a soul here for me to collect." She gestured with her chin toward the spot where the male zombie had fallen before the Morfran blasted him apart. Wisps of a bluish mist rose and swirled together. They grew to form a column and began to take on the shape of a man.

"But before I go, I'll say this: I saw the leather glove in that trunk. The gauntlet. I know its purpose, to call the falcon. If you give it to me, I will honor our bargain. But if you do not—" Her youthful features were anything but innocent. "If you do not, I will obtain it some other way. And then I will have both my falcon *and* my hound."

She whistled, and the pack of hellhounds sprang to their feet. The horse let out a terrifying whinny as she reared it back. The blue mist of the dead zombie's soul, now a transparent form the size and shape of his destroyed body, froze. The Night

Hag blew her hunting horn. Her hounds barked frantically and charged the zombie's shade. He screamed—a thin, muffled sound that came from somewhere beyond ordinary hearing—and ran, the hounds at his heels. Mallt-y-Nos dug sharp spurs into the sides of her steed and took off in pursuit. Her hunting horn blared furiously.

Within moments, they were gone, the sounds of the chase faded into silence.

And I was alone with the hurt, accusing stares of my aunt and the man I loved.

# 15

I DIDN'T GET A CHANCE TO EXPLAIN. BEFORE THE ECHOES of galloping hooves had receded, Boston police burst onto the scene. They streamed in from all directions, shouting and pointing guns. The missing security guards reappeared and convinced them that Kane, Mab, and I weren't the attackers. Even so, we were separated and taken to different areas of the hall to answer questions.

"Call Detective Daniel Costello," I insisted for what felt like the hundredth time. "I'm consulting for him on a related case."

"How about you take us through what happened again? Start with the time you arrived." The cop who was questioning me had a gray mustache, and his breath smelled like pizza, heavy on the anchovies.

I didn't see anyone use a phone, but within twenty minutes Daniel strode into the terminal. He looked like he'd been off duty; he wore a jacket thrown over a T-shirt and jeans. His rumpled curls and the dark circles under his eyes made me wonder if he'd been asleep. Still, his attitude was completely take-charge.

"I'll take the rest of Ms. Vaughn's statement later," he said to Anchovy Breath. "Right now, I need her assistance in questioning the previously deceased suspect." The cop looked surprised I'd been telling the truth.

"My aunt," I said to Daniel, gesturing to where Mab sat in a plastic chair, flanked by cops. "I need to talk to her."

"That's your aunt?"

"I was here to meet her flight."

"We need to question the PDH. I'll make sure your aunt knows where you are."

"But Daniel . . ." How could I explain that I needed to apologize for nearly attacking her? "She's injured. That zombie almost choked the life out of her."

"There's a doctor attending her. I'll make sure you're notified of any problem."

"But—"

"Vicky, this may be our only chance to talk to a PDH who survived a Morfran possession. For all I know, the suspect could explode at any moment. We have zero time to waste."

"She's not going to explode. The Morfran that possessed her was expelled and killed." *All of it,* I marveled, remembering the moment when the cawing stopped. "I'll explain how that happened, but right now I need to check on my aunt."

Daniel's mouth hung open as I turned and marched over to Mab. Seeing the expression on my face, the cops who surrounded her moved a few yards off. A fortyish woman with chin-length dark hair sat beside Mab. The stethoscope around her neck gave her away as a doctor, but she stood and identified herself, anyway. "Your aunt will be fine," she said. "There's no permanent damage, although those bruises will be tender for a while." I thanked her, and she left us.

I didn't see which way she went. All my attention was focused on Mab.

She wouldn't look at me. She sat very still, her head bent, looking at her hands, which lay folded in her lap. I sat beside her and reached out to place a hand on hers, then drew it back. With a quick motion she captured my hand and then gave it a quick *onetwothree* pat. She held it between hers. The coolness of her fingers made me think of summer mornings in Wales. Finally, she raised her bloodshot eyes to mine.

"Mab," I said, "I'm sorry."

"Hush, child." Her voice was a whisper. "It's not your fault."

"But I—" What I had done, or had been ready to do, was so terrible I couldn't get the words out.

"It wasn't you. It was the Destroyer in you." She patted my hand again and tried to smile, but all I could see were her exhausted face, her bruises, her red eyes. "No harm done. The Destroyer has gained much strength, but you can still defeat it."

*Could I?* I didn't say the words, but my face must have been one big question mark.

"That's why I'm here, child. To help you. Yes, the struggle is yours, but you will not face it alone. Now, go and do your job. That young detective looks rather impatient. Come back when you're finished. If I'm not here, wait for me. I need to heal these injuries."

The Cerddorion heal faster than humans, but I knew that wasn't what she meant. "You're going to shift? Is that safe?" If Mab changed her shape, she'd return to her human form good as new. But a shift could last for hours. And now, in a strange city, after a long flight and a traumatic attack? It felt too risky.

Mab gave my hand one last pat, dismissing my concern. "Don't fret. Over the centuries, I've gained control that most of our kind never have a chance to develop. I'll be here, and in my usual form, within the half hour."

I kissed my aunt's cheek and told her to be careful. She waved her hand and told me not to make a fuss. Across the terminal, Daniel gestured impatiently for me to come over.

He could wait one more minute.

I scanned the terminal, looking for Kane. I knew "sorry" wouldn't be enough. Maybe nothing would ever be enough to erase that shocked betrayal I'd seen in his eyes. There was no time now to explain, to try to fix things with him. Still, I needed to tell him how much I wanted to try.

But I couldn't. Kane was gone. I turned in a circle, surveying the hall. He was nowhere to be seen.

My heart a cold, heavy lump in my chest, I trudged over to where Daniel awaited me.

THE POLICE HAD REMOVED THE FEMALE ZOMBIE TO A cinder-block room deep in the bowels of the airport. After taking an elevator to a subbasement, Daniel and I went through a locked metal door and down several more flights of stairs. We emerged into a long, narrow hallway. Body-armored cops holding automatic weapons were stationed every ten yards. At the end of the hallway was a single door. It looked like the door to a bank vault, but behind it was no treasure. Behind it waited the zombie who'd nearly choked the life out of Mab.

*It wasn't the zombie's fault,* I reminded myself as a guard opened the door. It was the Morfran. Still, when I stood in the doorway and saw her sitting at the far end of a long table, her fingers drumming nervously on its wooden surface, all I could think of was those hands, locked around Mab's neck— squeezing harder, tighter—as my aunt's eyes bulged. My demon mark itched and grew hot; my fingers curled into fists. How *dare* she attack one of my own? I'd make her feel what Mab had felt. I'd—

*Wait. Stop. Not her fault.* The image of zombie hands choking Mab was replaced by one of my own arm, reaching for a sword to wield against my aunt. My nails bit into my palms. This zombie had been driven by a demonic force that pushed her from the inside. Of all people, I knew how that felt. The Morfran took over her will, just as the Destroyer was always pushing to take over mine. Now that the Morfran had been expelled from her, she was our best chance to understand what was happening.

"Vicky?" Daniel already seated, looked at me curiously. A folder was open in front of him. "They need to close the door."

"Sorry." I blew out a lungful of air and took a chair beside Daniel's. The door shut with a thud and the *shlick!* of bolts shooting home. One guard, armed with an automatic rifle, stayed inside. Daniel shrugged off his jacket, twisting around to hang it on the back of his chair. The grip of his gun protruded from his shoulder holster.

Undoubtedly, every single gun I'd seen was loaded with zombie droppers. If this zombie tried to attack, she'd never make it to this side of the table.

Not that she looked like she wanted to. She sat like . . . well, okay, like a zombie, stiff and awkward. She stopped drumming, slapping one hand over the other, and stared at a spot halfway along the table. Deep gouges from the falcon's talons furrowed her cheeks.

"Good evening," Daniel said. She didn't reply. He waited a few seconds, then cleared his throat and continued. Not even an eyelid twitched as she heard that she was being questioned in connection with tonight's attack and that the conversation was being recorded on video. He didn't read her rights, of course. Zombies don't have any.

"Please state your name," Daniel said.

Nothing.

Daniel glanced at me with raised eyebrows, and I shook my head. I didn't know her.

Daniel repeated his request, louder this time.

The zombie lurched forward and put her face in her hands. Zombies can't cry, but she gasped and her shoulders heaved as though she were sobbing. We waited. Suddenly she dropped her hands and pounded both fists on the table. The wood cracked.

"I didn't want to attack that lady." Desperation pushed her high-pitched voice to shrillness. "I tried not to, but I couldn't stop myself. Those birds . . ."

"We'll get to that," Daniel said. "First, I need you to tell me your name."

Her hands returned to her face, and she stayed silent for a long time. "Bonita." The muffled whisper barely made it through her fingers.

He wrote it down. "Bonita what?"

She shook her head, shoulders heaving again. "Wait," Daniel said. He leafed through the papers in his folder, then ran a finger down one of them. His finger stopped, and he looked up. "Bonita Scruggs?"

She nodded, letting her hands fall to the table, where they lay like stunned animals. "You gonna kill me?"

It was a valid question. The law offered no protections to zombies who got violent. But Daniel didn't answer her. "Bonita, you failed to return to Designated Area One after Police Commissioner Hampson issued a Code Red." He tapped the list of names he'd consulted. "Where were you during that time?"

"Nowhere."

"Listen," Daniel said, meeting her surly tone with gentleness, "I'd like to be able to report that you cooperated with this investigation."

"Why should I? You'll never believe me. Might as well go ahead and kill me right now."

He sighed. If he weren't packing a serious weapon, he'd look exactly like an exasperated high school teacher trying to collect missing homework.

Maybe I should try. "Bonita, we know what happened wasn't your fault. You were possessed."

Her head snapped toward me. "You know about the birds?"

"Crows, right? Filling your head with unbearable cawing."

"Yes," she whispered. "I woulda done anything to make it stop."

"That's why you need to talk to us," Daniel said, leaning forward. "You're a valuable witness because you survived that possession, and you can help us prevent it from happening to other PDHs."

"You don't have to say that." Daniel blinked, confused at Bonita's words. "PDH. I'm a zombie, and I know it." Her voice turned hard. "I also know what happens to zombies who do what I did tonight, whether they did it on purpose or not." She narrowed her bloodred eyes. "Right?"

"No one will kill you, Bonita," I said. "I won't let them. I promise."

Daniel scowled at me. I had no authority to make a promise like that. But so what? I meant what I said. I'd enlist Kane to help and then—

*Oh.*

My heart turned to lead and sank to my shoes. Kane had left the airport without saying good-bye. I doubted he'd be taking my calls.

Bonita, at least, seemed encouraged. She straightened in her chair and took a deep breath. "So you wanna know where I was?" A humorless laugh escaped her lips. "It's like I told you—nowhere. Or if it was somewhere, it wasn't like any place I've ever been."

"I'm not following you," Daniel said.

Bonita snorted. "You wouldn't want to follow me there."

"Let's start at the beginning." He shuffled through his papers, then picked one up and scanned its text. "According to records, you left Deadtown on Thursday at nine fourteen P.M. as part of a group of workers. The group was covered by a Class

B permit held by the We Klean 4U maintenance company. You were the only worker who didn't return." He set down the piece of paper and tapped it with his index finger. "Where did you go after you exited the checkpoint?"

"To work. I clean offices in a building on Boylston Street." She gave the address, and Daniel wrote it down.

"Was anyone with you there?"

"Just my friend Suzanne, but we work on different floors. The third floor was empty, except for me. Until *he* showed up."

"Who?"

"The Devil."

Daniel looked up sharply. I did the same. Bonita was dead serious.

"The *Devil*," she insisted. "I know it was. Even though at first I thought it was just some guy." Neither Daniel nor I said a word. Bonita's hand shook as she tucked a strand of hair behind her ear. "I'd almost finished vacuuming the hallway when I looked up to see a man walking toward me, fast. I didn't know what to do. We're supposed to keep a low profile because some of the tenants don't like having zombies clean their offices. It's usually not a problem, since we clean after hours. Anyway, all of a sudden there was this guy, and he looked *mad*."

"Can you describe him?" Daniel asked.

"Tall. Dark eyes with thick black lashes. Black hair, too, but pale skin. Unhealthy pale, like a vampire. But why would a vampire come after a zombie? He wore a black suit, and all that black made me think of an undertaker." Her gaze went distant, and she shuddered. "He looked like Death coming to get me."

It was my turn to shudder. She'd just described Pryce. Poor Bonita. I knew how it felt to have that scowling face approach, lips twisted in a sneer, intent on doing harm. Of course she'd think of death and devils.

"I started to apologize," Bonita continued. "Why, I don't know. I was only doing my job. But he looked so angry, like he wanted to hurt me. I stood there frozen, and he grabbed both my arms. I must have blacked out or something, because after that everything went dark." She hugged herself and rocked in her seat. "But I couldn't have passed out, because I remember how scared I was. His grip hurt my arms. I smelled the most awful smells—worse than the time a skunk died under my grandparents' back porch. And the sounds. Mean, horrible laughter. Screams. Sobbing. That's when I knew it. I'd died and gone to hell."

"That's one name for it." I turned to Daniel. "Somehow, Pryce pulled her into the demon plane."

He nodded, still watching Bonita. "What happened next?"

"The place I was in changed. It was still dark, but quiet all of a sudden. And instead of dead skunk it smelled musty, like a cellar. The Devil let go of my arms, pushing me away. I fell on a hard floor. It was cold, concrete. I scooted backward, trying to get away from him, but I hit a wall. I waited, like this"— she threw both arms across her face—"expecting red-hot pincers or a flaming pitchfork or whatever they use to welcome the damned to hell. But nothing happened. After a few minutes, I realized he was gone. I was alone."

Pryce had pulled Bonita through the demon plane to deposit her elsewhere. I remembered what Butterfly had said about Pryce's visits to a place in the Ordinary. "You said the place smelled musty. Can you remember anything else about it?"

"Pitch-black, like a cave. I never saw it, but I explored every inch. Concrete floor, like I said. Cinder-block walls. When I stood up, I couldn't reach the ceiling, even on my tiptoes. There was hardly any floor space, though. I couldn't lie down. When I slept, it was sitting up, my legs stretched out so my toes were up against the far wall and my back wedged into a corner."

"Did you try the door?" Daniel asked.

"I didn't even think there *was* a door at first. I screamed and screamed until my voice was gone because I was sure I was sealed into that place. But later, I don't know how much, the door opened. It slid sideways into the wall, and somebody stood there. You can bet I found my voice for more screaming then. I thought the Devil had come back for me. But it wasn't him. It was . . . I don't know what it was. Even in Deadtown, I never seen nothing like it."

"Please try to describe it, Bonita," Daniel said. "We can bring in a sketch artist later if that would help."

Bonita closed her eyes. Whether she was trying to remember or to blot the memory out, I couldn't tell. "There was some light in the hall, but it was dim and the . . . the thing stood in front of it. And it wore a robe, with the hood pulled up and forward. I tried to back away from it, but the cell was so small. It stepped inside and set down a tray of food and water on the floor—I don't mind telling you, I was hungry by then. I'm a zombie after all." She ventured a small smile, which turned almost immediately into a frown. "But I almost lost my appetite at what happened next. As the thing straightened, it pushed back its hood and peered at me. Its face was like a skull covered with old, dried-out skin. And it had fangs. Like a vampire's, but bigger. That made me start screaming all over again. The thing smiled, and it looked like those fangs grew a mile. Then it turned and left. There was another one in the hall—I saw it. The door slid back into place and I was alone again."

Daniel and I exchanged a look. Her jailers were Old Ones, members of a race of super-vampires trying to turn their undeath into true immortality. The Old Ones were ruthless; the zombie plague had been their test run, released on thousands of innocent people, of a magically enhanced virus that could "cure" death. Their leader, Colwyn, a fifteen-hundred-year-old former druid, had recently escaped from police custody. If Pryce and the Old Ones were working together, it was the worst kind of bad news.

"Time passed. I ate food when they brought it—two of 'em always came together. I slept. I tried not to think about what would happen to me. And then the Devil came back. All of a sudden, he was just there. He grabbed my arms again, and we entered that other darkness. The noisy, smelly one. But this time, there was light. It flickered, like it was from fires all around, but I never seen no flames."

"What happened then?"

"The Devil picked me up and threw me on a table. I thought for sure it was flaming-pitchfork time. He never let go of my arms, but he moved around behind my head and held me down from there. I struggled, but it didn't help. The Devil said, 'Hurry.' It took me a second to realize he wasn't talking to me. There was another man—he looked like the Devil, except he was older and had a beard. This one was a ghost. I could see that weird light flickering right through him." She swallowed. "And there was . . . there was . . ."

We waited. It was hard, watching Bonita struggle to get past the horror of the memory, but she needed to express it her own way. The bearded guy was obviously the shade of Myrddin, free to detach himself from Pryce in the demon plane. I had a pretty good idea who—or what—Bonita was about to describe, but I didn't want to put words into her mouth.

"It was horrible. *Horrible.* Huge, like a giant. But so . . . disgusting. It had blue skin all covered with warts, some of them big like tumors. I had to crane my neck back to see its face—and then I wished I hadn't. The firelight was coming from its eyes. And then it grinned at me. More fire was inside its mouth. It lit up rows of sharp, pointy teeth big as steak knives."

Difethwr, as I'd expected.

"The giant was a demon, Bonita," I said.

"I knew it! I knew I was in hell. The whole time, from the very first minute I saw the Devil, I prayed and prayed. It's how I kept from going crazy in that tiny cell. I promised, if I got out, I'd never do anything bad ever again." She crossed her heart as she said it, as she'd probably done hundreds of times in her cell. But then a look of defeat dimmed her eyes, and again she buried her face in her hands. "And then what happened? I did get out, only to do the worst thing I've ever done in my life. I tried to kill that lady." She dropped her hands and leaned forward. "I don't even know *why* I did that. I don't know her. I never saw her before tonight. But these voices filled my head. Screaming. It hurt so bad. They kept shrieking, 'Kill! Kill! Kill! Kill the lady!' Like a million of them. They didn't give me a choice."

Bonita confirmed my suspicions that Pryce was causing zombies to be possessed by the Morfran. But now we were coming to the part I really wanted to know—*how.*

"When did you hear those voices for the first time?" I asked.

"After the bearded ghost cut me."

"What happened?"

"Like I said, the Devil held me down on that table. He musta put all his weight on my arms." She rubbed her upper arms like she wanted to erase the feel of it. "Then the other one cut me. Here." She pulled down the neck of her T-shirt and pointed to her breastbone, marked by a vertical gash about six inches long. "The . . . the demon breathed on it. Fire. God, it hurt. I felt like my whole body was a red-hot coal. The ghost waved his hands over me and he said the same words, over and over again."

"What words?" I grabbed a spare pencil and a piece of paper from Daniel's stack. Even if Bonita didn't remember Myrddin's chant exactly, Mab might be able to make sense of it. And if we knew his spell, we could figure out a way to undo it.

"I don't know," Bonita said. "I didn't understand the words, but I heard them so many times it's like they're written in my brain. They sounded like . . ." She frowned, concentrating. I gripped the pencil.

Bonita screamed. She pushed back her chair and waved her arms crazily.

Three paces from Bonita, where a second before had been nothing but empty space, stood Pryce. He lunged toward the zombie. In a flash, Daniel drew his gun and fired. Black blood spurted from Pryce's chest, but before his knees even started to buckle, he disappeared. He was back in a wink, his wound healed—not even a spot of blood on his white shirt.

The guard by the door nailed Pryce with a rapid-fire blast of zombie droppers, and the same thing happened. Pryce disappeared before the bullets exploded. But this time, when Pryce reappeared, the Destroyer was with him.

Bonita fell to the floor and scrambled under the table. "No! No! No!" she screamed. I shouted in pain as my demon mark blazed to life. Difethwr leered at me, fire leaping behind its eyes. I couldn't look away. The guard shot again. The Destroyer absorbed the bullets. If anything, they made its inner fire burn hotter. I felt the burning in my own arm.

The Hellion released my gaze and turned toward the guard. Flames blasted from its eyes, pinning the screaming man to the wall.

Daniel was on his feet, shouting. He fired again, but the Destroyer moved in front of Pryce, shielding him. Its eye flames burned white-hot.

The guard moaned and then went silent. The Destroyer pulled back the flames, releasing him. As the guard slumped to the floor, the Hellion turned toward Daniel.

"Look out!" I yelled.

Daniel ducked under the table. Flames scorched the wall behind where he'd stood a moment before.

"Enough, Difethwr." Pryce's voice cut through Bonita's screams.

The Hellion knocked the table aside.

"I said, 'Enough'!"

Difethwr, furious, whipped its head around. Flames streamed from its eyes. They raced toward Pryce, halting an inch away from his face. The two of them stood there, deadlocked. Then, inch by inch, the Destroyer reeled back the flames until they were a mere glow in its eye sockets. It growled and turned away.

Pryce straightened the sleeves of his suit jacket. "Hello, cousin," he said, as though we'd bumped into each other on the street. "Ready to join our side yet?"

"Never."

Pryce looked surprised. "Haven't you been doing your homework? Surely the book wouldn't hide from you the delicious irony of what's to come."

My demon mark smoldered as I tried to block out the vision of me attacking a defenseless woman on Boston Common.

"She knows," the Destroyer said. "We can feel it in her."

Bonita was curled up in a corner. Pryce bent over and closed his hands around her arms. "Thanks for keeping this one safe for me. This evening's events have been most interesting, and I believe we have much to learn from them. See you in hell, cousin."

The Destroyer's rumbling laugh filled the room. Then the Hellion, Pryce, and Bonita—her eyes screwed shut, her voice wailing in despair—all disappeared.

# 16

"LET ME GUESS," DANIEL SAID, AS HE STOOD AND BRUSHED off his clothes. "They went to the demon plane."

"I'm afraid so." Poor Bonita, dragged back to hell so Myrddin and Pryce could figure out why and how the Morfran left her body. I didn't hold out much hope she'd escape a second time.

"Can we go after them?"

I shook my head. "I can perceive the demon plane, but it's like I'm looking at it through a window. I can't step into it bodily." Once, I'd been pulled physically into the demon plane by a Hellion, as Pryce had done to Bonita. I almost hadn't made it back.

"Damn it!" Daniel kicked the table. Then he bent over the fallen guard, feeling for a pulse. He wouldn't find one.

As he straightened, his expression grim, someone began working the lock mechanism in the door. The bolts shot back, and it opened to reveal a doorway full of gun barrels.

"Put down your weapons," Daniel said. "You're too damn late. What the hell took you so long?"

"Sorry, sir. We had two men monitoring the video. One of 'em tried to contact me over the radio, but then it went to static.

I sent Mike in, and Mike came running back yelling the guys in the video room were dead. Both of 'em. And their monitor showed this room empty and the table knocked over. We opened the door soon as we knew."

"Didn't you hear—?"

"Daniel," I interrupted, "it wouldn't have done any good. There would have been more deaths."

Daniel glanced at where Pryce had stood and taken several bullets. Spots of black blood marked the wall. Yet Pryce had disappeared into the demon plane and returned good—or bad—as new, in less than a second. "There's no way to kill him?"

"It would take something like a grenade, blow him to bits before he could pop back to the demon plane and repair the damage. Or else make him vulnerable by severing him from his shadow demon—he can't enter the demon plane without that connection." That's how I'd once defeated Pryce, all too temporarily. Now, however, Pryce was bound to the Destroyer. He could draw on the Hellion's demonic energy to give himself power and extend his life.

Out in the hallway, a slim man with close-cropped hair exited the stairwell door. He wore a dark suit and hurried over to us. "I got here as soon as I could," he said to Daniel. "Here's the phone you requisitioned."

"Vicky, this is my new partner, Ramón Sandoval," Daniel said, taking the phone. "Ramón, Vicky Vaughn is our demon expert."

"Nice to meet you," he said as we shook hands. His dark brown eyes showed friendliness, not a trace of the hostility that was the calling card of Daniel's previous partner.

"You, too," I said. I turned to Daniel. "Not that I was looking forward to seeing his smiling face or anything, but what happened to Detective Foster?"

Ramón laughed, and I liked him for it. Even Daniel let a smile quirk one side of his mouth upward. "He quit. Took an executive position with Humans First." Humans First was a political action committee pushing an anti-paranormal agenda.

"As a law enforcement liaison," Ramón added. "They're welcome to him, as far as I'm concerned."

"He claimed he'd been considering the move for a while,

but I think that being half strangled by a PDH was too much for him."

"Yeah. Hard to maintain his tougher-than-the-monsters image when word of that got around." I wanted to join their laughter, but the reference to getting strangled by a zombie made me need to check on Mab. That, and a deep-down, little-girl desire to reassure myself of her love.

"I have to find my aunt," I said, moving toward the stairwell. I hoped she'd shifted. Not only to heal, but to avoid Pryce and the Destroyer. Pryce had sent those zombies to kill Mab—both of them had gone straight for her. "Kill the lady!" Bonita had said the crows commanded. And according to Butterfly, Pryce needed to get rid of "some lady" to move forward with his plans.

I wasn't the Lady of the Cerddorion. Mab was.

"Wait, first let me give you this." Daniel held out the cell phone Ramón had brought. "Tonight when I got word of an attack at the airport, I couldn't get in touch with you. I didn't know you were in the middle of it. I need to be able to reach you at any hour. So keep this with you and don't turn it off."

"You know why I don't have one of those, right?" Cell phones can't withstand the energy blast that accompanies a shift. After I'd destroyed three in a single month, I was finished.

"Don't worry about that. If you blow it up, or even just lose it, let me know immediately and I'll get you another. We need to stay in close touch."

He programmed the number into his own phone, then made sure my new phone had his numbers in it. I felt kind of dumb as he showed me the basics of making and answering calls and listening to voice mail—my six-year-old nephew could do all that plus play games—but it wasn't my fault the technology changed so fast.

I took the phone and stuck it in my back pocket, then went to find Mab.

MAB WAITED FOR ME WHERE I'D LEFT HER, AND KANE SAT beside her. My heart leapt to see him, then sank as the thought hit me how badly I'd let both of them down. I stood in front of them, not knowing what to say. Mab had a feather stuck in her hair. Pigeon, by the look of it. Good choice for shifting in a city. As I plucked it away, I inspected her throat. The bruises were gone. Mab closed her hand around mine and squeezed.

Kane stood abruptly. "Let's be on our way."

"I thought you'd gone."

"I probably should have." His eyes locked onto mine, then looked away. "I had to make some calls. Let the rally organizers know I'm running late."

"The rally is still on?"

"Of course. After this . . ." He still wouldn't look at me as his arm swept across the hall. "We need it more than ever." He offered his hand to Mab. "Are you ready?"

"Indeed." She accepted his assistance in standing, and I noticed she was a little wobbly on her feet. Not surprising after a shift, but when I asked if she was all right, she assured me that she was.

And that was all we could manage to say to each other.

Mab took my arm and we followed Kane, who was already pushing her luggage trolley toward the doors, out into the night.

KANE'S BMW CARRIED US ALL BACK TO DEADTOWN: KANE, Mab, me, and the most awkward, uncomfortable silence I'd ever experienced. Mab sat in back, staring out the side window, her hand on the small suitcase beside her. I sat in front, inches from Kane yet feeling like we were on opposite sides of an impenetrable steel wall.

Who knew what the others were thinking? I didn't want to guess. But for me, most of my thoughts were of the kicking-myself variety. Kicking myself that I hadn't told Kane about the Night Hag's offer. That I hadn't told either of them about Dad. That I'd let Difethwr's rage take over, to the extent that I was ready to attack my own aunt.

*Shit.* The car may have held three passengers, but I was crowded out by remorse and regrets.

"I think it would be wise," Kane said, speaking to Mab, not me, as we neared Government Center, "to stow your weapons in my office vault, as we discussed earlier. The authorities might let you bring them into Deadtown, but you'll never get them out again. Not with the situation as it is now."

"Is there time before your rally?" Mab asked, her gaze never straying from the window. It was just past ten o'clock.

"There is. I don't take the stage until one."

"Then I agree."

Kane steered into the garage on New Sudbury Street where he paid an outrageous monthly fee for his reserved parking space. When he stopped the car, I unbuckled my seat belt and started to open the door.

"Wait here," he said.

"I was going to help you lug that trunk up to your office."

"No need. Keep your aunt company. I'll be right back." He turned around and peered at Mab. "Before I lock up the trunk, do you need anything out of it?"

"No, thank you. I already have it."

"Have what?" I asked. "Mab, Kane's right. Any weapons you bring into Deadtown now won't get out again."

"Not a weapon," Mab said. "The gauntlet." She still wouldn't look at me. "Thank you, Mr. Kane. Please do secure my . . . er, cargo."

Kane nodded and pulled back from the window. A few seconds later, the car's trunk opened. The whole car shifted as Kane lifted the heavy box. I watched him trudge toward the elevator, Mab's trunk bowing his broad shoulders. I thought about getting out of the car and helping, whether he wanted me to or not, but I didn't want to be brushed off again. I slumped in my seat.

But not for long. I turned and looked back at my aunt.

"Mab . . ." I began.

"Not now, child. I know you wish to talk, and we shall. But not now. At the moment, I'm tired. The shift healed my injuries, but it required energy I scarcely had. Most of all, I need to think. So please have some patience with an old woman."

"You're not old." My aunt had lived for more than three centuries, but she was the definition of vitality. I didn't like the tone of defeat in her voice.

Mab didn't answer, so I pressed forward with what I really wanted to say. "Mab, I'm sorry. Please believe that. Are . . . are things okay between us?" It was a question I'd never expected to have to ask my aunt, but her weariness and her refusal to look at me made me frightened.

Her face still turned toward the window, she waved a hand, then let it drop to her lap. "It's as I said before, child. The Destroyer has a strong hold on you." She paused. "Stronger than I'd imagined. That is why I must think now."

I turned back to stare through the windshield at the concrete wall. We sat in silence until Kane returned.


THE CHECKPOINTS WERE BUSY HEADING INTO DEADTOWN, although I didn't see a single car coming out. Kane swore under his breath as we joined the end of a line of cars leaving human-controlled Boston.

"Maybe people are coming in for your rally," I said.

"Or maybe they've elevated the code again."

But when we pulled up to the booth, the restriction level poster still indicated Code Yellow. I wasn't surprised. The recent attacks had come from zombies, and yellow restrictions kept them in Deadtown. Plus the full moon was almost here, so companies would want werewolf employees to clear their desks before heading off on retreat.

Kane passed our ID cards through the window. Mab still had the forged ID I'd gotten her the last time she was here, and no eyebrows were raised. The guard handed the cards back and raised the barrier, already looking past us to the next car.

A couple of businesses had reopened in the New Combat Zone. The convenience store remained closed, but Conner's and The Wild Side both had lights on and handwritten OPEN signs on their doors. As we passed Creature Comforts, a group of pedestrians pulled open the door. Inside business seemed brisk, not at all like during my last visit. Probably people having a couple of drinks before the rally. I was glad Axel was getting the business.

After we cleared the second checkpoint, it was only a few minutes' drive through the crowded streets to get to my building. Zombies were everywhere, thronging the sidewalks and spilling into the road. Yet pockets of emptiness surrounded the food carts stationed every few yards, the vendors looking dejected. The zombies still weren't eating.

With each block, the need grew to say something, *anything*, to Kane. Half a dozen times I turned to him, only to have his name die on my lips at the sight of his fixed stare, his rigid posture. The way he made such a point of *not* looking at me. When he pulled to a stop in front of my building, I still hadn't managed a word.

"Kane—"

He was already out of the car, opening Mab's door. I got out and removed her bag, setting it on the sidewalk. "Do you need help with that?" His gray eyes watched me over the roof of the car. At last he'd spoken to me, but his formal voice sounded more like a professional limo driver than my boyfriend.

"I've got it," I said.

He nodded and turned away. Damn it, I couldn't let him just leave. Not with things like this. As he opened the driver's side door, I raced around the car and put my hand on his arm. "I know you have to get to the rally, but can you wait a couple of minutes? I need to get Mab upstairs, but I'd like for us to talk." I'd spent more than enough time avoiding him and ducking conversations. I didn't want him to leave with bad feelings between us. For once, I was going to face the issue head-on.

If he'd let me.

"Please?" I added.

He tilted back his head, as if the answer was written on the sky. Then he looked at me and nodded. "I'd like that, too."

My heart surged. "Good. I'll be right back."

I picked up Mab's bag and ushered my aunt inside. I introduced her to the night doorman—a new guy, not Clyde—and told him she'd be staying with us for a while. Upstairs, Mab stretched out on the couch and closed her eyes. "Take your time, child," she said. "We'll talk after I've rested. You go and make things right with your young man."

*Make things right.* Was that even possible? Maybe not. All I knew was I had to try.

# 17

KANE STOOD BY HIS CAR, TALKING ON HIS CELL PHONE. HE ended the conversation as I walked over. He watched me but didn't shift his posture or open his arms to me. I stopped several feet in front of him, suddenly tongue-tied. I'd said we needed to talk, but now in the searchlight of his stare I didn't know what to do or say.

"You should have told me," he said.

Five words, each of them a distinct knife in my gut. Not because Kane was aiming to hurt, but because he was right.

"I promised Dad."

"You think I couldn't keep his secret? Me?" His mouth snapped shut and he clenched his jaw. "Juliet knew. You trusted her, but you didn't trust me."

"That was different. She microwaves things for him." Kane looked at me like I was crazy. Maybe I was. "What I mean is, I *didn't* tell Juliet. She was home one night when Dad came to see me and—"

"And he was obviously okay with her knowing. And *still* you didn't tell me. You didn't even bother to ask your dad if he'd mind." His expression clouded. "Or did you ask? Is he afraid I'll try to talk you into handing him over to the Night Hag to gain my freedom? Because . . ." Kane's voice trailed off. His eyebrows knit together as he thought. Then understanding widened his eyes. "He doesn't know about that, does he? No one does."

I looked at my shoes, unable to meet his gaze.

"Christ, Vicky, you've got yourself wrapped up so tightly in secrets it's a wonder you can breathe."

"The choice the Night Hag gave me. It's . . . it's impossible. I don't know what to do."

I expected him to yell; he had every right to be angry with me. But when he spoke, his voice was gentle. "Don't you see? That's exactly when you need to turn to others for help. We've had this conversation so many times before. You don't have to face everything alone."

I looked into his eyes then. They were alight with sincerity. And now he did open his arms, and I flew into them. Finally I could breathe again, and I drank in his scent. He hugged me tight and pressed his lips against my hair. Then gently, firmly, he straightened and held me at arm's length.

"Vicky, I understand that you don't want to hand over your father to the Night Hag. I wouldn't ask you to. I know it means a lot to you to have him back."

"It does. But there's more. The white falcon is mentioned in the prophecies—I did tell you that. And you saw what he can do."

"You mean kill the Morfran."

"Kane, there's never been a way to do that before. We could imprison the Morfran in slate, but we couldn't destroy it. With Dad's help, we can obliterate so much of the Morfran that Pryce will never be able to make his demons strong enough to attack. We can stop the war before it begins."

"Which can't happen if the Night Hag has the falcon in her control." He paused, thinking. "Mab told me, though, that no one knew until tonight that the falcon could kill the Morfran. Right?"

"That's right." The sharpness of his question brought on a twinge of guilt. He didn't trust me to tell him the whole truth, with good reason.

"When did the Night Hag approach you with this bargain?"

"I was still in quarantine."

"Vicky, that was three weeks ago! We could have used those weeks to figure out a plan. You, me, your father, Mab. We should be putting our heads together to beat the Night Hag, not let her win through your—" He bit his lip. "Through *our* inaction."

Something stung my eyes and suddenly Kane looked all blurred and wavery. "I can't protect you," I said. "I can't protect either one of you."

"Don't protect me; let me stand beside you." His thumb brushed a tear from my cheek. "I love you. And you told me you feel the same way. But if there's no trust, there's no love. There can't be." His voice was low, almost hoarse. "I need you to trust me, Vicky."

"I do." How could I explain it *was* love that made me want to shield him from the darkness that had swallowed me whole?

"No more secrets, then." He lifted my chin with his forefinger. "Promise?"

I nodded.

"We still have a couple of days before the full moon. Let's put those heads together and see what we can come up with."

I didn't hold out much hope, but it was a plan—and better than anything I'd been able to formulate as the problem had spun round and round on the Merry-Go-Round of Impossibility in my mind. At least we'd be trying to do something.

Kane kissed me—a long, deep, lingering kiss that held all the promise, all the feelings I'd feared my silence had killed. I moved closer, savoring the way our bodies fit together. His arms tightened around me.

Too soon, the moment was over. He stepped away, putting his hand on my cheek, his thumb lightly caressing my skin. "I've got to go," he said. "I don't want to. The unity rally could go to hell for all I care, but—"

"That's not true. And even if it were, I wouldn't want it to be." Kane's passion for social justice, his tireless efforts to bring people together for a greater cause—I loved these things about him. "Go ahead. I'll be there in time for your speech."

"You don't have to. You've got your aunt to look after."

I stood on tiptoe and raised my mouth to his. "I wouldn't miss it for the world," I murmured against his lips.

BACK IN MY APARTMENT, MAB WAS ASLEEP ON THE SOFA. I was glad. She'd had quite a day, thanks to jet lag, a zombie attack, a confrontation with the Night Hag, and a quick shift into a pigeon and back. Not to mention having her niece draw a sword on her.

I'd put things right with her. Kane's words—*you don't have to face everything alone*—made me believe that I could. But for now, I'd let her sleep.

I got a spare blanket from the closet. Mab lay on her back, one hand clutching her bloodstone pendant, her head turned slightly to the side. She looked peaceful. It was good to see the worry erased from her face, I thought as I gently spread the blanket over her. How could I have come so close to betraying her?

As I straightened, I heard a buzzing at my ear.

"So what are you gonna do next, oh fearsome aunt slayer—try to smother her with a pillow?"

Butterfly. Wonderful.

But wait. On second thought, maybe I did want to talk to this demon. I pointed down the hall. *I'm not chatting with an Eidolon in front of my aunt, even if she is sleeping. I'll talk to you in the bedroom.*

"Seriously?" The black insect hovered in front of my nose, its demon face perplexed. "What are you trying to pull?"

*I'm going into my bedroom and taking all my delicious guilt with me. You can follow me or go back to the demon plane.* I bent and kissed Mab's cheek, then turned out the lights and left the living room.

I shut the bedroom door behind me. A minute later came a *taptaptap*, like a moth bumping into a window screen. I opened the door. No Butterfly. Or so I thought until the demon ran past my foot. Then it shot into the air, zipped across the room, and alighted on my dresser.

"Since when do you knock?" I asked, closing the door. I kept my voice low so as not to disturb Mab. But I found it easier to shield my thoughts from the demon when I spoke to it out loud.

"I thought maybe you were setting up some kind of trap. So I made my entrance in a way you wouldn't expect it. Clever, huh?"

Whatever. "Listen, Butterfly, I need to talk to you. So if we could call a truce"—I couldn't believe I was saying that—"for just a few minutes."

"Talk? Great, let's talk. I got a whole list of conversation starters. How 'bout we discuss how you let Pryce and the Destroyer snatch poor Bonita out from under your nose? Or how you put your loved ones in danger because you couldn't bring yourself to tell them about the whole Night Hag thing? Or how you were all set to do battle with your beloved aunt until I stopped you? Or, speaking of battle, what about those visions you keep having of murdering innocent people? Yeah, I think we've got a lot to talk about."

"Do you know what the word *truce* means?"

"Hunger shrinks my vocabulary."

"Not as much as a bronze blade would." As best I could, I shielded the fact that I was bluffing. Although I hated to admit it, I needed this annoying demon right now.

A pause. "You've still got that dagger in your nightstand, haven't you?"

"You know I never sleep without a weapon in reach."

Butterfly launched itself from the dresser. It landed on my shoulder and belched. "So talk."

I fanned the putrid air away. "I need a favor."

The demon rocketed upward and ricocheted around the room, bouncing off the ceiling and hitting the walls like a butterfly-shaped pinball. I ducked as it whizzed past my cheek. Eventually, it landed on my headboard, its sawtooth wings trembling.

"Pardon me. I don't think I heard you right. I could've sworn you asked me for *another* favor. That's two in two days. Doesn't that mean you owe me your firstborn or something?" The demon frowned. "Except you wanna stay a shapeshifter, so that means you won't have a firstborn. So I guess you owe me . . . let's see . . ."

"Quit clowning around. This is important."

"Let me get this straight. You insult me. You threaten me. You torment me. You starve me to the very brink of death."

Butterfly flopped onto its back on my pillow and feebly waved its legs in the air. "And I'm pretty sure that you haven't yet gotten over that whole trying-to-kill-the-Eidolon obsession."

*I should have killed you when I first conjured you.* I tried to stuff that thought behind my mental shield before Butterfly picked up on it. Not exactly persuasive. Still, I *should* have killed the thing then. I'd been ready to. The only reason I hadn't was the demon had surprised me in a moment of weakness by unexpectedly using the magic word.

Hmm. The memory gave me an idea.

"P . . . puh . . ." The word refused to leave my mouth.

Butterfly rolled over and stood on all six legs again. "Did you say something?"

I licked my lips and tried again. "Please."

The demon staggered back like I'd dealt it a blow. I took advantage of its stunned silence and rushed on.

"You said you want to stop Pryce. Here's your big chance. We know he's allied with the Old Ones and they're providing him with a base somewhere in the city. I need you to find out where that base is and what he's giving the Old Ones in return for their cooperation."

"Oh, is that all? How 'bout I bring you his head on a platter while I'm at it?"

"That would be nice. But the location and the deal would be enough."

"And how do you propose I get this information? Just saunter up to him and ask?"

"You've brought me information from the demon plane before."

"Yeah, but that's just passing on rumors. Demons gossip a lot, sure. But if someone as nasty as your Pryce-Destroyer combo wants to keep a secret, ain't nobody gonna ask about it." The demon shook its head. "Besides, you say the base is in Boston. That's your turf. If I snuck into the Ordinary trying to do some fly-on-the-wall routine and Pryce noticed me, he'd squash me flat."

"But you're our best chance to find this place. If you could follow him out of the demon plane, you know, unobtrusively—"

"Unobtrusively my demon ass. If I materialize anywhere around the guy in this plane, his Hellion buddy will know in

a second. And if they catch me spying, I'm one dead Eidolon."
Butterfly's wings quivered in indignation. "Not that you'd mind.
But information flows two ways, you know. If they even suspected I was spying for you, they'd torture me until I spilled
everything I know about the contents of your messed-up head."

"I'm willing to risk that."

"Oh, *you're* willing to risk *my* life. Now, there's courage."

"Okay, forget it. I'll figure out another way to find them." I
should have known better than to ask a demon for help. Especially not my very own Eidolon. "Get out of here now. I've got
things to do."

"But—" the demon began.

The mark on my arm itched.

Butterfly snapped its mouth shut. "All right, all right. Don't
get angry. I hate it when you're angry. It's like a big salt shaker
full of yuck ruining your otherwise yummy emotions." The
demon sighed. "Anger's only edible when it cools off and turns
into regret. Fresh anger—too hot. Anyway, I can see I'm not
going to get a meal here tonight, so I'll be off." Its wings fluttered, and its body faded. "If I happen to hear anything about
you-know-who—in passing—I may be in touch. But don't
count on it."

"Believe me, I won't."

Butterfly winked out. Stupid Eidolon. At the airport, when
it said, "Stick with me, kid," I'd almost believed the thing was
on my side. Silly me. It was a demon, and I was a demon fighter.
Tonight, it had reminded me what I could expect from it: a big
fat load of nothing.

# 18

HALF AN HOUR LATER, I WAS TAPING A HASTILY SCRIBBLED
note on the front door to alert Juliet that Mab was asleep on
the sofa. Another note, including the number for my newly
acquired cell phone, awaited my aunt on the coffee table in
case she woke up. I locked up and headed for Kane's rally.

My street was deserted. I hoped that meant everyone was
at the rally. I checked my watch; it had started ten minutes ago.
Hurrying through the cool night air, I set off toward the Old
South Meeting House. The former church now served as Deadtown's town hall. The Council of Three held public meetings
here, and its steps had been the starting point for several protest
marches. Nice symbolism—this same building had launched
the Boston Tea Party in 1773.

Smells of smoke and wet ashes hung in the air as my
boots clicked along the sidewalk. I passed an abandoned food
cart, then another. The third, badly dented, lay on its side, its
contents disgorged and trampled beyond recognition. Apparently Deadtown's zombies hadn't recovered their collective
appetite.

Several yards ahead, a silhouette detached itself from a dark
wall and planted itself in the center of the sidewalk. I stopped.

Two more figures stepped from a doorway. My hand slipped inside my jacket, fingers closing around my pistol grip. I'd almost left the gun home—it didn't seem like the best accessory for a unity rally—but I was glad to have it now. My demon mark twitched and warmed.

Around the corner came a Goon squad patrol. Four big zombies, dressed in body armor and carrying evil-looking automatic rifles. The group on the sidewalk turned and strolled past the Goons, like that had been their intention all along. I left my pistol in its holster and zipped my jacket. I nodded to the Goons as I continued on my way, hoping Kane was building some unity at his rally. On Deadtown's streets, all I'd seen so far tonight was trouble.

THE RALLY HAD DRAWN A GOOD CROWD. AS I JOINED THE fringes, a zombie stepped aside and smiled, waving me closer. The mood here was upbeat, not like on the dark, deserted street. A woman's amplified voice carried through the night, and I craned toward the platform that had been erected over the steps of the Old South Meeting House. Several chairs had been set up at the side of the stage, and I picked out Kane sitting there. At the microphone stood the current speaker, dressed in a pearl gray suit and black pumps. "It took nearly three years for us to get a school . . ." she was saying, and I realized with a jolt I was looking at Tina.

No Barbie pink. No giant hoop earrings. No sparkly rhinestones. She looked like the zombie version of a young businesswoman making a presentation to the Chamber of Commerce.

I closed my dropped jaw and tuned back in. Tina was contrasting her experience as a high school student before and after the plague—first as a norm girl in Revere, then as a zombie in Deadtown.

"My old school was all about cliques. You belonged to one group, and you didn't make friends outside of it. There were the popular kids—that was my clique, as I'm sure most of you would guess." She beamed at the audience. "There were the jocks, the gamers, the drama club kids, the stoners, the overachievers . . . You know what I'm talking about. You probably had similar cliques when you were in school. And everything was all about which group you belonged to. To some of us, that was more important than classes."

She raised her hand and pointed at herself, nodding, causing a ripple of laughter among listeners.

"Then came the plague. And for those of us caught in it, suddenly there was just one group: the outcasts. Or the losers, or the freaks, or whatever you call people that the rest of the world wishes would go away. Like I said earlier, we waited almost three years even to have a school in Deadtown. When we got one, cliques didn't seem so important anymore. Hey, we were all outcasts together, so why make life hard for each other? In my school now, I'm friends with kids I never would have spoken to back in Revere. Most of my classmates are zombies, but there are some werewolves, too. Sounds like a really bad horror movie, right? *Deadtown High: Zombies vs. Werewolves*. But you know what? We get along.

"And you know why? Because now we want to learn stuff. Not just from our classes, but from each other. My friend Brendan knows everything about computers, and he's also teaching me martial arts." She did a karate move that brought more laughs and scattered applause. "My best friend, Jenna, she's an awesome negotiator who never met an argument she couldn't resolve. My other friend Sharon, who's a werewolf, is into finance and makes these amazing predictions about the stock market. People come to me for fashion tips, which you'd expect"—she twirled to show off her outfit—"but also to learn how to get rid of their personal demons. Because kids have their own demons to wrestle with. And I learned about demons from the best demon slayer in the business, who, by the way, happens to be a shapeshifter."

My doubts about Tina as demon-slaying expert were squashed by the lump in my throat.

"So, in conclusion, my point is this. Most things about being previously deceased well and truly suck. But for me, there's been one good thing, and that's the ability to look past stupid, meaningless differences and come together to support and learn from each other. And if us kids can do that at the DA-1 school, we can all do it." She looked around, as if expecting applause, but the audience was silent, every face watching her. "So . . .

um . . . go, unity!" As she pumped a fist in the air, the applause came, along with cheers and more pumping fists. Tina grinned and clasped her hands above her head, like a prizefighter. Then she skipped to the edge of the stage. Kane, standing, shook her hand, before she went down the steps. Kane went to the microphone to introduce the next speaker.

I skirted the edge of the crowd and caught up with Tina a couple of minutes later. When she saw me, she threw her arms around me in a hug that nearly broke my ribs.

"Nice job," I said, once I could breathe again. "The audience loved it."

"Yeah, they did, didn't they? I practiced, like, a gazillion times. Kane said not to say 'like' and 'you know' and 'stuff' and, you know, other stuff. That was hard. But I think I did okay."

"You did great."

"Thanks." Tina grinned, still riding high on the applause. "Anyway, I've gotta go. I'm getting interviewed. It's just PNN, so it's not like anyone will watch, but hey, TV is TV."

"You never know who might see it." The Paranormal News Network's largest audience was in Deadtown, but it was available nationwide. "Have fun."

"I will." But she didn't move away. She bit her lip and looked almost shy. "Um, Kane told me your aunt is visiting."

"That's right. We picked her up at the airport tonight."

"Did she . . ." Tina glanced around. "Did she come to my speech?"

"She's asleep in my apartment."

"Oh. I guess she must have been tired after flying across the ocean and all."

"She did have a very long day. We'll watch for your interview on PNN tomorrow."

"Awesome. They'll probably show part of my speech, too." The shy look returned. "Um, do you think it would be okay if I came over to see her? You know, to say hello and whatever."

"I'm sure Mab would love to see you. Just call first."

"Really?" She bounced on her toes, looking more like the Tina I knew. "Cool. Okay, I'll call tomorrow. Talk to you then." Another hug, and she disappeared into the meeting house while once again I checked for cracked ribs.

*  *  *

SEVERAL MORE SPEAKERS, ROUSING BURSTS OF MUSIC FROM an all-paranormal brass band between them, took the stage. All of Deadtown's main paranormal groups were represented: zombies, werewolves, and even vampires, who weren't normally into things like unity and togetherness. Most moving was Clyde, who'd traded his doorman's uniform for a cleric's robe. "I know that many of you lost your faith after the plague," he said. "Certainly, I've struggled with my own. Despite that, or perhaps because of it, I'd like to offer a simple prayer. Even if you don't believe, I hope you'll listen to the spirit that moves these words." By the time he'd finished his quiet, dignified appeal to heal breaches and bring people together, I was wiping tears from my cheeks. The female zombie beside me put an arm around my shoulder. If zombies could cry, there wouldn't have been a dry eye in the audience.

Then it was Kane's turn. He praised the speakers and thanked the audience for coming. He described some of the work he'd been doing to secure paranormal rights through lobbying and the courts. "I'm not going to talk about winning this fight," he said. "Fighting, warfare, battles—those are the wrong metaphors. If we try to fight, we will lose. We will lose in more ways than one. First, we possess neither the weapons nor the numbers to win an actual war. The forces that oppose us would smash our homes, our businesses, take away what little freedom we now have. Even worse, to my way of thinking, is that we would lose our ability to define ourselves. 'Look at them,' the powers-that-be would say. 'They're monsters. All they understand is violence. We *have* to destroy them—they give us no choice.'"

A couple of shouts came from the back of the crowd. A fight? Hecklers? From where I stood I couldn't see what was going on. Kane stared in that direction for a moment, then continued.

"What we face is not a fight," he said, "but it *is* a struggle. Think of the difference. Any thug can pick a fight."

"Fight! Fight! Fight!" What at first sounded like an echo of Kane's word turned into a chant. "Fight! Fight! Fight!" The voices came from multiple directions. I heard scuffling behind me and turned around to see a big zombie take a swing at a werewolf who wore a SECURITY T-shirt.

Kane raised his voice. "Struggle demands sacrifice. It demands discipline. It demands looking beyond the immediate situation to our long-term goal."

The security werewolf snarled and launched himself at the zombie. All around, scuffles broke out. Groups of zombies threw themselves at those standing at the edges of the crowd. It looked like a coordinated effort to interrupt Kane's speech.

The security werewolf and the zombie he was fighting crashed to the ground beside me. A bronze dagger was already in my hand. I didn't remember unsheathing it, but my burning demon mark urged me to use it. *Now.* Cut up the damn zombie's face. He wanted a fight? He'd picked the right rally.

Unity, my ass. I'd teach this assclown a lesson.

*"STOP!"* A thunderous roar exploded from the platform. It shook the ground and echoed off the buildings. Everyone froze. A thousand pairs of eyes turned to the platform.

Kane stood tall, his face a mask of barely constrained fury. His silver hair shining under the stage lights, he looked like an avenging angel. This was not a werewolf to be messed with. This was strength and power given form.

Kane took advantage of the crowd's silence. "This is exactly what they expect of us," he said in a low, deadly voice. "I thought we were coming together tonight for unity. Apparently not. So tell me, if you don't want unity, what *do* you want?"

He waited. Silence reigned for three, maybe four seconds. Then a voice yelled, "Kill all the bloodbags!"

Kane's gaze zeroed in on the heckler. "Really? That's what you want? Because if that's your goal, you can't complain when they start dropping bombs on Deadtown." He gestured, waving his arms around to imitate a fascist dictator on crack. " 'They're our enemies! Kill them all!' If that's the attitude you take, are you surprised when the other side looks at you the same way? The same anger. The same hatred. The same feeling of 'All our problems would be solved if only those other bastards didn't exist.' "

Again he waited. This time, the heckler stayed quiet. Kane shifted his stance, his gaze sweeping across the crowd. I put my dagger away, willing the heat in my demon mark to cool.

Nobody shook hands and started singing "Kumbaya," but no one threw a punch, either. A few zombies slunk away from the crowd's edges.

"Struggle, my friends," Kane said at last. "Not fighting the norms. And for God's sake not fighting each other—there's nothing they'd like more. But struggle. It's how we'll make our voice heard. It won't be easy, but we have to show we'll never give up. Because our goal—no matter how long it takes—is to be equal participants in society. That's my vision. But we have to be in it together. Because if you're not with me . . ." He didn't seem to know how to finish that sentence. He dropped the microphone, which landed with a *thunk* and squeal, and walked to the edge of the stage.

He hadn't made it down the first step before the chanting started up again. But this time, the chant wasn't "Fight! Fight! Fight!" Instead, a thousand voices called out his name.

"Kane! Kane! Kane!"

Even the zombie who'd attacked the security werewolf was chanting it.

"Kane! Kane! Kane!"

Kane stopped, his hand on the railing. He turned back to the crowd.

"Kane! Kane! Kane!"

I added my voice to the chant. We clapped with each repetition. All of Deadtown chanted in one voice, until the word exploded into a tumult of cheering.

By the time Kane took the stage again, his hand on his heart, even from where I stood I could see the tears shining in his eyes.


WHEN I FOUND HIM, KANE WAS ANSWERING A REPORTER'S questions. The moment he saw me, he pushed the microphone away and enfolded me in his arms.

He came home with me. Mab still slept on the sofa; Juliet was nowhere to be seen. We tiptoed down the hallway to my room and closed the door, so softly it made no click.

What we did next was more than lovemaking. It was a uniting, a coming together so profound that every cell of my body confirmed that nothing could ever, ever pull us apart. Not the

Night Hag, not the full moon, not the Destroyer's mark. Not even my own fears. Whatever we'd meant to each other before, we deepened those feelings. Whatever hurts or disappointment we'd inflicted on each other in the past, we erased them. Together, we became something more. Something indestructible. Something that would stand together and face whatever came our way, no matter what that might be.

# 19

I WOKE TO THE SOUND OF THE SHOWER RUNNING. HALF turning to check the time, I slid out from under Kane's arm. He murmured something I didn't catch, and then his eyes opened. When he saw me, pleasure filled those gray eyes, and he smiled sleepily. Troubles piled in jagged heaps all around us, but in the midst of them, we were together. I would not let him down again.

He ran his hand along my shoulder and down my arm. Just a fleeting touch, but electric sparks shot through me as I felt his warmth, as I turned and snuggled against him, enclosed in his pine-and-moonlight scent.

No, I would not let this man down.

"I thought maybe that was you in the shower," I said.

"What time is it?"

"I was just checking." I twisted around to see my bedside clock. "Almost seven." We'd managed about three hours' sleep.

Kane groaned and rolled onto his back. "Midnight rallies do not mix well with eight-to-five jobs."

"When did you ever knock off work at five?" Or start as late as eight, for that matter. I heard the bathroom door open. "The shower's free. If you get ready now, you can be at work on time."

He sat up and swung his legs over the edge of the bed. I watched the muscles ripple in his back as he stretched. Too bad Mab hadn't slept in for an extra hour. Kane stood and walked across the room to the closet. Mmm . . . it was *really* too bad. I sighed as he put on the bathrobe he kept at my place. I pulled on my T-shirt and sweatpants.

"Actually," he said, "I was planning to go in late. I think you, Mab, and I should discuss what to do about the Night Hag."

"Really?"

"We're almost out of time. The sooner we brainstorm how to handle the situation, the better." When I didn't reply, he sat beside me and took my hand. "What is it?"

"Last night, at the airport. When I . . ." I caught myself rubbing my demon mark and stopped. "She fell asleep so quickly last night. We haven't talked about it."

"How about this: I'll take my shower and get dressed, and then I'll wait in here. You take all the time you need. If you can't get matters resolved, then you and I will go out somewhere and talk over this Night Hag thing. But I think you will. Your aunt is the most reasonable, practical-minded woman I've ever met. More than that, though, she loves you. She *wants* to understand."

Kane kissed my cheek and headed for the bathroom. As I walked down the hall to face my aunt, I could only hope he was right.

I FOUND MAB IN THE KITCHEN, RUMMAGING IN THE CUP-board beside the stove.

"Where do you keep your kettle?" she demanded before I'd said a word. "I'm parched for a cup of tea."

"I'll heat you some water in the microwave," I said, taking down a mug.

"That beastly contraption? I'm quite certain Rose would go on strike if I attempted to install one of those in my kitchen."

We stood in silence as the microwave whirred. I watched the mug spin around on the turntable, unable to pull my gaze away. The couple of minutes it took to heat the water passed more like a couple of centuries. Only after I'd taken out the mug, dropped in a tea bag, and handed Mab her drink could I manage to meet her eyes.

There was no anger there. No disappointment. What I saw looked more like compassion.

Mab held the mug in both hands, as if warming them. "As I told you, child, what happened last night wasn't your fault. So we need not discuss it."

"But . . . at least let me tell you I'm sorry." If I left those words unspoken, I couldn't live with myself.

"Certainly. I accept your apology." She dunked the tea bag in the hot water several times. "But if you feel you must apologize, I'd prefer you do it for keeping your father's return a secret."

Right. There was that, too. "I promised Dad I wouldn't tell anyone. Not until he had a chance to talk to Mom."

"And you assumed I'd go running off to your mother with the news like some garden-variety village gossip. Honestly, Victory."

"I promised." Lousy as that excuse had turned out to be, it was the only one I had.

"And I'm pleased you're someone who keeps her promises. But surely you could have asked Evan if he'd make an exception for me. After all, he hasn't kept the secret himself."

It was the same argument Kane had made. And it was just as right the second time. I'd made a bad assumption. Mab was family, and I figured that Dad wanted to tell her in his own time, just as he would with Mom and Gwen and the rest of the family.

"This is no time to be keeping secrets from me, child. We are on the brink of war, and I must be able to count on you."

So we were back to that, the whole Lady of the Cerddorion thing. Last night's events proved I wasn't the Lady, and maybe now was the time to make my aunt understand that.

"Mab," I asked, "why did you come to Boston?"

"To help you assume your role."

Here we go again. "What role?"

Instead of answering, Mab dunked her tea bag a few more times. Then she walked over to the trash can and dropped it in. She got the milk out of the fridge and poured a few drops into her tea. She took a sip, and then added another drop.

"You," she said, looking at me over the rim of her mug, "are the Lady of the Cerddorion."

As I started to object, she cut me off by holding up one hand.

"I know what you're going to say." Mab pulled out a chair from the kitchen table. "Traditionally, that title belongs to Ceridwen, mother of our race."

"Actually—"

"Hush, child, and listen. The time has come for her to pass the title on. Sit down, you look pale. Shall I make you a cup of tea?"

"No, thanks." But an acute awareness of my coffee deficit suddenly hit me. I went through the motions of making a pot, my head spinning. Ceridwen, the goddess who'd created both shapeshifters and demi-demons, was sometimes called Lady of the Cerddorion. But that had nothing to do with me. If some long-lost goddess was passing on her title, it was going to Mab. I had to make her understand that.

I pulled the biggest mug I could find out of the cupboard and filled it before the coffee had finished brewing. Then I joined Mab, who sat at the table waiting for me.

"All right," I said. "I'm sitting down. But you're wrong, Mab."

She shot me one of her "don't be cheeky" looks, then cleared her throat. I had the feeling her next words were long rehearsed. "In the beginning, there was Ceridwen, mother to our race. She had two sons—"

"Avagddu and Taliesin." A classic story of the bad son and the good son, like Cain and Abel. Night and day, darkness and light. Even their names reflected the archetype: Avagddu means "utter darkness," while Taliesin was named for the shining beauty of his face. Avagddu was greedy and destructive; Taliesin was talented and wise from the day he was born.

Mab nodded. "The Morfran was formed by cries of hunger and rage that issued from Avagddu. He also created demons and became the progenitor of all demi-demons. Taliesin, the wizard and bard, was the first of our kind."

"I know all this, Mab." How could I not? *The Book of Utter Darkness* had burned the story into my brain.

"Let me explain in my own way, child," Mab said sharply.

But her tone softened as she continued. "Ceridwen gave part of her own nature to each child: Avagddu was created from the shadows within her spirit, and Taliesin from the light. Because of this, as her sons grew and thrived, she weakened. Her last act of magic before she faded away was to lay a burden upon the females of her line. Daughters of Avagddu would be barren. Daughters of Taliesin would lose their powers if they gave birth."

"So she cursed us. Both lines."

"I don't believe Ceridwen saw it as such. Looking at Avagddu's line, the Meibion Avagddu, she understood the lust for power that's fundamental to the race. After all, it came from the darkest places of her own soul. So she curbed that line by limiting its ability to propagate—or she tried to. By that time, her magic was weak and imperfect, and some female demi-demons have reproduced, although always with great difficulty."

"Her magic seems to have stuck it to our side pretty well." Every Cerddorion mother I'd ever known—my grandmothers, Mom, Gwen, countless second and third cousins—had lost her ability to shapeshift with motherhood. Gwen had never wanted anything besides her house in the suburbs and her family, but Mom had been an active demon fighter before she met Dad. She'd never talked about it much, but the decision couldn't have been easy for her. Shapeshifting powers or family—it was the impossible choice all Cerddorion females faced.

"Yes, well, some do see her action as 'sticking it,' as you put it, to her Cerddorion descendants, but I do not believe that is what Ceridwen intended. Her own children drained her, to the extent that she faded away. She did not want her daughters to suffer the same fate."

"That's a hell of a decision to make for someone else." For generations of someone elses. My race was small in number, but over the centuries so many Cerddorion women—tens of thousands of them, probably more—had been forced to choose.

"That's what a goddess does, child. She shapes the world, and we mortals must live with the results. Ceridwen's actions may have been shortsighted. They may even have been cruel. But she was trying to protect her children. She was trying to keep that which she had created in balance."

"Okay, so Ceridwen put limitations on both her lines." I already knew the effects of her actions; I didn't care much about the whys. "What does that have to do with me?" Other than the fact that I would never have children. That knowledge had never bothered me much—I'd made up my mind to be a shape-shifter and fight demons around the time Dad took the training wheels off my first bicycle. Still, it was an issue whose impact I'd felt lurking around the fringes of my relationship with Kane. He was a lone wolf now, but some day he'd want a pack of his own. To a werewolf, that meant starting a family. Sooner or later, one of us would have to sacrifice—either Kane would have to fight his instinct to start a pack or I'd have to give up shapeshifting.

But then, maybe I'd get lucky. Maybe I wouldn't survive the next full moon.

Mab rapped the table. "If you pay attention, I'll tell you what it has to do with you."

"Sorry." Just trying to find an upside to being shredded by the Night Hag's pack of hellhounds.

"After Ceridwen faded from the world, some believe she ceased to exist. Others believe she retired to another plane, one beyond our experience and understanding, to rest. To regather her strength."

"She's been gone for, what? Millennia. I'd say that, dead or retired, she's not coming back."

"But she *is*, child. Already she stirs." Excitement lit up Mab's face. She pulled on the silver chain she wore around her neck, bringing out the pendant that hung inside her shirt. "A spark of her dwells here. In my bloodstone."

"What do you mean?"

"Last night, after I was attacked, do you remember the state I was in?"

I nodded. I'd never lose that image of Mab collapsed, her face purple, angry red marks around her throat.

"I hadn't the strength to climb to my knees. I could barely utter a whisper. Yet when the Night Hag threatened you, I stood up—"

"And gave her what-for. Yes, I remember." Mab's voice had echoed through the terminal. Then, after the Night Hag was gone, Mab weakened again. It had taken a shift to restore her.

"For those few minutes, Ceridwen supported me. She lent me her strength so I could face our enemy."

A goddess, gone from the earth for centuries, now living in a rock and popping out when needed, like a genie in a bottle? For a moment, I wondered if near-strangulation had damaged Mab's brain. Yet I'd witnessed that surge of strength myself. "How do you know it's Ceridwen?"

"I know, child. It's as simple as that." She rubbed the bloodstone between her fingers. "Do you remember, during my previous visit here, that this stone was nearly drained of its power?"

"That's why you buried it when you got back to Wales."

"Yes. I left it deep in good Welsh soil for a fortnight. Over the years, I've done that many times to recharge its power. But this time when I dug it up, the bloodstone had changed." She leaned toward me, holding the stone flat on her palm. "Do you see? The color is richer now, its power stronger. It's even larger than it was before."

I inspected the stone. It was gray with green and red flecks, just as I remembered. But the colors sparkled, giving the stone depth, and it did seem bigger. I touched the polished surface. A vibration, slight but definite, emanated from the stone.

Mab closed her fingers around my hand. The stone's vibration buzzed through me. "Do you feel that, child? My bloodstone has been charged with the spark of Ceridwen. I don't know what form she will take, but I'm quite sure she is returning to our world."

"All right, if you believe that, I'll take your word for it." I pulled my hand away, and Mab returned the bloodstone to its place inside her shirt. My practical aunt had never been one for silly fantasies, but it was hard for me to make this leap with her. Her bloodstone was powerful in itself—I'd witnessed its life-restoring powers. Why bring some long-vanished goddess into it? Besides, it only confirmed my thoughts. "If Ceridwen has hitched a ride back from Dimension X or wherever via your bloodstone, then she's chosen *you*. That makes *you* Lady of the Cerddorion."

Pryce was trying to kill her, yes. Still, I was comforted by the thought that Mab was the Lady. For too long, I'd been on the front lines battling Pryce and his allies. If Ceridwen had chosen Mab for this role, I'd follow her anywhere. I'd throw every ounce of my strength into supporting her. I'd protect her with my life. Mab coming out of her retirement and leading the Cerddorion in battle against the demons: That felt like our best chance of winning.

But my aunt was shaking her head. "No, child. I'm not the one. That was never my fate. My job has been to hold back the darkness and prepare the way."

"But your bloodstone—"

"I've worn this bloodstone for centuries, child. Never in all that time has it held any spark of the divine. Not until it was touched by your blood." It was true that some of my blood had splattered the stone in a fight. But I still thought Mab was jumping to conclusions. And I was about to tell her so, when she slid from her chair and kneeled before me. "I've long suspected it, Victory. The prophecies, your father's dream-vision the night before you were born, they all pointed to it. But now I'm certain." She bowed her head. "Welcome, Lady."

# 20

"MAB, DON'T!" THE LAST THING I WANTED WAS MY AUNT on her knees in front of me. "Get up, please."

"You cannot know how long I've waited for the Lady to return," she murmured. But she returned to her chair.

"I'm sorry to say it, but you're jumping the gun. I'm not the Lady of the Cerddorion. I can't be."

"And what makes you think that?"

"This, for starters." I pulled up my sleeve to expose my demon mark. "And that vision I told you about—the one where I fought on the wrong side. I can't be the second coming of some goddess. There are things inside me . . . like last night—" I stopped, not sure how to express my fear that next time, the Destroyer would gain control. "I'm too flawed."

"Ceridwen was never perfect, child. Her story makes that clear. Don't forget that both lines—demon and Cerddorion—came from her. After centuries of struggle, they're reunited in you. It's this"—she tapped my demon mark with her finger—"that makes Ceridwen's return possible."

"You're wrong. Even Pryce believes you're the Lady." I told her how I'd pieced together this theory.

"Pryce's arrogance has always been his undoing, child. We need not pay the slightest attention to what he thinks."

"Except for the part where he's trying to kill you." And besides that, I remained unconvinced. If anyone should lead the Cerddorion in the coming war, it was Mab.

She tutted, then patted my arm. "Never mind that, child. I'll refrain from calling you 'Lady' if it troubles you. Just know that I am here to protect and serve you."

I didn't like it. For my whole life, I'd always looked up to Mab. She was so many things to me: teacher, mentor, taskmaster, drill sergeant, role model. What she *wasn't* was some kind of attendant who called me "Lady." If she honestly believed I was Ceridwen, take two, she was going to be disappointed. Big time.

"Let's not discuss it now." The briskness in Mab's voice made her sound more like herself. "Haven't we kept your young man waiting long enough?"

A blush crept into my cheeks. "You knew Kane was here?"

"I heard the shower running and, later, a door close. As it's past dawn, I assumed it wasn't your vampire roommate."

"He wants to have a conference about how to deal with Mallt-y-Nos."

"Very sensible. Why don't you fetch him, and we'll do just that?"

"All right. But no more 'Lady of the Cerddorion' stuff, okay?"

"As you wish."

That sounded way too much like some underling acquiescing to royalty, but I let it go. Mab would realize her mistake soon enough. This whole legend about the goddess returning sounded like nothing more than wishful thinking to me. Just as the war between demons and the Cerddorion reaches crisis mode, Mama Ceridwen returns to sort things out. Not bloody likely. I was surprised Mab could believe such a thing.

But Pryce believed it, so I'd have to be vigilant. I would not let him attack Mab again.

Down the hall, I tapped on the bedroom door and opened it. Kane, sitting on the edge of the bed, looked up from his phone. He was dressed in the suit he'd worn yesterday, his shirt a little rumpled from lying on the floor all night. A sexy look on him.

"Everything okay?" he asked.

"Basically, yes. A little weird. Mab's not angry at me, but she thinks I'm the reincarnation of an ancient Welsh goddess." Kane's eyebrows went up at that. "I'll hash that out with her later. Now, we need to figure out what to do about the Night Hag."

"A goddess, huh?" Kane stood and slipped his phone into his inner suit pocket. "Goddess of what?" He grinned and pulled me to him, his lips close to my ear. "After last night," he whispered, "I'm guessing goddess of sex."

I ignored the shiver that went through me. "Don't tease. This idea of hers is making things awkward between Mab and me. So please don't bring it up."

"I won't say a word."

In the kitchen, Mab had made herself another mug of tea. She was back to her usual self, acknowledging us with a brisk nod and suggesting we get down to business at once. I poured coffee for Kane and refilled my own mug, and we sat around the table.

That's when I noticed the glove lying on the tabletop. Crafted from thick leather, it was big enough for the hand of a large man—even Axel might be able to squeeze his paw into it. The glove was brown and looked soft from years of use and polishing. Its long cuff was decorated with undulating patterns embroidered in gold and silver thread—swirls and runes and symbols I didn't recognize.

"That's the glove you took from your trunk last night," I said.

"The gauntlet, yes. I thought it would be a good idea if Evan were to join us for this discussion. After all, the situation concerns him, as well." Mab picked up the gauntlet and fitted it onto her right hand. The fingers looked big and clumsy, and the cuff nearly reached her elbow.

She stood, holding her right arm out straight before her. In a loud, clear voice, she said, *"Hebog, tyrd!"*

The words meant *Falcon, come!* in Welsh.

She repeated the phrase twice more. The third time she said it, there was a change in the air, an electric charge. I took a breath; it was like inhaling lightning, a sharp, tingly feeling in my lungs. Kane grabbed my hand. Mab watched the ceiling, holding her arm before her. The gauntlet glowed with a pulsing light. The buzzing pressure grew.

A shape slammed through the ceiling, a hurtling white blur. Mab staggered back a step as the blur hit her arm. The blur took shape as a falcon, his talons grasping the gauntlet. The bird's head turned, taking in the room. When he saw me, his body relaxed and he folded his wings. "Hi, Vic." Dad greeted Mab, too. Although he stared at Kane, he didn't speak to him. Instead, he looked at Mab. "Well, that was weird. It's good to see you, but I'm not sure how I got here."

"Weird, yes," said Mab. "Almost as weird as being spoken to by a falcon in the voice of my long-dead nephew."

"Touché, old girl." He chuckled. "You should've seen your face."

"Weirdness aside, what happened, just now, when I called you here?"

The falcon tilted his head. "Do you remember those old science fiction films I used to watch? It was like being pulled into a tractor beam, like you sometimes see in those. However hard I strained, whichever way I tried to fly, it sucked me here."

"I used the gauntlet to call you. Can you leave it?"

Dad didn't move. He grunted and twisted, but he stayed where he was. "Nope. My talons won't let go."

"The white falcon is bound to this gauntlet unless I release him." Mab snapped her fingers. Dad hopped off the glove and perched on the back of a chair. He shook himself and started preening. Mab sat in her own seat, then turned to Kane and me. "Now you see why we must not allow the Night Hag to get possession of it."

Dad stopped preening. "The Night Hag? She knows about it?"

"She saw me with it last night." Mab took off the glove and laid it flat on the table, her fingers smoothing the leather. "Were you aware of it, Evan? Before I used it to call you, I mean."

"No, but the falcon was. Or at least, I got a flash of recognition when you called. There's a memory buried deep in this brain, but it feels old, something almost forgotten. Where did you get the gauntlet?"

"In the very distant past. It was a gift from Lord Arawn."

That surprised me. "Really?" I'd met Arawn in the Dark-lands, and he didn't seem like the gift-giving type. He'd loaned me a sword, but that didn't work out too well. During our brief acquaintance, the main thing Arawn had given me was an order to get out of his kingdom or die.

"As I said, child, it was long ago. I brought the gauntlet with me because you told me you'd brought the falcon into our world from the Darklands." She turned to Dad. "What she didn't tell me, Evan, was that you had come with him."

"I promised," I muttered, staring at the table. Kane, his hand still on mine, gave a squeeze.

"Vic, it would have been okay—" Dad began.

"Victory has not been entirely forthcoming with any of us—including you, I'm afraid. That's why we're meeting here now, to lay our cards on the table, as it were, so that everyone involved fully understands the situation."

Dad cocked his head at me. I'd gotten used to the falcon's constant sharp-eyed, almost angry expression, which never changed, no matter what Dad was feeling. Even so, guilt perme-ated my gut. I ignored the feeling. Time to stop trying to carry everything myself, as Kane said. I loved everyone sitting around this table, loved them so much it hurt sometimes. If anything ever happened to any of them . . . But they didn't want my protection. They wanted my trust. I took a deep breath.

"Dad, when I was in the Darklands, Kane followed me there. To bring me home."

The falcon's head swiveled to Kane. His stare lasted a full minute. "How did you get in?"

"The same way I did," I answered. "He made a deal with Mallt-y-Nos."

"She's well known to werewolves," Kane put in. "One of her titles is Mistress of Hounds. But normally she leaves us alone."

"What did you promise the hag?"

"He promised . . ." My voice cracked, and I couldn't seem to get any more words out. Kane moved his chair closer to mine and put his arm around my shoulders. A warm, gentle squeeze reassured me.

"I promised to join her pack for a year and a day."

"As a hellhound?"

"Yes. For the three nights of each full moon."

Kane and my father locked eyes across the table, Kane's steady gray-eyed gaze meeting Dad's bright, sharp one. With a start, I realized that this was the first time they'd met, not counting the business at the airport. *Oh, great.* I was glad we'd had no time for formal introductions. Dad, meet my werewolf boyfriend; he moonlights as a hellhound. Kane, meet my father, a talking falcon from the realm of the dead. Even under the best of circumstances—which these were not—we'd all be chowing down on supersize portions of awkward.

"Well, Vic," Dad said. "He looks strong. He might survive. You say he came for you in the Darklands? How come?"

"Because I love her." Despite our grim situation, Kane's words sent sparkles of pleasure through me. He sounded so natural, so sure.

"Really? Vic, are you two an item or something? Because I swear I can't remember you ever mentioning . . . what's his name again?"

Kane stiffened, but he didn't pull away. I could feel his questioning gaze on me, but I kept my own eyes on my father. "Kane, Dad. His name is Alexander Kane. And if you'd think for a minute, you'd realize my love life has never been a big topic of discussion between you and me."

"But he's a—"

*Don't say it, Dad.* "He's my boyfriend. And I—" I was going to say, "I love him," but my voice cracked again and Mab took the opportunity to tsk at all of us.

"Based on my own observations, Evan, I will attest to the fact that Victory and Mr. Kane are indeed in a serious and exclusive relationship."

*A serious and exclusive relationship.* How romantic. Why couldn't I get the L-word out in the easy way Kane said it? Damn it, I didn't want to leave any room for doubt.

"I love him, Dad." There. Not a hint of a crack. My words came out clear and strong. My father stared at me and didn't reply. I broke from his gaze and turned to Kane. He didn't speak either, but the soft glow in his eyes said everything.

Mab broke the silence. "Examining the validity of their relationship is not the purpose of this meeting. Although I'll admit it does affect our current problem. To catch you up, Evan, I'm sure you're aware that Mallt-y-Nos was furious when you escaped from her."

Dad quit staring at Kane. He chuckled and puffed out his chest feathers. "The old hag didn't have her claws on me for more than half an hour."

"She blames Victory. She's convinced that Vicky somehow stole you from her. She has sworn that at the next full moon, she will set her hounds—Mr. Kane among them—on Vicky in revenge."

Dad's chest deflated. "Vic, is this true?"

I nodded, miserable.

"The hag has offered Vicky a way out. She will release Mr. Kane from his promise on one condition."

The falcon's gaze fixed on the glove lying on the table. "If Vic hands me over."

"That's correct. So you see—"

"That's why you brought the gauntlet, isn't it?" Although the falcon's expression never changed, hurt permeated my father's voice. "You called me here to tell me that you're giving me to that horrible creature."

"No, Dad. It's not that simple."

"Of course it is. I understand, Vic. Your boyfriend gets his freedom, and the Night Hag leaves you alone."

"If we planned to do that, Evan, why would we be here now? We could have given Mallt-y-Nos the gauntlet at the airport last night."

"Without saying good-bye? You wouldn't be that cold, Mab." The falcon shook himself, and the sadness in Dad's voice deepened. "Honestly, Vic, I do understand. When you made your first bargain with the Night Hag, you never expected me to be part of it. You couldn't have known I'd use this body to leave the Darklands or that I'd abandon the hag the first chance I got. So I take responsibility. But . . . if you could hold off one more day, give me a chance to see your mother." He shook his head and spoke quietly, as if to himself. "I'm sorry now I wasted so much time getting up the courage to speak to her."

"Dad, stop." I rapped the table a couple of times to make him look at me. "We are *not* handing you over to the Night

Hag. In the first place, you should know me well enough to know I couldn't do that to you."

"And I couldn't let her sic her hellhounds on you. They'd rip you to bits."

"She'll probably do that anyway. Calling the hounds off was never part of the deal. All she offered was a one-for-one exchange: the falcon for Kane's release. That's where I got stuck. It's an impossible bargain. No matter how many times I thought it through, I couldn't come up with an acceptable solution."

"Besides," Mab put in, "there's even more at stake." Awe crept into her voice. "The white falcon can kill the Morfran."

"I was as surprised about that as anybody," Dad said. "In fact, I was planning to come over and discuss it before you called me here. I don't know if Vic told you, Mab, but I've been trying to read the book. And now I finally understand what it was telling me, telling the falcon part of this brain. The Morfran is the falcon's food." He clicked his beak in what was perhaps the avian equivalent of smacking one's lips. "Better than cheeseburgers."

"What happened last night, Evan?"

"I was perched on a rooftop near the harbor, looking out at the water and trying out different things I might say to Anne. I can't seem to figure out a way to break this"—he opened and closed his wings—"to her gently. So there I was, watching the planes come and go. Now that I think of it, Mab, I probably saw yours land. Anyway, all of a sudden there was this clamoring in my head. And hunger. Good lord, I've never felt so hungry. Like what I felt while reading the book, but stronger. I didn't even try to understand what was happening; I simply let this body act. I let the hunger guide me, and you saw what happened. The falcon wanted the Morfran."

"You expelled it from Bonita. That's the name of the zom—" I glanced at Kane. "I mean, the PDH who attacked Mab." Dad's talons hadn't done her face much good, but he'd saved her life by getting the Morfran out before it fed on her. Not that that mattered after Pryce grabbed her again.

"It's clear," Mab said, "that the falcon must remain at liberty to help us in the coming war. If we act now to destroy the

Morfran, Pryce's demon troops will never gain the strength to march out of Hell. We could *prevent* the war."

Silence fell upon the table. I closed my eyes against visions of Boston burning, of death and slaughter, of a bloody sword in my own hand. If only we could turn the path of fate so that instead of solidifying into reality, those visions would dissolve and fade like a bad dream. With the falcon's help, we might have a chance.

"So," Kane said, "let's look at what we're dealing with, point by point." His logical lawyer brain was taking control of the conversation. Good. He spoke dispassionately, holding up his free hand and counting off each point on his fingers. "One, there's my bargain with the Night Hag. Two, there's her threat to kill Vicky." He paused and looked at my father. "I've hired four of the country's top witches to shield her apartment during the full moon, if we can convince her to stay home."

"I already told you I can't promise that. And I still think you're wasting your money. That charm I wore didn't keep the Night Hag away; she blew it apart like dandelion fluff. When the Night Hag comes after me, nothing will stop her."

"Unless," Mab said, "we can think of a way to make Mallt-y-Nos call off her hounds." She nodded at Kane. "Please continue."

"Three"—he ticked off another finger—"the white falcon carries the spirit of Vicky's father. Four, the Night Hag wants the falcon. And five, the falcon can kill the Morfran—but only if it's free of the hag's control."

Each point felt like a hundred-pound weight settling on my shoulders. "See?" I said. "It's impossible."

"Hush, child. You can't think that way. There's always a solution." But the way the minutes stretched out, everyone staring gloomily at the table, seemed to contradict that notion.

"Okay." Dad's voice made me jump. "Let's say Vic did hand me over. Without the gauntlet, I mean—that was never part of the deal, right?"

"That's right."

"I'll escape again. The first time the hag sends me to dive-bomb some poor soul she's hunting, I'll fly away. Same as before."

"It's too risky." Mab shook her head. "Mallt-y-Nos would

not have proposed the exchange without some way of binding the falcon to her. If she gets her hands on you, Evan, I'm afraid there'll be no flying away this time."

"What about a substitute?" Kane said.

"Where would we get one?" I asked. "It's not like they sell white falcons at pet stores."

"True, but we might get something that's close enough. Remember when I was stuck in wolf form? Roxana Jade created a charm so that everyone who looked at me saw a German shepherd. We know that charm worked. If we got a different bird—a parakeet or a canary or something—and the charm gave it the appearance of the white falcon . . ."

"It wouldn't work." I shook my head. "The bird would have to wear the charm somewhere, and the hag will inspect every inch before she releases you."

"I believe Mr. Kane has the right idea," Mab said, her eyes alight. "Although we can effect the substitution much more simply. Victory, you will contact the Night Hag. Tell her you've agreed to the exchange, and set up a time and place."

"And then what? If not Dad or a charmed canary, what can I give her?"

"Me, of course. I'll shift into a white falcon."

# 21

I DIDN'T LIKE IT. IF HANDING DAD OVER TO THE NIGHT HAG was too risky, it was an equally bad idea to give her Mab. If anything went wrong, my aunt could end up as a hostage, or worse.

"Nonsense, child." Mab waved away my objections. "I've thought it through. We'll make a replica of the gauntlet, and you'll offer that to Mallt-y-Nos if—and only if—she promises to prevent her hounds from attacking you. She'll want to test it, of course. I'll be close by, and when she calls I'll arrive immediately. When she's convinced of the gauntlet's authenticity, I don't doubt she'll be willing to give whatever you want in exchange for it."

"But you said she must have some way of binding Dad to her. I don't want her doing that to you."

"I'm not a falcon, child. As soon as she's released Mr. Kane and vowed not to attack you, I'll resume my usual form."

Something would go wrong. I could feel it. I argued; I reasoned. I even considered pulling rank—if Mab really thought I was the Lady of the Cerddorion, maybe I should use that to my advantage. But I couldn't bear the thought of my aunt on her knees before me again. It wasn't right.

So eventually I agreed. I couldn't think of a better plan, and

I'd sacrificed weeks to my own indecision. As soon as darkness returned and she could ride forth, I'd call the Night Hag and set up our exchange.

Kane stood, announcing he had to get to the office. He said a general good-bye. Mab replied that it was a pleasure to see him again, but Dad fixed him with a cold predator's stare. I got up to walk him to the door.

"Your father doesn't like me." He said it as though puzzled. Kane was a charmer, and most people responded warmly to him. He had his enemies, of course, but they were usually political. His eyes held a question: *What did I do?*

I thought I knew. It wasn't anything Kane did; it was who he was. But that was Dad's problem, not Kane's, and I intended to have it out with my father as soon as Kane left.

"I'm sorry he was rude. You know how some fathers are. He's not used to the idea of me dating."

"Of you dating, or of you dating a werewolf?"

Kane was right on the money, but I didn't want to go there now. "It doesn't matter. Whatever the issue, it's his problem, not yours." My demon mark twinged as I thought about how unfair Dad was being. Kane had dedicated his life to fighting discrimination. He shouldn't have to face it from his girlfriend's father. "I'll make sure he understands that."

Kane pulled me into his arms for a kiss. "Thanks for standing by me. For saying what you said. Those are words I'll never get tired of hearing."

So before he left, we said them again.


WHEN KANE HAD GONE, I RETURNED TO THE KITCHEN. WITH each step across the living room, my irritation grew. My demon mark heated up to a slow burn, but the anger felt good. Dad had no right to judge Kane before he even knew him. It was an insult to both of us, and I wasn't going to put up with it.

I slammed open the kitchen door. "Dad," I yelled, "you were totally out of line."

Two heads turned to me. Mab muttered something about more tea and went over to the sink. My father's sharp, rainbow-eyed stare irritated me further. Okay, so it's impossible for a falcon to look contrite, but all I could see was defiance.

"You met my boyfriend for the first time, and you acted like . . . like . . . I don't even know what."

"Like a concerned father." Dad's voice was softer than his expression. "Two things, Vic. First, the whole thing was a complete surprise. I didn't know you had a boyfriend."

Was it really true I'd never mentioned Kane to my dad? I had a sinking feeling it was, but that only stoked the anger building inside me.

"Second," Dad continued, "the guy's a werewolf. There's no worse match for one of our kind—you know that, Vic."

I'd known it, but hearing him say the words made my simmering anger boil over into rage. I stood there unable to speak, my fists clenched. My demon mark felt like a hot coal inside my skin.

Dad went on. "I'm sure you like him, but you need to nip this thing in the bud before he gets serious. You know what werewolves are like. Once they start sniffing around, before you know it they're pressuring you to start a pack. It's not that I'm prejudiced or anything. It's their nature. Instinct is strong in werewolves. Sooner or later, it always wins out. And then where will you be? Stuck at home with a wolf cub while the demons run rampant."

The words gave voice to my own doubts, yet hearing them infuriated me. The kitchen dimmed as white-hot anger zeroed in on the falcon. I tensed, ready to lunge at the stupid bird. I'd wring its neck and toss its broken body aside like a limp rag. I'd—

"Victory." Mab's voice cut through the haze of anger. "Remember yourself."

I closed my eyes. The vision persisted—I could feel the bird's neck crack under my fingers, see the lifeless heap of feathers. *No. Stop. Not Dad.* I inhaled slowly, counting to five, feeling the air expand my lungs. I held it there, counting to five again. In my mind, my hands were still tight around the falcon's neck, but the edges of the vision blurred. I exhaled to another five counts, making an effort to empty my lungs. As I inhaled again, the vision dissolved.

In my mind's eye, my hands were empty. My father perched, unharmed, on the back of a chair. I kept my eyes closed, holding those images in place.

A few more rounds of focusing on my breathing drained away the anger. The demon mark's heat diminished to the level of a bad sunburn. I opened my eyes.

Where was Dad? The chair where he'd been perching was empty. Then I saw him on top of the fridge. He'd flown out of my reach. Yesterday I'd nearly gone after Mab with a sword. Today I'd been ready to wring my father's neck.

"You need to work on anger management, Vic."

"You're not the first to say so. But that doesn't make what you said okay."

The falcon ducked his head. "I'm only trying to protect you."

"I don't need protection. Not like that." *Deep breath, Vicky.* "My love life is my own business. Kane and I will work things out for ourselves."

"You really love him?"

"Yeah. I do." The effort of pushing away the anger collapsed my knees, and I sat down at the table.

"You can't argue with that, Evan." Mab came over with her mug of tea. "I understand your concern with Vicky's future. However, you'd do well to remember your own past. You may not be a werewolf, but I seem to recall that you once persuaded a skilled Cerddorion demon fighter to give up her career for you."

That ruffled Dad's feathers. "I didn't persuade Anne. It was her decision. Anyway, that was different. Vicky has a role to play."

"Only if she accepts it. And that's not a decision you—or I—can make for her." Mab glanced at me sidelong, and I wondered whether she was thinking about the Lady of the Cerddorion again. Because if it really was my choice, I could tell her right now: I didn't want the job. Nope. Mab was the Lady, not me. Not in a million years.

"All right," Dad said. He left his refrigerator perch and glided to a chair. "You're right, Vic. I was wrong. I'll apologize to the werewolf the next time I see him."

"The werewolf has a name, Dad. It's Kane." I reached out and scratched the falcon's head. He cooed and leaned into my hand, closing his rainbow-colored eyes. "I think you'll like him once you get to know him."

The falcon straightened, clucking. "We'll see. I mean, I'll

give it a shot. If he's important to you, I'll give him a chance. In the meantime, do you have any of those little cheeseburgers Juliet makes for me?"

I microwaved a package of sliders and put some bread in the toaster for Mab. I hadn't had time to pick up her favorite marmalade, but she graciously made do with strawberry jam.

By the time I brought everything over to the table, Dad and Mab had reached an agreement: As soon as the sun went down, the three of us would be at the Granary Burying Ground, the place where I'd imprisoned the Morfran Pryce had brought to Boston. Mab would release the Morfran from the old slate headstones, and Dad would kill it. I'd stand by to capture any Morfran that tried to escape. It was a good plan, and the sooner we could put it into action, the better.

Dad attacked the mini-cheeseburgers fiercely, devouring each in two bites. When he was finished, he stretched his wings and cleared his throat.

"I have an announcement," he said. "I'm going to take the plunge."

"You mean you're finally going to tell Mom?"

"Yes. Today. I don't want to put it off any longer."

"That's great, Dad. She'll be thrilled."

"You think so? I've been worried the whole situation will upset her."

"She's missed you for a long time." I knew how that felt. When Dad died, I thought I'd never get over my grief and guilt. When I found him again in the Darklands, it was clear things had changed, but I still had the essence of my father back. That's what counted.

"Ten years. But that's just it. By now, she's accepted that I'm dead. Gone. She's adjusted to the idea. We always told each other that if anything happened to one of us, we'd want the other to move on." His voice suddenly sounded small. "What if she has?"

"She's not dating anyone, if that's what you mean. She told me so."

"But don't you see? My return could mess up her life. I'm back, yes, but in this body." He opened and closed his wings. "It's painfully obvious that things can never be like they were between us. What if she doesn't want to be married to a bird? Or worse, what if she squelches her own life because she feels an obligation to this freak hybrid that holds some part of her long-lost husband? Or what if—"

"Come, come, Evan." Mab's no-nonsense tone cut Dad off mid-rant. "Stop torturing yourself. Best let her decide."

"Mab's right, Dad."

"I know. And now I realize that maybe I don't have all the time in the world. The Night Hag wants this body, and even if I escape her, it looks like the falcon will be on the front lines when Pryce leads the demons out of Hell. It'd be a real shame if I never got the chance to speak to Anne."

"It's the reason you escaped the Darklands," I said. "Sometimes you have to take risks." That was something I was learning, myself.

Dad didn't speak for a moment, staring into the distance. Then he blinked and puffed out his chest. "You're right," he said. "Let's do it. Today, before I lose my nerve again."

"We'll be rooting for you, Dad."

"You'll be doing more than that, Vic. At least, I hope you will. I need your help."

"What do you want us to do?"

"Set things up for me. Ring your mother, and tell her Mab is in town. Arrange a meeting in the park. Tell Anne to come alone."

It could work. Mom would love to see Mab, and she'd understand the need to get away from Gwen's house to do it. Gwen harbored bad feelings toward Mab, thanks to a twenty-year-old misunderstanding. Recently, Gwen had realized that past events were more complicated than she'd thought. She'd softened toward Mab, but only a little—not enough to invite her over. Now, when Dad revealed himself to Mom at the park, Mab and I would be there to offer them support. I had a feeling they'd need it.

"I would enjoy seeing your mother again, Victory."

"Okay." I turned to Dad. "What time do you want me to set up the meeting?"

"How soon can you drive out there?"

Wow, Dad really had made up his mind. "It depends. Let

me see what the restriction code is." If they'd raised the code back to red or orange after the zombie attack at Logan, I'd have trouble getting Mab out of Deadtown.

Dad paced back and forth on the table, pecking at cheeseburger crumbs, as I called the hotline to check.

"We're good," I told him. "It's still yellow. Let me call Mom and see what she says."

My luck held. Gwen had taken Justin, her youngest, to a swim class at the Y. Mom said she'd love to see Mab and could meet us at the park at ten.

"Okay, Dad," I said after I hung up. "You've got a date with destiny in two hours."

"Two hours?" It was hard to tell with a white falcon, but I could swear he paled a couple of shades. "Gotta go. I have to practice my speech."

"Evan, it's Anne," Mab said. "Your wife. The mother of your girls. A speech is not required."

The falcon bobbed his head in a distracted nod and took off, flying straight through the ceiling. He was off to meet his date with destiny.

# 22

I HALF DREADED THE DRIVE OUT TO NEEDHAM, BECAUSE I expected Mab to start up with her Lady of the Cerddorion talk again. But as soon as we got through the checkpoints, her eyes closed and her head lolled back against the seat. An occasional snore erupted from her sleeping face. Once or twice, she snorted so loudly she woke herself up, putting her hand on her chest and exclaiming, "Goodness!" before plunging immediately back into sleep.

As I drove, I thought about Dad's remarks about werewolves. About Kane. He was wrong to jump to conclusions before he'd gotten to know Kane, but some niggling doubt deep in my gut reminded me that not long ago I'd been thinking the same thing. *Face it, Vicky. It's exactly why you've always held back.*

It was true. The first time Kane invited me to join him at his werewolf retreat, I balked because I thought he wanted to change me. I'm a shapeshifter, not a werewolf, I'd insisted, worried he'd expect me to spend each full moon as a wolf. Worried he wanted more from me than I could give—like a family. Later, I was even ready to let him go, to end our relationship so he could pair off with a more suitable mate, only to find he wanted me.

He wanted *me*.

Even now, I could hardly believe it. Kane was the most eligible lone wolf in Boston. He could have his pick of sexy, smart, successful females of his own kind. Yet he wanted a shapeshifter with a stubborn personality and serious commitment issues.

I knew why the demon mark had tapped so easily into my anger at Dad: His words touched a fear I didn't want to admit. However much Kane and I loved each other—and I could no longer doubt that we *did* love each other—we'd never get our happily ever after. We couldn't. We were too different.

Beside me, Mab gave a decidedly unladylike snort and said, "Goodness!" This time, though, she sat up straight in her seat. She stretched both arms out in front of her, wriggling a bit as if working some kinks out of her shoulders. "Where are we?" she asked, leaning forward to peer through the windshield.

"Getting close. The park's a couple of miles more."

Mab watched the buildings go by as we drove down streets lined with single-family houses: colonials and Cape Cods. "So this is where Gwen has made her home. She's done well for herself."

"It's a good place for kids to grow up. And it's close enough to Boston that Nick's commute isn't bad. Gwen's on friendly terms with everyone in her neighborhood. She belongs to a book club and is on various committees. It's the life she always wanted."

"But not a life for you, eh?" I could feel Mab studying my profile as I kept my eyes on the road. "Child, no one is asking you to choose one life or the other. Don't give too much weight to your father's concerns. I'll admit, when I first met Mr. Kane I shared them to some degree. Although I can't claim to know him well, I've seen enough to believe your young man would never ask you to sacrifice what's important to you."

I couldn't help it; the thoughts I'd been having during the drive surfaced. "What if he can't help it, Mab? Instinct is a powerful thing."

"So is love. Perhaps what he loves in you is precisely the thing you're afraid of losing. He will fight hard to protect that, Victory. He won't ask you to give it up."

*Wow.* I was talking to Aunt Mab, battle-hardened demon

fighter, about my relationship—and what she was saying made sense. "Have you started moonlighting as an advice columnist or something? 'Ask Aunt Mab'—you'd have a readership of millions."

Mab laughed in a voiceless rush of air as she waved away my suggestion. "Given my own history, I hardly think anyone would be the slightest bit interested."

I was about to ask her what she meant, when she exclaimed, "Look, there's Anne!" Mom, sitting on a bench, stood when she saw the Jag. She looked good, her shoulder-length white hair and trim figure making her seem younger than her sixty years. Mab was opening the door before I'd finished parking.

They trotted to each other and embraced. By the time I got out of the car and walked over, they sat on the bench together, each gripping the other's hands as if afraid she'd float away.

Mom stood as I approached, and we hugged. It always amazed me how my mother's scent, vanilla and Jean Naté cologne, brought back my entire childhood in a rush. Instead of in this park, we could be standing in the kitchen of our old triple-decker in Somerville, schoolbooks open on the table and dinner simmering on the stove, waiting for Dad to get home. We both stepped back, and the image faded.

"Vicky, thank you for driving Mab all the way out here." Mom sat down and again took both of Mab's hands in hers. "I wish I could invite you back to the house, but . . ."

"I know," Mab said. "It's all right. Gwen and I are not precisely friends, but we have declared something of a truce. Perhaps she'll come around in time; perhaps she won't. Some things are beyond my control." Her shoulders rose and fell in a slight shrug. "I do regret, though, that I've been unable to meet the children. Maria seems a remarkable young girl."

"Gwen is very protective of them," Mom said. "Maria especially."

A flicker of sadness crossed Mab's face at the suggestion Maria needed protection from her. "I do understand. I must say, Anne, you're looking very well."

Mom smoothed her sleek white hair, even though it didn't need smoothing. "I'm getting old, Mab. But what can you do? It beats the alternative." She smiled. "You, on the other hand, seem to be getting younger. What's your secret?"

I wondered whether Mom knew Mab's true age—and if so, whether she'd want her own life to stretch over three centuries and more. Mab was strong and energetic, the most sensible person I knew. Lately, though, I'd caught glimpses of a deep emotion, sorrow perhaps, buried beneath Mab's brusque demeanor. Like in the car, when she'd alluded to her history. She never explained, and she never let it show for more than a moment, but something was there.

I wondered what it was.

I scanned the sky, watching for Dad to appear. The jitters in my stomach told me I was almost as nervous as he must be. I wanted this to go well for him. It *had* to—Mom would be as happy to have him back as I was. Wouldn't she? It had been such a joy to hear his voice and listen to his words, exasperating as they were sometimes. Yet that was part of it, too. Dad here, in real time, not locked away in memories that faded with each passing day. Yes, hearing that voice coming from a falcon's beak took a little getting used to, but . . .

And there was the problem, in that little word *but*. What if Mom couldn't handle it? Like Gwen, she'd chosen a normal life, one of mundane daily chores, family vacations, dinners around the kitchen table. In Florida, she lived in a retirement community where she played tennis, entered bridge tournaments, and attended classical concerts. Having your dead husband return in the body of a huge white bird was not part of that life.

I looked around again. No sign of the falcon. *Come on, Dad. Don't lose your nerve.*

Mom was asking Mab about Jenkins and his wife, Rose, who helped Mab run Maenllyd, her manor house in north Wales. As Mab launched into an anecdote about the garden, I excused myself and started walking the perimeter of the park. Maybe Dad was hiding somewhere, watching. If I spotted him, I could give him a pep talk.

I saw mothers pushing strollers. I saw kids zipping down slides, swinging from monkey bars, and kicking high into the air on the swings. I saw an empty potato chip bag blowing across the grass—I picked that up and dropped it in a trash can. But I didn't see the white falcon.

Had something happened to him? The Night Hag couldn't

attack in daylight, and Mab was keeping the gauntlet with her. I headed back toward the bench where my aunt and my mother sat together. I was almost ready to use the gauntlet to make Dad arrive and reveal himself.

"Vicky," Mom called as I approached. "Do you remember that Christmas at Maenllyd when you and Gwen snuck downstairs to spy on Father Christmas and caught Dad putting presents under the tree?"

I smiled. "He thought he was busted, but he managed to convince us he'd heard someone in the parlor and was checking to make sure Father Christmas had delivered the presents to the right address. He made it so real, I was sure I saw boot prints on the hearth."

"Your father always was quite the storyteller." Her smile was sad. "I do miss him. Not a day goes by when I don't."

A shadow soared over us, and something fell from the sky. Mom started as it landed in her lap. "Oh!" she exclaimed. "What on earth . . . ?" She looked up, searching overhead. So did I. But there was nothing there.

When I looked back at Mom, she was crying. She clutched a flower, pressing it to her chest. Mab, one arm around her, awkwardly patted her shoulder.

"What is it, Mom?"

She couldn't speak. Instead, she held out the flower. It was a long-stemmed rose, the petals a soft shade of lavender, with deep pink at the base.

"It's . . . it's not possible."

I sat down beside her. Mab pulled back as I enfolded Mom in a hug. But she squirmed free, eager to talk.

"This rose, it's special," she said, her cheeks shiny with tears.

"It's beautiful," I said. "I've never seen colors like that."

"That's just it." Clutching the flower, she dug a handkerchief from her purse and blew her nose. "Your father . . ." She paused as if searching for the right words. "Where to begin? With the flower show, I suppose. It was years ago, before we moved to the States. We'd been courting for some time, and I convinced Evan to accompany me to a flower show in Cardiff. Flowers were of no interest to him, but he agreed. I was in heaven—you know how I've always loved gardening—especially looking at the roses. There was one variety I couldn't stop admiring. Deep pink in the center and lavender in the petals. Evan said, 'Yes, yes, very nice,' but he said the same thing for each display. He seemed bored, to be honest, and happy when we left the show and went to a pub."

She stared at the rose, turning it in her fingers. Tears brimmed again. "The next day, he presented me with a rose like this one and asked me to marry him. Oh, Evan." She pressed the flower against her face, inhaling its fragrance. "How I do miss you."

Mab patted my mother's knee. "Those we love are never truly gone," she said quietly. "They live on in memory, of course, but sometimes they also return to us in unexpected ways."

Mom nodded, her tears dampening the rose petals, but she didn't reply.

"She's right, Anne." Dad's voice drifted down from above us. Mom stared, then jumped to her feet. The rose fell to the ground as she searched the branches.

"Evan?" She looked at Mab, then at me, her eyes asking us whether she'd lost her mind.

"It's me, love. But you might find me, um, somewhat changed."

The falcon dropped from the tree. Gently, he picked up the rose in his beak, then flew to perch on the back of the bench. Regarding my mother with rainbow eyes, he spoke around the stem.

"I couldn't let a little thing like death keep us apart. I came back because of you, my love. Only because of you."

# 23

MY MOTHER FROZE, HER RAPIDLY BLINKING EYELIDS THE only part of her that moved. Then she swallowed hard—once, twice. Slowly she lifted her hand and took the rose from the falcon's beak.

"How . . . ?" Her voice faltered in her inability to frame the question.

"It's a long story. Isn't it, Vic?" Mom's head swiveled toward me, then back toward the falcon as Dad continued speaking. "But we've got all the time in the world to tell it."

Mab cleared her throat.

"Well, not *all* the time in the world," Dad amended, "but enough. To make a start, anyway." Dad fell silent as a couple of young mothers pushed strollers toward us. They stopped, staring at the falcon—he was an unusual sight, even when he wasn't talking—and changed their course, hurrying off in the other direction.

When they were out of earshot, Dad said, "Anne, let's find a place where we can speak without gawkers. I know a quiet corner." The falcon launched into the sky, circled once, then landed again. "Will you follow me?" he asked.

Mom brushed the rose petals with her fingers. "Of course I will."

Dad let out a very falcon-like squawk and took off again. Watching the sky, Mom set out across the park. She walked quickly, stumbling here and there on the uneven ground. But she never took her eyes off the falcon that flew before her.

Mab still sat on the bench. I plopped down beside her, feeling like a tangled heap of limp noodles. "That was exhausting," I said. "But I think it went well, don't you?"

"I do. Anne is in a bit of shock, as may be expected. I felt the same when the falcon first spoke to me. She's probably wondering when she'll wake up." She smiled her thin smile. "Becoming reacquainted may well be more difficult than either of them anticipates, but I do believe they'll work out their differences."

An inactive shapeshifter who'd been widowed ten years ago, and her long-dead husband in the form of a man-falcon hybrid. Yeah, those were some differences to work out. But I agreed with Mab. If anyone could overcome differences like that, it was my parents.

The warm glow of that thought snuffed out as I wondered again about the differences that stood between Kane and me. I shoved the thought aside. I couldn't figure out the answer by myself, and anyway I was too tired to try.

The warm May sunshine played over my skin, making me drowsy. "Do you mind if I stretch out on the grass and take a nap?" I asked. "It's past my bedtime." Not that I had a normal bedtime, although like most of Deadtown I was up at night and slept during the day.

"Of course, milady. You sleep. I'll watch over you."

Had she called me lady again? Maybe I'd misheard her. I suddenly felt too sleepy to worry about it. The grass was soft and fragrant with new growth. I took off my jacket—the day was warm enough that I didn't need it—and rolled it up to use as a pillow. I lay on my back, an arm thrown over my eyes. It was good to feel the solid earth support my body, to let the stress drain from my limbs. To let go of the tension that propelled me through my days and nights. To know Mab was here, watching over me. Sleep crept into the edges of my consciousness, and I let it take me.

\* \* \*

"AUNT VICKY? IS THAT YOU?"

A girl's voice snatched away the warm blanket of sleep. I blinked and sat up, looking around.

Maria straddled her bicycle on a path about ten feet from where I'd been lying. Her blue eyes squinted at me from under her pink bike helmet.

"It *is* you!" She took off her helmet and shook out her long blonde hair. "What are you doing here? Are you coming over to our house? Where's Grandma?"

I shaded my eyes with my hand. "Shouldn't you be in school?"

She shook her head and rolled her eyes simultaneously. I wondered if the maneuver took practice. "It's Saturday."

"Is it? Guess I lost track." One of the hazards of having a job with no regular hours. I stood, brushing grass from my jeans. I retrieved my wrinkled jacket and shook it out.

"Why are you sleeping in the park?"

"Because I was tired." That earned me another eye roll. "What are you doing here?"

"Looking for Grandma. It was weird this morning. She was talking on the phone, and then she said she had to go to the park. I wanted to come with her, but she wouldn't let me. She said, 'Maybe later.' I figured it was later." Maria got off her bike and wheeled it over the grass. Suddenly she stopped, looking past me. "Do I know you?"

My heart nearly quit beating. Mab, sitting on the bench. In my disorientation, I'd forgotten she was there.

"Hello, Maria. I'm Aunt Mab."

"I thought so!" Maria dropped her bike and stood there, her eyes going from Mab to me and back again to Mab. "I recognize you from my dream."

Once, Maria had allowed Mab to pass through her dreamscape and into Boston. Doing so had saved my life. But since then Gwen had told Mab to stay away from her daughter. Other than that single encounter, Maria didn't know Mab at all.

"I'm very pleased to meet you in person at last," Mab said, extending her hand.

Maria glanced at me. Then she stepped forward and took

Mab's hand, standing very straight as she pumped it up and down. "Pleased to meet you, too," she said in her best grown-up voice. She let go, and her forehead wrinkled. "Why doesn't Mom want me to talk to you?"

Mab raised her eyebrows at me, then turned to Maria. "Your mother won't explain, and she made it clear it wasn't my place to weigh in. Lately it seemed like she was softening up a little, and I hoped—"

"Mom? Softening up? *Please.*"

"You must be patient with your mother, young lady. Many years ago, more than twenty now, she had a serious fright. It troubled her deeply, and I'm sad to say it led to a misunderstanding between her and me. We've made some progress in resolving it, but Gwen remains hurt and confused."

"After twenty years? That's longer than I've been *alive.* Why can't she just get over it already?"

"Maria." The sharpness in my own voice reminded me of Mab. "Don't be unkind."

"Sorry. But it's not fair to keep me away from my own great-aunt and not even tell me why."

The kid had a point. Yet I had no right to interfere with Gwen's parenting. Gwen had her blind spots, but she was a good mom.

Maria sat down on the bench beside Mab. "I thought you live in Wales."

"I do. I've come to Boston to help Vicky with a project."

"A project? You make it sound like arts and crafts. But it's not, I bet. It's about demons, right?"

"Among other things."

"That's my job, Maria," I said. "You know that."

But Maria couldn't take her eyes off Mab. "You're a shapeshifter, too?"

"I am. I understand you're well on your way to joining us."

Maria nodded solemnly. "I've had shifting dreams, where I become a bird or a fish or something. And I get that false face thing, when it feels like my face has turned halfway into an animal's, a couple of times a week. Oh, and Aunt Vicky taught me how to make my dreamscape into anything I want it to be. We talk on the dream phone sometimes. Don't we, Aunt Vicky?"

I nodded, but Mab was the one who spoke. "It won't be long before you're able to change your shape. How do you feel about that?"

"Scared, a little." Maria bit her lip. "If I become a shape-shifter, do I *have* to fight demons?"

"No, Maria," I said putting a hand on her hair. "You don't have to do anything you don't want to. If you want to learn about demons, I'll teach you. If not, well, shapeshifting can be fun."

"What kind of animal would you like to try out first?" asked Mab.

"I've been thinking about that," said Maria. "A seagull. I want to soar out over the ocean and see the waves from above." She looked up at the sky, then back at Mab. "Or maybe a cat. They're so graceful." She began a cat stretch and then spun it into a pirouette.

"Maria's a dancer," I told Mab.

"My friend Kelsey has a cat, and sometimes when I watch him, like when he jumps up onto a table by the window, I think he'd make a good dancer. I'd like to be able to move like that."

"Well, you decide," Mab said. "And once you have, let Vicky know."

"We'll spend some time together in your dreamscape so you can practice being that animal in your dreams," I said. "That makes things easier when it's time to shift for real."

Maria nodded but turned a shade paler. "What if shifting sneaks up on me and I'm not ready?"

"We won't let that happen," I said. "We'll try shifting on purpose. It won't happen for a while, but trying means when it *does* happen, it'll be under your control. Once you've decided, we'll tell your mom which animal you're focusing on. That way, on the off-chance that you start to shift when I'm not around, she'll be able to help."

"So first practice in my dreams and then start trying for real. That makes sense, I guess." Letting the subject drop, she looked around. "Where's Grandma? Did you see her?" Her eyes widened with comprehension. "Oh! She must have come here to see Great-Aunt Mab. Because Mom would never let her invite Mab home." She stopped and covered her mouth with both hands, as if worried she'd said something rude.

"It's all right, child," said Mab. "You're quite correct."

"But Grandma likes you. And Aunt Vicky likes you, so I wish—"

Maria never got to express her wish, because at that moment a car horn sounded from the street. She and I both spotted Gwen's minivan at the same time.

"Oh, no!" said Maria. "It's Mom. Quick, run!"

She sprinted over to where her bike lay on the grass and was halfway on it when I caught up with her. "Don't run, Maria. It would only make your mom angrier. Come back, and we'll talk to her like grown-ups."

Usually Maria liked being referred to as a grown-up, but not when it meant facing her mother's wrath. "I'm just a kid," she muttered, but she didn't get on the bike. With me beside her, she wheeled it to where Mab sat.

If we had decided to run, we could have been halfway back to Boston by the time Gwen had found a place to park; assembled the stroller and wrestled two-year-old Justin into it; grabbed the hand of Zack, her six-year-old; and stormed over to us.

Maria stood straight, but her chin quivered. I dropped my arm across her shoulders and pulled her close to my side.

"What do you think you're doing?" Gwen's enraged face looked at each of us in turn, including all three in her question.

"Hello, Gwen," said Mab quietly. "It's been a long time."

"And I had every intention of keeping it that way! I *told* you to stay away from my daughter. And Maria, you know perfectly well you're not supposed to talk to that woman."

Zack pulled away from his mother's grasp. "What woman? Aunt Vicky?" He peered around Gwen's legs to see Mab. "Oh. Not Aunt Vicky. Who are you?"

Gripping Zack by his shoulder, Gwen pushed him behind her. Her angry gaze burned holes in me. "I never expected you to betray me."

"Gwen, you're overreacting." I kept my voice level. "Nobody's betraying anyone. Let me explain."

"I don't want explanations! I want Maria to get in the van and come home with me. Now!" Gwen's shouts were attracting attention; a group of kids stopped their soccer game to stare. The two mothers who'd steered their strollers away earlier now angled them closer. Gwen didn't seem to notice, or maybe she didn't care. She continued laying into me.

"I asked you to help me with what Maria's facing, and the first thing you do is drag her off behind my back to meet that old bag. Well, forget it, Vicky. I can't trust you. Mom's here now. We don't need you."

"Yes, we do! *I* do!" Maria threw both arms around my waist.

"Maria, pick up your bike and get in the van."

"I won't! You can't run my life. You think you can, but I won't let you! Do you hear me? *I won't let you!*" She buried her face in my side, sobbing.

"What's going on here?" Mom hurried across the grass. I scanned the sky but didn't see Dad anywhere. "Gwen, what's got you and Maria so upset?"

"Upset? Who says I'm upset? I'm shocked, that's all. Shocked that I came out looking for Maria to learn that she'd snuck off to meet . . . to meet *her*." Looking like a Puritan at a seventeenth-century witch trial, Gwen pointed an accusing finger at Mab.

"That's not what happened." Mom's voice was calm, and Gwen let her arm fall to her side. "Vicky called to let me know Mab was in town, and we agreed to meet here. We chose the park specifically because we didn't want to upset you."

Gwen's mouth hung open, but her eyes narrowed in disbelief.

"It's true, Gwen," I added. "Mom told Maria she wanted to go to the park alone. Maria followed her."

"Gwendolyn." Mab's voice was quiet. "Although I was hurt by your refusal to introduce me to your children, I always respected it. We met today by accident."

"Not 'always,' " Gwen growled. At least she wasn't shouting anymore. "You barged into Maria's dream. The poor child didn't understand what was going on."

"She helped save Vicky's life," Mab said. "As did you not long after, when I entered your dreamscape to ask for your help." When my sister didn't answer, Mab pressed on. "It may be too much to expect that we'll ever be friends. But surely you know I'm not your enemy."

Justin bounced up and down in his stroller. "Birdie!" he shouted.

A white falcon perched on the next bench.

"Nice birdie!" Justin waved his arms and struggled to escape the stroller. "Want birdie!"

"Hush, Justin. Here, have some apple juice. Yummy." She dug a sippy cup out of a bag attached to the stroller and handed it to the boy.

"We've seen that bird a lot," Zack explained. "Mostly at the park, but sometimes at our house. Justin talks to it."

Justin threw his apple juice on the ground. "Birdie talk! Birdie talk!"

"Enough about the bird," Gwen said. "The point is, I'm Maria's mother. And I expect all of you—and that includes you, young lady—to respect my parenting decisions."

"Funny," said a voice from the next bench. "That sounds a lot like what I used to say when my older daughter insisted on coming home after curfew."

"Birdie talk!" screeched Justin, delighted.

"Hi there, Justin," continued the voice. "How's Grandpa's big boy?"

"Birdie Grandpa!"

"Holy cow," said Zack, giving himself an exaggerated smack on the forehead. "Justin was right!"

All the color drained from Gwen's face. She turned slowly. On the next bench sat the white falcon, no one else.

Mom stepped forward and took Gwen's arm. "It's your father, Gwen. He's come back to us."

"My grandpa is a *bird*?" Zack smacked his forehead again.

"There have been stranger things in this family," Gwen muttered. She wiggled her shoulders, as though trying to wake herself up. "Dad—?" She cut herself off as she looked around, taking in our growing audience.

"Obviously," she said, "we can't continue this conversation here. I suppose we'd better go back to the house. You, too." She nodded sharply at Mab, then paused. "If you'd like."

"I'd be delighted," Mab replied.

# 24

BY THE TIME MAB AND I ARRIVED AT GWEN'S HOUSE, MY sister had already put on the coffee and set out a selection of Danish on a silver tray. It was how she coped when she was nervous: becoming the World's Greatest Hostess. The Queen of England wouldn't have felt out of place seated with us in Gwen's living room for a midmorning snack.

Which is not to say that Mab was comfortable in this setting. She sat on the edge of her chair, her back board-straight. She balanced a full cup of coffee in her lap. Mab doesn't drink coffee, but she hadn't asked Gwen for tea, and Gwen hadn't offered.

Dad perched on the coffee table, letting Justin pat his head.

"Careful, Justin," Mom cautioned as the pats got too enthusiastic. "Gentle strokes, like this." Dad closed his eyes and sighed as Mom smoothed her slim fingers over his head and along the feathers of his neck. "See? Gentle."

"Gen'le," Justin repeated. "Nice birdie."

"That's right, sweetheart," Mom said, settling back in her chair. She grinned at Dad. In fact, she hadn't stopped grinning at Dad since we got here. It was like her smile held him here, near her. Dad watched her just as intently. He couldn't shape the falcon's beak into a smile, but his rainbow eyes were alight with happiness.

"Justin, honey, leave the birdie alone now," Gwen coaxed. "Here, do you want to play with your choo-choo?"

Justin ignored her. "Nice birdie."

"The birdie wants to . . . um, tell us his story now." She closed her eyes for a moment as though she couldn't quite believe those words had come out of her mouth.

"Story?" Justin asked, pausing in mid-stroke. "Birdie talk?" He sat on the floor and waited.

Dad flew up and perched on the sofa by Mom's shoulder, out of the toddler's reach.

"I take it, Dad, that today isn't the first time you've talked to Justin," Gwen said, not managing to filter the disapproval from her tone.

"He recognized me," Dad said.

"That's true!" Maria exclaimed. She sat cross-legged on the floor beside my chair. "One day we were at the park, and Justin pointed at the tree and shouted, 'Grandpa!' "

Zack laughed. "Yeah, and we looked up in the tree and saw the bird. I told Justin he was a silly billy." He stared at the falcon with round eyes. "But he was right. I guess *I* was the silly billy." He dropped to his hands and knees and crawled over to his brother. "Who's a silly billy?" he asked, waggling his head in Justin's face. Justin squealed with laughter.

"So here's what happened—" Dad began.

"Wait." Gwen held out a hand. "I'm not sure this is appropriate for the children to hear. Maria, why don't you take your brothers outside?"

*"Mom."* The word emerged in a well-practiced whine. "I'm not a child. I want to hear." This from the same girl who, half an hour ago, had exclaimed in a panic *I'm just a kid.* Eleven is such a fun age.

"It's all right, Gwen," Mom said. "I've heard Evan's story. There's nothing frightening in it. And I think perhaps it would benefit the children to understand how their grandfather came to his present condition. Leaving them in the dark would only cause confusion."

Maria leaned forward but didn't chime in. Smart girl. Gwen chewed her lip as she considered. "I suppose you're right," she said finally. "But I reserve the right to stop everything and send the children outside if I decide otherwise."

"Fair enough," Dad said, his voice covering Maria's squeak of protest.

Gwen pursed her lips, ready to cut him off.

"Well, then. Once upon a time, a man wandered into a far-off land . . ." Dad launched into the story of his time in the Darklands, framing it in fairy-tale language. To the younger kids, it would be just a story. To the rest of us, it was Dad's history.

As Dad spoke, faces turned toward him in rapt attention, I realized that this was the first time the whole family had been together. Ever. Dad died when Maria was a baby. He'd never seen Zachary or Justin. So it was nothing short of miraculous that Justin had looked at the falcon and seen his grandfather. A lump formed in my throat as I thought about how strong the bonds of family could be.

Would they be strong enough for Gwen and Mab to make peace? I hoped so, yet Gwen hadn't looked at Mab once since we'd arrived. Even while handing Mab that still-undrunk cup of coffee, she'd turned her head away. Now, Mab gazed sadly at Gwen, as though remembering the girl she used to be before things went wrong between them. Several lifetimes ago, long before her current incarnation, Mab had lost a sister, and she'd carried the pain of that loss ever since. Losing Gwen must have hurt nearly as much.

Dad was wrapping up his story. Justin, who'd lost interest, was pushing his choo-choo around the floor, making whispered train sounds.

"And so I hung around the neighborhood for the past few weeks, watching you all and getting my nerve up to speak to Anne. Although I've almost gotten used to this body now, I realize it's a shock to hear my voice coming out of this beak. I was . . . well, I was afraid it might be too freaky. That you wouldn't want me around."

"It is freaky, darling." Mom scratched his head, and he wriggled with pleasure. "But we definitely want you around." She looked pointedly at Gwen. "After all, we're Cerddorion. We've always known that the person is more important than the form."

Beside me, Maria gasped and sat up straighter, as though Mom's words had turned on a lightbulb in her head.

"Dad," Gwen said, making the word sound almost like a question, like she was still getting used to it. "Of course you're welcome here. But we'll have to set some ground rules."

"Sure, Gwennie. I don't want to cause problems with your neighbors."

"It's more than that, Dad. If the authorities find out, they'll force you to live in Deadtown."

"Hey!" I objected. Gwen made living in Deadtown sound like being shut up in some pitch-black, airless dungeon. We had our problems, but there were worse places to live. Personally, I wouldn't last two weeks in the suburbs.

Dad chuckled. "I'd like to see them try. I've seen the checkpoints, but those are street level." He stretched out his wings. "They don't control the airspace."

"Be that as it may, here are the rules. One, when you're outside, you act like a real bird. No talking. No . . . I don't know . . . no playing Frisbee or whatever. Two, try not to spend too much time here. At this address, I mean. People in the neighborhood have noticed you, and some have talked about bringing in a wildlife relocation expert. A falcon is a predator, and it makes folks nervous. Mrs. Baumann, three houses down, is terrified you're going to snatch her Chihuahua."

"Okay," Dad laughed. "Keep a low profile and no snatching the Chihuahua. No problem."

"I'm serious, Dad. I've worked hard to build a life here, to be accepted and fit in."

"And you think I'll mess that up."

Gwen's hands twisted in her lap.

"Perhaps I ought to look for my own place," said Mom. "Now that I've found Evan I'm not going to lose him again. I don't care what shape he's taken on."

"No, Mom, don't. I'm sorry. But, you know, it *is* a shock. I'm just trying to figure out how to adjust." Gwen pressed both hands over her eyes, as though dealing with a headache. But when she looked at Dad, her eyes were clear. "Dad, I'm happy you're back. I'm eager to get to know you again. I'm thrilled the kids will have their grandfather. But I need a little time to wrap my mind around the fact that their grandfather is a bird.

Yes, my heritage is Cerddorion. But I've spent most of my life trying to be normal. This is not normal, not even for our kind. Please be patient while I figure out how to make room for it in my life."

*Wow.* That was quite a speech, coming from Gwen. For so many years, she'd wanted nothing to do with being Cerddorion. She'd tolerated me because I was her sister and because she knew I wouldn't embarrass her by suddenly shifting into a donkey or something at a cocktail party. She'd wanted so badly for her daughter to grow up human, to be what Gwen considered a "normal" girl. Maybe being forced to accept that Maria was a shapeshifter was making Gwen reconsider her own relationship to our kind. She wasn't exactly embracing her heritage, but her willingness to make some room for it was a big step.

No one said anything, leaving Gwen's words to hang in the air like smoke. Even Justin quit *choo-chooing* and looked up. It struck me for the first time how out of place my sister must feel in our family. How strange it must be to step away from the people you grew up with, and then turn around to watch them, your nose pressed against an unbreakable window of your own making.

Gwen's face reddened as the silence stretched out.

Mab's cup clattered as she set it on the table in front of her. "I must say, Gwendolyn, you have a very lovely home."

Gwen blinked, and for the first time in an hour looked directly at Mab. "And *I* must say that I never expected to see you in it." They stared at each other across the coffee table.

"Nor did I expect to be here." Mab's voice stayed calm and level. "Thank you for inviting me."

Gwen barked a bitter laugh. "Why are you here, Mab? In Boston, I mean. No one told me you were coming." Gwen sounded a little hurt at the exclusion, and I remember how she told me, after Mab's last visit, that she'd almost attended the bon voyage party.

"I'm here to support Victory. She's preparing to face some challenges, and I've come to back her up."

"You? Playing backup?" Another sharp laugh. "I thought you always had to be front and center."

"Did you?" Mab's question, which sounded genuine, showed no sign she'd taken offense.

"You know, I've accepted that I was wrong about—" Gwen cut herself off as she glanced at her kids. "About what happened all those years ago. But that doesn't mean I like you. And it doesn't mean I want Maria to—" Again she stopped and looked around. Her mouth opened and closed as though she couldn't get the words out with so many people present.

I stood up. "I think Gwen and Mab could use a little time alone. Let's go outside, kids." Zack jumped up and ran into the kitchen, toward the back door. Justin toddled after him. Maria looked like she was going to protest, but when she saw my expression she unfolded her long legs and got up.

"Good idea," said Mom. "Evan, I'll close the garage door, and you can follow me out. The neighbors would have to peer in the windows to see us."

"Well, then it would serve them right," Gwen said, with a strained smile. She was trying, but everything about her—her face, her posture, her voice—was tight, ready to snap. I hoped I wasn't making a mistake, leaving her alone with Mab. But it had to be better than hashing out their differences in front of an audience.

"Would you like some tea?" Gwen's voice asked as I went through the kitchen. Yes, Gwen was tense, and maybe tying on her hostess apron was a way to avoid talking. But, on the other hand, maybe it was a start.


I'D EXPECTED A BARRAGE OF QUESTIONS FROM MARIA, BUT she held back whatever may have been bubbling up inside her. As I closed the kitchen door behind me, she'd already organized a game of Wiffle ball. Maria pitched, Zack swung an oversized plastic bat, and, whether Zack hit or missed, Justin scurried after the ball. He'd pick it up, run over to a spot about two feet from Maria, lift his arm as high as he could reach, and then hurl the ball at her feet.

As I sat on Gwen's deck watching the kids play, I wondered what was going on in the living room. I wasn't entirely sure that my impulse to clear everyone out had been a good one, but neither Mab nor Gwen had objected. That had to mean they wanted to talk, right? As Maria clapped and shouted, "Good one, Zack," I strained my hearing toward the house. No yelling.

Even though we were in the backyard and the living room faces the front, the windows were open, so if they were tearing each other apart in there I was bound to hear something.

I kept checking my watch as the minutes shuffled by in a slow parade. After twenty minutes that felt like two hours, the kitchen door opened. Mab stepped out, turning her head back inside and saying, "Yes, I'll be sure to tell her." She shut the door behind her and stood blinking in the bright sunlight. Her face gave nothing away.

The yard behind me was silent. Their game halted, all three kids stood staring. "It was nice meeting you, children!" Mab called, waving. She took my arm and propelled me toward the garage. "We must go now."

"Mab, what happened?"

"Patience, child. Let's be off first."

"I should say good-bye to Gwen."

"There's no need. She said she'll telephone you." Pushing open the garage's back door, she called, "Anne? Evan? We're on our way. I shall see both of you again soon."

"Bye, Mom. Bye, Dad," I shouted past her. I turned around and waved. "Bye, kids!"

Maria, already heading toward the house with a determined set to her jaw, threw up her arm in a wave without breaking her stride. I hoped Gwen was ready for the interrogation she was about to face.

By the time I'd backed out of the driveway and driven as far as Gwen's next-door neighbor, I couldn't stand the suspense any longer. "Come on, Mab, tell me. How did it go?"

Mab's head lay still against the headrest. Her eyes were closed, her lips pressed tightly together in a thin line. Her skin was papery white. She looked like she'd just emerged from a battlefield, rather than my sister's suburban living room. Then again, not all battles are fought on a field.

"Fine, child." Her eyes remained closed, and her hand went to the bloodstone pendant, pulling it from her shirt and closing her fingers around it. "Emotionally draining—for both of us, I think. Your sister and I have quite a long journey ahead if we're ever to reach common ground. But we've taken our first steps. The fact that Gwen was willing to set foot on that road at all is enormously encouraging to me."

"But what did she say?"

"I understand your curiosity. Even so, some things are private, child."

She fell silent, fingering the bloodstone. I bit my lip to hold back the questions that swirled through my mind. Some things were private, fair enough, but this feud had affected more than just the two of them. I thought of Maria's determined face as she marched into the house. It was great that Mab and Gwen had declared a truce—or at least, that's what Mab's words suggested—but what did that mean for Maria? What did it mean for the rest of the family? I wanted to ask Mab the myriad questions that Maria was no doubt firing at her mom right now, but Mab seemed so tired, lost in her own thoughts.

I watched the miles click by on the odometer. Five more miles, and I'd try again. We'd gone four-point-three when Mab cleared her throat and sat up straight.

"What are you doing next Saturday evening?"

"Saturday? As in a week from today? There's a full moon between now and then."

I didn't have to explain what I meant. Unless our plan to fool the Night Hag worked—and my doubts about that were the size of Mount Washington—I'd be hellhound chow by then. Not to mention the strong possibility there'd be another zombie attack, especially once Pryce figured out we were killing the Morfran.

"Yes, I know. Gwen has a horror of anything beyond what she considers normal. It was difficult to explain what we face over the next few days. Still, I did tell her we'd try our best to make it."

"Make it to what?"

"Dinner. A 'cookout,' I believe she called it. She's invited you, myself, and Mr. Kane. At five o'clock, so the children can join us. Anne and Evan, too. We mustn't disappoint her if we can help it."

And with those words, Mab told me all I needed to know. Gwen was trying. She would no longer be the iron-hard wedge splitting the family apart. She would let Mab interact with Maria—under her own watchful eye, no doubt, but as Mab said it was a first step. Gwen was creating a family event, with a wider, more inclusive definition of "family" than she'd ever allowed before. I felt a warm glow that she'd made Kane a part of it.

"We'll be there." If we managed to survive the week ahead.

BACK AT MY APARTMENT BUILDING, CLYDE WAS ON DUTY in the lobby. As soon as he saw Mab, he came out from behind his desk to fold her into a hug. Mab stiffened—she's not a hugger—but she lightly placed her hands on his back. Then again, I wouldn't have pegged Clyde as a hugger, either. After three or four seconds, he released her and stepped back.

"Welcome, welcome!" he exclaimed. "I heard a rumor you were back in town. How are things in Wales?" As a young man, Clyde had climbed several mountains in Europe; Mount Snowdon remained his favorite.

The two exchanged small talk for a few minutes, as I stood by and tried not to yawn. I'd managed a few hours of sleep after the rally, but going out to Needham had been hard work in some ways, and this was my usual time for sleeping. Still, before going up to my apartment, I had to compliment Clyde on his speech last night. "You have a real way with words," I told him. "I think everyone around me would have been moved to tears if . . . well, you know."

"If my kind were capable of crying. Thank you for saying so."

"I wish I'd been there to hear it," said Mab. "I'm afraid I succumbed to jet lag."

"I . . ." As he paused, Clyde turned bright red. Who knew zombies could blush? "I do have a copy, should you care to read it."

"I'd love to." Mab squeezed Clyde's arm as he sputteringly promised to print out his speech and have it ready for her at the desk. "I'm looking forward to it," Mab assured him as we headed for the elevators.

Upstairs, Mab said she wanted to spend some time looking over *The Book of Utter Darkness*.

"Is that a good idea?" I asked. "You should take a nap. We're going to be up all night exorcizing the Morfran." *The Book of Utter Darkness* wasn't exactly the kind of book you take to bed to help you nod off.

"Yes, I shall. But later. Now, I feel the book may be in the mood to reveal something to me."

"Well, be careful. Wake me up if you need me."

Mab crossed her arms and frowned. "I'm not a toddler terrified of bad dreams." Her expression softened a tad. "Good night. Or perhaps I should say good afternoon. At any rate, sweet dreams."

I started down the hallway, then turned around. "Are you sure you don't want my bedroom? I could have fresh sheets on the bed in two minutes."

"For heaven's sake, Victory, go to bed."

I did. As I snuggled into my soft pillows, pulling the comforter around me, I was glad Mab was willing to sleep on the couch. That was my last thought before the gentle tide of sleep washed over me.


SWEET DREAMS, MAB HAD SAID. BUT SHE'D BE BLUSHING crimson if she knew what I was dreaming now. Kane. And me. Alone, lying together in the empty darkness. Our bodies were clothed, I noticed with a pang of disappointment, but twined together. We were kissing, and everything was in the kiss.

His lips, so warm, pressed mine. His mouth went to my jaw, kissing and nibbling its way up to my ear and then along my neck. I leaned back my head, eyes closed, and shivered with the deliciousness of it. We were so close. It was like there was nothing else in the universe—only this closeness, this tingling warmth, his scent of musk and midnight forest.

I kissed his cheek, moving back to meet his mouth. The tip of his tongue flicked out, traced the shape of my lips. I inhaled deeply.

Something was wrong.

The scent I knew so well had changed. Beneath the pine and fresh air lurked an undertone of something unpleasant. Something heavy and rotten. Sulfur.

I pushed hard with both hands and scrambled backward. The face that now looked at me, the face I'd been kissing a moment ago, wasn't Kane's.

"Hello, cousin. Ready to join our side?" Pryce spoke the

same words he'd sneered at me in Logan. His face twisted with ugly laughter.

I didn't answer. I shook off my disgust, conjured a dagger, and struck, aiming for his evil heart.

Halfway through the strike, I faltered. Pain flared in my demon mark. My arm lost its strength and dropped to my side. My fingers released the dagger, which disintegrated before it hit the ground.

Pryce's laughing face distorted, growing larger, changing its shape and color. The laughter deepened; other voices joined in. Difethwr puckered its warty blue lips, making mock kissing noises. Demon voices roared.

The Hellion grew to massive size. I tried to conjure another weapon to fight left-handed, but nothing materialized. So I ran. All I wanted was to get away, to find a path out of this nightmare. The Destroyer's fingers, big as logs, closed around my waist. I screamed and thrashed as it lifted me to its face. Its cavernous mouth gaped, fringed with razor-sharp teeth twice my height. Fires burned deep in its gullet, and its stinking breath emerged in a cloud of sulfurous smoke. The Destroyer dangled me there like a morsel.

*This is a dream. It's not real. Wake up!*

A nasty blast of hot air blew over me as the Destroyer laughed again. "Here is thine awakening." Its mouth snapped shut and it lifted me higher, holding me at eye level. "Look, shapeshifter," the Hellion's many voices commanded. *Look, look, look, look.* The word came at me from all sides, from inside my own head. *Look, look.* I had no choice. I gazed into eyes the size of movie screens.

Hellflames burned there, but that wasn't all. A scene took shape. I recognized Boston Common, a terrified human woman running toward me for help. It was the same vision the book had given me. *No—not that.* I closed my eyes and turned my head away, but the scene continued to play itself out in my mind. Again I ran her through. Again I laughed at the horror in her eyes as she fell. Again I looked for others to kill.

"No," I whispered. I filled my mind with *no*, pushing the images away. *No, no, no.*

"It is thy destiny," the Hellion said.

*No, no, no.* I built a wall in my mind, each *no* a brick to keep the Destroyer out. *No, no, no, no, no.*

The Destroyer muttered something, but I couldn't hear it. I focused on *no. No, no, no. No . . . there is . . . no, no . . . another . . . no . . . another way. No, no, no.*

Confused, I paused in my litany of denial. As I did, words came through loud and clear: *There is another way.*

Who said that? My eyes flew open. Difethwr's own eyes held their flames, but the image of Boston was gone. Something had replaced that scene of horrible destruction—fear? Was it possible?

Could the Destroyer be afraid?

Difethwr roared and flung me away. I soared through empty air. My arms and legs thrashed as I fell and fell and fell . . . until I awoke with a start in my own bed.

My bedside clock read seven thirty-two. I had to check for the little red dot that indicated whether it was A.M. or P.M. Evening, good. I'd slept long enough to make it through the night that lay ahead. I flopped onto my back and waited for my pounding heartbeat to return to normal.

*Ugh.* Images from my dream swirled through my head. How could a dream that began so wonderfully turn so wrong? The only good thing was that I'd kept my clothes on. I rubbed my mouth, erasing Pryce's kiss. My body felt coated with foul-smelling slime. I threw aside the covers, grabbed my robe from the back of the door, and headed for the bathroom.

Voices drifted down the hall from the living room.

"Victory?" Mab called. "Is that you?"

"Shower," I yelled back. Whatever Mab wanted could wait. This might take a while.

Hot water spraying over me, I scrubbed and scrubbed until my skin was red. I wished I had sandpaper to remove the feeling of Pryce's kiss, of Difethwr's slime-dripping grasp. I wanted the memory of my own helplessness before the Destroyer to swirl down the drain. I wanted to bleach out the picture of myself on Boston Common, cutting down an innocent woman. It was going to take more than soap and a loofah to do that job.

As I toweled myself dry, I recalled that other voice, the one that had cut through my denial. *There is another way.*

Who had spoken? It wasn't Pryce, and it wasn't the Destroyer. The voice had seemed to come from inside my own mind, squeezing its words between the *no*'s I was mentally chanting. Yet Difethwr had heard it, too. The Hellion had seemed afraid, or at least disturbed. No, *afraid*. Fear had crept into its expression before it tossed me aside like an unwanted plaything.

Probably the voice had bubbled up from my own subconscious. Things like that always happen in dreams. Yet even though it spoke inside my mind, the voice wasn't my own.

*Another way.* Who'd said those words, and what could they mean?

# 25

I DRESSED IN JEANS AND A T-SHIRT, AND FINGER-COMBED MY
hair into some approximation of a style. Feeling less icky, I
entered the living room to find Tina playing with one of my
swords. She'd pushed aside the coffee table and stood in the
middle of the room, practicing lunges with all the grace and
balance of a one-eyed alley cat with four broken legs.

"Tina!" I snapped. "Put that away before you hurt yourself."

She staggered sideways in mid-lunge and swung around to
face me, knocking over a lamp in the process.

"Oops."

"What do you think you're doing? I told you never to touch
my weapons."

Tina licked her lips nervously. "Your aunt said it would be
okay." She bent over to pick up the lamp, nicking an end table
with the sword point.

"Do you seriously expect me to believe that?"

"But I did, child." Mab sat in a side chair. I'd been so
focused on Tina I hadn't seen her there.

Wait. Had aliens stolen my aunt and replaced her with a
copy? The Mab who'd trained me, tougher than any drill sergeant, would never let someone with Tina's inexperience touch

a sword, let alone fool around with it. I'd studied books for five long years before she'd let me practice with a wooden sword. And yet here she was, calmly watching as Tina played a bull while my living room played the china shop. A bull with a long, sharp sword.

None of these thoughts found their way out of my mouth, which simply gaped in astonishment.

"Isn't it awesome?" Tina gushed. She'd figured out that it was a good idea to set the sword aside while she righted the lamp and also a picture frame she'd knocked over. "Mab's teaching me to become a swordsman . . . er, swordsgirl? Whatever. I'm learning how to fight." She snatched up the heavy long sword and swished it around like a rapier. I grabbed it from her before she carved a figure eight in the sofa cushions.

Wordlessly, I turned to Mab.

"I know what you're thinking," she said. I doubted it. First proclaiming me Lady of the Cerddorion, and then encouraging Tina to play with swords? I couldn't begin to get my mind around those concepts. "But these are remarkable times," Mab went on. "We need to recruit all the support we can, and this young lady is willing."

"Right." Tina reached for the sword, and I stepped back to keep it out of her reach. "I've been willing for, like, *ever.*"

My voice returned as I faced Mab. "She became my apprentice less than a year ago, then quit after a couple of months. She's never been serious."

"I have so!" Tina's tone was indignant. "I read that whole book! You know I did, 'cause you helped me go over some of it." She was referring to *Russom's Demoniacal Taxonomy*, a basic demonology textbook. But you don't jump from one read-through of *Russom's* to swordplay; you just don't. Mab certainly never let me do that.

Keeping my body between Tina and the sword, I spoke to Mab. "You honestly believe she's ready to start working with weapons?"

"Honestly? No. But unfortunately we are not talking about a proper apprenticeship. We are preparing for war."

*War.* The word tolled an ugly note, like a cracked bell. It subdued even Tina, who quit trying to reach around me and stood quietly with her head down. Some wisps of blonde hair, escaped from her ponytail, hung in front of her face. She looked young and vulnerable, and suddenly the last thing in the world that I wanted was to drag her into this.

"It's not her war."

Mab's eyes swam with sadness. "If we can't stop it, child, this war will destroy everyone in its path."

# 26

WE COMPROMISED. TINA COULD CONTINUE TO PRACTICE, but only if she used a short sword of my choosing, one less likely to slice up the living room. I could hear Mab coaching her—"Widen your stance. There, that's better! Now, again"— as I went into the kitchen to brew coffee. *The Book of Utter Darkness* lay open on the table, where Mab must have left it. That was odd. Mab was the very definition of neat and tidy, not someone to leave things lying around. Maybe she wanted to show me something in the book. In my shock over seeing Tina waving around a long sword, I'd forgotten to ask Mab if the book had revealed anything while I slept.

I half turned toward the book, letting my gaze skitter across the open pages. Words formed in my mind: *There is another way.* The book slammed itself shut.

I jumped back. That was a new trick.

I pulled on Juliet's pink rubber gloves and tried to reopen the book. It wouldn't budge. I yanked the gloves off, tossed them aside, and tried again. No visions leapt at me when I touched the cover. But I still couldn't open the damn thing. It was like a solid block of wood.

*There is another way.* The words shimmered in my mind, then faded. The book remained stubbornly closed.

Coffee. That's what I needed. Sometimes, the best way to deal with a crazy world is to brew a good, strong pot.

I scooped some beans into the grinder and pressed the button. The machine's jarring *whirr* was the perfect soundtrack for my mood. As much as I tried to keep it out of my mind, I kept seeing Pryce's face, his heavy-lidded eyes fringed by black lashes, in the moment before I pushed him away. When I forced that image from my mind, it was replaced by Tina lunging and waving around my sword. I'd rather picture the grinder blades pulverizing coffee beans into dust.

Still, I needed my coffee. I turned off the grinder, but its harsh sound continued. *What the—?* I pushed the button several times, then yanked out the plug. The blades weren't turning, but the grating sound didn't stop.

Then I spotted the black butterfly perched on my coffee-maker. The grinding noise turned into speech. "Whoa, that was some dream," Butterfly said. "You've got enough weird stuff going on in that head of yours for an army of psycho-analysts to write a whole library of books."

"Did you find out where Pryce goes in the Ordinary?"

"I've been occupied with much more . . . interesting things." I swatted the demon off the coffeemaker and measured the water and grounds. Maybe if I ignored the thing, it'd go away.

Didn't happen.

"I wonder what the ol' werewolf boyfriend would think? Have you considered that?"

Exactly what I'd been trying my damnedest *not* to think about. I started the coffeemaker and searched the cupboard for my favorite mug.

"I'll tell you what he'd think of it," Butterfly continued. The demon didn't seem to realize I was ignoring it. "First of all, his poor, delicate werewolf-y feelings would be all hurt. I mean, another male trespassing on his territory, playing kissy-kissy with his female. And she liked it."

"I did not!" So much for ignoring the demon. There were no words for the repugnance I felt at its suggestion.

"Did so. You liked it a lot until you realized who it was."

"Exactly. I like kissing Kane. I *don't* like . . ." My words trailed off as I shuddered.

"Uh-huh. Well, here's the million-dollar question, sweetheart. When did your smooching partner switch from the wolf to the demi-demon? 'Cause I think I detected a few seconds there when you enjoyed playing kissy-face with you-know-who."

"You're wrong!" I slammed down the mug with such force I cracked it. Butterfly's suggestion spread nausea through my entire body. I desperately needed to gain control of this conversation—now.

"You know, my apprentice is practicing fencing moves on the other side of that door. Maybe I should invite her in here for a little target practice."

"You mean that teenage zombie?" Butterfly's laugh was a cross between a bray and a snort. "Go ahead. Want me to call her for you? She'd never get within an inch of me. But she'd destroy your entire kitchen trying, and your mortification when she found out you've got your very own Eidolon would be . . ." Butterfly sighed happily. "Delicious."

Okay, so maybe siccing Tina on Butterfly wasn't the answer. But I had other weapons. Positive thoughts and happy images usually force an Eidolon to back off. So I reached for a thought that felt good. It was spring. Everyone loves springtime in New England, right? I pictured the warm May sun in a clear blue sky, birds chirping, lilacs blossoming—the image didn't hold. The pleasant landscape coalesced into Pryce's damn face, his lips glistening from our kiss.

"Yum," Butterfly said. The only other sounds were the heavy, wet noises of a demon chewing and swallowing.

All right, if I couldn't banish Pryce's face, I'd use it. I merged the picture of that face with the Eidolon's munching sounds. Pryce's eyes remained half open, suffused with the pleasure not of kissing, but of eating. As he tipped his head back, he raised his hand. In his fingers was a fat, squirming maggot. One with the face of a demon. Just to be sure the image was clear, I mentally tattooed the word Butterfly along the demon's side. Pryce opened his mouth wide and bit the demon in half. His eyes closed with pleasure as he chewed.

Butterfly screamed. "Stop! That's terrible! Knock it off!"

"No fun being somebody else's snack, is it?"

"That's different."

"How?"

"It's different because . . . because . . . It just *is*."

I kind of liked this mental image of Pryce munching a maggot. It made me feel better in all sorts of ways. I kept it as clear as I could manage as I poured myself some coffee.

"Ow! *Ow!* All right, I'll starve. I only materialized to ask you something, anyway."

I sipped my coffee. I didn't need to hear any more questions about how Kane would react to that dumb dream. In my mind, Pryce licked his lips and moved the remains of the maggot closer.

"No!" Butterfly spoke quickly. "Listen, Uffern is in an uproar. Here's all I want to know: What in the name of all that's unholy did you do to the Destroyer?"

In a blink, I let the image of Pryce eating Butterfly disappear. "What do you mean?"

"Not an hour ago, the big, bad Hellion went squealing through the demon plane like a pig running away from the butcher and hauling Pryce with it. The two of them had this earthshaking argument. And if you think that's a figure of speech, you're wrong. Towers crumbled."

An hour ago. Just about the time I'd been jolted out of my dream.

"The thing is, I could've sworn I heard your name mentioned. Since you conjured me, that puts me at risk. So I ask again: What did you do?"

*There is another way.* Those words really had frightened the Destroyer. Problem was, I had no idea where they came from or what they meant.

"I don't know," I told Butterfly truthfully. "What did Pryce and Difethwr argue about?"

"You think I hung around to listen? I'm just a little demon, and so far they've overlooked me. But I'm *your* Eidolon. You conjured me, and that puts your mark on me. If either of those two bad boys catches wind of that, they'll torture me until I tell them everything I know. Since I don't know anything, they'd keep going just for fun—and that'd be way too much pain."

"Poor you." But I wasn't thinking about Butterfly's dilemma, I was thinking about why that voice in my head scared Difethwr.

"What voice?" Damn Eidolon was eavesdropping on my thoughts again.

"Don't ask me. Just a voice in a dream."

Butterfly fluttered around my head, like it was trying to peer into my mind to see my thoughts more clearly. I let it. I didn't know what had scared the Destroyer, so there was nothing to hide. Anyway, maybe Difethwr's reaction had nothing to do with the voice. Weird things happen in dreams. Maybe the Hellion had been startled by the sudden appearance of some image from my subconscious. God knows I've got enough scary stuff lurking in there.

"*That's* for damn sure," Butterfly commented. "Listen, I'm going to lie low for a while. Pryce is in a bad mood; the Destroyer is in a worse one. The last thing I need is for them to find common ground in tormenting me. So, with your permission . . ." Butterfly hovered near the ceiling. I knew what was coming, and crossed my arms over my torso. "Or without." The demon dive-bombed straight into my gut.

*Oof.*

Butterfly settled down and was quiet. No gnawing or stirring up feelings of guilt. The thing was probably listening to my thoughts, ready to run back to the demon plane with a report. On the other hand, Butterfly was probably right that Pryce and the Destroyer would get a kick out of torturing a personal demon, just because. Right now, it was probably best for both of us if the demon remained where it was.

"But you'd better *stay* quiet," I said out loud. "It might be worth sacrificing my kitchen to see Tina make her first demon kill." I never liked those cabinets, anyway.

IN THE LIVING ROOM, TINA HAD RETURNED THE FURNITURE to its usual arrangement and now sat on the sofa talking with Mab. A quick look around reassured me that the room had survived Tina's practice session more or less unscathed.

"Tina was telling me," Mab said, "what she's been studying at school."

Several possibilities leapt to mind: Passing Notes 101, Advanced Gossip, Workshop in Napping. But then I remembered what a good job Tina had done with her speech. I looked at her, eyebrows raised.

"Civil disobedience," Tina said brightly. "At first I thought it was gonna be something dumb, like, you know, being polite." She sat up extra-straight, chin high, and placed her hand on her chest. " 'Pardon me very much, but I do not believe that I wish to do as you say.' " She leaned back, grinning. "That's not it at all, though. It's really interesting, like Thoreau and Gandhi and stuff. People who've made the government pay attention by breaking stupid laws, but doing it in a nonviolent, nonthreatening way. So everyone sees how dumb the law is, and the government ends up looking like a big bully."

I nodded. "Kane would approve."

"He does. He even came in to talk to us."

I hadn't known that. But Kane and I had spent most of the last several weeks keeping our distance.

"Tina recited her speech for me," Mab said. "I was duly impressed. Between that and the copy of the speech your doorman so kindly sent up, I feel I've caught the rally's highlights."

Tina squirmed with pleasure. I knew how she felt. Hearing the words "duly impressed" from Mab was like winning the lottery. Yet, something was odd about Tina—something more than the fact that she was showing an interest in school. Then I realized what it was. She wasn't scarfing down every last bit of food from my kitchen.

"Do you want something to eat?" I asked.

"No, thanks."

"We've got ice cream. The chocolate almond kind you like."

The black tip of Tina's tongue darted out as she licked her lips. Then she shook her head.

"Tina is practicing a sort of civil disobedience," Mab explained.

"Hunger strike." Tina allowed herself a longing glimpse toward the kitchen, then squared her shoulders. "It's part of the protest."

"But . . ." I began. Zombies don't have to eat to survive. They just love to stuff their faces. It's one of their few pleasures. "When someone goes on a hunger strike, it's to show that they're willing to die over an issue. The person begins to starve, and public sympathy grows. It doesn't work that way with zombies, so what's the point?"

"Think about it. Deadtown doesn't produce any food, but we consume *tons*. We zombies are a gold mine for norm-owned food corporations. If we refuse to eat, they lose money. Gets their attention."

She had a point. Still, seeing Tina without a small mountain of food at hand was like seeing the ocean without any water—impossible, by definition.

"Yeah, I was hungry at first. But I'm so mad at the way they're treating us I've pretty much lost my appetite. Well, most of it, anyway. Other zombies say the same thing. Getting mad really wrecks your appetite."

Funny. Butterfly had said something like that, too, although Eidolons eat emotions instead of experiencing them.

Juliet appeared at the mouth of the hallway, yawning and stretching. Her short, slinky dress was a shade of red so dark it was almost black. With it she wore a pair of black, strappy sandals whose stiletto heels must have added four or five inches to her height. "Good evening," she said to the room in general.

"Wow," Tina said. "You look amazing."

Juliet smiled widely enough to show the tips of her fangs, accepting the compliment as her due.

"Off hunting?" I asked.

"I have a job."

"You're joking." Juliet hadn't worked a day in at least six centuries.

"You have a job. Why can't I? As a matter of fact, I happen to be working with the same hunky—and very juicy-looking—human detective that you are."

My face must have revealed my utter incomprehension, because her smile widened into a leer. "I'm a police consultant, too. And tonight I'm going out with Detective Daniel Looks-Hot-In-Tight-Jeans Costello."

*"Daniel?"*

Tina put both hands to her mouth and squealed with delight, like a preteen at a slumber party.

"Hang on," I said. "What are you talking about?"

"That zombie you interrogated at the airport—Bonita

Something-or-other. She indicated that Pryce is working with the Old Ones, yes? And since I'm the only vampire ever to escape the Old Ones' clutches, Daniel wants me to help locate their cell."

The Old Ones prey on vampires in much the same way vampires prey on humans. It was true that Juliet had been in their thrall and broken away. The Old Ones communicate telepathically, and during her time with them Juliet had learned to listen in on their conversations. She probably knew more about the Old Ones than anyone.

"We're going to drive around town, starting with locations they've used in the past, so I can listen for any telepathic chatter. It's going to be a very long night." She licked her lips as she adjusted the plunging neckline of her dress. "And Daniel and I will be in very close quarters."

"Juliet, you can't. This is business, not a date."

"Since when have I ever hesitated to mix business with pleasure?" She twirled her shiny dark hair around her finger as her eyes appraised me. "Do I *detect* some lingering interest in the detective?"

"Of course not." I cursed the crimson heat that rose in my cheeks. "But the man has a girlfriend. They live together. You can't barge in and help yourself."

She blinked a couple of times. "Why not?"

"Because—" The phone rang. It was Clyde, announcing that Daniel was waiting for Juliet downstairs. Wow. He was picking her up at our building. I had to meet him past the checkpoints. This almost *did* look like a date.

She smirked as she sauntered to the door, hips swaying with each step of those impossibly high heels.

"Wait," I said, "you'd better take a thermos of blood, because I guarantee you won't get lucky with Daniel."

One hand on the open door, Juliet turned around and winked. "Don't wait up."

"You're supposed to be doing a job!" The door clicked shut before I got the last word out.

"She is *so* awesome," Tina sighed. "I wish zombies could become vampires."

# 27

JULIET WASN'T THE ONLY ONE WITH A JOB TO DO THAT night. Gently but firmly, Mab told Tina it was time for her to go. "But it's early. I want to practice some more," Tina objected. She stood, but in slow motion.

"You may practice on your own," Mab said. "Victory and I have another matter we must attend to."

"Really? What?" Tina's face darkened as Mab and I exchanged glances. "Oh, come on. One minute you're training me to fight in some war and the next you won't even tell me what's going on, like I'm a child. It's not fair!"

*It's not fair* made her sound exactly like a child, but even so she had a point.

"You're right," Mab said. "If you're to be recruited to help us, you should know what we're facing."

"I'm right?" Tina quickly covered her astonishment with a grin. "Score one for the zombie."

"Do you remember what happened at the Paranormal Appreciation Day concert last winter?" I asked.

"Of course." She did a couple of stiff-legged zombie dance steps. "I almost became a pop star."

"I mean *besides* your fifteen minutes of fame."

"Oh." She bit her lip, frowning. "You mean those nasty bird thingies?"

I hoped Mab noticed the utter despair in the look I sent her way. "Those 'bird thingies' were materialized Morfran."

"Oh, right. And the Morfran is a spirit of hunger that's, like, the essence of all demons. It eats zombies. Your cousin set it loose on Deadtown to feed on us to strengthen his demons so they could attack Boston."

Okay, not bad. Maybe there was some hope for her.

"Those birds went after me," Tina said to Mab, lifting the hem of her T-shirt to show some places where the Morfran had gouged her midriff. Because zombies don't heal, the wounds were as raw as the day they'd happened. "But Vicky used her black dagger and imprisoned them. In slate," she added. "It has to be slate, right? So the Morfran can't get out."

"That's correct," Mab said. "The Morfran is bound to the slate, unless someone releases it. And releasing it is what we plan to do tonight."

"Why?" Tina's eyes widened as she clutched her torso protectively. "Won't those birds attack Deadtown?"

"That's what we're trying to prevent," I said.

"We won't let the Morfran attack anyone," Mab added. "We'll kill it before it can."

"You can kill it? Why didn't you do that before . . . you know, the concert?"

"We've only recently discovered how," Mab said. "So we must act quickly, tonight. It's our best opportunity to weaken our enemies."

"Enemies." Tina rolled the word around on her tongue as though tasting it. "You know, I always thought of enemies as the mean girls who make up rumors and send nasty texts. But you're talking about guys who, like, want to destroy the world as we know it. You're saying I've got *real* enemies." Her forehead wrinkled in thought. Then a grin cracked her pensive expression wide open. "That is so cool."

MAB SENT TINA OFF WITH A YARDSTICK TO USE AS A PRACtice sword. Tina cast a longing glance at my weapons cabinet, but she didn't argue. She promised to come back tomorrow night to demonstrate her progress.

As soon as the door closed behind her, I turned to Mab. "Teaching that zombie to fight is a disaster waiting to happen." In fact, if I were taking bets on Tina's middle name, I'd give *Disaster* the best odds.

"You forget, child, that I spent some time with *The Book of Utter Darkness* as you slept."

That made me pause. "The book mentioned Tina?"

"Not specifically, no. But it did make a reference to her kind, in the form of one of its riddles. One I hadn't encountered before: *The dead have no choice, and yet they must choose.*"

I didn't ask Mab what she thought it meant. We both knew that trying to interpret the book's riddles led to misunderstanding. And this one was a doozy. How can you choose when you have no choice? By "no choice," was the book talking about the Morfran-possessed zombies who were driven to murder against their wills? Or did it simply mean that death removes all options? Kane would talk about how political oppression took away zombies' ability to choose for themselves. See, that was the problem with the book—its prophecies came true, but you were never quite sure what they meant until after the fact.

"Whatever it may mean," Mab said, making me feel like she'd read my thoughts, "it seemed to me a good idea to let at least one of 'the dead' choose our side. Tina is strong, and she's eager. She's also deeply loyal to you."

"Are we talking about the same Tina?" The Tina I knew had stolen from me. She'd quit being my apprentice when something better came along, then begged to come back when "something better" hadn't worked out. She'd helped me a few times, too, but the girl was unreliable. Yes, she was strong, but she wasn't the person I'd want at my back in the thick of battle. Anyway, she'd probably get bored of practicing with the yardstick and quit when lunges made her thighs sore.

"I've told you before, child. Do not underestimate that young lady."

"All right. If you promise not to overestimate her."

"Fair enough."

"Mab," I asked, "did you get anything else from the book today?"

"No, child. After the line about the dead and their choices, the book went silent. So I took that nap you recommended." She yawned. "I wouldn't mind another before we begin our night's work."

I hoped she'd be spared any dreams like the one I'd had. "Mab, does the phrase 'There is another way' mean anything to you?"

"It's a very broad phrase, to be sure. After all, whatever path one chooses there is always another. Usually many more." She shook her head. "However, the book has never spoken that particular phrase to me, if that's what you mean. Why do you ask?"

"Pryce and the Destroyer invaded my dreamscape." A wave of revulsion shuddered through me at the memory of Pryce in that dream. No need to tell Mab about that part. "They were trying to convince me it was inevitable that I'd join their side. But a voice spoke in my mind. And that's what it said: 'There is another way.'"

"Whose voice?"

"I don't know. It seemed to come from somewhere inside my head, but it wasn't mine."

"That sense of doubling is common enough in dreams."

"True. But it didn't end with the dream." I told her what had happened in the kitchen, from the repetition of those words when I glanced at the book to Butterfly's claim that Difethwr had returned to the demon plane, upset and raging, around the time my dream ended.

Mab stretched out on the sofa. She put her hands behind her head, elbows out, considering. "It's hard to know what to think. Most likely, the voice came from within your own mind, arising from your subconscious as a defense against the attack on your dreamscape. When you glanced at the book, your subconscious put forth those words again, as a reminder that the horrible visions the book shows you are not inevitable. Of course, there is another possibility . . ." She looked me up and down as though inspecting for flaws.

"What?"

"That Ceridwen awakens within you."

Not that again. "Mab, I told you: I am *not* the second coming. So let's not go there."

"As you wish." How did she manage to acquiesce to me while making me feel like she'd won? Her voice shifted back to its usual crisp tone. "Anyway, child, it's most likely the first option, a reminder from your subconscious that you do have choices." With that, she turned on her side. "And now I must rest. You, child, should spend some time in meditation. We must be prepared."

I was dismissed. To be honest, I preferred that Mab—the one I grew up with, the one who confidently announced what would happen next—to the one who bowed her head and called me Lady. This new Mab was someone I didn't recognize.

DAD WAS ALREADY WAITING FOR US AT THE OLD GRANARY Burying Ground. Perched on a headstone in the moonlight, he looked like a poster for a spooky movie. The falcon's feathers glowed almost silver in the soft light, reminding me how little time was left before the full moon and Kane's transformation.

I surveyed the old graveyard. Row upon row of headstones stretched into the darkness. Some of the old stones tilted. Others had split, and the broken-off piece leaned against the portion that still stood. Some of those broken headstones were thanks to me, from when I'd slammed the Morfran into the old, fragile stones with too much force. I hated damaging the antique markers, but at the time I'd had no choice.

I could hear distant noises of traffic and sirens, but the cemetery itself was quiet. I opened my senses to the demon plane to see whether we had any company. Pryce undoubtedly knew by now that we could kill the Morfran; he'd probably tortured poor Bonita to learn every last detail of what happened at Logan. He'd be anticipating our project here tonight.

As always, becoming aware of the demon plane made me stagger with revulsion. Through the smoke and stink, I could hear the muffled cawing of thousands of birds, the Morfran trapped in the stones, shrieking with hunger and rage.

I listened, trying to judge. Was there less Morfran now than I'd put here back on Paranormal Appreciation Day? I thought so. Pryce needed Morfran for his experiments on the zombies, and this cemetery was the richest source around. We were lucky he hadn't released it all.

Returning to the human plane, relieved to purge my nostrils with the sweet scent of recently mown grass, I got ready to do the job I'd come here for.

Dad flapped over and landed on a tree branch. He seemed in a good mood. "I can't believe I didn't explain things to Anne sooner. We've missed a couple of good weeks because I was such a chicken."

His feathers puffed out, as though the body he inhabited took offense at his choice of word.

"I'm delighted you're both happy, Evan," Mab said. "Are you ready to get to work?"

"I know there'll be some adjustments," he went on, ignoring Mab's question. "But that's to be expected. I mean, we had our problems before. We didn't always see eye to eye, what with me being from the north of Wales and her from the south. Our current incompatibilities are a bit more dramatic, I'll grant that. Still, I'm optimistic we'll overcome them. It turns out absence really does make the heart grow fonder, at least in our case."

He was gushing like a teenager who'd just gotten a date for the prom, and we let him gush. It made me smile. Mab was smiling a little, too.

Dad saw our expressions and said, "Look at the pair of you, standing there grinning like fools. Did we or didn't we come here to work?"

"Ah, yes," Mab said drily. "Thank you for reminding me."

"Well, then." Dad puffed out his feathers again.

"Here's how we'll proceed," said Mab. "It's quite simple. I will release some Morfran from a stone. A small amount, to start."

"A test batch," I said.

"Precisely. The emerging Morfran will be materialized in its crow form. Victory, you'll wield Hellforged. Use large, slow circles to keep the crows in its orbit, but don't pull them in too close. Keep the Morfran in a holding pattern so that Evan may attack. I shall watch to ensure none escapes." She gestured southward. "Any Morfran that manages to break away will obviously travel toward Deadtown, seeking food. If I see any, Evan, I'll send you after it."

The gleam in Dad's eye showed how much he'd enjoy chasing down every last bit of Morfran.

"Is everyone clear?" Mab asked. Dad and I nodded.

Mab crossed her arms and nodded in return. "Victory, I don't imagine you'll need to return any Morfran to the slate—not unless we release too large an amount at one time. If all goes well, Evan will destroy whatever Morfran we release."

*If all goes well.* That's got to be how things happen sometimes, right? Maybe tonight would be our night for that.

"Let's go," Dad said. "I can hear the damn Morfran cawing. It's making the falcon hungry."

We got into position. Dad launched into the night sky and circled overhead. I held Hellforged in my left hand. When I was learning to use this dagger, the thing bucked like a bronco, getting away from me more often than I managed to hold onto it. But we'd learned to work together. Now, Hellforged felt warm in my hand, vibrating slightly as if anticipating tonight's job. I curled my fingers comfortably around the grip. I began tracing slow, wide, clockwise circles over my head. The motion always made me feel like I was twirling an invisible lasso. Cowgirl Vicky. Right.

Mab put her hand on a stone and tilted her head, as though listening. She straightened and went quickly to the next stone. Again, she laid her hand on it and listened. Satisfied, she traced a circle on the stone's surface, chanting an incantation. Then she produced a wooden stick and hit the stone.

A gong rang out. Mab touched the stone to muffle the sound. Not a good idea to attract attention. She held her hand in place as she struck the stone again.

One more hit, and the Morfran would emerge.

I tensed, preparing for the onslaught.

*Gong.*

A screeching mass of feathers, claws, and beaks exploded from the stone—and straight into Hellforged's orbit. I thought my arm would snap from the sudden, strong drag. I staggered but kept my arm moving. Big, slow circles. No need to rush. I wasn't pulling the Morfran in, merely holding it in place. The drag remained strong; it felt like I was stirring a huge vat of nearly hardened concrete. I quit straining so much, holding Hellforged lightly and concentrating on the motion.

When I felt sure I could handle this amount of Morfran, I looked up. More than a dozen crows with burning eyes circled overhead, moving with Hellforged. They flew silently, as though hypnotized. A couple of them jerked, like they were trying to break out of the enforced flight pattern, but Hellforged held them.

Far above the crows, another bird circled. At first, the falcon was barely a speck in the sky. Then, he dived. The speck hurtled earthward, growing bigger and bigger. His outstretched talons reached. He grasped a crow and tore it in two. Immediately the falcon ascended, gaining the height to dive again.

The drag on Hellforged lessened. Within minutes, all of the crows were dead. Heaps of bloody feathers littered the ground, steaming as the bodies dissolved. In moments, there was no trace left.

The falcon soared upward, screaming its triumph.

"Excellent," Mab said. She watched me rub my upper arm, which quivered from the exertion. "How do you feel, child?"

"Okay. But tomorrow I'm going to feel like I was in a one-handed weight lifting competition."

"We can trade tasks if you like."

"Maybe later. Let's keep going." The falcon alighted on a nearby headstone. "Dad, how about you? You okay?"

"Fine. I sort of move aside and let this body take over. The falcon feels *great*. He's doing what he was meant to do. I think we can handle a bigger batch, if you want to try that."

"Not too much bigger, I think," said Mab. "It requires effort to hold them in orbit. Pacing ourselves will allow us to accomplish more over the course of the night."

"You're the boss," Dad said. "Ready when you are." With a jump, he flapped his wings and took off into the sky.

I did another scan of the cemetery, paying attention to my demon mark as I looked around. If Pryce and Difethwr were nearby, I'd feel it. The mark remained quiet—or what passed for quiet these days. I nodded to Mab that I was ready for another round and began moving Hellforged in big circles over my head. She went to the next headstone.

We worked for hours, stepping it up to larger batches of twenty-five or thirty materialized crows. When my aching arm shook too much to raise over my head, Mab took Hellforged and taught me the releasing incantation. My first attempt freed too much Morfran, and the falcon took off after three crows that escaped and shot like arrows toward Deadtown. But Dad was faster. He got all three before they'd made it past the old Suffolk University campus.

Sometime around three in the morning, we took a break. Mab and I flopped down on the grass, and Dad perched on a headstone, preening his feathers. No one said much; we were all spent. I opened my senses to the demon plane, listening. Hard to tell, but by the reduced cawing I estimated that we'd gotten rid of a quarter of the Morfran trapped here.

Nice going.

"A few more nights of this, and it'll be gone," I said to Mab.

"Yes, child, but I doubt we'll have the luxury. Whatever is keeping Pryce occupied tonight, he will discover what we've done. We must destroy as much of the Morfran as we can before he tries to stop us."

"How do you think—"

To our left, the falcon's scream cut off my question. I leapt up, holding Hellforged in a fighting stance. A harsh cackle cut through the falcon's cries.

A skeleton with glowing eyes stood between two headstones, holding up a net in one bony hand. Inside the net, the white falcon struggled and shrieked.

# 28

"MINE!" THE NIGHT HAG SCREECHED. "AT LAST THE WHITE falcon of Hellsmoor is mine!"

"No!" I ran at her, Hellforged raised, forgetting its blunted blade. I'd lop off her damn hand to make her let go.

The hag whistled, and I nearly ran straight into the snapping jaws of the hellhound that jumped into my path. I stopped, spun. The hounds surrounded me.

When I looked at the hag again, she was a young woman with long, silky hair. Her eyes sparkled with laughter, but her lips twisted in a grimace.

"Mine." She gloated. "And your lover remains bound by his promise to me. All in all, I'd call this a good night's hunt."

She snapped her fingers, and the galloping of iron hooves sounded. Her fire-breathing steed appeared at her side. She grasped the saddle to swing herself up. Her hounds growled and snapped at me, keeping me back.

"Wait," said Mab.

The hag's head snapped toward Mab. Her face, now middle-aged and plump, frowned. She made a complicated whistle and pointed. Half her pack broke away to crouch in front of Mab, growling. Acid drool dripped from their huge fangs, sizzling as it hit the ground.

Mab lifted her hands to show she wasn't armed. "Mallt-y-Nos, you do not know what you're doing."

The Night Hag swung into her saddle. She looped the net around the pommel to make a bag. The falcon tore at the net with his beak and talons, but the fibers stayed intact. "Be still!" she commanded. A blue spark leapt from her finger and jolted the bird. He squawked and stopped moving.

"Stop!" I yelled. "You're hurting him!"

"Merely a little training. This bird will learn to do my bidding. A month or so tied to its perch and hooded, with barely enough food to keep it alive, should break its will. It'll be pleased enough to hunt for me then. If not, there's always this." She zapped another spark into the bird.

*Dad.*

"Mallt-y-Nos," Mab repeated. A hound lunged at her, but she ignored it, standing straight and staring fearlessly at the hag's crone face. "This is the white falcon of the prophecies. He can kill the Morfran. You have no right to take him."

"Haven't I?" The crone cackled like an evil witch escaped from a fairy tale. "I have possession. That's all the right I need. I've no interest in hunting Morfran. This falcon will chase whatever game *I* wish." Her lined, pallid face turned to me with an expression more snarl than laugh. "Perhaps I'll grant you a reprieve, until I've got this bird properly trained. Then I'll set both him *and* my hounds upon you, a full moon or two from now." Her skin turned greenish and shrank on her skull. "What a pleasure it will be to see his talons shred those smooth, pretty cheeks."

Before I could answer, Mab spoke. "Pryce needs the Morfran to conduct his war. Give us the time we need to destroy it."

"Why should I? What can you offer that will make it worth my while?"

"The gauntlet. With it, you won't need to break the falcon's will."

The Night Hag bit her lip, seeming to consider. "Perhaps I would take pleasure in the breaking."

"Perhaps. Yet a strong, proud falcon brings more honor to

its keeper than a spiritless one." When the hag didn't reply, Mab pressed on. "Pryce's plans are ambitious, you know. He intends to conquer not just the Ordinary, but the Darklands as well."

Mallt-y-Nos snorted, unimpressed. "If Lord Arawn cannot protect his realm, it's no concern of mine." Only few shreds of skin clung to her skull. Still, her smile was obvious. "I like war. Plenty of souls to chase. No, I possess the falcon now. The time for bargains is past."

"You cut our bargain short," I said. "The full moon is still two days away. I was going to summon you tomorrow to offer you both the falcon and the gauntlet in exchange for Kane's release."

"You lie. If you'd made that decision, why delay?"

"Because of the work we're doing here. Once that's finished, I have no use for the falcon. Why wouldn't I give him to you?" *Sorry, Dad. You know I don't mean it.* Still, I tried to sound sincere, hoping the Night Hag would believe me.

The hag's face, young again, jerked to the right. In one motion, her hounds stood tall, looking on the same direction. They trembled and whimpered, as though straining against invisible leashes.

"A soul!" she shouted. "The hunt is on!" She wheeled her horse to the right. Holding it in check, she glared over her shoulder at me.

"The hawk is mine, shapeshifter. As is the hound. You cheated me before, but I've won."

"You must listen—" Mab said.

"I'll tarry no longer. To the hunt!" She blew a long, curved horn. The hounds took off running. Mab leapt forward, reaching for the net bag that hung from the hag's saddle. Out of nowhere, a hound sprang at her. Mab cried out and clutched her arm, and the hag rode on.

Taking the falcon with her.

*Dad.*

We had to get him back.


MAB WAS ON HER KNEES, BENT OVER AND HOLDING HER injured arm against her chest. I ran to her. "Are you all right? Let me see the wound."

Her breathing was fast and shallow. "In a moment . . ." she whispered.

I laid my hand lightly on her shoulder, willing her some of my strength.

After a dozen heartbeats, Mab knelt up and extended her arm. Tooth marks ripped her skin in a ragged line, the edges black and curling. "It burns," she gasped.

"I'll call an ambulance."

"No." She pulled in her arm, pressing it to her chest and moving it slowly up and down. Light caught the silver chain at her neck, and I realized she was rubbing the injury against her bloodstone pendant.

The bloodstone that kept her youthful and strong.

I waited. Again Mab examined her arm. The torn skin was healing, and its color was better. After another minute's contact with the bloodstone, only faint white scars marked the places where the hellhound's fangs had sunk in.

"That will do," she said. "Now, we must figure out how to get Evan back. We've not a moment to lose."

"Can you call him with the gauntlet?"

"That might kill him. The Night Hag has put some kind of spell on that net to contain the falcon. I was watching. He should have been able to tear a hole in the bag easily, but he couldn't. If the falcon were called by the gauntlet now, he would batter himself to death trying to escape."

My heart plummeted. "What can we do?"

"Well, for a start you could open this damn bag and let me out." My father's voice emerged from the darkness.

"Dad?" I looked around. "Where are you?"

"Right here." I squinted toward the direction of his voice and saw something I'd never in a million years expected to see. Tina leaned against an obelisk, a net bag containing a falcon swinging from her hand.

"Ta-da!" She waved her other hand in a flourish.

She set the bag on the ground, opening it so the net lay flat. The falcon strutted to its edge, hesitated, then stepped onto the grass. He stretched his wings, folded them, and shook himself. Then he jumped into the air, flapping. After circling over our heads a few times, he landed on a tree branch.

"Feels safer up here," he commented. "Almost got me, didn't she?"

"How did *you* get him?" I asked Tina.

"I knew you guys were over here killing those bird thingies. I mean, um, the Morfran. I wanted to watch. You know, not get in the way or anything. Just be, like, an observatory."

"Observer," I corrected automatically.

"Whatever. Anyway, I snuck out of Deadtown, and when I got here, you were talking to that scary bitch on the big horse. It looked like a bad situation, so I stayed in the shadows. I couldn't hear much, but I saw the bird struggling in the bag. I knew it wasn't one of those Morfran thingies, because it was white. I felt sorry for it. When she zapped it I got mad." Tina put her hands on her hips. "I am *not* okay with cruelty to animals."

"I'm with you on that one, kid," said Dad's voice from the tree.

"I didn't even know he was, like, your dad. Not till he told me and I almost dropped the bag." She spent a moment scrutinizing my face. "I don't see a family resemblance." A one-shoulder shrug. "Anyway, like I said, I got mad. *Especially* thinking she was probably every bit as mean to her horse and all those dogs."

Trust Tina to look at a fanged, Volkswagen-sized, acid-drooling hellhound and see a nice doggy. "How did you get the falcon from the Night Hag?"

"Well, she blew that horn thing, and all of a sudden her dogs were running my way. A second later she galloped past on her horse. When I saw the bag, I reached out and grabbed it. I held tight, she kept riding, and it snapped. Just like that. All I knew was I didn't want her to hurt that beautiful bird again."

"Well done," said Mab. Tina beamed at the approval in her voice. "We owe you a debt of thanks, young lady."

"Really? So I can stay and watch you kill the Morfran? Or are you all finished?"

"Not finished," I said. "Not by a long shot. But I think we're done for tonight. Mab's injured. Dad's traumatized. And the Night Hag may come back."

"I think not, child. Once Mallt-y-Nos undertakes a hunt, she cannot leave it until she chases the soul into the next world.

It's near enough dawn now that she cannot complete her hunt and return here before sunrise. As for your other concern, my injury is quite healed."

"And your old man is holding up fine," Dad added.

"So we may as well do what work we can before daylight," Mab finished.

I didn't like it. We were pushing our luck to keep going now. Mab and Dad might insist they were okay, but I was ready to drop. When you're tired, you make mistakes. We couldn't afford another one of those.

Still, Dad and Mab insisted we continue, and I gave in. We did need to kill as much of the Morfran as we could while we had the chance.

Tina moved back into the shadows as we went to work. I was impressed with how quiet she stayed. Even though Mab and I had both warned her to let us concentrate as we worked, I'd expected at least a *Cool!* or an *Awesome!* to come our way. But Tina didn't say a word.

Finally, when Mab performed the ritual to release more Morfran from a headstone, nothing happened. She straightened, rubbing her back with both hands as though it ached. I didn't doubt it did—personally, I ached in places where I never knew I had muscles.

"The sun is up," Mab said. "That's all we can do for now."

Dad said good-bye and flew toward Needham. I hoped he'd grab a few hours' sleep, although if I had to bet, I'd put my money on his being at Mom's bedside when she woke up and spending every minute of the day with her.

I smiled at the thought. If you want to know what love really is, take a look at my parents. Nothing—not death, not metamorphosis—could keep them apart.

I could only hope that whatever Kane and I had was half as strong. We were going to need all the strength we could get.

"Are you ready to go home, child?" Mab's voice cut through my thoughts.

"I am. I think we've all earned a good day's sleep. Tina? You ready?"

There was no answer.

"Where's Tina?" I asked Mab.

We went over to where she'd been sitting. Although the sun

had crossed the horizon, the cemetery remained shrouded in shadow.

"Tina? Are you asleep? Better get up now, or you'll get sunburn on the way home." Tina was fussy about her complexion; she'd never expose her skin to the sun.

We found some crushed grass where Tina had sat to watch our Morfran extermination. But we didn't find Tina. Although we called, although we searched the whole cemetery, we couldn't find her.

Tina was gone.

# 29

"SHE PROBABLY WENT HOME BEFORE THE SUN ROSE," I SAID
to Mab as we approached the checkpoint. It was at least the
third time I'd made the assertion. "We told her not to disturb
us. She must have actually listened for once."

"We'd better make sure she arrived home safely," Mab
replied. "It would set my mind at ease."

Mine, too.

Getting through the first checkpoint wasted precious time.
The human guard took an excessive interest in Hellforged.
Despite the half-inch-thick sheaf of official approval forms
I carried, the guard wouldn't let us through until several
phone calls had been made and returned. When he was
assured for the fourth time that everything was legit, he
seemed disappointed, telling us that yes, we could go through
and take the dagger with us in exactly the same tone I'd imagine he'd use to tell his wife yes, she could take a younger,
sexier lover.

The zombie guard at the second checkpoint presented no
such problem. He didn't seem to care who or what entered
Deadtown.

Tina lived in a group home with several other young zombies. It was in the opposite direction from my building, but the detour would take us only a few blocks out of our way. I was as anxious as Mab to know that Tina was safe in her bed. It would let me sleep better in mine.

Day or night, there was always a house mother on duty at the group home's reception desk. This morning's attendant looked up as we entered. She was plump, with wire-rimmed glasses and her hair pulled back into a bun. Before the plague, her cheeks must have been rosy, her blue eyes full of twinkles. I always thought of her as a kind of zombie Mrs. Butterworth.

"Good morning, dear," she said, repeating the greeting when I introduced Mab. "I'm afraid we don't allow visitors after sunrise. Except in case of emergency, of course." Her pleasant smile didn't falter. "Is it an emergency?"

"I hope not. We're checking to make sure Tina got home okay."

"She didn't come in while I was on the desk, but I've only been here for half an hour. I'll check the book." She opened a red ring-binder that lay at her elbow. Twirling a stray tendril of hair around one index finger, she ran the other down the page. She shook her head and turned back a page. "Here's where she signed out last night. But she never signed in again." She flipped back to where she'd started. "No . . . no, there's no sign-in time." She closed the book and smiled at us. "Of course, this *is* Tina we're talking about. She's something of a free spirit."

I'd have laughed at the understatement if I weren't so worried. "She doesn't always sign in?"

"I'd say we're lucky if she remembers . . . oh, half the time. Of course, often the house mother on duty will sign in for her. We're not supposed to do that, but really, the point is knowing where the children are, not getting them to practice their signature."

Except Tina would bristle at being called a "child"—and we had no idea where she was.

"Is it possible to check her room?" Mab asked.

The house mother consulted the watch that squeezed her plump wrist. "It's a little late," she said dubiously. "Lights-out was ten minutes ago."

"That's not so very long. She probably isn't asleep yet. Even if she is, now would be a good time to remind her of the importance of signing in."

The house mother's pleasant smile turned crafty. "It would, wouldn't it? If Tina wants her beauty sleep, she can make an effort to follow the rules." She picked up a telephone and pressed a button. "In-house intercom," she commented as we waited. She tapped a finger on the desk, then shook her head. "No answer. Either she's fast asleep or she's not in her room. Sometimes she doesn't return all day." She put down the phone, then spread her hands. "With Tina, what can you do?"

WHAT *COULD* WE DO, I WONDERED, AS MAB AND I WALKED through the empty streets toward my building. Debris from the previous night's rally littered the ground. I stepped over a bent sign with a broken stick; it read WHAT PART OF HUMAN DON'T YOU UNDERSTAND?

"Wait," I said, stopping in my tracks. "I've got the cell phone Daniel gave me. We can call her."

"But the house mother tried that, child."

"That was an intercom. She didn't call Tina's cell phone. Tina never goes anywhere without that thing. She probably sleeps with it on her pillow."

Mab watched as I pressed random buttons on the phone, trying to remember how to bring up the contact list. Mab didn't even have an old-fashioned, rotary-dial landline in her house. She didn't see the need, although there had been plenty of times when I'd tried to convince her it would be useful to call her— not use the dream phone, not leave a message at the village pub. To Mab, the contraption in my hand must've looked like something out of a science fiction movie.

To be honest, it felt a little like that to me, too. Cell phones had changed, a lot, since I gave up trying to carry one. Now, the contact list eluded me. I gave up looking for it and entered Tina's number directly, a little surprised the phone let me do that.

*Pick up,* I thought. *Answer the phone so I can stop worrying about you. I won't even yell at you. Too much.*

But my call went to voice mail. I left a brief message asking Tina to call me back. I followed up with a text message, my thumbs as awkward as tree trunks on the tiny keypad. The message looked like some kind of code: R u ok? She'd understand that, right? Abbreviations like that were part of the secret language kids use for texting.

I pictured Tina squinting at it and scratching her head—"*Ruok*? What's that supposed to mean?"—then trashing the message without bothering to reply. After all, she didn't know I had a cell phone and wouldn't recognize the number.

I sent another text. Thisis vikcy. I realized my tongue was poking out the side of my mouth as I concentrated; I pulled it back in. Aree yuo okay Looking at the tiny letters on the screen, I was dismayed by the number of typos, but it was too hard to go back and fix them. Tina would understand. I hoped. At any rate, when we got home I'd call her from the number she'd recognize.

As I put my phone away, Mab commented that it certainly required a lot of time and effort for a device that was supposed to make life easier. I didn't disagree.

AS I UNLOCKED THE DOOR TO MY APARTMENT, BY FORCE of habit I pressed my ear to the door, listening for Juliet's TV. Silence. I hoped she hadn't already retired to her coffin for the day. I really wanted an update on her search for the Old Ones. Wherever the Old Ones were, Pryce wouldn't be far away.

But maybe I didn't need an update. The door swung open to reveal Pryce himself sitting in my living room.

"Hello, cousin. Hello, auntie. Do come in."

Pryce raised both hands, palms out, to show he wasn't holding a weapon. That didn't mean there wasn't one concealed somewhere in his double-breasted black suit.

I gauged the distance to my weapons cabinet. Pryce was in the way. I'd never get past him, unlock the cabinet, and grab something deadly.

"Don't stand there all day. I'm here to talk, not fight. And I believe what I have to say will be of interest to you both."

Mab and I exchanged a look, but neither of us made a move to enter the apartment.

Pryce heaved a dramatic sigh and stood up. I tensed. If he attacked, I wouldn't have time to extricate Hellforged from its sheath. But Mab was adept at magical fighting. If I distracted Pryce, she'd have enough time to summon a deadly ball of energy—

Pryce didn't move toward us. He disappeared.

Into the demon plane.

Before Mab or I could say a word, he was back. Tina struggled in his grasp.

"Let *go* of me, douche bag!" she shouted. Twisting, she stomped on his instep. Pryce swore and punched her, hard, in the head. Tina cried out in pain. Her eyes found me. "Vicky, help!"

The two of them winked out.

Pryce was back in a moment, once again sitting in the chair. He looked perfectly at ease, legs crossed, hands folded on his stomach. "Now are you ready to talk?"

I stepped inside. Mab followed me and closed the door behind us. Pryce motioned toward the sofa, but we stood where we were.

"Let her go," I said.

"Honestly, Pryce, this is low, even for you." Mab stood rigid beside me. "A mere child."

"Oh, dear. Such hypocrisy. As I recall, auntie, you attempted to kill me when I was 'a mere child.' And quite a bit younger than that creature."

"It's my greatest regret that I didn't succeed."

Pryce put his hands behind his head, elbows sticking out as he regarded us. "Neither of you has the slightest idea how to negotiate. I see this will take longer than I'd hoped."

"There's nothing to negotiate," I said. "Let Tina go, or I'll kill you."

Pryce laughed. "See what I mean? That's hardly impressive as an opening gambit. You've already tried to kill me nearly as many times as I've tried to kill you, and I'm stronger now than I've ever been. Sorry, cousin, but I can't say I fancy your chances."

"What do you want, Pryce?" Mab's voice was tight, dangerous.

Pryce didn't notice Mab's tone—or maybe he didn't care. "Ah, that's better. You see, cousin, Auntie Mab realizes that I'm in a position of advantage, so she looks to me to start negotiations. That's how the game works." He leaned forward and held up his index finger. "First, stop destroying the Morfran. If you don't, I'll kill that horrid zombie you both seem so fond of." He looked at Mab, then back at me. He laughed. "You think I can't do it? I've already released a significant amount of the Morfran from that cemetery and transferred it elsewhere. It's hungry. Unless you do as I say, I shall feed that Tina creature to it."

The image of Tina, screaming and shaking and clutching her head as the Morfran prepared to blow her apart, invaded my mind. We had to get her back.

"Second"—Pryce raised another finger—"you will give me Hellforged." He held out his hand, palm up, like he expected me to walk over and drop the dagger in it.

"No."

Anger lit Pryce's eyes. "The dagger is mine by right. The Cerddorion stole it from Uffern, many years ago. It is past time for its return."

"I won't." If something happened to the white falcon—as it nearly had tonight—Hellforged was our only line of defense against the Morfran. Giving it to Pryce would be like handing him written permission to set the Morfran loose on the world.

Pryce's eyes seemed to burn holes into mine as he stared at me. Then he laughed, showing his animal-like teeth, and sat back again. "All right," he said, "I'll allow you your illusion of power—for now. You'll give me Hellforged, and gladly, soon enough."

"You'll get that dagger from me when I stick it deep into your black heart."

Before Pryce could reply, Mab spoke. "You are too sure of yourself, Pryce. Your arrogance has led you astray before."

"Arrogance? I don't think so. In the past, my eagerness to see the ancient prophecies fulfilled may have made me a tad hasty. But I am greater now than I was then, you see. Now I have Difethwr's strength, plus my father's skill and knowledge, to support my ambition. And soon, I will have her as well." His long white finger pointed at me. "Not that I need her, mind you, but think of the blow to your side when your Last Great Hope abandons you."

"You're insane," I said.

"Thank you for the psychological analysis, cousin. But you're diagnosing the wrong subject. Auntie is the one who refuses to accept reality." He jutted his chin toward Mab. "She thinks you're the long-awaited Lady of the Cerddorion. But it can't be you. Difethwr made sure of that, by putting its mark on you."

I tried to ignore the slow burning that began in my forearm.

"You can feel it, can't you? The rage, the urge to destroy. Ever since I resurrected Difethwr, those feelings have become stronger. They're taking you over, from the inside. And there's nothing you can do about it."

*I can fight it,* I thought. *Like I've always fought it.*

Pryce's voice was suddenly at my ear, whispering, insinuating. "You wanted to fight Mab, didn't you? You wanted it, just like you wanted to wring your own father's feathery neck. The anger . . . it feels good. It feels right. It's your nature. And you want it."

I whirled around to shove him away from me, but my hands pushed empty air. Pryce still sat in his chair, smirking.

"Already your loyalties are shifting, cousin. You know I speak the truth. Deep down inside, you know." I couldn't even deny his words as a parade of images passed through my mind. Boston burning. A dead woman at my feet. The itch from my demon mark turned into a fire, a raging need to destroy. "When it is time," Pryce said, his voice low but oh, so sure, "you will come to me."

*There is another way.*

I blinked. The inner voice fled, but it took the horrible images with it.

I glanced at Pryce. He didn't recoil in fear, the way the Destroyer had in my dream. Either he hadn't heard the words, or they didn't scare him.

"Well, then." Pryce rubbed his hands together. "I won't say it's been a pleasure, but I do believe I've made my point. Stay out of that graveyard, or Tina dies."

Pryce winked at me. Then he disappeared, returning to the hell where he belonged.

•

# 30

"PRYCE HAS TINA."

Yes, I was stating the obvious. But maybe I was hoping the words wouldn't exit my mouth or, if they did, would be so ridiculous Mab would laugh and we could both go to bed.

Mab didn't laugh.

Instead, she paced back and forth across my living room. "Most likely, he's holding her with the others, those poor missing zombies. It is imperative that we find the Old Ones' base."

"Maybe Juliet located them last night." I went down the hallway, but the door to Juliet's room was closed. She must have climbed into her coffin as soon as she got home. There'd be no waking her until the sun dipped below the horizon.

Back in the living room, I picked up the phone. "I'll ask Daniel what they found out."

The odds were good that he was sleeping, too, after driving around Boston all night. And he'd be extra sleepy if he'd let Juliet—*Not going there*. I pushed that image from my mind.

Daniel answered on the second ring, and my first reaction was a wave of relief that my roommate hadn't had her way with him. But we had more important things to worry about, so I got right to the point.

"Did you find the Old Ones' base? Juliet was asleep when I got home."

"We uncovered several possibilities, but nothing definite yet. We're going out again tonight." A yawn sounded through the phone. "How did things go at the cemetery?"

"We made some progress. But Pryce has already taken a lot of Morfran out of there. And he has Tina."

"Tina?" Daniel was silent for a few moments as though trying to place the name. "Your zombie friend? But her name isn't on the list of missing PDHs."

"He snatched her from under our noses. And he says he'll kill her if we go back to the cemetery."

"Damn."

"We have to find them, Daniel. Tina's an innocent kid." Pryce would take great pleasure in infecting her with the Morfran and sending her as a weapon against me. He'd laugh with glee watching me fight off my own apprentice, only to stand by helplessly when the Morfran blew her to pieces. And he'd do it even if we complied with his demands. Staying out of the Burying Ground would only buy Tina some time. It wouldn't save her life.

"We're following up on some leads today," Daniel said. "Finding out who owns the buildings, getting search warrants. But Juliet admitted last night she never picked up anything more than a stray thought or a one-on-one conversation, nothing to indicate a group of Old Ones. Nothing about zombies or demons, either—the thoughts she overheard were mostly about where to hunt for dinner. We've mapped all the locations where she heard something, of course, and we're checking everything out. But we have to move cautiously because we don't want to tip them off. As far as Juliet could tell, they don't know we're looking for them. I'd like to keep it that way."

That was one piece of luck, however small. If the Old Ones thought their hiding place was secure, they wouldn't be moving the zombies any time soon. Of course, that didn't mean a thing if we couldn't find them.

Daniel promised to keep me informed, and we hung up. I shook my head at Mab, who watched me, worry lines etched around her eyes.

" 'Possibilities,' he said, but nothing definite. They're following up on all leads, blah blah blah. The upshot is they don't know."

"Would he tell you if they did?"

I considered. Daniel was all cop. He'd warned me to stay away from his investigations in the past. Even though he'd hired me as a consultant, would he hold back information to keep me out of his way? Probably. Yet, this case was different.

"I think he'd tell me. He'd want me there to handle any Morfran that emerged." Daniel had seen the effects of Morfran possession with his own eyes. "Anyway, Juliet would tell us." No norm could make Juliet do anything she didn't want to do. Even if she swore herself to secrecy, she'd do it with two perfectly manicured fingers crossed behind her back.

"She can't tell us anything now," Mab pointed out. "Not until nightfall."

My confidence sagged. If the police did know where Old Ones were hiding, the smartest time to raid the place would be during the day, when the creatures were sluggish and the Morfran couldn't materialize. Daniel might think he wouldn't need me during a daytime raid. He could be preparing such a raid right now.

And what if Tina got caught in the middle? What if she got hit by an exploding zombie dropper or hauled off to that top-secret holding facility? What if Pryce had already infected her with the Morfran and it was ticking away inside her, waiting for nightfall to turn her into a killer and then destroy her?

Without knowing where to find the Old Ones, there was nothing I could do. And I hated feeling helpless. I wanted to charge in somewhere, lop off some Old One heads, and skewer Pryce like shish kebab. I wanted to slash Difethwr with my flaming sword until the Hellion was a steaming mass of melted goo. Most of all, I wanted to open Tina's cell door and lead her to safety. But without the location, I couldn't do a thing. I looked at my weapons cabinet and thought about the tools of my trade. I could be loaded with pistols, bristling with blades, and it wouldn't do a bit of good. All weaponed up and no place to go.

Mab said we might as well try to sleep, so we could recharge for whatever was coming next. I knew she was right, but how could I sleep haunted by the image of Tina, crouched in a pitch-dark cell, waiting for me to rescue her? "Vicky, help," she'd cried out, fear clouding her eyes.

And I was going to bed.

While Mab was in the bathroom washing up, I called Kane.

"I'm at the office," he said when he answered.

"Still?" An all-nighter was extreme, even for Kane.

"I couldn't afford to miss another day of work, so I've been here trying to clear my desk before the full moon." He yawned.

I managed to get out about three words of my reply before he sensed something was wrong and insisted I fill him in. I told him everything—how we'd killed a significant amount of Morfran, how the Night Hag had captured Dad and almost made off with him, how Tina had rescued him only to be abducted herself. "We don't know where Pryce is holding her." My voice broke.

"Vicky." Kane's voice was soothing. "It's okay. I understand how much you hate not being able to act right now. I feel that way all the time, like when a judge issues a biased decision or a just cause gets choked by red tape. Our methods are different, but we both feel that impulse to help very strongly."

I was afraid anything I said would turn into a sob, so I didn't answer.

"Right now, the best thing you can do for Tina is get some rest. When the time comes to move forward, you need to be strong and clearheaded, not trembling with fatigue."

"You're right," I managed to squeak out. Mab had said the same thing.

"I need to take my own advice. I've been awake for more than twenty-four hours, and now's not the time to exhaust myself." In his pause, I knew we were both thinking about the strength he'd need to withstand the Night Hag. "I knew she rode through town last night, Vicky. The Mistress of Hounds. Ever since the moon started waxing, I feel her pull. It tugs at me more strongly each night. Last night, while I was trying to work, it nearly knocked me out of my chair, and I mean that literally. I felt that . . . that burning in my veins, and my body ached to change." Horror thickened his voice. "It couldn't, of course. Not until the first night of the full moon. But the pull felt so intense. I shouldn't have gotten sidetracked into organizing that rally. It was a good show of unity, but my focus should have been on resting, getting strong, and building up my resistance. I can't control the shape she forces on me, but whatever remains of me inside will fight her with everything I've got."

"I wish you were here," I whispered.

"So do I." Even over the phone, his longing was palpable. I shivered.

"And Vicky," he said. "Have faith in yourself. Tina does. Your aunt does. And I do."

I brushed at my suddenly damp eyes. "I have faith in you, too."

Given the impossible challenges we both faced, the words meant a lot. Everything, maybe.


MAB FELL ASLEEP AS SOON AS I TUCKED HER IN ON THE SOFA. I expected to spend several hours tossing and turning, but I must have been even more tired than I'd thought.

Sleep wrapped around me like a warm blanket. I let it hold me in the darkness. Tension drained from my limbs. Aches were soothed away. Worries that had sawed at my mind grew blunt and faded. Slowly, strength returned, filling me like a rising tide.

I didn't think any of these thoughts. But somehow I knew them as my mind drifted in the warm darkness.

Eventually, the texture of that darkness changed, its uniform blankness ruffled by puffs and billows. It looked like a rising mist in shades of inky black and charcoal. Slowly, the mist spread and thickened, and I realized why. Someone was calling me on the dream phone. But who? Not Mab, her colors, silver and blue, always appeared quickly. Maria? She was still mastering this form of communication. I watched the mist for traces of Maria's colors, candy-heart pink and sky blue, bleeding in, but the billows remained black and gray.

Black and gray? I didn't know anyone with those colors.

I turned my mind away from the signal that someone wanted to talk to me. The black-and-gray mist persisted. It expanded to fill my dreamscape.

Finally, I grew impatient. I didn't need to be solving puzzles in my sleep. "Who is it?" I demanded in a voice I hoped would scare the intruder away.

The mist whirled into a spiral. It looked like one of those satellite views of a hurricane. Coughing sputtered. The mist drew back. Then, the hurricane's eye spat out a small, dark shape.

Butterfly lay gasping at my feet.

"Holy crap," the demon wheezed. "You've got this dreamscape of yours locked up like Fort Freakin' Knox."

"There's a reason for that."

"Well, how else am I supposed to report to you? I can't materialize in daylight, and it's hours until dark. I figured getting into your dreamscape—you know, like a Drude—would be the easiest way." Drudes are the demons that manifest in dreams, causing nightmares. "Hah!" Butterfly continued. "Look at how bruised I got trying!" The demon shook a wing at me. I didn't see anything that looked like a bruise.

"I'm trying to get some rest," I snapped. "Did you say you have something to report to me?"

Butterfly ignored my words, fluttering around my dreamscape as though checking the place out. "So then I got smart. Instead of beating my poor wings against the barriers, I'd get you to *invite* me in. Brilliant, huh? I knew all about that Cerddorion dream-phone thing from rummaging around in your brain—"

"Yes, fine, brilliant idea. Write it up as a book, and you'll have the best-selling title in Uffern. But unless you actually do have something to report, get the hell *out* of my dreamscape. I mean it."

"Best seller, huh? Too bad we don't use money there. You try to barter an idea like that, some bigger demon steals it. Probably bites your head off in the process." Butterfly quit flitting around and landed at my feet. "Hey, how come your eyes are bugging out like that? You should try to relax when you sleep. That's what it's for, you know."

This was too much. I conjured a bronze sword. "Oh, right," Butterfly said, flying out of reach. "My report. Well, it was like this. I got tired of hanging out in your gut and not being able to feed. It's like, you know, going to an open-bar party when you're on the wagon. So I split and went back to my own realm.

And there I was, twiddling my thumbs. Figuratively speaking, of course, since I don't have any." Butterfly held up its two front legs to illustrate the point.

I gritted my teeth. Even in my dreamscape, my demon mark itched as I tightened my grip on the sword. This demon better have something to report that was worth the vast reserves of my patience it was squandering.

"To while away the time and distract myself from the fact you were starving me to death, I considered whether I should try to stop you from killing the Morfran in that cemetery. After all, it's the essence of all demons, including yours truly. From one way of looking at things, it was like you and your aunt and your father were all destroying little pieces of my soul. Except it wasn't. All that Morfran has nothing to do with me. I mean, I already *am*. Whatever Pryce wants that trapped Morfran for, it sure ain't for my benefit."

"You couldn't have stopped me if you'd tried."

"Heh." Butterfly's wings quivered with amusement. "You can believe that if you want to, I guess. Anyway, all of a sudden I heard this screaming. Now, screams are usually sweet ambrosia to any demon. But this . . ." The insect flew a quick loop-the-loop to show its agitation. "I wanted to cover my poor ears with my hands. And I would have, too, if I had, you know, ears. And hands."

"You heard Tina."

"Yeah, your zombie friend. I never heard such a racket. Enough to deafen all the demons of Hell."

Why hadn't I heard Tina screaming? I thought back. At first, I'd checked the demon plane frequently, watching for signs of trouble. But later the work was going so smoothly that I slacked off. After the Night Hag's departure, I'd been in a hurry, wanting to kill as much Morfran as possible before dawn. I'd kept my ears tuned to the human plane, listening for the Night Hag's return—and that was when Pryce snatched Tina and dragged her through Uffern.

I waited for Butterfly to gloat over my carelessness, but for once the demon didn't take the bait. "I'm not a Drude," it said in response to my thoughts. "I can't feed inside your dream-scape. I'll save that one for later, though. Thanks."

"Go on with your story."

"Pryce had a tough time with the zombie—the way she howled and struggled and hit at him, he could barely keep a grip on her. He had to call Difethwr to help. They were both so distracted, I figured this might be my one and only chance to follow them without being noticed. So I went for it."

The absurd rush of gratitude I felt was swamped by the urgency to hear more. "You know where Pryce took Tina? Tell me, *now*!"

"Cool your heels, lady. You want to hear it, you let me tell it in my own time. We're in your dreamscape. This whole conversation is taking maybe fifteen, twenty seconds of outside-world time."

I wanted to remind the Eidolon that "fifteen, twenty seconds" would be plenty of time for it to die a long, slow, painful death inside my dreams. Instead, I reminded myself that, for reasons I didn't understand, this demon appeared to be helping me.

"So, Pryce and Difethwr dragged the zombie through Uffern, and the whole way she's raising holy hell—so to speak. Heh heh. They stopped in front of this door and looked around. I hid in the shadows so they wouldn't see me." Not hard—Uffern was all flames and flickering shadows. "Pryce kicked open the door and dragged the zombie through."

"By himself?"

"Difethwr stayed on our side. The demons' side. I waited for it to cross the threshold, so I could scoot through before the door closed. But that didn't happen. Difethwr stayed put, but the door was closing. I had to creep along the floor, like this." Butterfly demonstrated, wings flat, its multiple legs taking stealthy steps. "When I was sure the Destroyer wasn't looking, I ran across the threshold. Immediately, I knew I was in your world. I was on a concrete floor in some hallway. No windows. I think it was underground. The place was filthy, with lots of junk lying around.

"Anyway, by the time I caught up with Pryce, he and some guy in a robe were shoving the zombie through a door. Once they locked her in, the screaming stopped and I could hear again. Soundproofing, I guess. I crawled as close as I dared. The guy in the robe was pulling up his hood; it had fallen back in the struggle. Whoa, man. Talk about *ugly*. He had the Crypt

Keeper's complexion and fangs like freakin' walrus tusks. He was complaining, and it took a minute for me to follow what he was saying, what with those ridiculous fangs and all. Something about how he wasn't sure that even the cauldron was worth all this trouble. Pryce said, 'Once you've been transformed, you'll thank me.'"

Of course. That was what Pryce was offering the Old Ones for their cooperation. The one thing Colwyn and his crew had always wanted: eternal life. Not as the decrepit, hideous creatures they'd become, but transformed into strong, powerful beings—into gods. After Pryce conquered the Darklands, he'd give its prize, the cauldron of transformation, to the Old Ones.

"Then," Butterfly continued, "Pryce asked Mr. Fangs how long before the virus would be ready. I didn't catch the exact answer, but I got the impression it would be soon. I did hear fangboy say that some was being readied for shipment."

"Shipment? Did he say where it was going?"

"'The first locations.' That was all I got."

The Old Ones, creators of the original plague virus, were making more and shipping it somewhere—multiple somewheres. And Pryce was threatening Tina to prevent us from destroying more Morfran. He planned to create more zombies and turn them into an unstoppable Morfran-driven army.

"Butterfly, this is bad. This is really, *really* bad. You need to tell me where Pryce took Tina."

The demon's voice turned crafty. "What's it worth to you?"

*Don't kill the thing yet, Vicky. It's got more information.*

"What do you mean?" I said, trying to sound all innocent. "You said you'd help me in hopes of saving your own sweet ass. Remember?"

"That was my starting position, sure. But I risked my 'sweet ass' to get some information, and I hit pay dirt. Emphasis on *pay*. You heard enough to know my info is good. You can save your little zombie friend and prevent Mr. Fangs from distributing plague virus to locations unknown. So I ask again: What's it worth to you, oh great demon slayer? How much do you want to save the world?"

Never, ever had I wanted to kill any demon more than I wanted to kill Butterfly at that moment. But I couldn't. Not yet. "What do you want?"

"You know, ever since you first conjured me, it's been nothing but, 'Get the hell away from me, Butterfly,' or 'I'm going to stab you with this bronze dagger, Butterfly,' or 'How about I humiliate you to death, Butterfly?' You only ever summon me when you want something. The rest of the time, you'd rather see me dead."

"What do you expect? You're a parasite."

Butterfly sniffed. "That doesn't mean that I don't have feelings. So here's what I want. I'll tell you where Pryce took your zombie friend—give you the actual address—if . . ."

I leaned forward, waiting.

"If you promise to be nice to me."

Okay, this *had* to be one of those moments when a dream went from feeling like everyday reality to Salvador Dali–land. "You want me to be *nice* to you?"

"Yeah, yeah, I know. A personality like yours, it's asking too much, isn't it?" Butterfly's voice went all pouty. "I knew you couldn't do it."

With an effort, I made the dagger I'd conjured vanish. "Define 'nice.'"

"What?" Butterfly's eyes fixed on my empty hand.

"When you say that you want me to be nice to you, what exactly do you mean?"

"Well, you won't threaten to kill me, for starters. That sort of talk puts a real crimp on a relationship."

"No threats. What else?"

"No actually *trying* to kill me either, of course. And no name-calling or humiliation."

"So basically you want me to grin and bear it while you torment me and get fatter on my emotions."

"A demon's gotta eat." Butterfly flew close, hovering inches in front of my face. "But no, actually, that's not what I mean. I thought maybe we could . . . you know, talk." Its beady eyes actually looked sincere, even hopeful.

"Let me make sure I understand. You want to me to sit down and have a friendly chat with you."

"Yeah." A forked tongue darted from its mouth. "And maybe just a *little* snack."

It went against everything I'd ever learned about demons. As soon as any demon got a toehold into your psyche, you killed it, the faster the better. And yet I'd been living with this one for weeks. It had stopped me from attacking Mab, and it had risked its life to find out where Pryce had taken Tina. Butterfly drove me crazy, but this demon also had information I needed.

"You promise you have the actual street address, here in the Ordinary, of where the Old Ones are holding Tina?"

"Yeah. When Pryce left, it was still dark in your world. Instead of following him back into the demon plane, I went outside. I know the address, all right."

I bit my lip, feeling I was about to make a terrible mistake. But Tina needed me. I had to find her. "All right. I'll be nice to you. For one hour."

"That's all I'm asking." For a moment, Butterfly looked almost weepy. But the sentimental expression hardened to a sneer. "Your head would explode if you tried for any longer than that."

Whatever. "You want to shake on it?"

Butterfly lifted its front leg. "No hands, remember? I'll accept a blood oath." I didn't like the sound of that, but before I objected Butterfly shot like a rocket through the air and landed on my shoulder. "So," it said, "you agree to be nice to me for one hour in exchange for the address of the Old Ones' base?"

"Yes, but—" Before I could get another word out, the demon chomped a chunk out of my neck. "Ow!" My hand reflexively swatted at the spot.

"No swatting, either. When you're being nice to me, I mean."

"Fine, fine. Give me the address."

"Pay attention. You don't want to forget it when you wake up." Butterfly buzzed the address in my ear, repeating the number and street over and over. When I felt like it was burned into my brain, I brushed the demon away. Gently, even. "Get ready," I said, spreading my arms wide. I brought my hands together in a loud clap. An explosion boomed, shattering my dreamscape and hurling Butterfly and myself each into our own realms.

# 31

I JUMPED OUT OF BED AND YANKED AT THE BLACKOUT shade. Bright sunlight dazzled me. Still day. I had time.

Ignoring the white spots that swam through my vision, I wrote down the address Butterfly had given me. It was in East Boston, not far from the airport. I clutched the paper in my hand as I rushed out to the living room to call Daniel.

Mab lay fast asleep on the sofa, a light blanket pulled up to her collarbone, her face pressed into the cushions. The sight of her there, so relaxed, so vulnerable, gave me pause.

Pryce wanted to kill her. I didn't doubt that for a moment. After all, both zombies had gone straight for Mab at the airport. My demi-demon "cousin"—and his plan to work with the Old Ones to distribute the zombie virus—had to be stopped. But what if Pryce had fed Butterfly that information and then sent the Eidolon to me to set up an ambush? I mean, a demon spying on its own kind in return for nothing more than an hour of civil conversation? It didn't add up. Demons—all of them—are creatures of greed and pure self-interest. The only way an Eidolon could come up with an offer like Butterfly's would be if it were getting a much more significant reward from another quarter.

Like Pryce.

It made sense. Everything Butterfly had told me was true: the address, the virus, Pryce's alliance with the Old Ones. But maybe my friendly neighborhood demon had left out the part where Pryce had given it the information on purpose, patted its misshapen little head, and sent it my way with his blessing.

Was Butterfly double-crossing me? If it was, that damn demon would soon learn that I defined "being nice" as putting it out of its miserable existence by dicing it into pieces with my sharpest bronze blade.

I couldn't trust Butterfly. I couldn't trust *any* demon. And I would not risk Mab's life by leading her into a trap.

Pryce had told Mab I wasn't the Lady of the Cerddorion. But I'd bet my best long sword that he thought she was—and therefore needed to be eliminated.

I set the phone in its cradle and returned quietly to my bedroom. As I dressed, I formulated my plan. First, I'd go to Kane's office and fill him in. He said he wanted to stand beside me. Okay, I'd let him. I could use his help. While there, I'd arm myself with weapons from Mab's trunk, still locked in Kane's vault. Then, we'd go to East Boston. If Butterfly's information checked out, I'd call Daniel. That way, Mr. Let-the-Professionals-Handle-It Detective couldn't tell me to keep away from the site—I'd already be there.

The clock on the wall told me it was a little past noon. With any luck, I'd be home safe and sound, ready to tell Mab of the Old Ones' defeat before she woke up.

I tiptoed through the living room and eased the front door open. I didn't let out my breath until I'd pulled it silently but firmly shut behind me.


DEADTOWN WAS AS QUIET AT NOON AS THE REST OF BOSton would be at two in the morning. I was glad to see that zombies were home behind their blackout shades, honoring the curfew, not roving around in gangs looking for things to smash and fights to pick. If Kane's rally had let them express their frustrations in a more constructive way, he'd really accomplished something.

Once I'd passed through the checkpoints, I entered a different world. The downtown streets bustled with humans going shopping, heading to appointments, and running lunch-hour errands. It was a beautiful spring day, with the kind of warm, sunny weather that fooled you into thinking summer had arrived. In my tank top, jeans, and light jacket, I was a little dressed-down compared to all the business-suited types, men and women, buzzing in and out of Kane's office building. Too bad. I was at work, too, but in my business dress-for-success didn't mean a tailored suit and high-heeled pumps. Those would only get in my way.

I rode the elevator to Kane's floor. As I pulled open the glass door to his office suite, his receptionist, Iris, smiled a greeting. Iris was a pretty and efficient human who kept Kane's law firm running smoothly, especially when the boss and his werewolf partners were on retreat.

"Vicky, hello," Iris said warmly. "You missed Kane by twenty minutes."

"Is he at lunch? I thought maybe I should peek into The Grill, but the office was on the way, so it made sense to stop here first." The Grill was Kane's favorite lunch spot.

"I can save you the trouble of going over there. He's not at lunch. He went home."

I remembered he'd admitted being tired, but I still thought he'd be here. Kane voluntarily going home in the middle of a workday was on a level with daisies sprouting from a three-foot snowbank in the middle of February.

"I know," Iris said. "Unheard of, right? He said he had to get some sleep. Said he'd been feeling a little run-down and wanted to rest up before the full-moon retreat." She frowned. "I hope the Detweiler pack isn't giving him trouble again. Their oldest sons are twins, and I hear they've been challenging every male in sight."

"I don't think that's it." The Night Hag gave "run-down" a whole new meaning—she'd drive her hounds until their paws were ragged shreds of bloody flesh, and then do it again the next night. I was glad Kane was giving himself time to prepare for his ordeal. He'd need it.

"You're probably right," Iris said. "Those Detweiler whelps are no match for him. So, do you want to use the phone?" Iris knew about my abysmal track record with cell phones; she wouldn't expect me to be carrying one. "I know he wouldn't mind if you called him at home."

"No, I don't want to disturb him. But I would like to get some things from the safe."

"That's fine. He told me a couple of days ago that you and your aunt have access. You know the combination, right?"

I assured her I did.

"Great, I'll let you in his office."

I followed Iris down the carpeted hall. The ring of keys in her hand jingled with each step. She stopped at Kane's door, fitted a key into the lock, and pushed the door open. "Take your time," she said, stepping back to let me pass. "The door locks automatically when you close it. Just pull it shut when you're done."

The keys jingled their way back toward the reception desk.

Kane's office looked the same as always—papers piled high on his desk, law books crammed into multiple bookcases, several diplomas adorning the wall, a KANE AND ASSOCIATES screensaver bouncing around his computer monitor—except for the vacuum at the center of it all created by his absence. His leather chair was swiveled to the side, as though he'd just stood up and would be back again in a minute. Even the air held his scent. I inhaled, feeling it warm my lungs and send tingles through me.

I sat down in his chair. *This is how he sees the world,* I thought. The windows along one wall revealed a spectacular view of the harbor, framed by tall buildings. An airplane drifted toward a runway at Logan. On his desk sat a framed photo I hadn't seen before. I leaned forward and picked it up. It showed the two of us, the ocean in the background. Kane had his arm around me, and I leaned against him. Wind ruffled our hair, and we were laughing, our faces lit up with the joy of being together.

I couldn't remember when the photo had been taken. The ocean suggested it was from the weekend we'd spent on Cape Cod last summer. Had it been nearly a year since we'd laughed that way? So many other things had pushed between us, turning our relationship into an obstacle course. I wanted this moment back—no, I wanted it again. And again and again. I wanted to be together, relaxed and easy and basking in uncomplicated happiness.

Should I call him? To say, "I love you, and I know we'll get through this." I reached for the phone, then paused. What if he was sleeping? He'd said himself he needed to rest and build up his strength. I knew he was worried about the full moon, but I also knew he hadn't admitted even half how much. He didn't need me to call him now to say, "Nice photo on your desk." He'd want to know what I was doing here, and when I told him he'd insist on going to East Boston with me. Part of me wanted him there, by my side. But another part said that was selfish, that I'd be draining his reserves exactly when he needed to replenish them.

The Night Hag intended to break him. I'd do whatever I could to support him.

I touched the glass over the photo, tracing Kane's cheek. This picture said so much. It showed that Kane believed in a vision of us, one that wasn't marred by demons and evil and blood and death. His vision was simple: us together, laughing. And I was grateful. It was a vision I could hold onto as I did what I had to do. A hope for coming out on the other side of all this and finding each other there.

Coming together again. Holding each other, maybe even laughing.

I set the photo back in its place. Then I opened Kane's safe to choose my weapons.


THE ADDRESS BUTTERFLY HAD GIVEN ME WAS IN EAST BOS-ton, a few blocks from a popular skate park. Narrow clapboard houses squeezed together amid auto-body shops and restaurant supply stores. I found the street, and then the number; the building itself appeared abandoned. Made of yellow brick, its single story squatted behind a six-foot chain-link fence, topped with coils of razor wire. Graffiti covered the walls and boarded-up windows.

Exactly the kind of place the Old Ones would slither into and call home.

I scouted as much of the building as I could without drawing attention to myself. Weeds sprouted throughout the small parking lot, which was gated and locked, and along the walkway to the front door. A wooden sign announced the building was AVAILABLE! and gave the name and phone number of a real estate firm. Much of the paint had flaked off, taking with it the last couple of digits in the phone number. I had a feeling no prospective buyers had looked at this building for a very long time.

Across the street a face watched me from the second story of a small house. East Boston is a diverse neighborhood, and its residents keep an eye out for each other. If anything had been going on in the abandoned factory, someone would have noticed.

I crossed the street and went up the short walkway to the house's front steps. The concrete walk was cracked, but petunias sprouted from window boxes. Grimy statues of mischievous gnomes peeked out from between the flowers. One of them, positioned to appear as any visitor mounted the steps, dropped his pants to greet you with a double-cheeked moon. Hostile or humorous? I'd find out when I rang the bell.

A buzzer sounded inside. I didn't have to ring a second time before a short woman in a flowered housecoat opened the door. She looked to be in her late sixties. Her gray-and-white hair was pulled back tightly from her face, barrettes catching potential stragglers. Sharp lines etched her forehead and the corners of her eyes, making her look like someone who scowled as much as she smiled. She was scowling now. Or maybe just squinting in the bright sunlight.

"Yeah?"

I spoke to her through the screen of the aluminum storm door. "Sorry to disturb you. I'm interested in the building across the street, and I wondered if you could tell me anything about it."

"That dump? Been empty for years. Used to be a factory making cardboard boxes. My Salvatore worked there. It's why we moved here, so he'd be close to his work. Then they closed down the place. Sal was out of a job, and we were stuck here. Story of my life."

"How long ago did it close?"

"Seven years. Sent all the jobs down south somewheres. Any work Sal's gotten since then has been half the pay at most. He was a security guard for a while at Boston Garden, but even at that job they fired him. Hired a bunch of zombies instead— they don't got to pay zombies minimum wage, you know." She shook her head, looking more tired than angry. "I don't know what this country's coming to."

"So you haven't seen any activity around this building?" I gestured across the street to remind her of what we were talking about.

"Seen? Nah. Heard? Oh, Lordy." She pressed both hands to her ears to show the extent of the noise. "At night, sometimes you hear these awful screams. Last night, for example. Stupid drunk kids, that's what it is. It was so bad I woke up Sal. I was sure they'd gotten hold of a stray cat and were torturing it. Not that I like the wild cats that have taken over this street. Nasty pests, scratch you as soon as look at you. But still. I told Sal to call the cops, but he said to ignore it and go to sleep."

"Did you?"

"Yeah. The screaming stopped, sudden-like. I figured they'd had their fun and done the poor thing in. Cops would've taken hours to get here, anyway. If they bothered to come at all. Think cops care about a stray cat?"

I thanked her for her time and went back down the path. The gnome mooned me again. Now, the statue seemed like neither a joke nor an expression of hostility—more like a comment from a disappointed woman who knew she was at the end of her road. She'd never get any further in life than where she was right now. So she'd plant flowers, but she'd also let the world know this was not where she'd intended to be.

I put petunias and bare-assed gnomes out of my mind and went to call Daniel.

WALKING ON MERIDIAN STREET, I FELT LESS CONSPICUOUS. There was more traffic here, along with the occasional pedestrian. A mother sat on the front steps of a triple-decker, holding her sleeping baby and enjoying the sunshine. I pulled out my cell phone and called Daniel. His work number went straight to voice mail. I didn't leave a message. Daniel had worked all night. He was probably home sleeping, like Kane and Mab and Juliet and everyone else with any sense at all.

I called him at home. The time to raid the Old Ones' hideout was in daylight, and I'd burned enough of that already.

It took four rings for him to pick up. "Costello," said a voice heavy with sleep.

"Daniel, it's Vicky. I know where the Old Ones are hiding."

His voice went from sleep-addled to alert in zero-point-two seconds. "Where?"

"East Boston." I gave him the address.

"Wait. Where did you get this information? Juliet and I didn't get to that part of town last night."

"A little birdie from the demon plane told me. My informant has been inside, Daniel. When Pryce grabbed Tina, it followed them through the demon plane and into this world. It saw Pryce hand Tina over to Colwyn."

"A demon informant. Are you sure you can trust what it tells you?"

The million-dollar question. "I'm sure this is the address. I spoke to a neighbor who confirmed she heard screaming there last night. That screaming must have come from Tina."

"Wait, you're *there*? Vicky, get away—now. This is a job for professionals; I'm sending in a paranormal SWAT team. I can't have a civilian screwing up the operation."

A hot tingling began in my demon mark, and I clenched and unclenched my fist. Daniel wouldn't even know where to send his damn professionals if it weren't for me. The tingling intensified to a slow burn. Stupid know-it-all cop. Without me, he'd be snoozing away in his nice, warm bed, while Tina and the others cowered in their pitch-dark cells.

*Tina.* I couldn't help her if I let the rage take over. I took a couple of deep breaths. The tingling settled back to an itch. One more breath made sure my voice remained steady.

"I'm not screwing anything up, Daniel. I'm telling you where you can find the Old Ones and the missing zombies." He started to say something, but I talked over him. "And I'm not leaving. A friend is in there, and I'm going to make sure she doesn't get hurt. I'll stay back and let your SWAT guys do their work, but I'm not going to be pacing my living room biting my nails and hoping *they* don't screw things up."

There was a long pause. "I could have you arrested."

*Push it down, Vicky. Don't let the anger win.* "You could. But you won't. You need my help."

Silence.

"Pryce is storing a significant amount of Morfran some-where in there. You need me to find it. And some of the zombies might be Morfran-possessed. We need to help them, not use zombie droppers to blow them away."

"I thought you said the Morfran only materialize at night."

"That's true, but I can see into the demon plane. Not far, just where it overlaps with this one. I can use that vision to locate the Morfran, so we can destroy it at nightfall."

I could almost see Daniel running a hand through his shaggy curls as he thought. "I don't like it. I didn't bring you into this to put your life at risk."

The anger I was holding back receded a little on its own. Daniel didn't think I was incompetent; he was trying to protect me. That was an impulse I could understand, even though I didn't want his protection.

"I'll stay back, I promise. But I have to be there. And Daniel, one more thing."

"What is it?" He sounded afraid to ask. He was right.

"You'll need a biohazard team, as well. The Old Ones are manufacturing plague virus."

"They're *what*? You tell me this as an afterthought?"

"It wasn't an afterthought." Rescuing Tina was my first priority. As a human, of course, Daniel would be most worried about the plague. "Pryce is having them ship it to multiple, undisclosed locations. My informant says they haven't sent any yet, but they're close."

He swore, quietly but packed with frustration. "This changes everything. Okay, I'll have to activate SWAT team B—all paranormals. After they've cleared the building, the biohazard team will go in to remove the virus and create a quarantine zone. You say there are houses nearby?"

"There's a row of them across the street."

"We'll do what we can to get them evacuated. It might be tricky, though. We need the element of surprise. That and daylight are the only advantages we have." He added that the team would be there within the hour. I agreed to meet them in a parking lot a block away.

I believed Daniel when he said he'd do his best to evacuate nearby residents. Even so, while I was waiting for the team I'd pay another quick visit to Mrs. Sal. Just to drop the hint that this would be a good afternoon to grab her neighbors and go shopping.

# 32

THE PARANORMAL SWAT TEAM ARRIVED IN A PANEL TRUCK disguised as a delivery van. It reminded me of the one that transported Daniel, his former partner, and me to the secure holding facility out in God-knows-where. Now, the back door opened, and a woman waved me in. I climbed inside, and she closed the door behind me.

Besides the driver up front, six team members sat on benches along either side of the van: four werewolves, an ogre (you can tell by the tusks), and a hook-nosed giant who looked so much like Axel he had to be another troll. The team wasn't dressed in body armor like the SWAT teams you see on TV. Instead, they wore black jeans and black sweatshirts, but the clothes were heavily embroidered with symbols of magical protection. In addition, a charm hung around each cop's neck. There was one female on the team—the werewolf who'd opened the door for me—and she looked tough enough that I'd think twice about tangling with her, no matter what phase the moon happened to be in.

Daniel wasn't present. Regulations kept humans a mile away from any suspected plague site. But the van carried communication equipment, which one of the werewolves fiddled with now. In a minute, Daniel's face appeared on the screen.

The ogre sat at the near end of a bench, his knees nearly hitting his chin. He scooted over to make room for me and I sat—well, *half* sat would be more accurate—balancing as best I could on the sliver of available bench.

The werewolf who'd established the communications link told Daniel everyone was here.

"Great," he said. "Team, I want you to meet Vicky Vaughn, who's lending us her expertise on demons and the Old Ones. We found this location thanks to her." This got me a couple of nods from various SWAT personnel, but most kept their eyes glued to the screen. Daniel took a couple of minutes to complete the introductions, announcing each team member's name and specialty. I'm sorry to say the information didn't stick. There were six of them, and only one of me, and I've never been good with names.

Preliminaries dispensed with, Daniel got down to business. The team was well informed about the Old Ones, especially their powers and vulnerabilities. A few months ago, the Old Ones were a mere legend—most vampires didn't even believe in them. But recent events had changed all that. This SWAT team knew that if an Old One gets his fangs into a body, he can drain it dry in less than a minute. They knew that the Old Ones never sleep, although they grow lethargic in the daytime. And they knew that silver is the best weapon against them. Each team member was supplied with silver bullets, two silver knives, and silver-plated handcuffs. The werewolves wore special gloves made of some thin, high-tech material that let them handle those items.

"I've seen silver burn through Old Ones' flesh," I said. "But be aware that, when we broke them up last winter, they were working on a cure to make them impervious to silver." They'd used Juliet as a guinea pig, and the experiments had nearly killed her. "We don't know how far they might have advanced that project."

From the screen, Daniel spoke. "Given our current information, although silver may not kill the Old Ones, it should weaken them enough to subdue them. Also, like all undead they don't do well in sunlight. If possible, break out some windows; the light will disorient them."

"That's true," I agreed. "Their vision weakens in daylight. But remember that there are hostages in there, too. We want to avoid injuring them if possible."

"What about those hostages?" the female werewolf asked. "They're all PDHs, right? We understand some of them may be possessed by a demonic spirit."

"The Morfran. It can't materialize in daylight, so you won't have to deal with it directly. But yes, it's possible that some of the zombies in that building are Morfran-possessed." *Not Tina,* I thought. *Please not Tina.* I didn't let my voice betray my fear. "If that's the case, the Morfran could drive its host to a murderous frenzy. So be careful."

"All PDHs are to be taken into custody so we can watch them and make sure they're clean," Daniel said. "No exceptions." I had a feeling that last comment was directed at me.

"But don't kill any," I emphasized, "even if a zombie attacks you. We know how to exorcise the Morfran. Remember, these folks are victims."

There were no more questions, and other than, "Please be careful. One of those zombie hostages is just a kid," I couldn't think of anything else to add. Daniel gave the team the green light to do their reconnaissance.

Two werewolves left, and the ogre sitting next to me slid over, so I finally had enough bench to sit on. The scouting werewolves took along thermal imaging equipment to scan the building for cold spots. The Old Ones' icy body temperature would show up black, giving us an indication of the locations and number of Old Ones in the building. Zombies don't produce body heat, either, but their skin is the same temperature as their surroundings. The Old Ones are like walking blocks of ice.

Nobody said much while we waited for the team members to return. Daniel cut the communication link so he could talk to the biohazard team, waiting in their own van at a different location. The SWAT guys sat with their eyes closed and their heads back, meditating to strengthen their magical defenses. They'd need it. The Old Ones are adept at magical warfare, able to call up energy and wield it as a lethal weapon. They're no slouches at sword fighting, either.

I thought of Tina, practicing lunges in my living room, and my heart constricted. Right now, she was probably curled up in a tiny cell like the one Bonita described. Alone, scared, and in darkness, not knowing where she was or what would happen to her. I *had* to get her out of that place. In fact, I vowed, if she made it out in one piece, I'd take the kid back as my apprentice, if only to keep an eye on her.

Two sharp raps on the van door made me jump and almost fall off the bench. The others opened their eyes calmly as the scouts returned. They got Daniel back on the link and uploaded thermal images of the building. They'd found eight Old Ones—our team was outnumbered, but not by much. "We couldn't scan the basement, though," a werewolf explained. "There could be more down there."

"Probably at least two," I suggested. "That's where they keep the zombies, and Bonita said they always came in pairs when they brought her food. So we should assume another two guards, at least, on that level."

Ten ancient super-vampires—maybe more—to six highly trained paranormal cops. Even with our daylight advantage, it could go either way. I'd fought the Old Ones before. I could tip the advantage to our side. But Daniel wouldn't hear of it.

"You're here as a consultant, Vicky, and I appreciate your help in that role. But you haven't trained with this team. You don't know their procedures. I hate to say it, but you'd get in the way. So I'm telling you—no, I'm *ordering* you: Stay in the van."

None of the team looked at me, and I was glad my crimson face evaded scrutiny. The humiliation heated my demon mark, making me want to strike out at something—anything, since Daniel was out of reach. Instead, as the van started rolling toward the target site, I focused on slowing my breathing, willing the demon mark to cool. Whatever was about to go down, Hellion-fueled rage wouldn't help.

The recon images showed that the cold spots were concentrated at one end of the building. As the team conferred with Daniel to formulate an attack plan, leaving me out, the uneasy feeling that had taken root in my gut began to sprout. Could I trust Butterfly's information? The information, yes. The Old Ones were in that building. But what about the demon's intention?

Was this a trap?

"Good luck, team," Daniel said. The screen went blank.

The ogre reached across me to open the door. "Wait!" I touched his arm. He looked at my hand as though it might be something to eat. Then his hard, tiny eyes met my face. His tusks gleamed.

"Remember that this tip came from a demon," I said, looking at the ogre but speaking to the whole team. "Pryce is powerful in the demon plane. He may have passed me this information to set a trap."

"We know that." The hard eyes softened a degree. "But thanks." Then he opened the door and stepped quietly out. For a monster the size of a gorilla, he was light on his feet. The others followed, silent.

The ogre wore a headset linking him to the van's communication system, which the driver had now taken over. When the team was in position, the ogre notified us. Then we heard his whispered command, "Go, go, go, *go!*"

We heard shattering glass and the explosion of flash-bang grenades.

We heard shouts of "Police! Down on the floor, now!"

We heard rapid-fire shots.

And we heard a soul-rending scream of fear and pain.

After that, we heard static. Nothing else.

"Shit," said the driver. "Something's—"

I didn't hear the rest of his sentence. I was already out the door and running toward the building.

My boots slapped the pavement as I sprinted to the opening they'd cut in the fence. Wire ripped my jacket, catching a sleeve as I squeezed through. I yanked free and darted to the open door, drawing a sword as I went.

Inside, I found myself standing in a long hallway. Sounds of fighting erupted from the far end. Moving quickly, I advanced along the hall, staying quiet and watching the shadows for hidden enemies. The corpse of an Old One lay on the floor. I raised my foot to step over it, but a hand grabbed my ankle and yanked me off balance. *Not dead.* I fell sideways, using the momentum to turn and ram my sword into the damn thing's throat. Flesh sizzled as the silver blade entered the desiccated body. The Old One gurgled. The hand relaxed and fell away.

Good. Silver still did its job. The feel of the blade finding its target, the death rattle, strength slipping away—these things sped up my adrenaline-accelerated pulse. I wanted more.

The hot, prickling demon mark urged me forward. I paused, trying to suppress the feeling. It grew. I struggled for a moment, then I let it go. I was here to win. Not merely to stop my enemies but to crush them. To drive in my sword and exult in their annihilation. Instead of resisting the Destroyer, I'd draw strength from the demon that had marked me.

That mark raged with fire that raced up my arm. It ignited my heart, my brain. There would be death—and I would bring it.

Impatient to join the battle, I ran forward. I passed another body that made me pause. This one, in a mechanic's coveralls, had been decapitated. A few feet away the head of a male zombie stared at me. Then it blinked. His mouth moved, but the severed vocal cords couldn't produce sound. His black tongue licked his lips, and I realized the words he was trying to say.

"Help me."

How in hell can you help a headless zombie? Maybe an undead surgeon could put him back together, but there was nothing I could do. Not even put the poor guy out of his misery. My attempt at a reassuring smile a sickly failure, I left him where he lay.

*Almost there.* From the room at the end of the hall came the grunts, scuffles, and shouts of fighting. Blades clashed. Someone bellowed in pain. Why no gunshots? I quickened my pace. My demon mark spouted flame, reflected in my blade. The need to be in the thick of it, to color my sword with blood and gore, gripped me. I'd stood by for too long. Only death—hot, steaming, bloody death—would satisfy.

I stepped inside. In the semidarkness, it was hard to tell who was what. Zombies, robed Old Ones, SWAT team members—all roiled and writhed in a noisy, pounding mass of violence.

A scream, primal, coming from some place far beyond me, tore itself from my throat. Raising my sword, I plunged into the fight.

# 33

DARKNESS. PAIN. MY FACE LAY ON SOMETHING HARD, rough. It scraped my cheek when I moved.

Could I sit up? Yes. My muscles screamed, but I managed. My fingers clutched something. A sword hilt. Good. I had protection.

I squinted into the darkness through watery eyes, trying to figure out where I was. My brain thudded like a cotton-stuffed drum: *throb throb throb.* A thought pushed its way through the thickness: Bonita's cell. I stretched my arms widely, feeling with my fingers, testing with my sword. No walls within reach. In the distance, a car horn honked. I sniffed, inhaling scents of diesel fumes and salt air. Not a cell, then. I was outside. But where? I could think of no place in Boston where the darkness could be so complete.

How did I get here? And what the hell happened in the abandoned factory? I probed my memory, but the cottony, sludgy feeling wouldn't clear. I remembered making my way down the hall, my demon mark aflame, excitement building as I neared the fight. I remembered my lust for violence, my blood-chilling battle cry in a voice that wasn't mine. But then everything collapsed into a flashing kaleidoscope of tumbling images. Blade hitting blade. Blade sinking into flesh. Screams. Thuds. And blood—so much blood. Fountains of it. Rivers. Oceans.

I couldn't tease the images apart. I saw the blossoming of a sudden wound and didn't know whether it was mine or another's. I felt myself step over a body but couldn't tell whose it was, not even friend or foe. And through it all, a voice whispered in my mind. Not my own thoughts—I was sure of that. A voice outside of me, seeking a way in, wanting something from me. But I couldn't find the shape or meaning of the words. It was like trying to listen to someone speaking underwater. The words bubbled toward me, but I couldn't make them out. When I tried now to recall, to listen, my fragmented memory went blank.

Nothing.

My eyes had adjusted to the darkness, which wasn't as absolute as I'd first thought. I needed to figure out where I was. Everything would fall into place then, and I could move forward. I hoped.

The phone Daniel had given me had a GPS. I'd find out where I was, and then I'd call my apartment. Mab would pick up. She must be frantic with worry by now.

I tried again to dredge up a memory from the raid. But I couldn't. I couldn't remember. Mab wasn't the only one who was worried.

Daniel's phone wasn't in my pocket. Damn it, it *had* to be. I stood, feeling every blow and cut I couldn't remember, and checked all my pockets. My clothes were torn and stiff with blood. My hands were sticky with it. But the phone was gone.

So were most of the weapons I'd carried. All I had was the sword in my hand. It, too, was tacky with blood, both hilt and blade.

Okay. No phone, but the plan hadn't changed. I'd determine my location, and then I'd find a phone to call Mab.

I seemed to be in the middle of an alley between two tall buildings. No streetlights shone here, but the darkness seemed thinner ahead, so I went that way. It amazed me that there could be a pocket of such deep darkness in a city the size of Boston, especially so near the full moon. Overhead, the sky was uniformly black. No moon, no stars. Despite the sunny afternoon, heavy clouds must have blown in. But now, in this alley, there wasn't a whisper of wind.

I moved slowly, left hand in front of me, my right gripping my sword as I shuffled through the inky night toward the lesser darkness. Each step sent pains of every description surging through me. Twice I stumbled over unseen objects in my path. But I kept going. When I exited this alley, I'd be on a street. There would be lights, traffic, people, signs. It would be like stepping back into the world.

Except it wasn't. I reached the alley's mouth and leaned against the corner of the building. There was a street here, yes, but everything was still so dark. I couldn't see the far curb, let alone a street sign. Distant sounds of traffic were audible, but muffled. I shook my head, trying to clear it. What was wrong with my senses? And where was the source of the light I'd seen while in the alleyway?

*There.* A glimmer in the darkness. I squinted, and it took shape, grew steadier. A flame burned. I went toward it.

As I got closer, I could make out the source: a fire burning inside a barrel. A figure stood by it, warming his hands. One of Boston's homeless? Maybe he could tell me where we were, why everything was so dark.

The man stared into the fire, the flames giving his wrinkled, bearded face a maniacal air. He wore a torn raincoat, belted at the waist. His old, gnarled hands writhed around each other in the heat. His shoes were mismatched—one was an old work boot, the other a running shoe held together with duct tape. He didn't look up as I approached.

"Excuse me," I said, standing back a little in the darkness so my bloody appearance wouldn't alarm him. "I'm lost. Could you tell me where we are?"

The old man cackled, still staring at the flames as though hypnotized. His grin revealed a mouth missing more teeth than it held. I wasn't sure he'd understood my question, so I asked again. No answer. His laughter was the only sign he'd heard me.

This man couldn't help. I turned away, wondering which way I should go in all that darkness, when the cackling stopped.

"Yes, I can tell you where we are." The deep baritone voice didn't match the old man's high-pitched laugh.

When I turned around, the man stood in the same place by the fire. But the face that now stared at me wasn't the face of the old homeless man.

"Pryce." My aching fingers tightened their grip on my sword.

"You've been here before. The world between the worlds. Limbo, humans call it."

Yes, I'd been in Limbo before. A place of lost things, of wandering souls. It was a borderland between the human and demon planes, a place touching both but belonging to neither. Pryce had once sent a demon to pull me into Limbo and attack me there.

Not again. I brought my sword forward and stepped out of the darkness. *Aim for the bastard's heart.*

As soon as the firelight touched me, my hand released my sword. It fell to the ground and my arm dropped to my side, shaking.

Pryce kicked the sword away.

"Not here, cousin. Not now. I thought Limbo would be a good place for a truce. Allow us both some breathing room."

"I didn't agree to a truce."

"Not in so many words. But notice how you were unable to strike me. That's new, isn't it? My bond with Difethwr is good for that much, anyway. The Hellion has grown strong enough in me that you cannot raise your marked arm against me, just as you cannot raise it against the demon that marked it."

Was he telling the truth? I tried to flex my fingers. Limp, they wouldn't obey. But we were in Limbo, and the rules were different here. Pryce's claim might be a trick to make me believe I could no longer fight him.

Whether or not that was true in the real world, I couldn't fight him here.

"Where's Tina?" I demanded.

"I haven't given her to the Morfran yet, if that's what you're asking. But she's unimportant."

"Not to me, she isn't. Let her go."

Pryce kept talking as though I hadn't spoken. "What's important is what happened this afternoon. Tell me, cousin, what *did* happen?"

His question stabbed into my mind but didn't illuminate a damn thing. I stared into the flames, trying to make them into images, shape them into memories.

"You don't remember, do you? Well, you were in an exquisite killing frenzy. It must have felt like a trance. Difethwr was quite proud."

The tingling in my demon mark felt like a confirmation. I said nothing.

"It's been a long time coming," Pryce continued, "but at last it's happened."

I wasn't going to take his bait. I would not ask him what had happened. I didn't want to hear it—not from Pryce. I kept feeling around inside my mind, looking for the truth. But it was like that truth was locked away in a place I couldn't reach.

Pryce sighed. "So that's how you're going to be, is it? Very well. I could describe today's events to you, but you'd think I was lying. However, you cannot deny the truth of your feelings. You've noticed, haven't you? How the Destroyer's grip on you has strengthened. How small annoyances set off an anger that mushrooms into rage. And that rage—it's been harder to control, hasn't it? There have even been times when, perhaps just for a moment or two, you haven't *wanted* to control it." I stared at the flames, unable to reply. Pryce's voice, low and insinuating, buzzed in my ear. "When you thought how good it would feel to give in and *destroy*. The cause didn't matter. Everything was in the release. The crushing, the utter destruction. You've wanted that, cousin—and know it."

The flames parted like a curtain, and I was back in that hallway. The bodies on the floor. The screams and clashing of swords. The excitement heating my veins. Then each flame became an image, those flashes of memory I couldn't fit together. A spurt of blood. A wound gaping. Light flashing off a blade. A mouth contorted in pain. A bloody hand, its fingers going slack around a hilt. I closed my eyes, willing away both the images and the excitement they called up in me.

Pryce's voice whispered, close. "This afternoon, you got what you wanted. You finally gave in."

A grunt of pain. Blood spilling on a concrete floor.

"You stormed into that room like the spirit of Death itself.

You didn't care who or what you killed. You wanted only to destroy. And you did."

That sweet moment of triumph when flesh gave way to steel.

"The entire SWAT team is dead. Much of that is your doing. We lost some on our side, too—again, largely thanks to you. You *were* the Destroyer, finally and completely possessed."

I recalled the voice I'd heard, probing at my consciousness. Could it have been Difethwr? The Destroyer taking control, directing me, egging me on. I could hear those burbling echoes, but the words still eluded me. No. I wouldn't believe it. The Destroyer had touched me, but my will was my own. Always.

I shook off the images that crowded me and stared squarely into the black holes of Pryce's eyes. "You're lying."

"Didn't I tell you? I knew you'd say that. Well, I won't waste my breath attempting to convince you. The truth is in your bones now, cousin. It's in your blood. It's in your *soul*. When you accept that you belong to the Destroyer—and, through the Hellion, to me—your memories will return." He passed his hand over the flames, and again I stood in a doorway, my sword raised, watching a struggling mass. All I wanted was to throw myself in. My heart surged, and then the image winked out.

In its place was Pryce's smile. "I can help you," he said. Insidious words from a demi-demon. "Come with me now. Not to the Ordinary, where nothing but trouble awaits you. We'll go to my realm. Difethwr waits for you there. In Uffern, you can train to work *with* your Hellion master, stop fighting against what you've become. And after you've learned to serve that . . . thing, you'll be fit to serve me." He gripped my arm. "It's your destiny."

I yanked my arm away. "I've told you before, Pryce. I will never join your side."

He looked at me for a long time, then shook his head. "This stubbornness of yours is so tiresome." He waved a dismissive hand. "At least I won't have to endure it much longer. You *will* join me, and you'll be glad to do so. But I don't have to talk myself silly attempting to convince you. You'll convince yourself, from the inside. Your feelings already know."

Out in the real world, a siren wailed. Another joined it. The sound was muffled, but louder than any outside noises that had so far made their way into Limbo.

"Those sirens are coming for you," Pryce said in his bored voice. "In the Ordinary, you'll be arrested for murder. If you had agreed to return with me to Uffern, you'd be beyond their reach. But I've withdrawn my offer for the moment." His eyes, already impossibly black, somehow darkened. "You must understand where your true loyalties lie. Call me when you tire of languishing in a human prison."

The fire flared up, and the homeless man laughed and stared at the flames. Again the fire flared. I stood in the middle of a semidark room, gripping my sword. Bodies lay everywhere. Blood covered the floor.

I was the only living creature there.

# 34

TIRES SCREECHED. A BULLHORN ANNOUNCED THE ARRIVAL of the police. *Shit.* They'd be on top of me in moments. I stood in a room filled with dead bodies, with a bloody sword in my hand and no memory of what happened. They'd arrest me for sure. If they didn't shoot me on sight.

I had to be out of here before cops stormed the place, and there was only one way to do that. I threw aside my sword and prepared to shift.

To what? What creature could get me out of here?

*Feral cats.* Mrs. Sal's complaint about the pests that had taken over the neighborhood waved like a banner in my mind. A wild cat could slink past the cops. And it would pass unnoticed through the streets.

"This is the police. The building is surrounded."

I thought of gray fur and whiskers. Sharp teeth. A long tail.

"Throw down any weapons and come to the door with your hands on your head."

Claws. Glowing eyes with slitted pupils. Muscles tensed to pounce.

Footfalls pounded, inside. Coming down the hall.

The energy built. Sounds sharpened as my ears changed

shape, slid to the top of my head. My skull contracted, my field of vision widened. Smells, so many smells.

The bullhorn droned, but its words blurred together into mere sound.

My arms lengthened, nails sharpening into claws. The energy built some more. Whiskers sprouted, sensing the movements of air currents. Energy, more and more, getting stronger. Fur covered me. Then the energy blasted out, and I changed.

BLOOD. HUNGRY. WANT TO TASTE IT. WAIT—LISTEN. LOUD noises, angry noises. Coming fast. Trouble—angry sounds mean trouble.

I spring. Legs running as paws hit ground. I run, fast, away from angry sounds.

Dark place ahead, good for hiding. I run into darkness. Slow, stop. Creep away from noisy humans. Be quiet. Stay close to wall. Stay quiet. Hunger rumbles in my belly. My tongue wants the taste of blood.

*What was that sound?*

Too much noise. Too dangerous.

A doorway. Silent, I creep through. Dust here. Old smells, stale. No food.

Blood smell pulls me back. Hungry. I turn, watch. Stay low. Creep. Cautious.

Noisy humans stomp through the blood room. Too many. Too loud. Can't get near the blood.

Need to go. Run away. Find food.

My side touching the wall, I creep. Stay in shadows. A window lets in light. Open. I wait, watch. Crouching, ready.

*Now.*

I run to the light. Jump. Up, over, out. I run, ground hard under paws. Air fresher, clearer. I run from noisy humans.

Quieter now. Slowing down. Hungry. Food. Want food.

I stop, lift my nose. Sniff.

Over there, a movement. Pigeon pecks in the dirt.

Pigeon unaware. I crouch. I'll catch it, eat it.

I crouch, tense. Legs tight, ready to spring. I watch. Creep forward. Watch. Creep. Crouch lower. Tense, trembling. Watch . . . watch . . . *spring!*

Claws grab nothing. Pigeon above, in tree.

Hungry.

I sniff again. Where is food?

For a long time I hunt. On grass. In wide streets. On narrow streets. Other cats hiss, "Get away!" Sometimes I fight. Sometimes I run. Always, hunger rumbles.

Light dims. Hunger pinches me. Trotting, sniffing for food smells. I turn into narrow street, behind human dwellings. Sometimes food is here. Noises come from buildings. Food smells come from open window. I stop, sniff. Want food.

A door opens. Yellow light spills out. I freeze. A human watches me.

Run? But food smells hold me.

"Here, kitty." Hand stretches out, stops. Waits. "Do you want some milk?

I step toward human. Wait. Step, step, step. Stop. Safe? Danger? More steps. Stop again. I lift my nose, stretch forward. Legs tense, ready to run. I sniff. Human scent. Soap. And more. Warm, milky smell. Good. Want to taste.

Hand moves. I jump back, hiss. Tense, ready to run.

"*Shh*. It's all right." Human sounds are quiet, soft. Not fighting sounds. Hand turns, opens. I sniff more. Good smells. Milky.

"I don't want to scare you off, so I'll move real slow." Hand goes away. I stretch forward, feet planted, sniffing. Too close. I back up. Tense, watching.

"My, you are a skittish one. But I can tell you're hungry. Here, how about this?"

Something is on the ground. Milk smell is strong. In my belly, hunger roars. Food, close by. Crouch. Step forward. Milk smell fills my nose. Another step.

Stop. Where is human? Will she fight me for this milk?

No. She's backed away, sits on steps. Watches. I watch back. Want to taste the milk. She stays still, doesn't move.

"Go ahead, kitty." Soft sounds, quiet sounds.

One paw forward. Stop. Look up. She sits and watches. I step, then again. I taste the milk. Good. Hunger wants more, wants it all. I drink, milk good and wet on my tongue. Stop. Look. Human sits. My milk. Mine. I drink it all, lick up each drop.

"Gone already? Poor thing. You must be starving. I'll get you some more."

Hand reaches. My food! Mine! I want to scratch, bite. Protect my food. Mine. But soft sounds continue, soothing. Food in my belly feels good. No scratching. No biting. Milk dish gone. I lick my muzzle. I sit and groom.

"Here you go." Good smell. Milk again. Mine. I lap fast, drinking goodness.

A touch on my head.

No! I jump back. Spit. Hiss. No touching!

"All right, all right. I guess you don't like to be petted. I'll just watch you drink your milk."

Human backs off, sits. Milk smells good. I come forward, drink. No more touches. Just noises. Quiet, nice. "I wish I could keep you. But I don't think you'd like living in an apartment. I'll leave some milk out for you, though. Here, on the back porch. And an old pillow you can use for a bed. Maybe I'll see you in the morning."

Milk dish empty. Goes away. Comes back full. Human goes inside, light goes off. Darkness. Milk. Full belly. Warm.

I clean my fur, licking all over. Warm. Full. Clean.

I find a soft place and curl up to sleep.


THAT NIGHT, I DREAMED OF RUNNING HARD ON FOUR PAWS down dark alleyways. I dreamed of fighting, of eating, of watching small creatures—birds, mice—and then pouncing. Eventually, the dream changed. A big gray tomcat, stinking of piss and musk, challenged me. We fought; he tore my leg. As the pain grew, another cat attacked. Then another, and still another. They bit me all over, tearing my flesh, ripping out my sleek fur in bloody clumps. Pain raked my body and twisted my limbs. My body swelled and stretched.

Energy blasted out.

I was awake. It was dark—no, dim. I could see my hands clasping each other inches from my face. Was it twilight? Dawn, maybe. I remembered darkness, but was that experience or dream? My body tried to curl itself on a pillow, but mostly I lay on rough wood planks. I sat up and tried to figure out where I was.

"How . . . how did you do that?"

The voice—a woman's—made me jump. I picked up the pillow I'd been sleeping on and held it in front of my bare torso while I looked around to see who'd spoken.

I was on the back porch of a triple-decker. A woman stood at the door, watching me with wide eyes. She had short hair, like mine, and she wore a blue bathrobe over striped pajamas. One of her hands clutched the doorframe; the other gripped a saucer. Behind her was a brightly lit, warm-looking kitchen.

"You, um, must be cold," she said. She set the saucer on a counter behind her and unbelted her robe. "Here." She handed it to me.

"Thanks." I took the robe and managed to get it around me while still clutching the pillow to my front. Clothes never survive a shift. You'd think that after all these years I'd be used to returning to my human form without a stitch of clothing, but there was something inherently awkward about making naked conversation with a stranger. Especially a stranger who'd just witnessed an ordinary-looking cat transform into a person.

I set the pillow on the porch floor and stood, pulling the belt tight around my waist. "Thanks," I repeated, trying to work some cat hair off my tongue without being obvious about it. I let her question of "how?" hang unanswered between us. There wasn't any easy way to explain. Instead, I offered a weak smile as my mind tried to sort out all the images and impressions that crowded it. The SWAT raid. Dead bodies. Pryce. Limbo. More dead bodies. Shifting. Running. Hunger. Fighting. Milk and warmth.

It was the dead bodies that haunted me.

I had to call Kane, find out what was happening. But Daniel's cell phone was long gone. I hadn't had it in Limbo, and it sure as hell wouldn't have survived the energy blasts of my shifts.

"Can I use your phone?" I asked. If that went well, maybe I'd push my luck and borrow some clothes.

"I thought you were a cat." She twisted around to see the saucer of milk on the counter.

"I was. I'm a shapeshifter." Something about this woman was familiar. I raised my head and sniffed the air between us. Her scent made me feel warm and safe. "You fed me."

"We get a lot of strays around here. Usually they run away from me." She made no move from where she stood. "I'm Kaysi."

"Hi, Kaysi." I hesitated. Should I tell her my name? Pryce had said the police believed I'd attacked the SWAT team. If he was telling the truth—a big *if*—my name and picture would be all over the news.

Kaysi made my decision for me. "You're Vicky, aren't you? I read about you in the paper. It said Vicky somebody, a shape-shifter."

*Uh-oh.* "Listen, Kaysi, I don't want to bother you. If I could just use your phone to make one quick call, maybe borrow some clothes, I'll be out of here in five minutes. It'll be like you never saw me."

"Never saw you? How could I forget seeing . . . that?" Lost for words, she gestured at the spot on her back porch where a blast of energy had transformed a sleeping cat into a naked, disoriented woman.

Somewhere down the street, a car engine started. Kaysi leaned out and looked around. Then she beckoned to me. "You'd better come inside."

THE LINOLEUM FLOOR OF KAYSI'S KITCHEN FELT TOASTY under my bare feet. Cream-colored walls glowed warmly in the overhead light. A clock told me it was a little before seven. Beside the clock hung a calendar that showed three kittens snuggling in a basket. As I looked around, I could see that Kaysi was a big-time cat lover. The mug she held, the dishtowel beside the sink, the pot holders over the stove, the placemats on the kitchen table—all were adorned with pictures of cats. Cats sleeping, cats frolicking, cats sitting and staring through half-closed eyes. No wonder she'd been kind enough to feed a twitchy stray.

A newspaper lay on the table, open to a two-page spread whose headline shouted "Massacre in East Boston." It showed a picture of the factory, surrounded by police cars. And there was a photo of me—the one from my paranormal ID card. It looked like a mug shot.

"You were there." Kaysi gestured toward the paper.

I nodded. What could I say?

"The story says the police are looking for you. It says you're armed and dangerous."

"Well, at least you know I'm not armed." I smiled my goof-iest grin, hoping it made me look harmless, and turned the bathrobe pockets inside out. "Kaysi, I won't lie to you. I was there supporting the SWAT team. Something went wrong. I blacked out, and I don't know what happened after that."

"I don't think you're dangerous. You know why?" She stretched out her hands, showing backs crisscrossed with thin white scars. "We have lots of wild cats in this neighborhood. I like to help them. They eat the food I leave out, but whenever I try to get near them, they do this. They scratch and bite." She turned her hands back and forth, examining them, then picked up her mug. "The cat I fed last night didn't do that. She spit and backed away, but she didn't scratch or bite me, not even a nip. She was wary, but she wasn't mean." Kaysi sipped, her expression thoughtful. "Animals are purer than people. They don't lie or try to hide who they are. And that cat was you. I don't believe you'd hurt anyone."

I didn't know how to reply. Her clear blue eyes were trusting, sure.

"Anyway," Kaysi said, setting her empty mug in the sink, "you can stay here as long as you like. I won't tell anyone. You must be hungry." She glanced at the saucer that still sat on the counter. "Would you like a, um, a glass of milk?"

"I'd love some coffee if you can spare it. Black, please."

A tiger kitten chased an unraveling ball of string around the mug Kaysi handed me. The coffee inside was strong and hot. She pointed out the phone and said she'd go look for some clothes that might fit me. What she meant was that she was giving me privacy to make my call.

"I won't be more than a couple of minutes," I said.

"Take your time." She disappeared down a hallway. A door closed.

Kane has a special prepaid phone, registered under a false name, for emergencies—like now. I pressed *67 to mask Kay-si's number and called the emergency phone. As I dialed, I thought about what Kaysi had said. Her simple love of animals had convinced her I wasn't a killer. I only wished I could be as certain.

KANE PICKED UP ON THE FIRST RING. "ARE YOU SAFE?"

"For now."

"Good. Don't tell me where you are." He didn't have to explain why. If he didn't know where I was, he wouldn't have to lie about it to the cops. "Vicky, that botched raid is all over the news. What happened?"

"I don't know. I was in the van, listening over the two-way radio. Something went wrong . . . there was a scream. So I went in. But when I reached the fighting . . . I blacked out. When I came to, it looked like a slaughterhouse. Kane, the whole team was dead."

"And you don't remember anything at all about the fight?"

I told him the parts I did remember—the bodies in the hallway, the surge of power in my demon mark, the fragments of combat.

The silence lengthened. "I wish you'd kept me in the loop," he said finally.

"I intended to. I went to your office, but you'd gone home to sleep, and I remembered how tired you said you were. I didn't want to interrupt your rest before . . . you know, tonight."

Another pause, longer, hung between us. So much was packed into that one little word, *tonight*. The first night of the full moon. Kane's transformation into a hellhound. The Night Hag on the hunt for me.

"All right," Kane said. "Get me up to speed now. Tell me everything that happened since I last saw you."

"I got a tip about where Pryce and the Old Ones were holding Tina."

"A tip from whom?"

"Butterfly."

"That damn guilt demon," he growled. "And you trusted it?"

"The tip was good. I've told you before—Eidolons can't lie."

"But they can manipulate. You told me that, too."

It was true. And that was exactly what I'd been afraid of— that Butterfly was leading me into a trap set by Pryce. The next time that Eidolon dared to show its damn face, I'd kill it. No truces, no niceness. Just one dead demon.

"As I said, the tip was good. And Tina's *life* was at stake." Fear gripped me. "Do you know what happened to her? Is she safe?"

"There's been nothing about her in the news. Details are sketchy. So far, all the reporting is focusing on the SWAT team casualties. And you." *And me.* I wished finding out what had happened was as easy as turning on the news. "All, right, so the demon gave you this tip. Then what?"

"After I stopped at your office, I checked out the site. I talked to a neighbor. I called Daniel, and he organized the raid. He couldn't be on site because of the virus threat."

"Wait, *what* virus threat?"

There had been nothing on the news about the factory being a suspected plague virus lab. The authorities might cover up that information to prevent a panic—I'd seen them do that before. But they'd also have come up with a reason to keep humans away. According to Kane's description, and confirmed by the newspaper photo on Kaysi's table, cops and journalists swarmed over the site.

So the biohazard team hadn't found any virus.

My eye on the clock, I resumed my narrative. "Daniel emphasized I was there as a consultant—not to fight. So after I debriefed the team, I waited in the van, until I heard that scream."

Kane didn't speak, but I knew what he was thinking as clearly as if the phone could broadcast his thoughts. He was thinking that once again, I had to go rushing in. And yes, he was right. If someone was in trouble and I could help, I *did* have to go rushing in. It's part of who I am.

But today, "who I am" felt like a wide-open question. Had I helped those cops? Or had I sent them to their deaths? Even worse, had I been the one to kill them?

"I saw Pryce," I said.

"During the raid?"

"After. When I blacked out I ended up in Limbo somehow, and Pryce was there, waiting. He . . . he told me the Destroyer possesses me now. That its power makes me kill without caring what I destroy. He said that's what happened to the SWAT team." At that moment, the full horror of Pryce's claim hit me, *really* hit me, for the first time. "He said I killed them, Kane. And he said I'll keep killing." My voice couldn't make it through the last sentence without cracking.

For so long, I'd fought the Destroyer, pushed down the rage it created in me. But the Hellion had grown stronger, and I was so tired. Maybe Pryce had a point. Maybe some part of me did want to quit struggling and give in.

I stifled a sob. My greatest fear—and it was coming true.

"Vicky, listen to me. I know you. I've seen the Destroyer's hold on you, yes. But I've also seen how hard you fight. How deep your reserves are. You are stronger. Do you hear me? *You are stronger.*"

The certainty in his voice, his unshakable belief in me, touched me inside. Something small and tight stirred, like a long-buried seed groping toward a hint of warmth in the frozen ground. I wasn't sure Kane was right. In fact, I greatly feared he was wrong. But *he* believed his words, and that meant something. It meant a lot.

"Thank you," I whispered.

"I want so badly to hold you right now. This wasn't how I pictured saying good-bye, not today." The frustration in his voice shifted into something else. "But you stay strong, my love. Stay strong, and . . . and tonight I'll do my best to do the same."

I nodded, tears running down my face, knowing he couldn't see and yet knowing he understood.

# 35

BEFORE WE HUNG UP, KANE SAID MAB WANTED TO SPEAK
with me.

"Mab's there?" Surprise gave me back my voice.

"I'm at your apartment. I figured you'd get in touch if you
could—call me or your home phone, or contact Mab using that
dream-phone thing you do. However you managed it, I wanted
to be there."

I didn't have words for the feelings that swelled in my chest.
So instead, I asked him to put Mab on.

"We probably won't talk again," he said. Tonight was the
full moon, and he had to travel to the werewolf retreat in Princeton. "I'll leave this phone with your aunt. And Vicky . . ." His
voice wavered. "Please know that, whatever happens, I
love you."

"I love you, too," I whispered. "Whatever happens."

A moment later, Mab's brisk voice took over the line. "Victory, child, are you all right?"

"I am." I cleared my throat. Now wasn't the time to give
way to mushy feelings. "I'm recovering from a shift. Vicky
Vaughn went into the Old Ones' hideout, but a feral cat came
running out."

"It must have been a desperate situation."

"It was." I briefly repeated what I'd told Kane, bringing Mab up to speed on yesterday's events. "A kind animal lover gave me a saucer of milk and a bed for the night. And this person barely blinked an eye when I shifted back to my usual form."

"Can you stay out of sight until this evening?"

"I'll manage." I wasn't going to take advantage of Kaysi's hospitality—after all, I was a fugitive from justice. I'd find another place to hide. Boston had no shortage of empty buildings.

"See that you do. I've contacted the Night Hag. You're to give her the falcon tonight."

"Where?"

"Your photo was all over the news by late afternoon, so I knew the exchange couldn't take place here. And, needless to say, the witches your Mr. Kane hired for protection are suddenly unavailable. At any rate, I asked Mallt-y-Nos to suggest a spot. We're meeting there at midnight. Do you know a place called . . ." In the pause I could hear papers rustle. "Fenway Park?"

"The baseball stadium?"

"Oh, is that what it is? I assumed it was some sort of green space."

Green space. If that's what you want to call the Green Monster, the green-painted, thirty-seven-foot-high wall that flanks left field. I flipped through the paper. There wasn't a game tonight. But how were we supposed to get inside?

We'd figure it out as we went.

"Can you find your way there?" I asked.

"Certainly." Mab's tone could have been either amusement or annoyance. It was hard to tell without seeing her expression.

"If you need a map, Juliet can print one out from her computer."

"For heaven's sake, child, don't worry about me. Take care of yourself. Rest if you can. Meditate. Focus on staying pure; it will give you strength. I'll meet you at Fenway Park at eleven."

I still didn't like it. If Mab got lost, or if I ran into a problem, neither of us would have a way to contact the other. The dream phone wasn't an option while we were both awake.

"I really think you should have Juliet print you out a map. Tell her to mark Gate A on Yawkey Way. I'll meet you there."

"All right." This time, Mab's sigh made it clear she was more than a little annoyed by my concerns. "Although honestly, you'd do well to remember that I've had three centuries of experience in getting from one place to another." Her tone softened, but there was steel beneath it. "And Victory . . . do listen to what Mr. Kane said. The Destroyer is strong, but you *are* stronger. You can draw on that strength whenever you choose, but you must believe in it. Ponder that today."

I promised her I would, and we said good-bye.

"Thanks, Kaysi," I called down the hallway as I hung up the phone.

She appeared a moment later, a bundle of clothes in her arms. "I hope these will fit," she said, cocking her head as she inspected me. "You're a little taller than I am. Skinnier, too."

"They'll be fine. I really appreciate it."

"I have to get ready for work. Feel free to eat some breakfast and make more calls. After I'm gone, you can take a shower, grab a nap on the couch—whatever you need. Just be sure to lock the door if you leave."

"If there's anything I can do to repay you . . ."

"Don't worry about that. Just do whatever's necessary to find out what happened. When I see in the paper that you've cleared your name, I'll be proud I helped."

Suddenly, I couldn't think of anything to say. I held out my arms to accept the stack of clothes.

"Good luck," Kaysi said. She turned and went back down the hall. A door closed, and the shower started running.

A box of cereal stood on the table. I poured myself a bowl and refreshed my coffee. There was milk in the fridge, of course. Kaysi kept a good supply for any hungry cats that might wander by.

As I ate, I thought about Mab's advice. *Meditate. Focus on being pure.* Easy for her to say. She wasn't marked by a Hellion. Ten years ago, the Destroyer had touched me with its essence. I'd struggled to control it, and often I'd succeeded, but never had I been able to push it out. Over time, that essence had infected my own, intertwining with it like ivy creeping up a brick wall, insinuating itself, claiming a stronger, deeper hold, weakening the mortar until it crumbles and the wall collapses.

From the newspaper on the table, my own face stared at me. What if that disastrous SWAT raid had been my collapse?

That's what Pryce wanted me to believe.

But, damn it, who said Pryce got to define me? I didn't know what happened. I searched my memory for some clue. Sifting through images, I worked my way back, past my hours as a prowling cat, past my encounter with Pryce in Limbo. I focused on the moment I'd stood in the hallway, sword drawn, ready for a fight.

A fight with whom? I'd rushed into the building to defend the SWAT team. To drive back any Old Ones who threatened them. But what had been my intention when I threw myself into the fight? To protect—or to destroy?

My mind wouldn't go there. Each time I tried to picture myself stepping into the room where the SWAT team struggled with the Old Ones, blackness descended like the curtain falling prematurely on a play. I tried to peer through that darkness, but it was no use. My memory stayed stubbornly blank.

Although I couldn't picture the scene, I could almost remember a voice. Not shouting and grunting, as you'd expect in a fight, but murmuring. Indistinct, it gently probed the edges of my consciousness, searching for a way in. There were words, so soft and muffled I couldn't make them out.

The Destroyer, urging me on? Possibly, but it didn't feel that way. The Destroyer was pure rage. This voice was softer, and the tone was . . . I couldn't pin it down, but it felt more like a question than a command. Gentle, cajoling. Not brutal or harsh. Yet the sounds also thrummed with power, like lightning contained in a silken box.

I strained to listen, to recognize the voice, to make out the words. My efforts yielded nothing but a headache. I shouldn't try so hard so soon after shifting back to my human form. I blinked, focusing on the spoon in my hand. It was lifted halfway to my mouth, the bowl filled with soggy cereal. I raised the spoon and swallowed the cereal, even though I no longer felt hungry. Mab was right. I needed to recover from the shift. I'd fill my stomach, clean up, and rest. Maybe then I'd have the strength to figure out what had happened.

By the time Kaysi entered the kitchen, dressed and ready for work, I'd eaten a second bowl of cereal.

"I'm usually home before six," she said, pulling on her jacket, "but tonight I was going to meet some friends after work. I can cancel if you think you'll need my help."

Again I marveled at her belief in me, a complete stranger. "Don't change your plans for my sake. I'll be gone long before you finish work."

"Well, be careful. With your picture in the paper and probably all over TV, too, someone might recognize you. Just remember: You can stay here as long as you like."

"Thanks, Kaysi." I wasn't sure yet where I'd go, but I wouldn't impinge on her kindness any more than I had to.

"There's one other thing. But you have to promise you won't say no."

I've never been able to make a promise without knowing what it was, so I just stared at her.

"I know you don't have any money, so I want you to take this." She held out a twenty dollar bill. "If you want, we'll consider it a loan."

"Kaysi, I—"

"*Take* it." She shook the bill at me. "You'll be doing me a favor. If I'm worrying about you out there without a cent, I won't be able to concentrate at work. You wouldn't want me to get fired, would you?"

I met Kaysi's eyes—blue and shining with sincerity—as I wordlessly accepted the bill. "Thanks," I repeated. "I'll pay you back as soon as I can. For everything."

She shrugged like everything she'd done for me was no big deal. "Whenever. You know, there have been times in my life when things got hard and I wished somebody would give me a break, even a little one. Usually nobody does. So I'm happy I can do that for you." She glanced at the wall clock. "I'd better get to work."

She was out the door before I could thank her one more time.

I WAS IN THE SHOWER WHEN IT OCCURRED TO ME THAT THE cops might arrive at any moment. What if Kaysi had pretended to help me so she could call the police as soon as she was safely away from the house?

The thought had barely formed before shame washed over

me, hotter than the water that stung my skin. Was that how my mind worked—automatically assuming that anyone who helped me couldn't wait to turn around and stab me in the back?

I didn't believe Kaysi would turn me in. Even so, I hurried through my shower and got dressed quickly. With a little concentration, I was able to change my shape so the borrowed clothes fit. Not a full-blown shift—after last night, I was out of those until the other side of the full moon—but a trick that lets me alter the dimensions of my usual form. It's great for those days when putting on my jeans requires extra tugging. Now, I focused on making my body fit the dimensions of the faded jeans and gray T-shirt Kaysi had given me. I checked the mirror. The effect was good. My face was a little fuller, and I'd lost a couple inches of height. My features, hairstyle, and hair color were still my own, but the change in build might be enough of a disguise for me to move around Boston unnoticed. I certainly hoped so. I had hours to get through before tonight's showdown.

MORE WARMTH AND SUNSHINE. IT WAS THE KIND OF GLORI-ous spring day that rewards Bostonians for enduring the long winters. I bought some cheap sunglasses and a baseball cap at a dollar store. Nobody looked at me twice as I roamed around the city. For a while, I rode the subways, hiding behind a *Boston Globe* someone had left on a seat. I left the T at Copley Square and tried to grab a nap in the public library, but I'd barely closed my eyes before a librarian rapped on the table and whispered, "No sleeping." So I moved on to Boston Common, where I lay down on the grass in some shade, threw my arm over my eyes and slept for the better part of an hour. But sleeping in the open isn't easy, especially when an entire police force is looking for you, so again I moved on.

The afternoon passed in a blur of coffee shops, bus-stop benches, and window-shopping. Not wanting to be seen and having no place to hide is a bad combination. Still, on the crowded streets no one regarded me with suspicion.

Fast-food burgers for both lunch and dinner gave me indigestion but helped me stretch out my funds. If not for those twenty dollars, my day would have much harder—and hungrier.

Once this was all over, I'd definitely do something nice for Kaysi.

Assuming I lived to see morning.


I SPENT THE LAST TWO HOURS BEFORE MY RENDEZVOUS with Mab at the Boston University student union. It wasn't far from Fenway, and nobody cared if you slept there. In fact, sleeping with an open book on one's lap seemed a popular activity.

At ten thirty, I stood, stretched, and left the union. I walked along Commonwealth Ave. toward Kenmore Square. By ten minutes to eleven, I stood on Yawkey Way in front of Gate A, staring at the shuttered green doors in Fenway Park's high brick walls and wondering how the hell we were going to get inside.

Five minutes later, Mab arrived with the answer: a grappling hook. She regarded me skeptically. "You can make it over the wall, can't you?"

I stood straight, and released the energy that had changed my body shape. In moments, I was back to my usual self. "Fit as ever," I said.

For some reason, the skepticism didn't leave Mab's expression. She merely turned and heaved the hook upward. It flew two stories into the air, then landed behind the Fenway Park sign. Mab yanked the rope; the hook caught and held. "I'll go first," she said. "If you need help, I'll haul you up."

"I won't, but go ahead."

Mab scrambled up the wall and disappeared onto the roof. In a moment, her face popped over the edge. "Come, child."

I looked up the street, then down. It was deserted. I tugged on the rope; it held. I braced my legs against the brick wall and began my ascent. Okay, so maybe I didn't climb the two stories as fast as Mab, but I got there.

Mab pulled up the rope. We made our way across the roof, over a fence, and down another wall. In minutes, we stood on the field.

The full moon cast silvery light over everything, from the grass to Pesky's Pole to the famous Green Monster. Rows of seats stretched up into darkness. The field had been mown recently, the smell of cut grass mingled with the cool night air.

"Here is your athame," Mab said, handing me a dagger. "It's never been used as a weapon, so it will help you create a strong circle. Notice, though, that the blade is bronze. It can serve as a backup weapon if needed."

I tested the dagger's blade. A thin line of blood appeared. Unlike some ritual daggers that were purposely blunted, such as Hellforged, this one was sharp. Hellhounds are demons, and if any got too close tonight, the dagger would do some damage. As would the sword Mab handed me now.

I didn't want to think about what these weapons would do to Kane in hellhound form, so I put it from my mind. Maybe everything would go as planned.

And maybe the Night Hag would show up, kiss me on the cheek, and offer to adopt me.

My doubt must have shown in my face, because Mab put her hand on my arm. "Remember, child," she said, "I'll be here to protect you, and I can do that in two ways. The first is to defend you physically. If there's an attack while I'm still in falcon form, rest assured the falcon will not let anyone near you. But of course I'll shift back to this form as soon as possible so I can wield my sword."

"Thanks, Mab." There was no one I'd rather have on my side in a fight.

"Physical defense is merely one sort of protection, and it's the weaker of the two. I want you to wear this." She grasped her pendant and lifted its chain over her head, then held it out to me.

I watched it swing from her hand. "But that's your bloodstone." The source of Mab's power and longevity. She always wore it, even when she changed her shape.

"Not mine alone. Your blood has become part of it, too."

"Just a drop or two." Over the centuries, Mab had infused the stone with her own blood many times. The pendant was an essential part of my aunt, and I didn't like the thought of her being without it. A few months ago, when the stone was stolen, Mab had grown feeble and old with terrifying speed. Her vitality had returned only with the bloodstone.

"Take it," she urged. "You may return it to me after we've dealt with Mallt-y-Nos." I didn't flinch or pull away as she lifted the necklace over my head. The bloodstone rested in the center of my chest. The stone was warm and pulsed slightly, as though it had its own beating heart.

"Good." Mab's crisp tone conveyed her satisfaction. "Now, here is the gauntlet. It was crafted by Mr. Kane's witch friend, Roxana, and her circle working overtime." I wondered how much that had cost. "When you give it to the Night Hag, tell her to put it on, raise her arm, and thrice shout, *'Hebog, tyrd!'*"

*Falcon, come!* The same Welsh command Mab had used to call Dad. The gauntlet I held was a good copy. The leather, worn smooth, was darker on the fingertips, suggesting age. It even smelled old. I couldn't tell whether the silver embroidery matched the original exactly, but if I didn't know better, I'd swear this was Mab's glove. Roxana and her witches had given Kane his money's worth.

"I'll be waiting close by," Mab said. "When I hear the call, I'll fly in."

I thought of my time as a cat the night before, the taking over of the feline brain, the kaleidoscope of images, instinct, and sensation. I didn't ask whether Mab would have the presence of mind to stick with the plan once she shifted. Her centuries of experience gave her control far beyond that of any other shapeshifter. Like me, for instance. Last night, with the waxing moon almost full, the cat had taken over entirely. Yet even on the first night of a full moon, Mab would stay in control.

*"Pob lwc."* She touched her papery lips to my forehead. "Good luck, child."

Mab backed away a few paces. Closing her eyes, she raised her face toward the sky. Energy shimmered around her, beginning at the top of her head and cascading down her body. The energy flared, and from the light a falcon shot skyward.

Beautiful. It was the cleanest shift I'd ever seen. No pain, no contortion, no agonizing in-between stage. Just intention, energy, change. I wished I could shift half that well.

Time to create my circle of protection. For a moment, I wished Kane's expensive witches were here to build a professional-strength circle. Of course, they'd refused to do the job, what with me being a fugitive from justice and all. We were lucky they'd made the gauntlet. Still, as I stood in the pitch-dark field all alone, I wouldn't have minded some backup.

*You have backup. Trust in it.*

"Mab?" If anyone could figure out how to replicate Dad's talking-falcon trick, it would be my aunt. Yet the voice had seemed to emanate from inside my head.

No answer.

Could the voice be the Destroyer's? Instinctively, I checked my demon mark. It was cool and slightly itchy, but as soon as my attention was on it, I felt a flare of heat. I willed it down, and it subsided back to an itch.

*Focus, Vicky.* It was almost midnight. The Night Hag would be here soon. If she came upon me with a half-cast circle, she'd snatch the glove and order her hounds to attack. No question.

I faced east and called the first quarter. Immediately, I felt a change in the air, an electricity that seemed pulled from the ground, the sky, even past games played on this field. Sparkles of energy that lingered after Mab's shift were taken up and spun into the bubble of protection I wove. I turned to the south, then the west, then the north, calling each quarter in turn. Energy illuminated the field. Over my heart, the bloodstone glowed and pulsed.

Turning back to the east, I completed the circle. It closed with a *pop!* The cool night air grew comfortably warm, like bathwater.

I was ready.

*Bring it on, hag.*

I listened. The protective sphere muffled outside noises, but soon a frenzied baying sounded in the distance. As the pack approached, the pain that drove the hellhounds became audible, twined into each howl and cry. *Kane.* Kane was among them, feeling that frantic need to outrun the inescapable pain. Willing to do anything to make it stop.

But not for long, if all went well. If our plan worked, only minutes remained before he was free of his promise and back in my arms.

If all went well.

Fiery eyes gleamed as the pack bounded toward me. I tensed, reinforcing the circle with my will. Hounds charged, fangs bared as they came closer. Closer. A yelp sounded. Five feet away, the pack leader crumpled as though he'd hit a brick wall. Others clambered over him, only to come to the same abrupt halt. They prowled along my circle's barrier, growling.

From behind them came the slow, steady *clop clop* of a horse's hooves. Mallt-y-Nos may have sent her hounds speeding toward me, but now she made it clear that she kept our appointment at her leisure. She emerged gradually from the darkness, moonlight glinting off the glossy hair of her youthful aspect. Slowly, she steered her horse around the perimeter of the circle that protected me. As she made her circuit, she grew plumper, older, more wrinkled. She aged more, losing flesh, becoming skin and bones. When she halted before me, a dried-out corpse stared down at me from her mount. The horse shot fire from its nostrils and pawed the ground.

"I'm told you have something for me." Coming from that horrible face, rotting flesh hanging off its skull, her demand made me shudder.

My fingers tightened on my sword's grip. I had something for her, all right. A sharp blade to sever her ever-changing head from her body. It would serve her right, with all the misery she'd caused. To Kane, and also to countless frightened, lost souls.

But especially to Kane.

Yet attacking the Night Hag wouldn't do Kane or me any good. The hag was a spirit, not a demon; the bronze of my blade wouldn't harm her. I held up the gauntlet. "Here is what you need to call the falcon," I said. I didn't say *which* falcon.

The hag's eyes fixed greedily on the glove. "Give it to me." She reached forward. A sharp, sizzling noise crackled from my protective sphere. She drew back as though she'd touched fire. "Let me into your circle," she said, blowing on her fingertips, "and we'll conclude our bargain."

"Not so fast. If I give you this gauntlet, will you release Kane from his promise to serve as your hellhound?"

Her gaze, youthful again with sparkling eyes, never left the glove as she nodded. "If the gauntlet calls and holds the white falcon of Hellsmoor, I will."

There was no way she'd get the white falcon of Hellsmoor. But if Mab fooled her until she released Kane from his bargain, that wouldn't matter. "All right," I said. "I'll let you in—but alone. No horse, no hounds."

The young woman's elegant eyebrows came together in a fierce scowl, but Mallt-y-Nos dismounted. The horse reared up and exhaled a blast of flame from its nostrils, shrieking out a whinny to make the dead tremble in their deep-buried coffins. The hag raised her hand, and the horse stilled. She turned to me, her face plump, her hair graying. She looked least threatening in her middle-aged aspect—not that it fooled me for a second. "Let me in," she said.

As I watched, her flesh drooped and wrinkled; her cheeks sagged into jowls.

"Now!" she demanded. "Or our deal is void."

Whispering an incantation, I gestured with the athame, cutting a doorway in the sphere of protection. Mallt-y-Nos, a scowling old woman now, hobbled through.

I resealed the circle behind her. Gnarled, clawlike hands reached for the gauntlet. "Give it to me," she repeated.

I passed the gauntlet into the skeletal hands of death.

The Night Hag didn't even glance at my face as she took the glove. She turned it in her hands, inspecting it, reading the spells embroidered on the leather. I prayed the copy was accurate, because Mallt-y-Nos knew what she was looking at.

She slid her bony hand into the glove. As she flexed her fingers, testing the leather, her face and body grew young again. She smiled, dimpling her cheeks, and held her arm out in front of her, eyes scanning the night sky.

"You have to call it," I explained. "Shout, '*Hebog, tyrd!*' three times, and the falcon will come to you."

Narrowed eyes regarded me suspiciously.

"*Hebog, tyrd,*" she said.

A car horn sounded somewhere toward Lansdowne Street, but the sky remained empty.

"Louder," I urged.

"*Hebog, tyrd!*"

A shadow passed over her upturned face. A white falcon soared directly above us.

"*Hebog, tyrd!*" she screeched, excited now.

I readied the athame as the bird plummeted toward us.

*Soon . . . soon . . . now!* I swept my arm overhead, just in time for the falcon to plunge into the protected space. The Night Hag grunted as the bird hit the gauntlet, forcing her arm down. When she raised it again, her middle-aged aspect cackled in glee.

"Oh, my pretty, pretty birdie," she crooned, petting the falcon. "You've come back to me." Suddenly, she backhanded the bird. *Mab!* The force of the blow made me cringe, but I didn't interfere. I couldn't. The falcon squawked but stayed where it was, its talons gripping the gauntlet. The Night Hag chuckled. "Ah, so you *are* mine. You'd like to fly away after that, wouldn't you? But the gauntlet keeps you here." Again she petted the bird, stroking its feathers, tickling the underside of its beak.

Enough. I wanted Kane and Mab both free of this cruel hag. "I've given you the gauntlet and with it the falcon," I said. "Now it's your turn. Release Kane from his bargain."

"Not yet." The hag's middle-aged face squinted at me like a medieval housewife who suspects she's being cheated at the market. "I have a question for you."

"That wasn't part of our deal."

"Even so. Before I give up my newest hound, I must be satisfied."

"What do you want to know?"

"The white falcon has a role to play in the coming war between the realms. According to some of the old prophecies, you cannot win without it. So why are you willing to give me this bird?"

"If what you say is true, then why do you insist on having the falcon? Pryce and the demons will win."

She snorted. "What care I who rules this realm, so long as I have souls to hunt? But you, Victory Vaughn, you do care. So I ask again: Why give me this bird?"

In the darkness beyond the circle's boundary, the hellhounds of Mallt-y-Nos paced and growled. They sniffed the ground, their noses outside the perimeter, yelping and whining with frustration. I watched them, wondering which one was Kane. My heart ached with not knowing.

"Why? There can be only one reason. For love."

"Love!" The falcon had to adjust its grip as the old crone

doubled over, laughing. "You would let this world be destroyed," she said, straightening and wiping tears from her eyes, "for the love of one of my hounds?"

"He's not your hound. You have the falcon. Release him—now."

Her withered hand stroked the bird's head. I could almost see Mab's grimace at the touch. "How do I know you're not trying to trick me? I must test this falcon on a hunt to be certain. Meet me here again at this time tomorrow. If I'm satisfied, I'll release the hound."

Tomorrow? Even Mab couldn't make a shift last twenty-four hours. I pushed down the panic welling up inside me. *Careful, Vicky, don't give anything away.*

"This isn't a used car lot. You don't get to take the falcon for a test drive. Either fulfill your promise, or return the falcon to me."

"And if I don't?"

I raised my sword by the merest inch. Not to threaten her— yet—but to remind her I had it. The weapon wouldn't kill her, but she'd feel its bite. Trapped inside the circle and unable to set her hounds on me, she couldn't keep the falcon if I wanted to take it from her. I'd lop off her arm, yank away the gauntlet, and cast the severed limb aside. And she knew it.

"All right. A bargain is a bargain." She shook the falcon off. The bird jumped to the ground, stretching its wings for balance. "My show of good faith," she said. "I'll call it to me when our deal is done.

The Night Hag turned and walked to the edge of the circle. "Let me out. I need to touch the hound to release him."

Heart pounding, I went to the edge of the circle and made the motions to cut another door: up, across, down. I paused, waiting for the Night Hag to signal she was ready to pass through before finishing the last stroke.

Mallt-y-Nos nodded. I completed the doorway, and the Night Hag moved toward her waiting hounds. Then, one foot beyond the circle and the other still inside, she turned to me.

"Fraud!" she shrieked. "Cheat! You *are* trying to trick me!"

"I'm not—"

"The eyes! The white falcon of Hellsmoor has rainbow eyes.

This bird"—she flung it away, outside the circle—"does not. Our deal is void. Kill her!"

As a single creature, the hellhounds leapt to their feet. I ran at the hag, shoving hard with both hands to push her out of the circle. But Mallt-y-Nos held her ground. She raised an arm, and a sound like ice cracking rang out.

The circle was breaking.

The cracks raced around the sphere, shattering it into fragments. Shards of energy rained down on my face and arms like electric snowflakes.

The falcon shot into the sky.

The Night Hag grinned.

And the hellhounds charged.

# 36

THE BRONZE OF MY BLADE FLASHED AS I BROUGHT IT around to fend off the first lunging hound.

*Kane!* screamed my mind. *Which one was Kane?*

No time for guessing games. I ducked and twisted. Jaws crashed together an inch from my shoulder. I drove upward with the dagger, catching the leaping hound under its front leg. Flesh sizzled as black blood spurted out. The hound howled. The rotten stink of sulfur made me gag.

A true demon. At least it wasn't Kane.

As I yanked out the blade, another hound snapped at my left arm. A third got its fangs into my right ankle and shook its head, trying to drag me down. I wouldn't last ten seconds if I fell. I slashed the dagger across its shoulder and, with my other hand, swept the sword in a wide arc. Black blood cascaded over inky fur, and its muzzle released my ankle. The hounds fell back, keeping beyond the blade's reach. They crouched and growled and sprang, only to jump back as the blade swished toward them.

Where was Mab?

The Night Hag's cackle sounded over her hounds' barks and

yips. Her bow held ready, she scanned the sky, then turned back to her present entertainment. Mab must be shifting. If she tried to swoop in as a falcon, the hag would shoot her out of the sky.

Pain sliced into my left thigh as a hound ducked beneath my blade and sank its teeth into me. Its acid saliva burned. I stabbed the hound's flank, but the jaws held tight. Behind it another hound crouched, growling, its red, fiery eyes on my throat.

Teeth grabbed my ankle. Stars of pain exploded in my vision as I heard a sickening crunch. I slashed the hounds that held me, but they wouldn't let go. My flesh tore, and the wounds burned, burned, burned. I couldn't move.

The crouching hound leapt.

I brought up my sword.

Midway through its jump, the hound grunted. Its legs flailed as it twisted. My blade scored its side. The hound landed heavily and lay as if stunned. I hacked at the hounds that held me, stabbing over and over, until one let go, then the other. Acid ate at my ripped skin, and I feared my ankle was broken, but my bronze had left the hellhounds in even worse shape. They'd collapsed on their sides. Smoke poured from their wounds, and their bodies deflated. Neither tried to get up.

I spun to finish off the other hound, the one who'd leapt at my throat. The creature had regained its feet and stood, shaking off its fall. I lifted my sword to extinguish the crimson fire in those hellish eyes.

"Stop!" Something burst from my chest and buzzed straight to my ear. "Not that one!" Butterfly shouted. "Look at the blood."

Bright red drops fell from the hound's coat and splatted on the ground.

Red blood. Not black. This wasn't a true hellhound.

"Kane?"

A furious screech erupted from my right. The hound went rigid. An earsplitting yowl emerged from its clenched jaws. It fell to the ground.

"I commanded you to kill her!" the Night Hag shrieked.

The hellhound—Kane—writhed in agony. Flames shot

from his ears and nose. They consumed his body, crisping his fur and contorting his limbs.

I started toward him, but pain sliced through my ankle. It wouldn't hold me. I kept going, half dragging, half hopping. Whatever I had to do to reach him.

Another hound charged me from the left. I drove my blade deep into its body. A thick, choking cloud of burning sulfur obscured my vision.

"Kane!" I shouted.

His answer was a growl.

*"Obey me, hound!"*

At her words, a nightmare vision thrust itself through the smoke: a massive hellhound, his lips drawn back over sharp, gleaming fangs, his entire body in flames. Pain blinded his eyes to everything but its target—my throat. He growled again, ears back. His muscles twitched as he prepared to attack.

I couldn't raise my sword. I would not hurt Kane.

Butterfly spoke. "You *totally* owe me." The black insect shot into the air. Kane sprang, and the Eidolon dive-bombed the attacking hound. It flew straight into his jaws.

The jaws snapped shut.

The force of Kane's leap propelled him into me, knocking me backward. He stood with his paws on my shoulders, his jaws working as he chewed. Acid drool poured over me, dotted with fragments of black wings.

Kane stopped chewing. He looked at me and growled. He lowered his head, sniffing. I looked into his eyes, red and flaming and totally alien from the cool gray ones I knew so well. I searched them for some sign, any sign, of Kane.

For maybe ten seconds, we looked at each other. The hound cocked his head.

"Enough!" shouted the hag. "You have failed me, you pathetic cur. Pack—rip her apart!"

From all sides hellhounds lunged at us. Kane snarled and crouched, then got his fangs into the throat of one. A shake of his head tore the throat wide open. Black blood spurted. The hound gasped and fell.

I scrambled to my feet. Kane paced before me, hackles raised. Only two hellhounds remained in fighting shape. They circled, making low, guttural sounds.

The standoff didn't last. A stream of fire blasted into Kane, somersaulting him across the field.

His agonized howl stabbed through my heart as it escalated to a scream. I slashed at the hounds that tried to block my way and, ignoring the pain in my ankle, ran toward him. A hound grabbed my calf from behind. I fell. I lay on my front, my arms up to protect my head and neck.

Teeth tore into my arm and pulled. I stabbed blindly. A yelp sounded, and the teeth let go, only to grab my shoulder. The hound shook, shredding my flesh into hamburger.

"Hounds!" A hunting horn blast split the night wide open. My attackers paused. "Leave her. Come!"

Hoofs galloped away. The hounds abandoned me where I lay and ran after them, baying.

Cautiously, I sat up. Two of the fallen hounds had risen and now staggered toward left field, where Mallt-y-Nos spurred her steed.

A few yards ahead of me, a fire died to embers.

*Kane.*

I crawled toward his prone body. The odor of scorched fur and charred flesh made me retch, but I kept going. *I'm coming, Kane.* Just a few more feet. *Hang on.* I was almost there. Almost . . . And then I looked down at the remains of my lover.

Kane lay curled on his side. Smoke streamed from his body. His fur was gone, his flesh blackened. I wanted to feel for a pulse, but I was afraid my touch would be torture to his burned skin. I put my hand in front of his muzzle. No whisper of breath stirred. Carefully, I probed his neck. Almost too hot to touch, the skin crackled under my fingers. I couldn't find any sign of life pulsing through his veins.

*Kane.*

She'd killed him. He'd tried to protect me, and she'd burned the life out of him for it.

*Kane.*

Gently, I lowered my lips to his face. The stench of burned meat filled my nostrils. I kissed him. My lips lingered on his hot, charred skin. Then I threw back my head and wailed out my pain and fury. Across the field, the hellhounds howled in reply.

I would kill her.

I would make the Night Hag suffer for what she'd done, and then I'd obliterate her from all the worlds.

Now was no time for restraint.

Difethwr had marked me. Now, Difethwr could lend me its power. Kane's burned body lying before me, I called upon the Destroyer.

"Difethwr!" Rage gave me back the language that grief had turned into an inarticulate howl. "Destroyer! I invoke our bond. Help me crush my enemy!"

I quit trying to control my demon mark. Instead, I unleashed the torrents of my rage and channeled them straight into it. The mark heated, glowed red. A jet of flame flared out from it. My body blazing with hatred, I climbed to my feet.

I pulled the Destroyer's power into me. The bones of my ankle knit themselves together. I stood tall, strong, ready to take my revenge. I sprinted in the direction the Night Hag had gone. My ankle strengthened and my wounds healed as I ran. My power swelled. The flame brightened, lighting up the stadium like someone had flipped on the floodlights. I kept my focus on the Night Hag. I could destroy her. I could destroy anything. I *was* the Destroyer.

*There is another way.*

The voice made me stumble, but I swatted it aside like a pesky gnat. There was only one way, and that was to destroy.

Destroy.

Ahead, I could see a crowd. Who was there, what they wanted, how they got in—I didn't care. Sounds of fighting reached me. I welcomed them. I would add to their music, composing a symphony of pain and death, building it to a crescendo.

And then I would destroy the symphony. Rip up the score, smash the instruments, slaughter the players.

The Night Hag's horse stood beside the crowd. The hag gazed skyward, her bow poised. She tracked a white falcon that soared overhead.

Mab?

The falcon dived into the crowd. Crows erupted into the sky. The crowd parted, and I glimpsed Mab in its midst, wielding a flaming sword, her face bloody. She was surrounded by zombies.

So the falcon wasn't Mab. He was the real falcon, the white falcon of Hellsmoor, my father. The Night Hag would either capture him or kill him.

But not if I killed the hag first.

*Help Mab.*

The voice in my mind was imperious, not to be denied. Its words flamed with urgency and command. But my demon mark burned hotter. I raised my sword and charged the Night Hag.

My blade sliced into her arm. Her arrow flew in a low arc, missing the falcon.

The Night Hag's face, a bare skull, spit gobs of fire at me.

*Help Mab.*

The voice nudged at my mind. I ignored it.

Mallt-y-Nos had nocked another arrow. She aimed at my face.

"Difethwr, help me!" I shouted. "Destroy her!"

*There is another way. Let me in.*

In an inferno of hellfire, the Destroyer itself appeared on the field. The Hellion was ten feet tall, more. It was massive, magnificent. For several long seconds it regarded me. Then it directed its eyeflames at the Night Hag's horse. The animal screamed, then fell. Mallt-y-Nos jumped to the ground.

A cry arose from the fighting.

*Help Mab.*

Of course. I couldn't kill the Night Hag with a bronze blade. But Difethwr could destroy anything. I'd let the Destroyer do its work. My aunt needed my help.

Mab was surrounded by half a dozen zombies. They reached for her, yelling, desperate to kill. Her flaming sword held them back, but she looked tired. If Mab's reserves were low, I had what she needed.

Her bloodstone.

"Mab!" My aunt's head snapped toward me. I raised the pendant. "I'll throw it to you!"

I pulled. But the chain wouldn't lift over my head.

*No. You may not.*

As Mab watched me, two zombies charged her, knocking her down. The entire crowd swarmed on top of her.

"Mab!"

The falcon zoomed down from the sky. Its talons tore into

the topmost zombie, and a flock of Morfran shot into the sky. The falcon gave chase.

One zombie down. But there were too many others for Mab to handle.

I yanked at the pendant. It stayed put as though glued to my neck.

*Let me in. I can save her.*

"I'll save her!" I shouted, not knowing whom I addressed.

*Let me in. I will aid your friends and crush your enemies.*

Who spoke? The Destroyer? A sharp yelp drew itself out into a long howl of pain, and I turned to see one of the Night Hag's remaining hounds on its back, its stiff legs beating the air, as it rolled in flames that streamed from the Hellion's eyes and hands. No, Difethwr was otherwise engaged. Its voice was not the one filling my head.

Then whose?

"Who are you?" I said aloud.

*There's no time. Let me in—now. Or Mab will die.*

That did it. A bad idea? Probably. But I had no time to ponder the consequences.

"All right! I . . . I let you in." Whoever the hell you are.

Mab's pendant grew suddenly, unbearably hot in my hand. Before I could open my fingers to drop it, the bloodstone exploded into a million fragments.

My hand. Oh, God, my hand!

The explosion had blasted it clean off—I was sure of it. Below my elbow was nothing but pain. I couldn't see through the blood and grit in my eyes.

The pain turned into a buzzing that raced up my arm and spread through my body. It was energy, but an energy stronger and more vital than I'd ever felt. I had the sensation of being borne high in the air, yet my feet remained on the ground. I could feel electric wires of power shoot through my soles and draw energy from the earth's core. Energy that raised me, expanded me.

I flexed my electrified fingers. Good. They were still there. I wiped my eyes and looked at my hand. Glowing with golden light, it sparkled all the way up to the elbow, like I'd plunged it into a vat of glitter.

For the first time in ten years, I couldn't see the Destroyer's mark on my skin. The glitter covered it entirely.

"Victory!"

Mab's half-strangled cry seemed to come from far below me. When I looked toward the sound, I saw with a double perspective—from my own height and at a bird's-eye view of fifteen or twenty feet in the air. I shook my head to clear it, but the double perspective remained.

No time to worry about that. I had to save Mab.

A pile of zombies pinned her down. The reek of Morfran, hot and hungry and sulfurous, curled in my nostrils. Enraged, unappeasable cawing jarred my ears. If I could wrest out the Morfran, the zombies would lose their drive to kill.

And without knowing *how* I knew, I realized I could do it.

I stretched my hands—both glowing, one glittering—toward the zombies. I clenched both hands into fists, as though grasping handfuls of sand. Then, flinging my arms skyward, I opened my hands and shouted, *"Ewch nawr!"*

*Go now.* Why had the words come out in Welsh?

The sky blackened with crows. The white falcon shot like a meteor into their midst. From my higher perspective, I could see the excited, hungry gleam in his eyes.

On the ground, the zombies rolled away from Mab and staggered to their feet. Dazed, they wandered randomly or simply stood and stared.

Mab lay on her back. She was bleeding and bruised, but she was alive.

"Are you all—?" A fireball slammed into my chest. The ball was huge and dense, packed with intense energy. It should have killed me. It didn't even make me stagger. My own energy field embraced the fireball, absorbed it. The light around me glowed brighter. My upper perspective soared higher.

Below, Pryce stood scowling between two zombies. A second fireball shimmered in his hands. "So it's you after all," he said and hurled the fireball at my face.

I wanted to duck, but my body refused. Instead, my hands raised themselves and caught the fireball. The energy ruptured into sparks that raced up my arms and fizzed through my body.

I was a pillar of fire, a column of lightning. My power reached for the sky.

Pryce angled his head and looked upward, twenty feet above my head but meeting my higher gaze. He backed away. "Difethwr!" he shouted. "Destroy her! Do it now and we've won!"

The Hellion stomped toward me, expanding as it came closer. It was ten feet tall, fifteen, twenty. Its steps shook the ground. I mustered the energy that buzzed through me, gathering it, focusing. I held it in my fingertips, ready to shoot.

Difethwr stopped ten feet in front of me. Somehow, I stood eye to eye with the giant demon. I looked directly into the hellfire smoldering behind its eyes and between its open jaws. I summoned more energy. The Destroyer's hellflames brightened as it gathered its own strength.

This was it. One chance. Do or die.

I'd knock the Destroyer onto its Hellion ass. And then I'd blast that ass into oblivion.

I could do it. I *knew*. Just like I'd known I could somehow yank the Morfran out of those zombies.

I raised my arms, both of them. The demon mark no longer held me back. I pointed at Difethwr and summoned the energy that would obliterate the Hellion—forever this time.

Pain gripped my right forearm. My demon mark glowed red-hot through the glitter that coated my skin. Fire erupted from the mark, exploding and sparking like a Roman candle.

My arm lost its strength and dropped to my side.

Difethwr's laughter brightened the flames that burned inside it and over its skin. I stared into the Hellion's eyes and saw death.

"Get her, you stupid Hellion!" screamed Pryce. "You're stronger!" Difethwr didn't budge. Bellowing a battle cry, Pryce raised his sword and ran at me.

Hellflame blazed hotter. Difethwr turned its massive head. Fire streamed from its eyes, knocking Pryce to the ground and pinning him there. The demi-demon screamed and writhed. The Destroyer held him in the flames. It moved toward him. Each step shook the ground. Pryce's screams escalated, clawing the night air. I wanted to cover my ears against the sound, but my right arm remained obstinately limp.

Within minutes, Pryce fell silent.

The Destroyer bent over Pryce, poked at his torso with a clawed foot. No response. Difethwr straightened to its full height, looking once more into the eyes of my upper perspective.

"Know this," the Destroyer said. "The shapeshifter is *mine.*" And with a puff of sulfurous smoke, the Hellion vanished.

# 37

PRYCE WAS ... DEAD?

I couldn't believe it. I'd seen his fallen body on the ground before, after he'd infected himself with the zombie virus, but still he'd come back. Now, I mimicked the Destroyer, nudging his body with my foot. No response.

Mab would know. I turned to my aunt, only to find her kneeling before me as she had that day at my apartment.

"Lady," she said, bowing low and placing a hand on her chest.

I was going to tell her to knock it off, to remind her of her promise. But when I opened my mouth, a voice I didn't recognize came out.

"You have served me faithfully," the voice said. "I am well pleased."

That was *not* how I talk to my aunt. But I couldn't articulate the apology I wanted to issue.

"Lady," Mab said. "If I may be so bold, one who deserves punishment is fleeing." She flicked her eyes toward the northeast corner of the field.

With my normal vision, I could see nothing in the darkness. With my higher, keener vision, I saw the Night Hag creeping away.

"Mallt-y-Nos!" The voice that issued from my throat had more authority than I'd ever felt in my life. The Night Hag froze. *"Tyrd!"* the voice commanded. *Come.* The same word the hag had used to call the falcon.

Slowly, fighting every movement, the Night Hag turned and lurched toward me. For the first time in all my encounters with her, her appearance didn't change. She was the dried-out corpse of someone who'd died centuries ago: yellow skin, thin and wrinkled, sunken eyes, a few strands of hair still clinging to the scalp. When she was within ten feet of me, she kneeled, looking as though every downward inch cost her a thousand years.

"My lady," her voice croaked through long-decayed lips.

"You have overstepped your bounds," I said. Except it wasn't me. The strange voice continued to speak through me. "On what authority do you hunt one whose time has not come?"

The Night Hag whimpered instead of answering.

"On what authority do you hunt the one chosen by me?"

"I didn't know."

"That does not matter. You have abused your power. You will learn how it feels to be abused."

My right hand—working again—stretched itself forward. As the Night Hag cowered, energy streamed through my pointing finger. I didn't know the intention of the power that worked through me. I simply watched.

The limbs of Mallt-y-Nos contorted. She howled as her arms lengthened and her legs thinned. Her neck grew shorter and thicker. Her ears swiveled to the top of her head, becoming black triangles. Her chin and nose merged and stretched into a muzzle.

Energy blasted out, so intense I had to shield my eyes. When I could look again, I could see what the Night Hag had become.

A hellhound.

Her howling turned to baying, then shortened to a yelp as I, or the power working through me, jolted powerful energy into her. "Run, hound!" my voice ordered. The new hellhound took off and disappeared into the night.

"Run to hell," I muttered, watching it go.

A sound, a throat clearing, caught my attention. Mab still knelt in front of me, her hands crossed on her chest. Again, I wanted to tell her to stop it, to get up and be Aunt Mab again. But that other voice pushed its way past mine.

"What is it?"

"Lady," Mab said, her eyes on the ground. "There is one who requires your assistance. My niece would ask it of you." Still keeping her head down, she gestured across the field.

Toward Kane.

*Yes!* The thought swelled in my mind. If this entity that had taken over my body—it was Ceridwen, it *had* to be—could help Kane, she needed to get on it now. I tried to direct my (our?) feet toward where he lay on the field, but they didn't budge. Slowly, seemingly of its own accord, my head turned the way Mab had pointed.

*Help Kane!* I thought. *I let you in. You owe me.*

"We need to have a talk, I think, about who owes whom." Yet as her words issued from my own mouth, my feet started to work. I (we?) walked across the field.

Kane lay as I'd left him. My heart clenched to see him there, curled tight against the final agony of his burning, his skin seared and scorched. It was too late. Goddess or not, there was nothing Ceridwen could do for him. Nothing anyone could do.

My heart was a hollow ball of pain, but the tears that pressed my eyes wouldn't flow. *She* wouldn't let them.

"You underestimate our power," my own voice scolded. "But you shall see."

Power rose through me and sizzled in my fingertips. My knees bent themselves until I knelt beside Kane. Moving of their own accord, my hands touched two places on his body: between his eyes and over his heart. Unfamiliar words of some unknown language issued from my lips. Energy rose from the earth, flowed from the sky. It passed through me and poured into him.

Beneath my hand, Kane twitched.

I added my will to Ceridwen's, calling energy and directing it to him. But I infused that energy with love. I visualized it swirling through my heart and absorbing everything I felt for Kane, everything I wanted for him. For us.

*Come back to me.*

His eyelids fluttered.

My body jerked to its feet, and my legs sprinted down the

field. An energy blast like I'd never seen flashed through the stadium. It knocked me face forward onto the grass. My ears rang from the *boom!* Fighting Ceridwen's will to stay down, I struggled to my knees and turned to look at Kane.

Fizzling energy lit a circle of scorched earth twenty feet in diameter. In its center stood a wolf.

Not a hellhound, a wolf. His silver fur glowed in the moonlight.

*Is he . . . ?* I wanted to ask the question out loud, but my voice wasn't my own.

"He's no longer a hellhound," came Ceridwen's answer in my voice. "Nor shall he be one again."

Ceridwen relaxed her grip on my body, allowing me to stand. I held out my hand. My left one, the one not marked by a demon or coated with glitter. The wolf trotted over to me and sniffed. The gray eyes that searched me were Kane's. He sat, remaining perfectly still as I dropped again to my knees. I threw my arms around him and buried my face in his ruff. His heart beat free and strong. I could smell his scent of pine woods and cool air.

*Thank you, goddess.*

I don't know why—maybe she was moved enough to let us have our moment—but Ceridwen answered in my mind instead of through my mouth. *I restored his life*, she said. *But breaking the curse, that was your doing. Out of love for you, he bargained away his freedom. Your love has returned it to him.*

And then Ceridwen receded. She relinquished control of my body and shrank into a tiny spark that settled somewhere in the back of my brain. I felt almost myself again. Enough that I pushed Ceridwen aside to worry about later and turned all my attention to holding Kane.

And that's exactly what I did. Right up until the moment when the stadium floodlights blazed on and the police told us we were surrounded.

AT LEAST THEY DIDN'T COME IN FIRING. THAT HAD TO BE A good sign, right?

"Help me!" I whispered to Ceridwen. No response. I could feel that spark of her presence, but it was muted, silent. Great time to take a nap. Maybe she didn't care if the shapeshifter she'd chosen to inhabit got her ass hauled off to that underground paranormal prison.

Figures in body armor kept rifles trained on us as, step by step, they approached. Kane growled. "Shh," I said, stroking his fur. An attacking werewolf would be shot full of silver bullets, no matter who he was the other twenty-eight days of the month. Kane's muscles trembled as though longing to spring, but he stayed seated beside me.

Until a dart thwacked into his side. Kane jumped to his feet, but his legs buckled under him. He toppled forward, his muzzle hitting the dirt first, as the tranquilizer took full effect.

Per bullhorned instructions, I lay on my front with my hands on the back of my head. I expected frisking, handcuffing, the works. But it didn't happen. Minutes passed. I didn't move. Finally, a voice—Daniel's—told me I could get up. He even reached down a hand to help.

A quick glance around the field showed me the situation. Two dozen cops had herded the zombies into a group. An ambulance crew tended Mab. And Kane . . . Kane slept inside a werewolf cage with silver-plated bars.

Shit. Leaving the retreat during a full moon could be a death sentence for a werewolf.

"Kane didn't leave Princeton of his own will," I said. "He was forced." As quickly as I could, I explained about the Night Hag.

Daniel looked skeptical. "So far, there have been no reports of werewolf attacks in the city tonight. As long as it stays that way, I'll make sure he's returned to the retreat."

"Thanks."

He shrugged. "I'm in homicide. It's not my job to police werewolves. Not unless one of them kills somebody."

Which made yesterday's events come crashing back. As in me, armed and dangerous and wanted for murder.

"Um, not that I'm suggesting it or anything, but how come I'm not under arrest?"

Daniel's expression darkened. "Why didn't you call me? I've been trying to get in touch with you since yesterday afternoon."

"Why didn't I? Does 'armed and dangerous' ring a bell?"

"That was Commissioner Hampson's doing," Daniel's new partner, Ramón, said as he approached from the left. "We knew you tried to protect the SWAT team, but Hampson . . ." He lifted his hands in a what-can-you-say gesture.

"You knew I tried to protect them?" If so, that was a hell of a lot more than I knew. Not that I was about to volunteer that piece of information. "How?"

"Video," Daniel replied. "Each team member had a camera in their helmet. That's standard procedure now. It took a while, but we pieced together what happened from going through the videos. Of course, we need your version of events as well, given that you're an eyewitness."

That might be tricky, since the whole fight was still a black hole in my memory. I didn't know how to tell him that.

"We have video of you entering the room," Ramón continued, "and attacking that Old One." He grinned. "Nice hit, by the way. Sliced that ugly head right off. You must have been as surprised as we were when the Old One picked up his head and reattached it."

*Surprised* wasn't the word for it. But I didn't like the implication: The Old Ones were getting closer to their goal of true immortality—and therefore harder than ever to kill.

"After that," Daniel continued, "you disappear from the videos. All of them. Did you go for help? Why didn't you call me?"

"I was . . ." How do you explain Limbo to a couple of norms?

"We can take your statement later," Ramón said. "The important thing is that we have irrefutable evidence of what happened to each and every team member. You're in the clear."

In the clear. What beautiful words. Kaysi would feel vindicated.

AFTER PROMISING TO MEET WITH DANIEL AND RAMÓN THE next day, I was free to go to Mab. She lay on a stretcher, her face pale. When she saw me, her lips stretched in a thin smile.

"I don't know how to address you," she said. "Lady or child?"

I took her hand in mind. Her fingers felt thin and cold. "My name's still Vicky."

She lifted my hand and turned it back and forth. The glitter that coated it sparkled in the light, and her smile broadened. "So it is."

"Mab," I said. "Your bloodstone. It's . . ." I didn't know how to tell her. "It's gone."

"Of course, child. How else could Ceridwen return?"

I stared.

"For all these years," Mab said, "for more lifetimes than anyone should have to endure, I kept the bloodstone for her. And now she has made use of it."

"But what's going to happen to you?" The bloodstone had always been the source of Mab's vitality.

"At long last, child, I'll be able to rest." She must have seen the stricken look on my face because she added, "But not yet. The battle isn't over. Much work remains for both of us."

The EMTs stepped in then, saying that they had to get Mab to the hospital. She squeezed my hand, said, "I'll be fine, child," and then was gone.

Before I went home, I walked past the corralled zombies. The cops were starting to load them into vans. I scrutinized each face, but I didn't see anyone I knew. As far as I could tell, Tina was still missing.

I MADE IT HOME WITHOUT INCIDENT. WHEN I CALLED MASS General, the nurse told me that Mab was in "fair" condition and admitted for observation. She put me through to my aunt's room, and Mab forbade me from coming to visit. "I'll be out tomorrow," she insisted. "Stay home and sleep, child. You need it."

So I did. Maybe a better niece would have needed more convincing, but I was exhausted. If only I could get some sleep, everything that had happened would make more sense. And I'd wake up strong enough to face the next battle, whatever it might be.

Yet as soon as my body relaxed into sleep, Ceridwen woke up. Her presence flamed into my dreamscape, lighting up the usual darkness with sparkles of silver and gold. The light swirled. It solidified into a female shape, and she stepped forth. She was beautiful, with golden hair, rosy skin, and dark eyes.

She wore a simple gown, belted at the waist, its hem brushing the ground.

My greeting to her: "Go away."

I expected, maybe even hoped, to annoy her, but the goddess merely tilted her head and laughed. Shimmering, iridescent butterflies formed from the silvery sound and fluttered around her head, alighting like ornaments in her long, golden hair. They reminded me of Butterfly, the only Eidolon in history to sacrifice itself for its host, and for a moment I felt an inexplicable sadness.

*Get over it, Vicky,* I told myself. *You're better off without that demon. It was a pain in the ass.*

*A pain in the ass who saved yours,* I told myself back in a voice that sounded suspiciously like Butterfly's.

I'd never know whether Butterfly had deliberately led me into Pryce's trap at the empty factory. That made me a little sad, too. I'd almost enjoy listening to its sputtering self-justification. But I couldn't forget that fact that Butterfly had prevented Kane and me from killing each other.

I couldn't puzzle out the Eidolon's motives now, though, because Ceridwen spoke. "One freely invited is not so easily dispatched," she said. Her voice rang softly, like wind chimes.

"You call that 'freely'? I was desperate."

"Still, you could have refused. And do not be ungrateful for the gifts I have given you. For one, I saved the life of our servant, Mab."

"Mab is no one's servant."

Ceridwen tilted her head, her brown eyes puzzled. "It's no insult. She has served me faithfully for many years. What else would you have me call her?"

"Just Mab."

She shook her head like I wasn't making sense. The butterflies in her hair made a shimmering cloud around her head, then settled again. She continued her litany of gifts. "I restored the life of your lover. I transformed Mallt-y-Nos, although that was a just punishment for her overreaching. She misused her power appallingly. Still, she'll no longer hunt you before your time, so I count that as a gift."

"What will happen to her?"

"She'll remain a hellhound. I expect by now she's found her

way to Uffern to join the other demons there." Her voice sounded bored, as though the transformed Night Hag was of no further interest. "But we haven't mentioned my greatest gift to you." She inclined her head toward my glittering right hand. "A share of my power. With time you will learn what that means, but one benefit you'll see immediately is that it will help you control your demon mark."

Maybe. I'd felt the Destroyer's power push against Ceridwen's back in Fenway Park. I didn't want my body to become their battleground.

"Look," I said. "You're right. I can't even begin to express my gratitude for what you did tonight. You got the Night Hag off my back and saved the two people I love most in the world. But this is my body. No offense, but there's no room for two inhabitants."

"You invited me freely," she insisted.

"To save Mab! I let you in only for that. You're acting like somebody who gets invited over for dinner and moves in permanently. Who does that? Nobody!"

Ceridwen held out a finger and studied the butterfly that alighted there. She didn't speak.

I looked at my glittering hand. I'd washed and scrubbed, but it hadn't come clean. It sparkled in shades of gold, silver, and scarlet. "These are fragments of the bloodstone, aren't they?"

"They are. Fragments imbued with my power."

"What will happen to Mab? That bloodstone kept her young and strong."

"She will now live out the normal life span of a Cerddorion woman aged forty. Yes, her vitality will fade, as must happen with all mortals, but gradually. She'll not feel the effects of her three centuries. That was my gift to her." The butterflies began to circle Ceridwen, creating a shining cloud. "You'll find that I'm a generous goddess . . . to those who serve me well."

Energy flashed. Ceridwen and her cloud of butterflies vanished. But her words lingered in my dreamscape, fading slowly like the afterimage of a fireworks display. Somehow, they sounded less like a promise of generosity than a threat.

# 38

THE DAY OF GWEN'S COOKOUT DAWNED GRAY AND OVER-
cast, but by noon the sun had pushed apart the clouds. I sat
beside Kane as he drove west on the Mass Pike toward Needham. My hand rested on his leg, above the knee. From time to
time he put his hand on mine and gave a gentle squeeze. Since
our reunion after his full-moon retreat, we hadn't talked about
that night. We hadn't felt the need to. What we did need was
to touch each other. I'm not talking about passionate embraces
and hungry reclaiming of each other's bodies, although there
was that, too. I mean holding hands, sitting thigh-to-thigh,
brushing fingertips against an arm or cheek—the sorts of small
gestures that say *I'm here, I acknowledge you, we're together.*

Soft classical music—Kane said he put it on for Mab, who
sat in back, but it was a piece I'd heard him choose many
times—played through the car's sound system. No one said
much, and I had time to think about the events of the past few
days.

Pryce was dead. Really dead. The corpse Daniel showed
me when I went in to give my account of the SWAT raid looked
like a thousand-year-old mummy, shrunken and desiccated.
The Destroyer had done its job thoroughly.

"But why?" I'd wondered aloud to Mab after I picked her up from the hospital. She'd healed her injuries herself by shifting into a mouse, frightening a nurses' aide in the process. When the doctor could find no trace of Mab's former injuries, he had to discharge her.

"Why would the Destroyer kill Pryce? Think, child." Although I'd never liked it when Mab implied I wasn't thinking hard enough, it was miles better than hearing her call me Lady.

"Well, Butterfly told me they were fighting. And Hellions don't like to answer to anyone. So when the Destroyer saw its chance, it turned on Pryce."

"Those things are true, certainly. But think also of what the Destroyer said after the Lady came forth."

*The shapeshifter is mine.*

"Pryce recognized you as the Lady of the Cerddorion," Mab continued. "He believed that the Lady would thwart his plans. And so she did."

"Not in battle," I said thoughtfully, "but merely by showing up. Ceridwen manifested, and it was end-of-story for Pryce."

"Precisely. But it wasn't Ceridwen alone, child. It was *you*. The Destroyer killed Pryce, at least in part, to prevent Pryce from killing you."

Which meant Difethwr had plans for me. I wasn't exactly eager to find out what they were.

Did Difethwr's plans include the Old Ones? Tina was still missing. Daniel had confirmed that Tina wasn't one of the Morfran-possessed zombies at Fenway Park. Neither had she been found in the raid on the abandoned factory. I'd gone back there myself. The cops were long gone, and I could wander the place at will. I explored every square inch. I found the basement cells Bonita had described. I even found the cell Tina had occupied. My heart sank when my flashlight revealed the words scrawled in bubble gum–pink lipstick on the concrete wall: *Vicky help me!!!* The words blurred, and I had to blink fast to clear my eyes.

According to Daniel, Tina was one of several zombies still missing. He believed the Old Ones still held them, and he continued working with Juliet to try to find out where. (Judging from Juliet's increasingly sexy outfits and increasingly bad moods when she came in each morning, Daniel had successfully resisted her charms.) In the meantime, Tina's plea for help haunted my dreams.

I would find her. I would. And I'd punish the Old Ones for her suffering.

That brought forth a flare from the spark that now burned constantly in the back of my mind. Ceridwen loved that kind of talk. After centuries on the sidelines, she was ready for action.

It was a struggle to keep her in her place. For Ceridwen, having a physical body again was better than a kid's first trip to Disney World. Whatever I was doing—having a cup of coffee, taking a shower, walking through the streets of Deadtown—Ceridwen pushed herself forward and tried to take over. She loved TV almost as much as Juliet did. The last straw, though, was when Kane returned from his retreat. As he pulled me into his arms and pressed his lips against mine, the double perspective returned and suddenly it wasn't just me he was kissing.

I'd pushed him away then. I wasn't willing to share him with *anyone*, not even a goddess who lives inside my head.

It was Kane who helped me find the solution. Not a great one, I'll admit, but it works. At least for now. "Ceridwen came forth when the bloodstone exploded, right? And now fragments of the bloodstone are embedded in your skin. What happens if you cover them up?"

Excellent question. Before Ceridwen could stop me, I ran into the kitchen and shoved my hand into one of Juliet's hot-pink rubber gloves. *Ah. Blessed relief.* The double perspective disappeared, and when the bedroom door closed, it was just Kane and me.

Since that night I'd tried other gloves—leather gloves, knitted gloves, up-to-the-elbow opera gloves—but only that flamingo-pink rubber one did the trick. I wore it now. Hell, I wore it all the time. Ceridwen might be powerful. She might be the Lady of the Cerddorion, the mother of my race. But this was my body, and I liked being in control of it. Even if I won Fashion Don't of the Year.

Kane placed his hand on my ungloved one. I loved the warmth of it, the feeling of his skin on mine. No bloodstone glitter, no demon mark. Not even a stupid pink glove. Of all the claims on me, this one—from the man I loved and who loved me in return—was the one I accepted. This was the one I wanted.

"AUNT VICKY!" SIX-YEAR-OLD ZACK RAN TO ME AS WE GOT out of the car. He stopped and stared. "How come you're wearing that glove?"

"So I can help your mom with the dishes later," I said, ruffling his hair. I fully expected to be called a silly billy, but Zack was already tugging at Kane, wanting to show him the backyard trampoline. I smiled. It made me happy that Gwen's kids liked Kane.

Maria sidled up to Mab, looking shy. She hid both hands behind her back.

"Mom said I could give you these." Her right hand clutched a bouquet of flowers from Gwen's garden.

"Why, thank you, Maria. How lovely. Shall we put them in some water?" Mab glanced at Gwen, eyebrows raised. After a moment's hesitation, Gwen nodded. Maria led Mab into the house.

That left Gwen and me alone in the driveway. Gwen stared at my pink-gloved hand, then decided not to ask. Instead, she gave me a peck on the cheek.

"Where's Mom?" I asked.

"On the patio, helping Nick get the steaks started."

"Steaks?" I'd expected Gwen's husband to whip up hamburgers and hot dogs.

"Dad's favorite, so Mom insisted." Gwen rolled her eyes. So Dad had graduated from mere cheeseburgers. Mom was spoiling him. "He's in the garage," Gwen continued, "keeping out of sight. But other than Mrs. Baumann, who's still worried about her Chihuahua, I think the neighbors have gotten used to having him around." She laughed. "He's been great with Justin. They're inseparable. And you should hear Justin talking now. That child has picked up more words from a talking falcon . . ." I couldn't tell how much sadness permeated her smile. Maybe only a hint—for the dreams of a normal, middle-class life that had been swept away by the tsunami of her family.

Gwen took my arm, and together we walked toward the

patio. "So what's up with this glove?" she asked. "Not a look I'd have chosen for you—"

"Mom!" Maria staggered out of the house, looking pale and clutching her stomach. Mab was right behind her. "I don't feel good."

"What is it, sweetheart?" Gwen held out her arms, and Maria threw herself into them. Gwen scowled. "She's awfully hot."

"I think it's time," Mab said.

Time? Oh, no.

"It can't be. Not yet." Gwen frowned and felt Maria's sweaty forehead. "There's a bug going around . . ."

Maria gasped and doubled over. The edges of her form blurred and wavered. She coughed, but the sound came out as a succession of animal noises—*meow, chirp, moo, hiss.*

Mab was right. Maria was making her first shift. And months earlier than anyone had anticipated. We hadn't prepared her. She wasn't ready.

Gwen clutched her daughter to her. Her panicked face turned blindly back and forth between Mab and me.

"Maria." Mab laid a gentle hand on the girl's shoulder. "You told me you wanted to be a seagull, remember? Tell me what you like about seagulls."

"No!" Maria jerked away. Her voice was nearing hysteria. "I don't want to shift. I can't! I want my mom!" A sob caught her voice. "Mommy, help me!"

Gwen stood stiff as a post. I'd never seen my sister look so helpless. She hadn't shifted in over a dozen years.

My turn. "Maria, it's okay. You won't do this alone. Listen to what Mab said. Think about a seagull, soaring out over the ocean."

Energy built. Downy feathers sprang from the back of Maria's neck.

"No! I don't want to be a seagull."

"I'll get Anne." Mab rushed back toward the patio.

"What about a cat, then?" I said brightly, like this was supposed to be fun. "Remember how you said they're so graceful, like dancers?"

Maria didn't answer, but a tail—an orange tiger stripe—

began to sprout from her the base of her spine. At the same time, her arms began to stretch into wing shapes.

This was bad. If Maria didn't focus on one form, the shift could tear her apart. It could kill her.

"Maria." I kept my voice quiet and calm. "It's okay. You can be a seagull or a cat or whatever you want. But you need to choose."

"No, I don't *want* to. I changed my mind!" she wailed. "Mommy! Make it stop, please!"

The cat's tail lengthened. Whiskers sprang forth, and her ears changed shape and migrated higher on her head. At the same time, feathers sprouted all over her body. Her arms became more winglike, while her legs shriveled and shortened, like a bird's.

The energy continued to build. When Mom and Mab appeared, Kane close behind, it was almost at the flashpoint. Maria was resisting too strongly. She wasn't going to survive.

Maria screamed.

The energy blasted out.

"Stop." Suddenly, I saw the scene from twenty feet above. My hands grabbed the blast of energy and held it. Fragments of bloodstone sparkled and sizzled. The pink rubber glove lay on the ground. "I will not see one of my children destroyed in this way." The words issued from my mouth. Although I hadn't spoken them, I agreed with every word.

Maria looked at me with a face that was part-cat, part-bird, part-child. Her wide eyes moved upward. Her head tilted back until she stared high above her head. She looked directly into Ceridwen's eyes. "Can you help me?" she whispered.

"I can," Ceridwen answered in my voice. "But you must choose."

"I already did. But I . . . I didn't tell anyone. I want to be a falcon, like Grandpa."

"And so you shall. Trust me, child."

Maria swallowed hard, but then she nodded. She closed her eyes.

I could feel Ceridwen constrain the energy, like a dam holding back a vast reservoir of water. My body shook with her effort. Then, slowly, particle by particle, she fed it back to the trembling child. Maria's body resumed its normal shape. At a signal from me, Gwen stepped back. Then Ceridwen sent more energy into Maria in a strong yet gentle pulse. One moment there was an eleven-year-old girl. The next, a white falcon stretched her wings.

What a beautiful, perfect shift.

"Well," said Dad, landing beside his granddaughter. "What have we here? Want to go for a soar, kiddo?"

Maria's beak opened and emitted the piercing cry of a falcon. Together, the two magnificent birds launched themselves skyward.

Mab managed to catch Gwen as she fainted.

"Whoa!" exclaimed Zack. "Mom—" He noticed his mother's condition. "I mean, Grandma, did my sister just turn into a bird?"

"Maria birdie!" Justin exclaimed, clapping his hands.

Ceridwen bent my body. Using my hand, she picked up the pink rubber glove. Her voice spoke in my mind. *I will honor your wishes—for now—taking this glove as a signal you wish to have this body to yourself. But it is only through my courtesy. The time is coming when, whatever either of us wishes, we must work together.*

My sparkling fingers still tingled with power. As I pulled the glove over them, I knew I was doing so only with Ceridwen's permission. The goddess's voice faded, yet her words were distinct. *Two more gifts have I given you today: your privacy and the child's life. Do not take them for granted.*

Again, I felt the threat that laced her tone.

I didn't realize how badly my hands were shaking until Kane took both of them in his. "Are you all right?" he asked.

Was I?

A goddess had taken up residence in my body and was keeping count of the "gifts" she'd bestowed upon me—each one, I was sure, with miles of strings attached.

A Hellion, its essence still burned into my arm, laid claim to me.

The Old Ones remained at large. Tina was missing. Mab's bloodstone had shattered. The war between the realms still loomed.

Yet somehow, with Kane's hands holding mine, I could look into his eyes and believe that nothing was insurmountable. No trace of tortured hellhound lingered in those gray eyes. In them, I saw intelligence and loyalty, steadiness and strength. I saw belief in me. I saw love.

Whatever was coming, we'd face it together. How many times had he told me that? But now I could see it. And I think he saw the same thing.

"Yeah," I said. "I'm all right."

And if there was any hint of contradiction—a whisper in my mind, a twinge in my demon mark—I didn't pay attention.

Kane put his arm around me. Together, we watched my father and my niece soar through the blue suburban sky.

# ABOUT THE AUTHOR

**Nancy Holzner** grew up in western Massachusetts with her nose stuck in a book. This meant that she tended to walk into things, wore glasses before she was out of elementary school, and forced her parents to institute a "no reading at the dinner table" rule. It was probably inevitable that she majored in English in college and then, because there were still a lot of books she wanted to read, continued her studies long enough to earn a master's degree and a PhD.

She began her career as a medievalist, then jumped off the tenure track to try some other things. Besides teaching English and philosophy, she's worked as a technical writer, freelance editor, instructional designer, college admissions counselor, and corporate trainer.

Nancy lives in upstate New York with her husband, Steve, where they both work from home without getting on each other's nerves. She enjoys visiting local wineries and listening obsessively to opera. There are still a lot of books she wants to read.

Visit Nancy online at www.nancyholzner.com and facebook .com/NancyHolznerBooks.

FROM AUTHOR
**NANCY HOLZNER**

# DARKLANDS

## A DEADTOWN NOVEL

Boston's demons have been disappearing, and Vicky's clients are canceling left and right. While fewer demons might seem like a good thing, Vicky suspects foul play. A missing Celtic cauldron from Harvard's Peabody Museum leads her to an unwelcome conclusion: Pryce, her demi-demon cousin and bitter enemy, is trying to regain his full powers.

But Pryce isn't acting alone. He's conjured another, darker villain from Vicky's past. To stop them from destroying everything she loves, she'll have to face her own worst fear—in the realm of the dead itself.

### PRAISE FOR THE DEADTOWN NOVELS

"Fresh and funny."
—Karen Chance, *New York Times* bestselling
author of *Tempt the Stars*

"Zombies, demons, and a sassy slayer…
An incredibly realized world."
—Chris Marie Green, author of *Deep in the Woods*

"[An] excellent series."
—*Bitten by Books*

nancyholzner.com
facebook.com/NancyHolznerBooks
facebook.com/ProjectParanormalBooks
penguin.com

M1332T0613

Explore the outer reaches
of imagination—don't miss these authors
of dark fantasy and urban noir who take you
to the edge and beyond . . .

| | |
|---|---|
| Patricia Briggs | Anne Bishop |
| Simon R. Green | Marjorie M. Liu |
| Jim Butcher | Jeanne C. Stein |
| Kat Richardson | Christopher Golden |
| Karen Chance | Ilona Andrews |
| Rachel Caine | Anton Strout |

penguin.com/scififantasy